The Secret Heirs
COLLECTION

July 2019

August 2019

September 2019

October 2019

Secret Heirs: Billionaire's Pleasure

SHARON KENDRICK

KATE HEWITT

HEIDI RICE

MILLS & BOON

First Published in Great Britain 2019
By Mills & Boon, an imprint of HarperCollins *Publishers*
1 London Bridge Street, London, SE1 9GF

SECRET HEIRS: BILLIONAIRE'S PLEASURE
© 2019 Harlequin Books S.A.

Secrets of a Billionaire's Mistress © Sharon Kendrick 2017
Engaged for Her Enemy's Heir © Kate Hewitt 2017
The Virgin's Shock Baby © Heidi Rice 2017

ISBN: 978-0-263-27677-0

MIX
Paper from
responsible sources
FSC™ C007454

This book is produced from independently certified FSC™ paper
to ensure responsible forest management.

For more information visit: www.harpercollins.co.uk/green

Printed and bound in Spain by CPI, Barcelona

SECRETS OF A BILLIONAIRE'S MISTRESS

SHARON KENDRICK

For three fabulous writers who helped with the
Australian detail in my 100th book,
ARoyal Vow of Convenience.

Helene Young & Margareta Young for the
inspiration and the insight - and Rachael Johns,
for the Tim-Tams!

CHAPTER ONE

RENZO SABATINI WAS unbuttoning his shirt when the doorbell rang. He felt the beat of expectation. The familiar tug of heat to his groin. He was half-tempted to pull the shirt from his shoulders so Darcy could slide her fingers over his skin, closely followed by those inventive lips of hers. The soft lick of her tongue could help him forget what lay ahead. He thought about Tuscany and the closing of a chapter. About the way some memories could still be raw even when so many years had passed and maybe that was why he never really stopped to think about them.

But why concentrate on darkness when Darcy was all sunshine and light? And why rush at sex when they had the whole night ahead—a smorgasbord of sensuality which he could enjoy at his leisure with his latest and most unexpected lover? A woman who demanded nothing other than that he satisfy her—something which was easy since he had only to touch her pale skin to grow so hard that it hurt. His mouth dried. Four months in and he was as bewitched by her as he had been from the start.

In many ways he was astonished it had continued this long when their two worlds were so different. She was not his usual type of woman and he was very definitely not her type of man. He was into clean lines and minimalism, while Darcy was all voluptuous curves and lingerie which could barely contain her abundant flesh. His mouth curved into a hard smile. In reality it should never have lasted beyond one night but her tight body had been difficult to walk away from. It still was.

The doorbell rang again and the glance he shot at his wristwatch was touched with irritation. Was she daring to be *impatient* when she wasn't supposed to be here for another half hour? Surely she knew the rules by now...that she was expected to fit around his schedule, rather than the other way round?

Barefooted, he walked through the spacious rooms of his Belgravia apartment, pulling open the front door to see Darcy Denton standing there—small of stature and impossible to ignore—her magnificent curls misted with rain and tugged back into a ponytail so that only the bright red colour was on show. She wore a light raincoat, tightly belted to emphasise her tiny waist, but underneath she was still in her waitress's uniform because she lived on the other side of London, an area Renzo had never visited—and he was perfectly content for it to stay that way. They'd established very quickly that if she went home after her shift to change, it wasted several hours—even if he sent his car to collect her. And Renzo was a busy man with an architectural practice which spanned several continents. His time was too precious to waste, which was why she always came straight from work with her overnight bag—though that was a largely unnecessary detail since she was rarely anything other than naked when she was with him.

He stared down into her green eyes, which glittered like emeralds in porcelain-pale skin and, as always, his blood began to fizz with expectation and lust. 'You're early,' he observed softly. 'Did you time your visit especially because you knew I'd be undressing?'

Darcy answered him with a tight smile as he opened the door to let her in. She was cold and she was wet and it had been the most awful day. A customer had spilt tea over her uniform. Then a child had been sick. She'd looked out the window at the end of her shift to discover that the rain had started and someone must have taken her umbrella. And Renzo Sabatini was standing there in the warmth of his palatial apartment, looking glowing and delectable—making the assumption that she had nothing better to do than to time her visits just so she would find him half-naked. Could she ever have met a man more arrogant?

Yet she'd known what she was letting herself in for when she'd started this crazy affair. When she'd fought a silent battle against everything she'd known to be wrong. Because powerful men who dallied with waitresses only wanted one thing, didn't they?

She'd lost that particular battle and ended up in Renzo's king-size bed—but nobody could say that her eyes hadn't been open at the time. Well, some of the time at least—the rest of the time they'd fluttered to a quivering close as he had thrust deeply inside her until she was sobbing with pleasure. After resisting him as hard as she could, she'd decided to resist no more. Or maybe the truth was that she hadn't been able to stop herself from falling into his arms. He'd kissed her and that had been it. She hadn't known that a kiss could make you feel that way. She hadn't realised that desire could make you feel as if you were floating. Or flying. She'd surrendered her virginity to him and, after his shocked reaction to discovering he was her first lover, he had introduced her to more pleasure than she'd thought possible, though in a life spectacularly short on the pleasure front that wouldn't have been difficult, would it?

For a while things had been fine. More than fine. She spent the night with him whenever he was in the country and had a space in his diary—and sometimes she spent the following day there, too. He cooked her eggs and played her music she'd never heard before— dreamy stuff featuring lots of violins—while he pored over the fabulously intricate drawings which would one day be transformed into the glittering and iconic skyscrapers for which he was famous.

But lately something had started to niggle away inside her. Was it her conscience? Her sense that her already precarious self-worth was being eroded by him hiding her away in his palatial apartment, like a guilty secret? She wasn't sure. All she knew was that she'd started to analyse what she'd become and hadn't liked the answer she'd come up with.

She was a wealthy man's plaything. A woman who dropped her panties whenever he clicked those elegant olive fingers.

But she was here now and it was stupid to let her reservations spoil the evening ahead, so she changed her tight smile into a bright smile as she dumped her overnight bag on the floor and tugged the elastic band from her hair. Shaking her damp curls free, she couldn't deny the satisfaction it gave her to see the way Renzo's eyes had darkened in response—although her physical appeal to him had never been in any question. He couldn't seem to get enough of her and she suspected she knew why. Because she was different. Working class, for a start. She hadn't been to college—in fact, she'd missed out on more schooling than she should have done and nearly everything she knew had been self-taught. She was curvy and red-headed, when usually he went for slender brunettes—that was if all the photos in the newspapers were to be believed. They were certainly mismatched on just about every level, except when it came to bed.

Because the sex was amazing—it always had been—but it couldn't continue like this, taking her on an aimless path which was leading nowhere. Darcy knew what she had to do. She knew you could only fool yourself for so long before reality started hurting and forced you to change. She'd noticed Renzo was starting to take her for granted and knew that, if it continued, all the magic they'd shared would just wither away. And she didn't want that, because memories were powerful things. The bad ones were like heavy burdens you had to carry around with you and she was determined to have some good ones to lighten the load. So when was she going to grab the courage to walk away from him, before Renzo did the walking and left her feeling broken and crushed?

'I'm early because I sent your driver away and took the Tube instead,' she explained, brushing excess raindrops from her forest of red curls.

'You sent the driver away?' He frowned as he slid the damp raincoat from her shoulders. 'Why on earth would you do that?'

Darcy sighed, wondering what it must be like to be Renzo Sabatini and live in an enclosed and protected world, where chauffeur-driven cars and private jets shielded you from rain and snow and the worries of most normal folk. Where people did your shopping and picked up your clothes where you'd left them on the bedroom floor the night before. A world where you didn't have to speak to anyone unless you really wanted to, because there was always some minion who would do the speaking for you.

'Because the traffic is a nightmare at this time of day and often we're forced to sit in a queue, moving at a snail's pace.' She took the coat from him and gave it a little shake before hanging it in the cupboard. 'Public transport happens to have a lot going for it during the rush hour. Now, rather than debating my poor timekeeping can I please have a cup of tea? I'm f-f-freezing.'

But he didn't make any move towards the kitchen as most people might have done after such a wobbly request. He took her in his arms and kissed her instead. His lips were hard as they pressed against hers and his fingers caressed her bottom through her uniform dress as he brought her up close to his body. Close enough for her to feel the hardness of his erection and the warmth of his bare chest as he deepened the kiss. Darcy's eyelids fluttered to a close as one hard thigh pushed insistently against hers and she could feel her own parting in automatic response. And suddenly her coldness was forgotten and tea was the last thing on her mind. Her questions and insecurities dissolved as he deepened the kiss and all she was aware of was the building heat as her chilled fingers crept up to splay themselves over his bare and hair-roughened torso.

'Hell, Renzo,' she breathed.

'Is it really hell?' he murmured.

'No, it's…' she brushed her lips over his '…heaven, if you must know.'

'That's what I thought. Are you trying to warm your hands on my chest?'

'Trying. I don't think I'm having very much luck. You do many things very well, but acting as a human hot-water bottle isn't one of them.'

'No. You could be right. My skills definitely lie in other directions. Perhaps I could demonstrate some of them to you right now.' He moved his hand from her bottom and curled his fingers round hers as he guided her hand towards his groin. 'In which case I think you'd better join me in the shower, don't you?'

She couldn't have said no even if she'd wanted to. One touch from Renzo was like lighting the touch-paper. Two seconds in his arms and she went up in flames.

In the bathroom, he unzipped her drab beige uniform, soft words of Italian falling from his lips as her breasts were revealed to him. Disproportionately big breasts which had always been the bane of her life, because she'd spent her life with men's attention being constantly homed in on them. She'd often thought longingly of a breast reduction—except who could afford an operation like that on the money she earned waiting tables? So she'd made do with wearing restrictive bras, until Renzo had taught her to love her body and told her that her breasts were the most magnificent thing he'd ever seen. To enjoy being suckled or having his teeth tease the sensitive flesh until she was crying out with pleasure. He'd started to buy lingerie for her, too—the only thing she'd ever allowed him to buy for her and only because he'd insisted. He couldn't understand why she wouldn't let him spend money on her, but her reasons were raw and painful and she had no intention of letting him in on her secret.

But she let him buy her pretty underclothes, because he insisted that it enhanced their sex play—balcony bras and tiny matching panties, which he said made the most of her curvy hips. And didn't it make her feel rather decadent when she was at work, knowing she was wearing the finest silk and lace beneath the drab check of her waitress uniform? Hadn't he told her that he *wanted* her to think about him when he wasn't there? That when he was far away on business he liked to imagine her touching herself until she was wet between the legs and her body bucking helplessly as she thought about *him*. And although his fantasy about how she lived when he wasn't there was just that—fantasy—she couldn't deny that it also turned her on. But then, everything about Renzo Sabatini turned her on. His tall and powerful frame. His black hair and black eyes and those dark-rimmed spectacles he wore when he was working on one of his detailed plans. That way he had of watching her as she moved around the room. And stroking her until she was trembling with helpless need for him. Like now.

Her dress fell to the floor and the delicate underwear quickly followed. A master in the art of undressing, her Italian lover was soon as naked as she, and Darcy sucked in an instinctive gasp when she saw how aroused he was.

'Daunting, isn't it?' His sensual lips curved into a mocking smile. 'Want to touch me?'

'Not until I've got hot water gushing over me. My hands are so cold you might recoil.'

'I don't think so,' he said softly.

His eyes glittered as he picked her up and carried her into the wet room, where steaming water streamed down from a huge showerhead and the sensory impact of the experience threatened to overwhelm her. Hot water on icy skin and a naked Renzo in her arms. In the steamy environment, which made her think of a tropical forest, his lips were hungry, one hand stroking between her legs while the other played with one aching nipple. The warm water relaxed her, made her aware of the fierce pounding of her heart and the sudden rush of warmth at her groin. She ran her hands over the hard planes of his body, enjoying the sensation of honed muscle beneath his silken olive skin. Boldly she reached down to circle his erection, sliding her thumb and forefinger lightly up and down the rocky shaft the way she knew he liked it. He gave a groan. Hell. *She* liked it, too. She liked everything he did to her…and the longer it went on, the more difficult it was to imagine a life without him.

She closed her eyes as his fingers moved down over her belly until they were tangling in the wet hair at the juncture of her thighs. One finger took a purposeful route farther, until it was deep inside her and she gave a little yelp of pleasure as he strummed the

finger against swollen flesh, the rhythmical movement taking her closer to the edge. And now it was
her turn to writhe her hips against him, wanting release—and wanting oblivion, too.

'Now,' she breathed. 'Make love to me now.'

'You are impatient, little one.'

Of course she was impatient. It had been nearly a
month since she'd seen him. A month when he'd been
hard at work in Japan, before flying to South America
to oversee the enormous new hotel complex he'd designed which was creating a lot of waves in the high-
octane world of architecture. And yes, there had been
the occasional email—an amusing description about
a woman who had propositioned him after a boardroom meeting, which Darcy had managed to laugh
off and act as if it didn't hurt. He'd even phoned her
once, when his plane had been delayed at the airport
in Rio de Janeiro and presumably he must have had
time to kill. And even though she'd been battling
through the wind on her way back from the discount
supermarket at the time, she'd managed to find shel-
ter in a shop doorway and make like it was a normal
conversation. She'd tried to tell herself that she didn't
mind his total lack of commitment. That they didn't
have an ordinary relationship and that was what made
it so interesting.

He'd told her right from the start what she could
expect and what she must not expect, and number
one on his list had been commitment, closely followed by love. She remembered turning round as he'd
spoken, surprising an unexpectedly bleak look in his
gaze—unexpected because those ebony eyes usually
gave nothing away. But she hadn't probed further be-

cause she'd sensed he would clam up. Actually, she never probed—because if you asked someone too many questions about themselves, they might just turn around and ask them back and that was the last thing she wanted.

And she had agreed to his emotionally cold terms, hadn't she? She'd acted as if they were the most reasonable requests in the world. To be honest, she hadn't been able to think beyond the next kiss—and every kiss had the effect of binding her ever tighter to him. But several months had passed since he'd extracted that agreement from her and time changed everything. It always did. Time made your feelings start to deepen and made you prone to foolish daydreams. And what could be more foolish than imagining some kind of future with the billionaire designer with his jet-set lifestyle and homes all around the world? She, without a single qualification to her name, whose only skill was her ability to multitask in a restaurant?

She pressed her lips against his shoulder, thinking how best to respond to his question—to show him she still had some control left, even if it was slipping away by the second. 'Impatient?' she murmured into his wet, bare skin. 'If I'm going too fast for you, we could always put this on hold and do it later. Have that cup of tea after all. Is that what you'd like, Renzo?'

His answer was swift and unequivocal. Imprisoning her hands, he pushed her up against the granite wall of the wet room, parted her legs and thrust into her, as hot and hard as she'd ever felt him. She gasped as he filled her. She cried out as he began to move. From knowing nothing, he'd taught her everything and she had been his willing pupil. In his arms, she came to life.

'Renzo,' she gasped as he rocked against her.

'Did you miss me, *cara*?'

She closed her eyes. 'I missed…this.'

'But nothing else?'

She wanted to say that there *was* nothing else, but why spoil a beautiful moment? No man would want to hear something like that, would they—even if it was true? Especially not a man with an ego the size of Renzo's. 'Of course,' she said as he stilled inside her. 'I missed you.'

Did he sense that her answer was less than the 100 per cent he demanded of everything and everyone? Was that why he slowed the pace down, dragging her back from the brink of her orgasm to tantalise her with nearly there thrusts until she could bear it no more?

'Renzo—'

'What is it?'

How could he sound so calm? So totally in control. But control was what he was good at, wasn't it? He was the master of control. She squirmed. 'Don't play with me.'

'But I thought you liked me playing with you. Perhaps…' he bent his head to whisper in her water-soaked ear '…I shall make you beg.'

'Oh, no, you won't!' Fiercely, she cupped his buttocks and held him against her and he gave an exultant laugh as at last he gave her exactly what she wanted. He worked on her hard and fast, his deep rhythm taking her up and up, until her shuddered cries were blotted out by his kiss and he made that low groaning sound as he came. It was, she thought, about the only time she'd ever heard him sound helpless.

Afterwards he held her until the trembling had subsided and then soaped her body and washed her hair with hands which were almost gentle—as if he was attempting to make up for the almost-brutal way he'd brought her gasping to orgasm. He dried her carefully, then carried her into the bedroom and placed her down on the vast bed which overlooked the whispering treetops of Eaton Square. The crisp, clean linen felt like heaven against her scented skin as he got into bed beside her and slid his arms around her waist. She was sleepy and suspected he was, too, but surely they needed to have some sort of *conversation* instead of just mating like two animals and then tumbling into oblivion.

But wasn't that all they were, when it boiled down to it? This affair was all about sex. Nothing except sex.

'So how was your time away?' she forced herself to ask.

'You don't want to know.'

'Yes, I do.'

'All good.' He yawned. 'The hotel is almost complete and I've been commissioned to design a new art gallery just outside Tokyo.'

'But you're tired?' she observed.

His voice was mocking. '*Sì, cara.* I'm tired.'

She wriggled her back against him. 'Ever thought of easing off for a while? Taking a back seat and just enjoying your success?'

'Not really.' He yawned again.

'Why not?' she said, some rogue inside her making her persist, even though she could sense his growing impatience with her questions.

His voice grew hard. 'Because men in my position don't *ease off.* There are a hundred hot new architects who would love to be where I am. Take your eye off the ball and you're toast.' He stroked her nipple. 'Why don't you tell me about your week instead?'

'Oh, mine was nothing to speak about. I just *serve* the toast,' she said lightly.

She closed her eyes because she thought that they might sleep but she was wrong because Renzo was cupping her breasts, rubbing his growing erection up against her bottom until she gave an urgent sound of assent and he entered her from behind, where she was slick and ready.

His lips were in her hair and his hands were playing with her nipples as he moved inside her again. Her shuddered capitulation was swift and two orgasms in less than an hour meant she could no longer fight off her fatigue. She fell into a deep sleep and sometime later she felt the bed dip as Renzo got up and when she dragged her eyelids open it was to see that the spring evening was still light. The leaves in the treetops outside the window were golden-green in the fading sunlight and she could hear a distant bird singing.

It felt surreal lying here. The prestigious square on which he lived sometimes seemed like a mirage. All the lush greenery gave the impression of being in the middle of the country—something made possible only by the fact that this was the most expensive real estate in London. But beyond the treetops near his exclusive home lay the London which was *her* city. Discount stores and tower blocks and garbage fluttering on the pavements. Snarled roads and angry drivers. And somewhere not a million miles from here, but which felt as if it might as well be in a different universe, was the tiny bedsit she called home. Sometimes it seemed like something out of some corny old novel—the billionaire boss and his waitress lover. Because things like this didn't usually happen to girls like her.

But Renzo hadn't taken advantage of her, had he? He'd never demanded anything she hadn't wanted to give. She'd accepted his ride home—even though some part of her had cried out that it was unwise. Yet for once in her life she'd quashed the voice of common sense which was as much a part of her as her bright red hair. For years she had simply kept her head down and toed the line in order to survive. But not this time. Instead of doing what she knew she *should* do, she'd succumbed to something she'd really wanted and that something was Renzo. Because she'd never wanted anyone the way she'd wanted him.

What she was certain he'd intended to be just one night had become another and then another as their unconventional relationship had developed. It was a relationship which existed only within the walls of his apartment because, as if by some unspoken agreement, they never went out on dates. Renzo's friends were wealthy and well connected, just like him. Fast-living powerbrokers with influential jobs and nothing in common with someone like her. And anyway, it would be bizarre if they started appearing together in public because they weren't really a *couple*, were they?

She knew their relationship could most accurately be described as 'friends with benefits,' though the benefits heavily outweighed the friendship side and the arrogant Italian had once told her that he didn't really have any female *friends*. Women were for the bedroom and kitchen—he'd actually said that, when he'd been feeling especially uninhibited after one of their marathon sex sessions, which had ended up in the bath. He'd claimed afterwards that he'd been joking but Darcy had recognised a grain of truth behind his words. Even worse was the way his masterful arrogance had thrilled her, even though she'd done her best to wear a disapproving expression.

Because when it boiled down to it, Darcy knew the score. She was sensible enough to know that Renzo Sabatini was like an ice cream cone you ate on a sunny day. It tasted amazing—possibly the most amazing thing you'd ever tasted—but you certainly didn't expect it to last.

She glanced up as he walked back into the bedroom carrying a tray, a task she performed many times a day—the only difference being that he was completely naked.

'You're spoiling me,' she said.

'I'm just returning the favour. I'd like to ask where you learned that delicious method of licking your tongue over my thighs but I realise that—'

'I learned it from you?'

'Esattamente.' His eyes glittered. 'Hungry?'

'Thirsty.'

'I expect you are,' he said, bending over to brush his lips over hers.

She took the tea he gave her and watched as he tugged on a pair of jeans and took his glass of red wine over to his desk, sitting down and putting on dark-framed spectacles before waking his computer from sleep mode and beginning to scroll down. After a couple of minutes he was completely engrossed in something on the screen and suddenly Darcy felt completely excluded. With his back on her, she felt like an insignificant cog in the giant wheel which was his life. They'd just had sex—twice—and now he was burying himself in work, presumably until his body had recovered enough to do it to her all over again. And she would just lie back and let him, or climb on top of him if the mood took her—because that was her role. Up until now it had always been enough but suddenly it didn't seem like nearly enough.

Did she signal her irritation? Was that why he rattled out a question spoken like someone who was expecting an apologetic denial as an answer?

'Is something wrong?'

This was her cue to say no, nothing was wrong. To pat the edge of the bed and slant him a compliant smile because that was what she would normally have done. But Darcy wasn't in a compliant mood today. She'd heard a song on the radio just before leaving work. A song which had taken her back to a place she hadn't wanted to go to and the mother she'd spent her life trying to forget.

Yet it was funny how a few random chords could pluck at your heartstrings and make you want to screw up your face and cry. Funny how you could still love someone even though they'd let you down, time after time. That had been the real reason she'd sent Renzo's driver away. She'd wanted to walk to the Tube so that her unexpected tears could mingle with the rain. She'd hoped that by coming here and having her Italian lover take her to bed, it might wipe away her unsettled feelings. But it seemed to have done the opposite. It had awoken a new restlessness in her. It had made her realise that great sex and champagne in the shadows of a powerful man's life weren't the recipe for a happy life—and the longer she allowed it to continue, the harder it would be for her to return to the real world. Her world.

She finished her tea and put the cup down, the subtle taste of peppermint and rose petals still lingering on her lips. It was time for the affair to fade out, like the credits at the end of the film. And even though she was going to miss him like crazy, she was the one who needed to start it rolling.

She made her voice sound cool and non-committal. 'I'm thinking I won't be able to see you for a while.'

That had his attention. He turned away from the screen and, putting his glasses down on the desk, he frowned. 'What are you talking about?'

'I have a week's holiday from work and I'm planning to use it to go to Norfolk.'

She could see he was slightly torn now because he wasn't usually interested in what she did when she wasn't with him, even if he sometimes trotted out a polite question because he obviously felt it was expected of him. But he was interested now.

'What are you doing in Norfolk?'

She shrugged her bare shoulders. 'Looking for a place to rent. I'm thinking of moving there.'

'You mean you're leaving *London*?'

'You sound surprised, Renzo. People leave London all the time.'

'I know. But it's…' He frowned, as if such an option was outside his realm of understanding. 'What's in Norfolk?'

She'd been prepared to let him think that she just wanted a change—which was true—and to leave her real reasons unspoken. But his complete lack of comprehension angered her and when she spoke her voice was low and trembling with an anger which was directed as much at herself as at him.

'Because there I've got the chance of renting somewhere that might have a view of something which isn't a brick wall. As well as a job that doesn't just feature commuters who are so rushed they can barely give me the time of day, let alone a *please* or a thank you. The chance of fresh air and a lower cost of living, plus a pace of life which doesn't wear me out just thinking about it.'

He frowned. 'You mean you don't like where you're living?'

'It's perfectly adequate for my *needs*,' she said carefully. 'Or at least, it has been until now.'

'That's a pretty lukewarm endorsement.' He paused and his frown deepened. 'Is that why you've never invited me round?'

'I guess.' She'd actually done it to save his embarrassment—and possibly hers. She'd tried to imagine him in her humble bedsit eating his dinner off a tray or having to squeeze his towering frame into her tiny bathroom or—even worse—lying on her narrow single bed. It was a laughable concept which would have made them both feel awkward and would have emphasised the vast social gulf between them even more. And that was why she never had. 'Would you really have wanted me to?'

Renzo considered her question. Of course he wouldn't, but he was surprised not to have got an invite. You wouldn't need to be a genius to work out that her life was very different from his and perhaps if he'd been confronted by it then his conscience would have forced him to write a cheque, and this time be more forceful in getting her to accept it. He might have told her to buy some new cushions, or a rug or even a new kitchen, if that was what she wanted. That was how these things usually worked. But Darcy was the proudest woman he'd ever encountered and, apart from the sexy lingerie he'd insisted she wear, had stubbornly refused all his offers of gifts. Why, even his heiress lovers hadn't been averse to accepting diamond necklaces or bracelets or those shoes with the bright red soles. He liked buying women expensive presents—it made him feel he wasn't in any way *beholden* to them. It reduced relationships down to what they really were…transactions. And yet his hard-up little waitress hadn't wanted to know.

'No, I wasn't holding out for an invite,' he said slowly. 'But I thought you might have discussed your holiday plans with me before you went ahead and booked them.'

'But you never discuss your plans with me, Renzo. You just do as you please.'

'You're saying you want me to run my schedule past you first?' he questioned incredulously.

'Of course I don't. You've made it clear that's not the way you operate and I've always accepted that. So you can hardly object if I do the same.'

But she was missing the point and Renzo suspected she knew it. *He* was the one who called the shots because that was also how these things worked. He was the powerbroker in this affair and she was smart enough to realise that. Yet he could see something implacable in her green gaze, some new sense of determination which had settled over her, and something else occurred to him. 'You might stay on in Norfolk,' he said slowly.

'I might.'

'In which case, this could be the last time we see one another.'

She shrugged. 'I guess it could.'

'Just like that?'

'What were you expecting? It had to end sometime.'

Renzo's eyes narrowed thoughtfully. Up until a couple of hours ago it wouldn't *really* have bothered him if he'd been told he would never see her again. Oh, he might have experienced a faint pang of regret and he certainly would have missed her in a physical sense, because he found her enthusiastic lovemaking irresistible. In fact, he would go so far as to say that she was the best lover he'd ever had, probably because he had taught her to be perfectly attuned to the needs of *his* body. But nothing was for ever. He knew that. In a month—maybe less—he would have replaced her with someone else. Someone cool and presentable, who would blend more easily into his life than Darcy Denton had ever done.

But she was the one who was doing the withdrawing and Renzo didn't like that. He was a natural predator—proud and fiercely competitive. Perhaps even prouder than Darcy. Women didn't leave *him*... He was the one who did the walking away—and at a time of *his* choosing. And he still wanted her. He had not yet reached the crucial boredom state which would make him direct her calls straight to voicemail or leave a disproportionately long time before replying to texts. Lazily, he flicked through the options available to him.

'What about if you took a holiday with me, instead of going to Norfolk on your own?'

He could tell from the sudden dilatation of her eyes that the suggestion had surprised her. And the hardening of her nipples above the rumpled bedsheet suggested it had excited her. He felt the sudden beat of blood to his groin and realised it had excited him, too.

Her emerald eyes were wary. 'Are you serious?'

'Why not?'

He got up from the chair, perfectly aware of the powerful effect his proximity would have on her as he sat down on the edge of the bed. 'Is that such an abhorrent suggestion—to take my lover on holiday?'

She shrugged. 'It's not the type of thing we usually do. We usually stay in and don't go out.'

'But life would be very dull if only the expected happened. Are you telling me that the idea of a few days away with me doesn't appeal to you?' He splayed his palm possessively over the warm weight of her breast and watched as her swanlike neck constricted in a swallow.

She chewed on her lip. 'Renzo—'

'Mmm…?'

'It's…it's quite difficult to think straight when you're touching my nipple like that.'

'Thinking in the bedroom can be a very overrated pastime,' he drawled, subtly increasing the pressure of his fingers. 'What's to think about? My proposition is perfectly simple. You could come out to Tuscany with me. I need to make a trip there this weekend. We could spend a few days together and you would still have time to go to Norfolk.'

She leaned back against the pillows and her eyes closed as he continued to massage her breast. 'You have a house there, don't you?' she breathed. 'In Tuscany.'

'Not for much longer. That's why I'm going. I'm selling it.' The pressure on her breast increased as his voice hardened. 'And you can keep me company. I have to take an earlier flight via Paris to do some business but you could always fly out separately.' He paused. 'Doesn't the idea tempt you, Darcy?'

His words filtered into her distracted mind as he continued to tease her exquisitely aroused nipple and her lashes fluttered open. His black eyes were as hard as shards of jet but that didn't affect the magic he was creating with the slow movement of his fingers as she tried to concentrate on his question.

Her tongue flicked out to moisten her lips. Of course a few days away with him tempted her— but it wasn't the thought of flying to Tuscany which was making her heart race like a champion stallion.

He tempted her. Would it be so wrong to grab a last session of loving with him—but in a very different environment? Because although his apartment was unimaginably big, it had its limitations. Despite the pool in the basement, the heated roof terrace and huge screening room, she was starting to feel like part of the fixtures and fittings. Couldn't she go out to Italy and, in the anonymous setting of a foreign country, pretend to be his *real* girlfriend for a change? Someone he really cared about—rather than just someone whose panties he wanted to rip off every time he saw her.

'I guess it does tempt me,' she said. 'A little.'

'Not the most enthusiastic response I've ever had,' he commented. 'But I take it that's a yes?'

'It's a yes,' she agreed, relaxing back into the feathery bank of pillows as he turned his attention to her other aching breast.

'Good.' There was a pause and the circular movement of his fingers halted. 'But first you're going to have to let me buy you some new clothes.'

Her eyes snapped open and she froze—automatically pushing his hand away. 'When will you get it into your thick skull that I'm not interested in your money, Renzo?'

'I think I'm getting the general idea,' he said drily. 'And although your independence is admirable, I find it a little misguided. Why not just accept gracefully? I like giving presents and most women like receiving them.'

'It's a very kind thought and thank you all the same,' she said stiffly, 'but I don't want them.'

'This isn't a question of *want*, more a case of *need*

and I'm afraid that this time I'm going to have to insist,' he said smoothly. 'I have a certain…*position* to
maintain in Italy and, as the woman accompanying
me, you'll naturally be the focus of attention. I'd hate
you to feel you were being judged negatively because
you don't have the right clothes.'

'Just as you're judging me right now, you mean?'
she snapped.

He shook his head, his lips curving into a slow
smile and his deep voice dipping. 'You must have
realised by now that I prefer you wearing nothing
at all, since nothing looks better than your pale and
perfect skin. But although it's one of my biggest fantasies, I really don't think we can have you walking
around the Tuscan hills stark naked, do you? I'm just
looking out for you, Darcy. Buy yourself a few pretty
things. Some dresses you can wear in the evenings.
It isn't a big deal.'

She opened her mouth to say that it *was* a big deal
to her but he had risen to his feet and his shadow was
falling over her so that she was bathed in darkness
as she lay there. She looked up into lash-shuttered
eyes which gleamed like ebony and her heart gave a
funny twist as she thought about how much she was
going to miss him. How was she going to return to a
life which was empty of her powerful Italian lover?
'What are you doing?' she croaked as he began to
unzip his jeans.

'Oh, come on. Use your imagination,' he said
softly. 'I'm going to persuade you to take my money.'

CHAPTER TWO

RENZO LOOKED AT his watch and gave a click of impatience. Where the hell *was* she? She *knew* he detested lateness, just as she knew he ran his diary like clockwork. In the exclusive lounge at Florence airport he crossed one long leg over the other, aware that the movement had caused the heads of several women instinctively to turn, but he paid them no attention for there was only one woman currently on his mind—and not in a good way.

The flight he had instructed Darcy to catch—in fact, to purchase a first-class ticket for—had discharged its passengers twenty minutes earlier and she had not been among their number. His eyes had narrowed as he'd stared at the hordes of people streaming through the arrivals section, fully expecting to see her eagerly pushing her way through to see him, her pale face alight with excitement and her curvy body resplendent in fine new clothes—but there had been no sight of her. A member of staff had dealt with his irritation and was currently checking the flight list while he was forced to consider the unbelievable... *that she might have changed her mind about joining him in Italy.*

He frowned. Had her reluctance to take the cash he had insisted she accept gone deeper than he'd imagined? He'd thought she was simply making a gesture—hiding the natural greed which ran through the veins of pretty much every woman—but perhaps he had misjudged her. Perhaps she really *was* deeply offended by his suggestion that she buy herself some decent clothes.

Or maybe she'd just taken the money and done a runner, not intending to come here and meet him at all.

Renzo's mouth hardened, because wasn't there a rogue thought flickering inside his head which almost wished that to be the case? Wouldn't he have welcomed a sound reason to despise her, instead of this simmering resentment that she was preparing to take her leave of him? That she had been the one to make a decision which was usually *his* province. He glanced again at his wristwatch. And how ironic that the woman to call time on a relationship should be a busty little red-headed waitress he'd picked up in a cocktail bar rather than one of the many more eligible women he'd dated.

He hadn't even been intending to go out the night he'd met her. He'd just planned to have a quick drink with a group of bankers he'd known from way back who had been visiting from Argentina and wanted to see some London nightlife. Renzo didn't particularly like nightclubs and remembered the stir the six men had made as they'd walked into the crowded Starlight Room at the Granchester Hotel, where they'd ordered champagne and decided which of the women sipping cocktails they should ask to dance. But Renzo hadn't been interested in the svelte women who had been smiling invitingly in his direction. His attention had been caught by the curviest little firecracker he'd ever seen. She'd looked as if she had been poured into the black satin dress which had skimmed her rounded hips, but it had been her breasts which had caused the breath to dry in his throat. *Madonna, che bella!* What breasts! Luscious and quivering, they had a deep cleavage he wanted to run his tongue over and that first sight of them was something he would remember for as long as he lived.

He had ended up dancing with no one, mainly because he'd been too busy watching her and his erection had been too painful for him to move without embarrassment. He'd ordered drinks only from her, and wondered afterwards if she noticed he left them all. Each time he'd summoned her over to his table he could sense the almost palpable electricity which sizzled in the air—he'd certainly never felt such a powerful attraction towards a total stranger before. He'd expected her to make some acknowledgement of the silent chemistry which pulsed between them, but she hadn't. In fact the way her eyelids had half shielded her huge green eyes and the cautious looks she'd been directing at him had made him think she must either be the world's greatest innocent, or its most consummate actress. If he had known it was the former, would he still have pursued her?

Of course he would. Deep down he recognised he wouldn't have been able to stop himself because hadn't he been gripped by a powerful hunger which insisted he would never know peace until he had possessed her?

He'd been waiting outside when eventually she had emerged from the club and had thanked the heavens for the heavy downpour of rain which had been showering down on her. She hadn't looked a bit surprised to see him as she'd opened up her umbrella and for a moment it had crossed his mind that she might take a different man home with her every night, though even that had not been enough to make him order his driver to move on. But when he'd offered her a lift she'd refused, in an emphatic manner which had startled him.

'No, thanks.'

'No?'

'I know what you want,' she'd said, in a low voice. 'And you won't get it from me.'

And with that she'd disappeared into the rain-wet night and Renzo had sat in the back seat of the limousine, watching her retreating form beneath her little black umbrella, his mouth open and his body aching with frustration and unwilling admiration.

He'd gone to the club the next night and the weekend when he'd returned from a work trip to New York. Some nights she'd been there and some she hadn't. He'd discovered she only worked there at weekends and it had only been later he'd found out she had a daytime job as a waitress somewhere else. Extracting information from her had been like trying to get blood from a stone. She was the most private woman he'd ever met as well as the most resistant and perhaps it was those things which made Renzo persist in a way he'd never had to persist before. And just when he'd been wondering if he was wasting his time, she had agreed to let him drive her home.

His voice had been wry as he'd looked at her. *'Madonna mia!* You mean you've decided you trust me enough to accept the lift?'

Her narrow shoulders had shrugged, causing her large breasts to jiggle beneath the shiny black satin of her dress and sending a shaft of lust arrowing straight to his groin. 'I guess so. All the other staff have seen you by now and you've been captured on CCTV for all eternity, so if you're a murderer then you'll be apprehended soon enough.'

'Do I look like a murderer?'

She had smiled then, and it had been like the sun coming out from behind a cloud.

'No. Although you look just a little bit dangerous.'

'Women always tell me that's a plus.'

'I'm sure they do, though I'm not sure I agree. Anyway, it's a filthy night, so I might as well get a lift with you. But I haven't changed my mind,' she'd added fiercely. 'And if you think I'm going to sleep with you, then you're wrong.'

As it happened, she was the one who'd been wrong. They'd driven through the dark wet streets of London and he'd asked her to come in for coffee, not thinking for a moment she'd accept. But maybe the chemistry had been just as powerful for her. Maybe her throat had also been tight with tension and longing and she'd been finding it as difficult to speak as he had, as she'd sat beside him in the leather-scented car. He'd driven her to his apartment and she'd told him primly that she didn't really like coffee. So he'd made her tea flavoured with peppermint and rose petals, and for the first time in his life he'd realised he might lose her if he rushed it. He'd wondered afterwards if it was his unfamiliar restraint which had made her relax and sink into one of his huge sofas—so that when at last he'd leaned over to kiss her she'd been all quivering acquiescence. He'd done it to her right there—pulling her panties down and plunging right into her—terrified she might change her mind during the long walk from the sitting room to the bedroom.

And that had been when he'd discovered she was a virgin—and in that moment something had changed. The world had tipped on its axis because he'd never had sex with a virgin before and had been unprepared for the rush of primitive satisfaction which had flooded through him. As they'd lain there afterwards, gasping for breath among all the cushions, he'd pushed a damp curl away from her dewy cheek, demanding to know why she hadn't told him.

'Why would I? Would you have stopped?'

'No, but I could have laid you at the centre of my big bed instead of the sofa if I'd known this was your first sexual adventure.'

'What, you mean like some sort of medieval sacrifice?' she'd murmured and that had confused him, too, because he would have expected high emotion at such a moment, not such a cool response.

Had it been her coolness which had made him desire her even more? Possibly. He'd thought it would be one night, but he'd been mistaken. He'd never dated a waitress before and he acknowledged the cold streak of snobbery in his nature which told him it would be unwise to buck that trend. But Darcy had confounded him. She read just as many books as an academic he'd once dated—although admittedly, she preferred novels to molecular biology. And she didn't follow the predictable path of most women in a sexual relationship. She didn't bore him with stories of her past, nor weigh him down with questions about his own. Their infrequent yet highly satisfying meetings, which involved a series of mind-blowing orgasms, seemed to meet both their needs. She seemed instinctively to understand that he wasn't seeking a close or lasting connection with a woman. Not now and not ever.

But sometimes an uncomfortable question strayed into his mind to ask why such a beauty would have so willingly submitted her virginity to a total stranger. And didn't he keep coming up with the troublesome answer that maybe she had been holding out for the highest bidder—in this case, an Italian billionaire…?

'Renzo?'

The sound of her voice dragged him away back into the present and Renzo looked up to see a woman walking through the airport lounge towards him, pulling behind her a battered suitcase on wheels. His eyes narrowed. It was Darcy, yes—but not Darcy as he knew her, in her drab waitress uniform or pale and naked against his pristine white sheets. Renzo blinked. This was Darcy in a dress the colour of sunshine, dotted with tiny blue flowers. It was a simple cotton dress but the way she wore it was remarkable. It wasn't the cut or the label which was making every man in the place stare at her—it was her youthful body and natural beauty. Fresh and glowing, her bare arms and legs were honed by honest hard work rather than mindless sessions in the gym. She looked *radiant* and the natural bounce of her breasts meant that no man could look at her without thinking about procreation. Renzo's mouth dried. Procreation had never been on *his* agenda, but sex most definitely was. He wanted to pull her hungrily into his arms and to kiss her hard on the mouth and feel those soft breasts crushing against him. But Renzo Sabatini would never be seen in any airport—let alone one in his homeland—making such a public demonstration of affection.

And wasn't it time he reinforced the fact that no-body—nobody—ever kept him waiting?

'You're late,' he said repressively, throwing aside his newspaper and rising to his feet.

Darcy nodded. She could sense his irritation but that didn't affect her enjoyment of the way he was looking at her—if only to reassure her she hadn't made a terrible mistake in choosing a cheap cotton dress instead of the clothes he must have been expecting her to wear. Still, since this was going to be the holiday of a lifetime it was important she got it off to a good start and the truth of it was that she *was* late. In fact, she'd started to worry if she would get here at all because that horrible vomiting bug she'd had at the beginning of the week had really laid her low.

'Yes, I know. I'm sorry about that.'

He commandeered her wheeled case and winced slightly as he took her hand luggage. 'What have you got in here? Bricks?'

'I put in a few books,' she said as they set off towards the exit. 'Though I wasn't sure how much time I'd have for reading.'

Usually he would have made a provocative comment in response to such a remark but he didn't and the unyielding expression on his face told her he wasn't ready to forgive her for making him wait. But he didn't say anything as they emerged into the bright sunshine and Darcy was too overcome by the bluest sky she'd ever seen to care.

'Oh, Renzo—I can't believe I'm in Italy. It's so beautiful,' she enthused as she looked around, but still he didn't answer. In fact, he didn't speak until his shiny black car had pulled out of the airport and was heading towards a signpost marked Chiusi.

'I've been waiting at the damned airport for over an hour,' he snapped. 'Why weren't you on the flight I told you to get?'

Darcy hesitated. She supposed she could come up with some vague story to placate him but hadn't she already shrouded so much of her life with evasion and secrets, terrified that someone would examine it in the harsh light of day and judge her? Why add yet another to the long list of things she needed to conceal? And this was different. This wasn't something she was ashamed of—so why not be upfront about the decision she'd made when he had stuffed that enormous wad of cash into her hand and made her feel deeply uncomfortable?

'Because it was too expensive.'

'Darcy, I *gave* you the money to get that flight.'

'I know you did and it was very generous of you.' She drew in a deep breath. 'But when I saw how much it cost to fly to Florence first class, I just couldn't do it.'

'What do you mean, you couldn't do it?'

'It seemed a ludicrous amount of money to spend on a two-hour flight so I bought a seat on a budget airline instead.'

'You did *what*?'

'You should try it sometime. It's true they ran out of sandwiches and the tea was stone-cold, but I saved absolutely loads of money because the price difference was massive. Just like I did with the clothes.'

'The clothes,' he repeated uncomprehendingly.

'Yes. I went to that department store you recommended on Bond Street but the clothes were stupidly overpriced. I couldn't believe how much they were asking for a simple T-shirt so I went to the high street and found some cheaper versions, like this dress.' She smoothed the crisp yellow cotton down over her thighs and her voice wavered a little uncertainly. 'Which I think looks okay, doesn't it?'

He flashed a glance to where her hand was resting. 'Sure,' he said, his voice sounding thick. 'It looks okay.'

'So what's the problem?'

He slammed the palm of his hand against the steering wheel. 'The problem is that I don't like being disobeyed.'

She laughed. 'Oh, Renzo. You sound like a headmaster. You're not my teacher, you know—and I'm not your pupil.'

'Oh, really?' He raised his eyebrows. 'I thought I'd been responsible for teaching you rather a lot.'

His words made her face grow hot as they zoomed past blue-green mountains, but suddenly Darcy was finding the sight of Renzo's profile far more appealing than the Tuscan countryside. He was so unbelievably gorgeous. Just the most gorgeous man she'd ever seen. Would she ever feel this way about anyone again, she wondered—with a chest which became so tight when she looked at him that sometimes it felt as if she could hardly *breathe*? Probably not. It had never happened before, so what were the chances of it happening again? How had Renzo himself described what had happened when they first met? *Colpo di fulmine*—that was it. A lightning strike—which everyone knew was extremely rare. It was about the only bit of Italian she knew.

She sneaked another glance at him. His black hair was ruffled and his shirt was open at the neck—olive skin glowing gold and stunningly illuminated by the rich Tuscan light. His thighs looked taut beneath his charcoal trousers and Darcy could feel the sudden increase of her pulse as her gaze travelled along their muscular length. She'd rarely been in a car with him since the night he had seduced her—or rather, when she had fallen greedily into his arms. She'd hardly been *anywhere* with him other than the bedroom and suddenly she was glad about something which might have bothered other women.

Because with the amazing landscape sliding past like a TV commercial, she thought how easy it would be to get used to this kind of treatment. Not just the obvious luxury of being driven through such beautiful countryside, but the chance to be a bona fide couple like this. And she mustn't get used to it, because it was a one-off. One last sweet taste of Renzo Sabatini before she began her new life in Norfolk and started to forget him—the man with the cold heart who had taught her the definition of pleasure. The precise and brilliant architect who turned into a tiger in the bedroom.

'So what exactly are we going to be doing when we get to this place of yours?' she said.

'You mean apart from making love?'

'Apart from that,' she agreed, almost wishing he hadn't said it despite the instant spring of her breasts in response. Did he need to keep drumming in her sole purpose in his life? She remembered the hiking shoes she'd packed and wondered if she'd completely misjudged the situation. Was he planning to show her anything of Tuscany, or would they simply be doing the bed thing, only in a more glamorous location? She wondered if he had sensed her sudden discomfiture and if that was the reason for his swift glance as they left the motorway for a quieter road.

'The man who is buying the estate is coming for dinner,' he said, by way of explanation.

'Oh? Is that usual?'

'Not really, but he's actually my lawyer and I want to persuade him to keep on the staff who have worked at Vallombrosa for so long. He's bringing his girl-friend with him, so it'll be good to have you there to balance the numbers.'

Darcy nodded. To balance the numbers. Of course. She was there to fill an empty chair and warm the ty-coon's bed—there was nothing more to it than that. Stupidly, his remark hurt but she didn't show it—something in which she'd learned to excel. A child-hood of deprivation and fear had taught her to hide her feelings behind a mask and present the best ver-sion of herself to the world. The version that prospec-tive foster parents might like if they were looking for a child to fit into their lovely home. And if sometimes she wondered what she might reveal if that mask ever slipped, she didn't worry about it for too long because she was never going to let that happen.

'So when were you last abroad?' he questioned, as they passed a pretty little hilltop village.

'Oh, not for ages,' she answered vaguely.

'How come?'

It was a long time since she'd thought about it and Darcy stared straight ahead as she remembered the charity coach trip to Spain when she'd been fifteen. When the blazing summer sun had burned her fair skin and the mobile home on the campsite had felt like sleeping in a hot tin can. They were supposed to be grateful that the church near the children's home had raised enough money to send them on the supposed trip of a lifetime and she had really tried to be grateful. Until somebody had drilled a peephole into the wall of the female showers and there had been a huge fuss about it. And someone had definitely stolen two pairs of her knickers when she'd been out swimming in the overcrowded pool. Somehow she didn't think Renzo Sabatini's Tuscan villa was going to be anything like that. 'I went on a school trip when I was a teenager,' she said. 'That was the only time I've been abroad.'

He frowned. 'You're not much of a traveller, then?'

'You could say that.'

And suddenly Darcy scented danger. On the journey over she'd been worried she might do something stupid. Not something obvious, like using the wrong knife and fork at a fancy dinner, because her waitressing career had taught her everything there was to know about cutlery.

But she realised she'd completely overlooked the fact that proximity might make her careless. Might make her tongue slip and give something away—

something which would naturally repulse him. Renzo had told her that one of the things he liked about her was that she didn't besiege him with questions, or try to *dig deep* to try to understand him better. But that had been a two-way street and the fact he didn't ask about *her* past had suited her just fine. More than fine. She didn't want to tell any lies but she knew she could never tell him the truth. Because there was no point. There was no future in this liaison of theirs, so why tell him about the junkie mother who had given birth to her? Why endure the pain of seeing his lips curve with shock and contempt as had happened so often in the past? In a world where everyone was striving for perfection and judging you, it hadn't taken her long to realise that the best way to get on in life was to bury all the darkness just as deep as she could.

But thoughts of her mother stabbed at her conscience, prompting her to address something which had been bothering her on the flight over.

'You know the money I saved on my airfare and clothes?' she began.

'Yes, Darcy. I know. You were making a point.' He shot her a glance, his lips curving into a sardonic smile. 'Rich man with too much money shown by poor girl just how much he could save if he bothered to shop around. I get the picture.'

'There's no need to be sarcastic, Renzo,' she said stiffly. 'I want you to have it back. I've put most of it in an envelope in my handbag.'

'But I don't want it back. When are you going to get the message? I have more than enough money. And if it makes you feel better, I admire your resourcefulness and refusal to be seduced by my wealth. It's rare.'

For a moment there was silence. 'I think we both know it wasn't your wealth which seduced me, Renzo.'

She hadn't meant to say it but her quiet words reverberated around the car in an honest explanation of what had first drawn her to him. Not his money, nor his power—but him. The most charismatic and compelling man she'd ever met. She heard him suck in an unsteady breath.

'*Madonna mia,*' he said softly. 'Are you trying to tempt me into taking the next turning and finding the nearest layby so that I can do what I have been longing to do to you since last I saw you?'

'Renzo—'

'I don't want the damned money you saved! I want you to put your hand in my lap and feel how hard I am for you.'

'Not while you're driving,' said Darcy and although she was disappointed he had turned the emotional into the sexual, she didn't show it. Because that was the kind of man he was, she reminded herself. He was never emotional and always sexual. She didn't need to touch him to know he was aroused— a quick glance and she could see for herself the hard ridge outlined beneath the dark trousers. Suddenly her lips grew dry in response and she licked them, wishing they *could* have sex right then. Because sex stopped you longing for things you were never going to have. Things other women took for granted—like a man promising to love and protect you. Things which seemed as distant as those faraway mountains. With an effort she dragged her attention back to the present. 'Tell me about this place we're going to instead.'

'You think talking about property is a suitable substitute for discovering what you're wearing underneath that pretty little dress?'

'I think it's absolutely vital if you intend keeping your mind on the road, which is probably the most sensible option if you happen to be driving a car.'

'Oh, Darcy.' He gave a soft laugh. 'Did I ever tell you that one of the things I admire about you is your ability to always come up with a smart answer?'

'The *house*, Renzo. I want to talk about the house.'

'Okay. The house. It's old,' he said as he overtook a lorry laden with a towering pile of watermelons. 'And it stands against a backdrop that Leonardo should have painted, instead of that village south of Piacenza which is not nearly as beautiful. It has orchards and vineyards and olive groves—in fact, we produce superb wines from the Sangiovese grape and enough olive oil to sell to some of the more upmarket stores in London and Paris.'

The few facts he'd recited could have been lifted straight from the pages of an estate agent's website and Darcy felt oddly disappointed. 'It sounds gorgeous,' she said dutifully.

'It is.'

'So...why are you selling it?'

He shrugged. 'It's time.'

'Because?'

Too late, she realised she had asked one question too many. His face grew dark, as if the sun had just dipped behind a cloud and his shadowed jaw set itself into a hard and obdurate line.

'Isn't one of the reasons for our unique chemistry that you don't plague me with questions?'

She heard the sudden darkness underpinning his question. 'I was only—'

'Well, don't. Don't pry. Why change what up until now has been a winning formula?' His voice had harshened as he cut through her words, his hands tensing as a discreet sign appeared among the tangle of greenery which feathered the roadside. 'And anyway. We're here. This is Vallombrosa.'

But his face was still dark as the car began to ascend a tree-lined track towards an imposing pair of dark wrought-iron gates which looked like the gates of heaven.

Or the gates of hell, Darcy thought with a sudden flash of foreboding.

CHAPTER THREE

'HOW ON EARTH am I going to converse with everyone?' questioned Darcy as she stepped out onto the sunny courtyard. 'Since my Italian is limited to the few words I learnt from the phrasebook on the plane and that phrase about the lightning strike?'

'All my staff are bilingual,' Renzo said, his show of bad temper in the car now seemingly forgotten. 'And perfectly comfortable with speaking your mother tongue.'

The words mocked her and Darcy chewed on her lip as she looked away. Mother tongue? Her own mother had taught her to say very little—other than things which could probably have had her prosecuted if she'd repeated them to the authorities.

'Pass Mummy that needle, darling.'

'Pass Mummy those matches.'

'If the policewoman asks if you've met that man before, tell her no.'

But she smiled brightly as she entered the shaded villa and shook hands with Gisella, the elderly housekeeper, and her weather-beaten husband, Pasquale, who was one of the estate's gardeners. A lovely young woman with dark hair helped Gisella around the house and Darcy saw her blush when Renzo introduced her as Stefania. There was also a chef called Donato, who apparently flew in from Rome whenever Renzo was in residence. Donato was tanned, athletic, amazingly good-looking and almost certainly gay.

'Lunch will be in an hour,' he told them. 'But sooner if you're hungry?'

'Oh, I think we can wait,' said Renzo. He turned to Darcy. 'Why don't we take a quick look around while our bags are taken to our room?'

Darcy nodded, thinking how *weird* it felt to be deferred to like that—and to be introduced to his staff just like a real girlfriend. But then she reminded herself that this was only going to work if she didn't allow herself to get carried away. She followed him outside, blinking a little as she took in the vastness of his estate and, although she was seeing only a fraction of it, her senses were instantly overloaded by the beauty of Vallombrosa. Honeybees flitted over purple spears of lavender, vying for space with brightly coloured butterflies. Little lizards basked on baked grey stone. The high walls surrounding the ancient house were covered with scrambling pink roses and stone arches framed the blue-green layers of the distant mountains beyond. Darcy wondered what it must be like growing up somewhere like here, instead of the greyness of the institution in the north of England, which had been the only place she'd ever really called home.

'Like it?' he questioned.

'How could I not? It's beautiful.'

'You know, you're pretty beautiful yourself,' he said softly as he turned his head to look at her.

Remembering the way he'd snapped at her in the car, she wanted to resist him, but the light touch of his hand on her hip and brush of his fingers against her thighs made resistance impossible and Darcy was shaking with longing by the time they reached the shuttered dimness of his bedroom. It was a vast wood-beamed room but there was no time to take in her surroundings because he was pulling her into his arms, his lips brushing hungrily over hers and his fingers tangling themselves in her curls.

'Renzo,' she said unsteadily.

'What?'

She licked her lips. 'You know what.'

'I think I do.' His lips curved into a hard smile. 'You want this?'

Sliding down the zip of her cotton dress, he peeled it away from her and she felt the rush of air against her skin as it pooled to the ground around her ankles. 'Yes,' she breathed. 'That's what I want.'

'Do you know,' he questioned as he unclipped her lacy bra and it joined the discarded dress, 'how much I have been fantasising about you? About this?'

She nodded. 'Me, too,' she said softly, because the newness of the environment and the situation in which she found herself was making her feel almost *shy* in his presence.

But not for long. The beat of her heart and the heat of her blood soon overwhelmed her and had her fumbling for his belt, her fingers trembling with need. Very quickly she was naked and so was he—soft, shuttered light shading their bodies as he pushed her down onto the bed and levered his powerful form over hers. She gripped at the silken musculature of his broad shoulders as he slowly stroked his thumb over her clitoris. And she came right then—so quickly it was almost embarrassing. He laughed softly and eased himself into her wet heat and for a moment he was perfectly still.

'Do you know how good that feels?' he said as he began to move inside her.

She swallowed. 'I've... I've got a pretty good idea.'

'Oh, Darcy. It's you,' he groaned, his eyes closing. 'Only you.'

He said the words like a ragged prayer or maybe a curse—but Darcy didn't read anything into them because she knew exactly what he meant. She was the first and only woman with whom he hadn't needed to wear a condom, because her virginity had elevated her to a different status from his other lovers—he'd told her that himself. He told her she was truly pure. He'd been fascinated to find a woman of twenty-four who'd never had a lover before and by her fervent reply when he'd asked if she ever wanted children.

'Never!'

Her response must have been heartfelt enough to convince him because in a rare moment of confidence he told her he felt exactly the same. Soon afterwards he had casually suggested she might want to go on the pill and Darcy had eagerly agreed. She remembered the first time they'd left the condom off and how it had felt to have his naked skin against hers instead of *'that damned rubber'*—again, his words— between them. It had been...*delicious*. She had felt dangerously close to him and had needed to give herself a stern talking-to afterwards. She'd told herself that the powerful feelings she was experiencing were purely physical. Of course sex felt better without a condom—but it didn't *mean* anything.

But now, in the dimness of his Tuscan bedroom, he was deep inside her. He was filling her and thrusting into her body and kissing her mouth until it throbbed and it felt so amazing that she could have cried. Did her low, moaning sigh break his rhythm? Was that why, with a deft movement, he turned her over so that she was on top of him, his black eyes capturing hers?

'Ride me, *cara*,' he murmured. 'Ride me until you come again.'

She nodded as she tensed her thighs against his narrow hips because she liked this position. It gave her a rare feeling of power, to see Renzo lying underneath her—his eyes half-closed and his lips parted as she rocked back and forth.

She heard his groan and bent her head to kiss it quiet, though she was fairly sure that the walls of this ancient house were deep enough to absorb the age-old sounds of sex. He tangled his hands in her hair, digging his fingers into the wayward curls until pleasure—intense and unalterable—started spiralling up inside her. She came just before he did, gasping as he clasped her hips tightly and hearing him utter something urgent in Italian as his body bucked beneath her. She bent her head to his neck, hot breath panting against his skin until she'd recovered enough to peel herself away from him, before falling back against the mattress.

She looked at the dark beams above her head and the engraved glass lampshade, which looked as if it was as old as the house itself. Someone had put a small vase of scented roses by the window—the same roses which had been scrambling over the walls outside—and all the light in that shadowy room seemed to be centred on those pale pink petals.

'Well,' she said eventually. 'That was some welcome.'

Deliberately, Renzo kept his eyes closed and his breathing steady because he didn't want to talk. Not right now. He didn't need to be told how good it was—that was a given—not when his mind was busy with the inevitable clamour of his thoughts.

He'd felt a complex mixture of stuff as he'd driven towards the house, knowing soon it would be under different ownership. A house which had been in his mother's family for generations and which had had more than its fair share of heartbreak. Other people might have offloaded it years ago but pride had made him hold on to it, determined to replace bad memories with good ones, and to a large extent he'd succeeded. But you couldn't live in the past. It was time to let the place go—to say goodbye to the last clinging fragments of yesterday.

He looked across the bed, where Darcy was lying with her eyes closed, her bright red hair spread all over the white pillow. He thought about her going to Norfolk when they got back to London and tried to imagine what it might be like sleeping with someone else when she was no longer around, but the idea of some slender-hipped brunette lying amid his tumbled sheets was failing to excite him. Instinctively he flattened his palm over her bare thigh.

'And was it the perfect welcome?' he questioned at last.

'You know it was.' Her voice was sleepy. 'Though

I should go and pick my dress up. It's the first time I've worn it.'

'Don't worry about it.' He smiled. 'I'll have Gisella launder it for you.'

'There's no need for that.' Her voice was suddenly sharp as her eyes snapped open. 'I can do my own washing. I can easily rinse it out in the sink and hang it out to dry in that glorious sunshine.'

'And if I told you I'd rather you didn't?'

'Too bad.'

'Why are you so damned stubborn, Darcy?'

'I thought you *liked* my stubbornness.'

'When appropriate, I do.'

'You mean, when it suits *you*?'

'Esattamente.'

She lay back and looked up at the ceiling. How could she explain that she'd felt his housekeeper looking at her and seeing exactly who she was—a servant, just as Gisella was. Like Gisella, she waited tables and cleared up around people who had far more money than she had. That was who she was. She didn't want to look as if she'd suddenly acquired airs and graces by asking to have her clothes laundered. She wasn't going to try to be someone she wasn't—someone who would find it impossible to settle back into her humble world when she got back to England and her billionaire lover was nothing but a distant memory.

But she shouldn't take it out on Renzo, because he was just being Renzo. She'd never objected to his high-handedness before. If the truth were known, she'd always found it a turn-on—and in a way, his arrogance had provided a natural barrier. It had stopped her falling completely under his spell, forcing her to be realistic rather than dreamy. She leaned over and brushed her mouth against his. 'So tell me what you've got planned for us.'

His fingers slid between the tops of her thighs. 'Plans? What plans? The sight of your body seems to have completely short-circuited my brain.'

Halting his hand before it got any further, Darcy enjoyed her brief feeling of power. 'Tell me something about Vallombrosa—and I'm not talking olive or wine production this time. Did you live here when you were a little boy?'

His shuttered features grew wary. 'Why the sudden interest?'

'Because you told me we'd be having dinner with the man who's buying the place. It's going to look a bit odd if I don't know anything about your connection with it. Did you grow up here?'

'No, I grew up in Rome. Vallombrosa was our holiday home.'

'And?' she prompted.

'And it had been in my mother's family for generations. We used it to escape the summer heat of the city. She and I used to come here for the entire vacation and my father would travel down at weekends.'

Darcy nodded because she knew that, like her, he was an only child and that both his parents were dead. And that was pretty much all she knew.

She circled a finger over the hardness of his flat belly. 'So what did you do when you were here?'

He pushed her hand in the direction of his groin. 'My father taught me to hunt and to fish, while my mother socialised and entertained. Sometimes friends came to visit and my mother's school friend Mariella always seemed to be a constant fixture. We were happy, or so I thought.'

Darcy held her breath as something dark and steely entered his voice. 'But you weren't?'

'No. We weren't.' He turned his head to look at her, a hard expression suddenly distorting his features. 'Haven't you realised by now that so few people are?'

'I guess,' she said stiffly. But she'd thought…

What? That other people were strangers to the pain she'd suffered? That someone as successful and as powerful as Renzo had never known emotional deprivation? Was that why he was so distant sometimes—so shuttered and cold? 'Did something happen?'

'You could say that. They got divorced when I was seven.'

'And was it…acrimonious?'

He shot her an unfathomable look. 'Aren't all divorces acrimonious?'

She shrugged. 'I guess.'

'Especially when you discover that your mother's best "friend" has been having an affair with your father for years,' he added, his voice bitter. 'It makes you realise that when the chips are down, women can never be trusted.'

Darcy chewed on her lip. 'So what happened?'

'After the divorce, my father married his mistress but my mother never really recovered. It was a double betrayal and her only weapon was me.'

'Weapon?' she echoed.

He nodded. 'She did everything in her power to keep my father out of my life. She was depressed.' His jaw tightened. 'And believe me, there isn't much a child can do if his mother is depressed. He is—

quite literally—helpless. I used to sit in the corner of the room, quietly making houses out of little plastic bricks while she sobbed her heart out and raged against the world. By the end of that first summer, I'd constructed an entire city.'

She nodded in sudden understanding. Had his need to control been born out of that helplessness? Had the tiny plastic city he'd made been the beginnings of his brilliant architectural career? 'Oh, Renzo—that's... *terrible*,' she said.

He curled his fingers over one breast. 'What an innocent you are, Darcy,' he observed softly.

Darcy felt guilt wash over her. He thought she was a goody-goody because she suspected he was one of those men who divided women into two types— Madonna or whore. Her virginity had guaranteed her Madonna status but it wasn't that simple and if he knew why she had kept herself pure he would be shocked. Married men having affairs was hardly ground-breaking stuff, even if they chose to do it with their wife's best friend—but she could tell him things about *her* life which would make his own story sound like something you could read to a child at bedtime.

And he wasn't asking about *her* past, was he? He wasn't interested—and maybe she ought to be grateful for that. There was no point in dragging out her dark secrets at this late stage in their relationship and ruining their last few days together. 'So what made you decide to sell the estate?'

There was a pause. 'My stepmother died last year,' he said flatly. 'She'd always wanted this house and I suppose I was making sure she never got her hands on it. But now she's gone—they've all gone—and somehow my desire to hang on to it died with her. The estate is too big for a single man to maintain. It needs a family.'

'And you don't want one?'

'I thought we'd already established that,' he said and now his voice had grown cool. 'I saw enough lying and deceit to put me off marriage for a lifetime. Surely you can understand that?'

Darcy nodded. Oh, yes, she understood all right. Just as she recognised that his words were a warning. A warning not to get too close. That just because she was here with him in the unfamiliar role of girlfriend, nothing had really changed. The smile she produced wasn't as bright as usual, but it was good enough to convince him she didn't care. 'Shouldn't we think about getting ready for lunch?' she questioned, her voice growing a little unsteady as his hand moved from her breast to the dip of her belly. 'Didn't...didn't Donato say it would be ready in an hour?'

The touch of her bare skin drove all thoughts from Renzo's mind until he was left with only one kind of hunger. The best kind. The kind which obliterated everything except pleasure. He'd told her more than he usually told anyone and he put that down to the fact that usually she didn't ask. But she needed to know that there would be no more confidences from now on. She needed to know that there was only one reason she was here—and the glint of expectation in her eyes told him that she was getting the message loud and clear. He felt his erection grow exquisitely hard as he looked at the little waitress who somehow knew how to handle him better than any other woman.

'I employ Donato to work to my time frame, not

his,' he said arrogantly, bending his head and sucking at her nipple.

'Oh, Renzo.' Her eyes closed as she fell back against the pillow.

'Renzo, what?' he taunted.

'Don't make me beg.'

He slid his finger over her knee. 'But I like it when you beg.'

'I know you do.'

'So?'

She groaned as her hips lifted hungrily towards his straying finger. 'Please…'

'That's better.' He gave a low and triumphant laugh as he pulled her towards him. 'Lunch can wait,' he added roughly, parting her thighs and positioning himself between them once more. 'I'm afraid this can't.'

CHAPTER FOUR

'THIS?' DARCY HELD up a glimmering black sheath, then immediately waved a flouncy turquoise dress in front of it. 'Or this?'

'The black,' Renzo said, flicking her a swift glance before continuing to button up his shirt.

Her skin now tanned a delicate shade of gold, Darcy slithered into the black dress, aware that Renzo was watching her reflection in the glass in the way a hungry dog might look at a butcher, but she didn't care. She found herself wishing she had the ability to freeze time and that the weekend wasn't drawing to a close because it had been the best few days of her life.

They'd explored his vast estate, scrambling up hilly roads to be rewarded with spectacular views of blue-green mountains and the terracotta smudge of tiny villages. Her hiking boots had come in useful after all! He'd taken her to a beautiful village called Panicale, where they'd drunk coffee in the cobbled square with church bells chiming in stereophonic all around them. And even though Renzo had assured her that May temperatures were too cold for swimming, Darcy wasn't having any of it. She'd never been any-

where with a private pool before—let alone a pool as
vast and inviting as the one at Vallombrosa.

Initially a little shy about appearing in her tiny bikini, she'd been quickly reassured by the darkening
response in his eyes—though she'd been surprised
when he'd changed his mind and decided to join her
in the pool after all. And Renzo in sleek black swim
shorts, olive skin gleaming as he shook water from
his hair, was a vision which made her heart race. She
could have spent all afternoon watching his powerful body ploughing through the silky water. But he'd
brought her lazy swim to a swift conclusion with
some explicit suggestions whispered in her ear and
they had returned to his bedroom for sex which had
felt even more incredible than usual.

Was it because her senses had been heightened by
fresh air and sunshine that everything felt so amazing? Or because Renzo had seemed unusually ac-
cessible in this peaceful place which seemed a world
away from the hustle and bustle of her normal life?
Darcy kept reminding herself that the reasons why
were irrelevant. Because this was only temporary. A
last trip before she moved to Norfolk—which was
probably the only reason he had invited her to join
him. And tonight was their final dinner, when they
were being joined by Renzo's lawyer, who was buying the Sabatini estate.

Their eyes met in the mirror.

'Will you zip me up?'

'Certo.'

'So tell me again,' she said, feeling his fingers
brushing against her bare skin as he slid the zip of the

close-fitting dress all the way up. 'The lawyer's name is Cristiano Branzi and his girlfriend is Nicoletta—'

'Ramelli.' There was a moment of hesitation and his eyes narrowed fractionally. 'And—just so you know—she and I used to have a thing a few years back.'

In the process of hooking in a dangly earring, Darcy's fingers stilled. 'A *thing*?'

'You really are going to have to stop looking so shocked, *cara*. I'm thirty-five years old and in Rome, as in all cities, social circles are smaller than you might imagine. She and I were lovers for a few months, that's all.'

That's all. Darcy's practised smile didn't waver. Just like her. Great sex for a few months and then goodbye—was that his usual pattern? Had Nicoletta been rewarded with a trip abroad just before the affair ended? But as she followed Renzo downstairs she was determined not to spoil their last evening and took the champagne Stefania offered, hoping she displayed more confidence than she felt as she rose to greet their guests.

Cristiano was a powerfully built man with piercing blue eyes and Darcy thought Nicoletta the most beautiful woman she'd ever seen. The Italian woman's sleek dark hair was swept up into a sophisticated chignon and she wore a dress which was obviously designer made. Real diamond studs glittered at her ears, echoing the smaller diamonds which sparkled in a watch which was slightly too loose for her narrow wrist. Darcy watched as she presented each smooth cheek in turn to be kissed by Renzo, wondering why she hadn't worn the turquoise dress after all. Why hadn't she realised that of *course* the Italian woman would also wear black, leaving the two of them wide open for comparison? How cheap her own glimmering gown must seem in comparison—and how wild her untameable red curls as they spilled down over her shoulders towards breasts which were much too large by fashionable standards.

'So...' Nicoletta smiled as they sat down to prosciutto and slivers of iced melon at a candlelit table decorated with roses. 'This is your first time in Italy, Darcy?'

'It is,' answered Darcy, with a smile.

'But not your last, I hope?'

Darcy looked across the table at Renzo, thinking it might bring the mood down if she suddenly announced that they were in the process of splitting up.

'Darcy isn't much of a traveller,' he said smoothly.

'Oh?'

Something made her say it. Was it bravado or stupidity? Yet surely she wasn't *ashamed* of the person she really was. Not unless she honestly thought she could compete with these glossy people, with their Tuscan estates and diamond wristwatches which probably cost as much as a small car.

'To be honest, I don't really have a lot of money to go travelling.' She slanted Nicoletta a rueful smile. 'I'm a waitress.'

'A *waitress*?' Nicoletta's silver fork was returned to her plate with a clatter, the dainty morsel she'd speared remaining untouched. 'That is a very unusual job.' There was a slightly perplexed pause. 'So how did you and Renzo actually meet?'

Darcy registered the faint astonishment on Nicoletta's face, but what had she expected? And now she had dropped Renzo in it. He was probably going to bluster out some story about how he'd bumped into her in a bookshop or been introduced at a party by a friend of a friend. Except he'd told her very specifically that he didn't like lies, hadn't he?

'I met Darcy when she was working in a nightclub in London,' Renzo said. 'I walked in with some visiting colleagues and saw her serving cocktails to the people on the next table. She turned round and looked at me and that was it. I was completely blown away.'

'I'm not surprised,' murmured Cristiano. 'I have never seen hair as bright as yours before, Darcy. I believe this is what they call the show-stopping look?'

The compliment was unexpected and Darcy met Renzo's eyes, expecting to find mockery or anger in them but there was none. On the contrary, he looked as if he was *enjoying* the praise being directed at her and suddenly she wanted to turn and run from the room. Or tell him not to look at her that way because it was making her fantasise about a life which could never be hers.

She cleared her throat, trying to remember back to when she'd worked in that very hip restaurant which had been frequented by the media crowd. To remember how those high-profile people used to talk to each other when she arrived to offer them a bread roll, which they inevitably refused. They used to play everything down, didn't they? To act as if nothing really mattered.

'Oh, that's quite enough about me,' she said lightly. 'I'd much rather talk about Tuscany.'

'You like it here?' questioned Nicoletta. 'At Val-lombrosa?'

'Who could fail to like it?' questioned Darcy simply. 'There can't be anywhere in the world as beautiful as this. The gardens are so lovely and the view is to die for.' She smiled as she reached for a piece of bread. 'If I had the money I'd snap it up in a shot. You're a very lucky man, Cristiano.'

'I'm very aware of that.' Cristiano's blue eyes crinkled. 'Nobody can quite believe that Renzo has put it on the market at last, after years of everyone offering him vast amounts of money to sell it. And he won't say what has suddenly changed his mind.'

But Darcy knew why. She'd seen the pain in his eyes when he'd talked about his parents' divorce and suspected his stepmother's death had made him want to let all that painful past go. He hadn't said that much but it surprised her that he'd confided in her at all. For a little while it had made her feel special—more than just his 'friend with benefits.' But that was fantasy, too. It was easy to share your secrets with someone you knew was planning to leave you.

Except for her, of course. She was one of those people whose secrets were just too dark to tell.

Course after course of delicious food was served—stuffed courgette flowers, ultra-fine pasta with softshell crab and a rich dessert of cherries and cream—all accompanied by fine wines from Renzo's cellar. Nicoletta skilfully fired a series of questions at her, some of which Darcy carefully avoided answering but fortunately Nicoletta enjoyed talking about herself much more. She waxed lyrical about her privileged upbringing in Parioli in Rome, her school in Swit-

zerland and her fluency in four languages. It trans-
pired that she had several dress shops in Rome, none
of which she worked in herself.

'You should come visit, Darcy. Get Renzo to buy
you something pretty.'

Darcy wondered if that was Nicoletta's way of
subtly pointing out that the cheapness of her clothes
hadn't gone unnoticed, but if it was, she didn't care.
All she could think about right then was being alone
with Renzo again as she tried not to focus on time
slipping away from them. She returned to their room
while he waved their guests goodbye and was naked
in bed waiting for him when at last he came in and
shut the door behind him.

'You were very good during dinner,' he said, un-
buckling the belt of his trousers.

'Good? In what way?'

'A bewitching combination. A little defiant about
your lowly job,' he observed as he stepped out of
his boxer shorts. 'And there's no need to look at me
that way, Darcy, because it's true. But your heartfelt praise about the property pleased Cristiano very
much, though he's always been a sucker for a pretty
girl. He's going to keep Gisella, Pasquale and Stefania on, by the way. He told me just before they left
for Rome.'

'So all's well that ends well?' she questioned
brightly.

'Who said anything about it ending?' he murmured, climbing into bed and pulling her into his
arms so that she could feel the hard rod of his arousal
pushing against her. 'I thought the night was only
just beginning.'

They barely slept a wink. It was as if Renzo was determined to leave her with lasting memories of just what an amazing lover he was as he brought her to climax over and over again. As dawn coated the dark room with a pale daffodil light, Darcy found herself enjoying the erotic spectacle of Renzo's dark head between her thighs, gasping as his tongue cleaved over her exquisitely aroused flesh, until she quivered helplessly around him.

She was slow getting ready the next morning and when she walked into the dining room, Renzo glanced up from his newspaper.

'I need to leave for the airport soon,' she said.

'No, you don't. We'll fly back together on my jet,' he said, pouring her a cup of coffee.

Darcy sat down and reached for a sugar cube. *Start as you mean to go on. And remember that your future does not contain billionaire property tycoons with an endless supply of private transport.*

'Honestly, there's no need,' she said. 'I have a return ticket and I'm perfectly happy to go back on FlyCheap.'

The look he gave her was a mixture of wry, indulgent—but ultimately uncompromising. 'I'm not sending you back on a budget airline, Darcy. You're coming on my jet, with me.'

And if Darcy had thought that travelling in a chauffeur-driven car was the height of luxury, then flying in Renzo's private plane took luxury onto a whole new level. She saw the unmistakable looks of surprise being directed at her by two stewardesses as they were whisked through passport control at Florence airport. Were they thinking she didn't look like Renzo's usual *type*, with her cheap jewellery, her bouncing bosom and the fact that she was clearly out of her comfort zone?

But Darcy didn't care about that either. She was just going to revel in her last few hours with her lover and as soon as he'd dismissed the flight crew she unzipped his jeans. As she pulled down his silk boxers she realised this was the last time she would ever slide her lips over his rocky length and hear his helpless groan as he jerked inside her mouth. The last time he would ever give that low, growling moan as he clamped his hands possessively around her head to anchor her lips to the most sensitive part of his anatomy. Afterwards, he made love to her so slowly that she felt as if she would never come down to earth properly.

But all too soon the flight was over and they touched down in England where his car was waiting. Darcy hesitated as the driver held open the door for her.

'Could you drop me off at the Tube on the way?'

Renzo frowned, exasperation flattening his lips. 'Darcy, what is this? I'm not dropping you anywhere except home.'

'No. You don't have to do that.'

'I know I don't.' He paused before giving a flicker of a smile. 'You can even invite me in for coffee if you like.'

'Coffee?'

'There you go. You're sounding shocked again.' He shook his head. 'Isn't that what normally happens when a man takes a woman home after the kind of weekend we've just had? I've never even seen where you live.'

'I know you haven't. But you're not interested in my life. You've always made that perfectly clear.'

'Maybe I'm interested now,' he said stubbornly.

And now was too late, she thought. Why hadn't he done this at the beginning, when it might have meant something? He was behaving with all the predictability of a powerful man who had everything he wanted—his curiosity suddenly aroused by the one thing which was being denied him.

'It's small and cramped and all I can afford, which is why I'm moving to Norfolk,' she said defensively. 'It's about as far removed from where you live as it's possible to be and you'll hate it.'

'Why don't you let me be the judge of that? Unless you're ashamed of it, of course.'

Furiously, she glared at him. 'I'm not *ashamed* of it.'

'Well, then.' He shrugged. 'What's the problem?'

But Darcy's fingers were trembling as she unlocked her front door because she'd never invited *anyone* into this little sanctuary of hers. When you'd shared rooms and space for all of your life—when you'd struggled hard to find some privacy—then something which was completely your own became especially precious. 'Come in, then,' she said ungraciously.

Renzo stepped into the room and the first thing he noticed was that the living, dining and kitchen area were all crammed into the same space. And…his eyes narrowed…was that a narrow *bed* in the corner?

The second thing he noticed was how clean and unbelievably tidy it was—and the minimalist architect in him applauded her total lack of clutter. There

were no family photos or knick-knacks. The only em-
bellishment he could see was a cactus in a chrome pot
on the window sill and an art deco mirror, which reflected some much-needed extra light into the room.
And books. Lots of books. Whole lines of them,
neatly arranged in alphabetical order.

He turned to look at her. She had been careful
about sitting in the Tuscan sun but, even so, her fair
skin had acquired a faint glow. She looked much
healthier than she'd done when she'd arrived at Vallombrosa, that was for sure. In fact, she looked so
pretty in the yellow dress with blue flowers which she
had stubbornly insisted on laundering herself, that he
felt his heart miss a beat. And suddenly Renzo knew
he wasn't ready to let her go. Not yet. He thought
about the way she'd been in his arms last night. The
way they'd taken their coffee out onto the terrace at
Vallombrosa to stare at the moon, and he'd known a
moment of unexpected peace. Why end something
before it fizzled out all of its own accord, especially
when it still had the potential to give him so much
pleasure?

He glanced over towards her neat little kitchenette.
'So... Aren't you going to offer me coffee?'

'I've only got instant, I'm afraid.'

He did his best to repress a shudder. 'Just some
water, then.'

He watched as she poured him a glass of tap
water—he couldn't remember the last time he'd drunk
that—and added an ice cube. But when she put the
drink down on the table, he didn't touch it. Instead,
he fixed her with a steady gaze.

'I've had a good weekend,' he said slowly.

'Me, too. Actually, it was more than good.' She gave him a quick smile. 'Thank you.'

There was a pause. 'Look, this move to Norfolk seems a little…hasty. Why don't you stay in London a bit longer?'

'I told you why—and now you've seen for yourself my reasons. I want to start living differently.'

'I can understand that. But what if I told you I had an apartment you could use—somewhere much bigger and more comfortable than this? What then?'

'What, just like that? Let me guess.' Her emerald gaze bored into him. 'Even if you don't have one available, you'll magically "find" an apartment for me? Browse through your extensive property portfolio or have one of your staff discreetly rent somewhere? Thanks, but no, thanks. I'm not interested, Renzo. I have no desire to be a "kept woman" and fulfilling the stereotype of being a rich man's mistress, even if that's the way I'm currently heading.'

Her stubbornness infuriated him but it also produced another spark of admiration. How could a woman with so little be so proud and spirited and turn down an offer anyone else in her position would have leapt at? Renzo picked up the iced water and sipped it before walking over to the window and looking out at a red-brick wall. He wondered what it must be like to wake up to this view every morning, before putting on some drab uniform to spend the rest of the day carrying trays of food and drink.

He turned round. 'What if I asked you to delay going to Norfolk?'

She raised her eyebrows. 'And why would you do that?'

'Oh, come on, Darcy,' he said softly. 'You may have been an innocent when I bedded you, but you're not so innocent now. I have taught you a great deal—'

'Perhaps there's some kind of certificate I could nominate you for, if it's praise you're after?'

He gave a low laugh, turned on by an insolence he encountered from nobody else. He could see the wariness on her face as he took a step towards her, but he could also see the darkening of her eyes and the sudden stiffness of her body, as if she was using every bit of willpower not to give into what she really wanted. And Renzo knew enough about women to realise that this wasn't over. Not yet.

'It's not praise I want,' he said softly. 'It's you. I'm not ready to let you go.' He reached out to smooth down her riotous curls and felt the kick of lust as he pulled her into his arms. 'What if I told you that I liked the way you were with Cristiano and Nicoletta? That I find you charming in company as well as exquisite in bed and that maybe I'd like to take you out a little more. Why shouldn't we go to the theatre, or a party or two? Perhaps I've been a little selfish keeping you locked away and now I want to show you off to the world.'

'You make it sound as if I've passed some sort of hidden test!' she said indignantly.

'Maybe you have,' came his simple reply.

Darcy was torn, because his words were dangerous. She didn't want him *showing her off to the world*. What if someone remembered her? Someone who knew who she really was? And yet Renzo was only echoing the things she'd been thinking. Things she'd been trying and failing to deny—that she wasn't yet ready to walk away either.

'What if I gave you a key to my apartment?' His voice broke into her thoughts.

'A key?' she echoed.

'Why not? And—just so you know—I don't hand out keys every day of the week. Very few people are given access to my home because I value my privacy very highly.'

'So why me? To what do I owe this huge honour?'

'Because you've never asked me for anything,' he said quietly. 'And nobody's ever done that before.'

Darcy tried telling herself it was just another example of a powerful man being intrigued by the unfamiliar. But surely it was more than that. Wasn't the giving of a key—no matter how temporary—a sign that he *trusted* her? And wasn't trust the most precarious yet most precious thing in the world, especially considering Renzo's lack of it where women were concerned?

She licked her lips, tempted beyond reason, but really—when she stopped to think about it—what was holding her back? She'd escaped her northern life and left that dark world behind as she'd carved out a new identity for herself. She'd been completely underqualified and badly educated but night classes had helped make up for her patchy schooling—and her sunny disposition meant she'd been able to find waitressing work whenever she had put her mind to it. She wasn't quite sure where she wanted to be but she knew she was on her way. And who would possibly remember her after all this time? She'd left Manchester for London when she was sixteen and that was a long time ago. Didn't she deserve a little fun while she had the chance?

He was watching her closely and Darcy was savvy enough to realise her hesitation was turning him on. Yet she wasn't playing games with him. Her indecision was genuine. She really *was* trying to give him up, only it wasn't as easy as she'd imagined. She was beginning to suspect that Renzo Sabatini was becoming an addiction and that should have set off every alarm bell in her body because it didn't matter if it was drink or drugs or food—or in this case a man—addictions were dangerous. She knew that. Her personal history had taught her that in the bleakest way possible.

But now he was pulling her against him and she could feel all that hard promise shimmering beneath the surface of his muscular body. Enveloped by his arms, she found herself wanting to sink further into his powerful embrace, wanting to hold on to this brief sense of comfort and safety.

'Say yes, Darcy,' he urged softly, his breath warm against her lips. 'Take my key and be my lover for a little while longer.'

His hand was on her breast and her knees were starting to buckle and Darcy knew then that she wasn't going to resist him anytime soon.

'Okay,' she said, closing her eyes as he began to ruck up her dress. 'I'll stay for a bit longer.'

CHAPTER FIVE

THE LIMOUSINE SLID to a halt outside the Granchester Hotel as Renzo was caressing Darcy's thigh and he found himself thinking that she'd never looked more beautiful than she did tonight. Hungrily, he ran his gaze over the emerald shimmer of her gown, thinking that for once she looked like a billionaire's mistress.

He gave an almost imperceptive shake of his head. Didn't she realise that, despite her initial reluctance, she was entitled to a mistress's perks? He'd tried to persuade her that it would be easier all round if she enjoyed *all* the benefits of his wealth and made herself more available to him by giving up her lowly job, but she had stubbornly refused to comply. She'd told him he should be grateful she was no longer working in the nightclub and he had growled at the thought of her curvy body poured into that tight black satin while men drooled over her.

But tonight, a small victory had been won. For once she'd accepted his offer of a custom-made gown to wear to the prestigious ball he was holding in aid of his charity foundation, though it had taken some persuasion. His mouth flattened because where once her stubborn independence had always excited him, her independence was starting to rankle, as was her determination to carry on waiting tables even though it took up so much of her time.

'The princess is supposed to be smiling when she goes to the ball,' he observed wryly, feeling her sequin-covered thigh tense beneath his fingers. 'Not looking as if she's walking towards her own execution.'

'But I'm not a princess, Renzo. I'm a waitress who happens to be wearing a gown which cost as much as I earn in three months.' She touched her fingertips to one of the mother-of-pearl clips which gleamed like milky rainbows against the abundant red curls. 'If you must know, I feel like Cinderella.'

'Ah, but the difference is that your clothes will not turn into rags at midnight, *cara*. When the witching hour comes you will be doing something far more pleasurable than travelling home in a pumpkin. So wipe that concerned look from your face and give me that beautiful smile instead.'

Feeling like a puppet, Darcy did as he asked, flashing a bright grin as someone rushed forward to open the car door for her. Carefully, she picked up the fishtail skirt of her emerald gown and stepped onto the pavement in her terrifyingly high shoes, thinking how quickly you could get used to being driven around like this and having people leap to attention simply because you were in the company of one of the world's most powerful men. What was not so easy was getting rid of the growing feeling of anxiety which had been gnawing away inside her for weeks now—a sick, queasy feeling which just wouldn't shift.

Because she was starting to realise that she was

stuck. Stuck in some awful limbo. Living in a strange, parallel world which wasn't real and locked into it by her inability to walk away from the only man who had ever been able to make her feel like a real woman.

The trouble was that things had changed and they were changing all the time. Why hadn't she realised that agreeing to accept the key to his apartment would strengthen the connection between them and make it even harder for her to sever her ties with him? It had made things…*complicated*. She didn't want her heart to thunder every time she looked at him or her body to melt with instant desire. Her worst fears had been realised and Renzo Sabatini had become her addiction. She ran her tongue over her lips. She knew he was bad for her yet she couldn't seem to give him up.

Sometimes she found herself longing for him to tire of her and kick *her* out since she didn't have the strength to end it herself. Wouldn't such a move force her to embrace the new life in Norfolk which she'd done absolutely nothing about—not since the day he'd given her his key and then made her come on the narrow bed in her humble bedsit, which these days she only ever visited when Renzo was away on business?

She could hear him telling his driver to take the rest of the night off and that they'd get a taxi home when the ball was over and she wished he wouldn't be so thoughtful with his staff. No wonder they all thought the world of him. But Darcy didn't need any more reasons to like him. Hadn't it been easier not to let her heart become involved when their affair had been more low-key, rather than this new-found openness with trips to the opera and theatre and VIP balls?

And now he was taking her arm and leading her towards the red-carpeted marble staircase where the paparazzi were clustered. She'd known they were going to be there, but had also known she couldn't possibly avoid them. And anyway, they weren't going to be looking at *her*. They would be far too busy focussing on the Hollywood actress who was wearing the most revealing dress Darcy had ever seen, or the married co-star she was rumoured to be having an affair with.

Flashbulbs exploded to light up the warm night and although Darcy quickly tried to turn her head away, the press weren't having any of it. And wasn't that a TV camera zooming in on her? She wondered why she had let the dress designer put these stupid clips in her hair which meant she couldn't hide behind the usual comforting curtain of her curls. This was the most high-profile event they'd attended as a couple but there had been no way of getting out of it—not when it was Renzo's foundation and he was the man who'd organised it.

She felt like a fox on the run as they entered the ballroom but the moment she was swallowed up by all that glittering splendour, she calmed down. The gilded room had been decked out with giant sprays of pink-and-white cherry blossoms, symbolising the hope which Renzo's foundation brought to suffering children in war-torn areas of the world. Tall, guttering candles gave the place a fairy-tale feel. On a raised dais, a string quartet was playing and the exquisitely dressed guests were mingling in small chattering groups. It was the fanciest event she'd ever attended and dinner had been prepared by a clutch of award-winning chefs. But the moment the first rich course was placed in front of her, Darcy's stomach did an intricate kind of twist, which meant she merely pushed the food around her plate and tried not to look at it. At least Renzo didn't notice or chide her for her lack of appetite as he might normally have done—he was too busy talking to fundraisers and donors and being photographed next to the diamond necklace which was the star lot for the night's auction.

But after disappearing into one of the restrooms, where a splash of her face with cold water made her queasiness shift, Darcy became determined to enjoy herself. *Stop living so fearfully*, she chided herself as she chatted attentively whenever she was introduced to someone new and rose eagerly to her feet when Renzo asked her to dance. And that bit felt like heaven. His cheek was warm against hers and her body fitted so snugly into his that she felt like one of those salt and pepper shakers you sometimes found in old-fashioned tea rooms—as if they were made to be together. But they weren't. Of course they weren't.

She knew this couldn't continue. She'd been seduced into staying but if she stayed much longer she was going to have to tell him the truth. Open up about her past. Confess to being the daughter of a junkie and all the other stuff which went with it. He would probably end their affair immediately and a swift, clean cut might just be the best thing. She would be heartbroken for a while of course, but she would get over it because you could get over just about anything if you worked at it. It would be better than forcing herself to walk away and having to live with the stupid spark of hope that maybe it *could* have worked.

'So… How is the most beautiful woman in the

room?' He bent his head to her ear. 'You seem to be enjoying yourself.'

She closed her eyes and inhaled his sultry masculine scent. 'I am.'

'Not as bad as you thought it was going to be?'

'Not nearly so bad.'

'Think you might like to come to something like this again in the future?'

'I *could* be persuaded.'

He smiled. 'Then let's go and sit down. The auction is about to begin.'

The auctioneer stepped onto the stage and began to auction off the different lots which had been donated as prizes. A holiday in Mauritius, a box at the opera and a tour of Manchester United football ground all went under the hammer for eye-watering amounts, and then the diamond necklace was brought out to appreciative murmurs.

Darcy listened as the bidding escalated, only vaguely aware of Renzo lifting a careless finger from time to time. But suddenly everyone was clapping and looking at *them* and she realised that Renzo had successfully bid for the necklace and the auctioneer's assistant had handed it to him and he was putting it on *her* neck. She was aware of every eye in the room on them as he fixed the heavy clasp in place and she was aware of the dazzle of the costly gems.

'In truth you should wear emeralds to match your eyes,' he murmured. 'But since diamonds were the only thing on offer they will have to do. What do you think, *cara*?'

Darcy couldn't get rid of the sudden lump in her throat. It felt like a noose. The stones were heavy and the metal was cold. But there was no time to protest because cameras were flashing again and this time they were all directed at her. Sweat beaded her forehead and she felt dizzy, only able to breathe normally when the rumour went round that the Hollywood star was exiting through the kitchens and the press pack left the ballroom to follow her.

Darcy turned to Renzo, her fingertips touching the unfamiliar stones. 'You do realise I can't possibly accept this?' she questioned hoarsely.

'And you do realise that I am not going to let you give it back? Your tastes are far too modest for a woman in your position. You are the lover of a very wealthy man, Darcy, and I want you to wear it. I want you to have some pretty jewels for all the pleasure you've given me.'

His voice had dipped into a silken caress, which usually would have made her want to melt, but he made it sound like payment for services rendered. Was that how he saw it? Darcy's smile felt as if someone had stitched it onto her face with a rusty needle. Shouldn't she at least try to look as a woman *should* look when a man had just bought something this valuable? And wasn't she in danger of being a hypocrite? After all, she had a key to his Belgravia home—wasn't that just a short step to accepting his jewels? What about the designer dress she was wearing tonight, and the expensive shoes? He'd bought those for her, hadn't he?

Something like fear clutched at her heart and she knew she couldn't put it off any longer. She was going to have to come clean about her mum and the children's home and all the other sordid stuff.

So tell him. Explain your aversion to accepting gifts and bring this whole crazy relationship to a head, because at least that will end the uncertainty and you'll know where you stand.

But in the car he kissed her and when they reached the apartment he kissed her some more, unclipping the diamond choker and dropping it onto a table in the sitting room as casually as if it had been made of paste. His hands were trembling as he undressed her and so were hers. He made love to her on one of the sofas and then he carried her into the bedroom and did it all over again—and who would want to talk about the past at a moment like that?

They made love most of the night and because she'd asked for a day off after the ball, Darcy slept late next morning. When she eventually woke, it was getting on for noon and Renzo had left for the office long ago. *And still she hadn't told him.* She showered and dressed but her queasiness had returned and she could only manage some mint tea for breakfast. The morning papers had been delivered and, with a growing sense of nervousness, she flicked through the pages until she found the column which listed society events. And there she was in all her glory—in her mermaid dress of green sequins, the row of fiery white diamonds glittering at her throat, with Renzo standing just behind her, a hint of possessiveness in the sexy smile curving his lips.

She stood up abruptly, telling herself she was being paranoid. Who was going to see, or, more important, to *care* that she was in the wretched paper?

The morning slipped away. She went for a walk, bought a bag of oranges to put through the squeezer and was just nibbling on a piece of dry toast when the doorbell rang and Darcy frowned. It never rang when Renzo wasn't here—and not just because his wasn't a lifestyle where people made spontaneous visits. He'd meant what he said about guarding his privacy; his home really was his fortress. People just didn't come round.

She pressed the button on the intercom.

'Yes?'

'Is that Darcy Denton?' It was a male voice with a broad Manchester accent.

'Who is this?' she questioned sharply.

'An old friend of yours.' There was a pause. 'Drake Bradley.'

For a minute Darcy thought she might pass out. She thought about pretending to be someone else—the housekeeper perhaps. Or just cutting the connection while convincing herself that she didn't have to speak to anyone—let alone Drake Bradley. But the bully who had ruled the roost in the children's home had never been the kind of person to take no for an answer. If she refused to speak to him she could imagine him settling down to wait until Renzo got home and she just imagined what he might have to say to him. Shivering, she stared at her pale reflection in the hall mirror. What was it they said? Keep your friends close but your enemies closer.

'What do you want?'

'Just a few minutes of your time. Surely you can spare that, Darcy.'

Telling herself it was better to brazen it out, Darcy pressed the buzzer, her heart beating out a primitive tattoo as she opened the door to find Drake standing there—a sly expression on his pockmarked face. A decade had made his hair recede, but she would have recognised him immediately and her blood ran cold as the sight of him took her back to a life she'd thought she'd left for ever.

'What do you want?' she asked again.

'That's not much of a welcome, is it? What's the matter, Darcy? Aren't you going to invite me in? Surely you're not ashamed of me?'

But the awful thing was that she *was*. She'd moved on a lot since that turbulent period when their lives had merged and clashed, yet Drake looked as if he'd been frozen in time. Wearing clothes which swamped his puny frame, he had oil beneath his fingernails and on the fingers of his left hand were the letters *H*, *A*, *T*, *E*. *You have no right to judge him*, she told herself. He was simply another survivor from the shipwreck of their youth. Surely she owed him a little hospitality when she'd done so well for herself.

She could smell stale tobacco and the faint underlying odour of sweat as she opened the door wider and he brushed past her. He followed her into the enormous sitting room and she wondered if he was seeing the place as she had seen it the first time she'd been here, when she'd marvelled at the space and light and cleanliness. And, of course, the view.

'Wow.' He pursed his lips together and whistled as he stared out at the whispering treetops of Eaton Square. 'You've certainly landed on your feet, Darcy.'

'Are you going to tell me why you're here?'

His weasel eyes narrowed. 'Not even going to offer me a drink? It's a hot day outside. I could murder a drink.'

Darcy licked her lips. *Don't aggravate him. Tolerate him for a few minutes and then he'll go.* 'What would you like?'

'Got a beer?'

'Sure.'

Her underlying nausea seemed to intensify as Darcy went to the kitchen to fetch him a beer. When she returned he refused her offer of a glass and began to glug greedily from the bottle.

'How did you find me?' she asked, once he had paused long enough to take a breath.

He put the bottle down on a table. 'Saw you on the news last night, walking into that big hotel. Yeah. On TV. Couldn't believe my eyes at first. I thought to myself, that can't be Darcy Denton—daughter of one of Manchester's best known hookers. Not on the arm of some rich dude like Sabatini. So I headed along to the hotel to see for myself and hung around until your car arrived. I'm good at hanging around in the shadows, I am.' He smiled slyly. 'I overheard your man giving the address to the taxi driver so I thought I'd come and pay you a visit to catch up on old times. See for myself how you've come up in the world.'

Darcy tried to keep her voice light. To act as if her heart weren't pounding so hard it felt as if it might burst right out of her chest. 'You still haven't told me what you want.'

His smile grew calculating. 'You've landed on your feet, Darcy. Surely it's no big deal to help out an old friend?'

'Are you asking for money?' she said.

He sneered. 'What do you think?'

She thought plenty but nothing she'd want *him* to

hear. She thought about how much cash she had squirrelled away in her bank account. She'd amassed funds since she'd been with Renzo because he wouldn't let her pay for anything. *But it was still a pitiful amount by most people's standards, and besides…if you gave in to blackmail once then you opened up the floodgates.*

And she didn't need to give into blackmail because hadn't she already decided to tell Renzo about her past? This might be the push she needed to see if he still wanted her when he discovered who she really was. Her mouth dried. Dared she take that risk?

She had no choice.

Drawing her shoulders back, she looked straight into Drake's shifty eyes. 'You're not getting any money from me,' she said quietly. 'I'd like you to leave and not bother coming back.'

His lip curled and then he shrugged. 'Have it your own way, Darcy.'

Of course, if she'd thought it through properly, she might have wondered why he obeyed her quite so eagerly…

Renzo's eyes narrowed as the man with the pockmarked face shoved his way past, coming out of *his* private elevator as if he had every right to do so. His frown deepened. Had he been making some kind of delivery? Surely not, dressed like *that*? He stood for a moment watching his retreating back, instinct alerting him to a danger he didn't quite understand. But it was enough to cast a shadow over a deliciously high mood which had led to him leaving work early—

something which had caused his secretary to blink at him in astonishment.

In truth, Renzo had been pretty astonished himself. Taking a half-day off wasn't the way he usually operated, but he had wanted to spend the rest of the afternoon with Darcy. Getting into bed with her. Running his fingers through her silky riot of curls. Losing himself deep in her tight, tight body with his mouth on her breast. Maybe even telling her how good she made him feel. Plus he'd received an urgent message reminding him that he needed to insure the necklace he'd spent a fortune on last night.

After watching the man leave the building, Renzo took the penthouse elevator where the faint smell of tobacco and beer still tainted the air. He unlocked the door to his apartment just as Darcy tore out of the sitting room. But the trouble was she didn't look like the Darcy of this morning's smouldering fantasies, when somehow he'd imagined arriving home to see her clad in that black satin basque and matching silk stockings he'd recently bought. Not only was she wearing jeans and a baggy shirt—her face was paler than usual and her eyes looked huge and haunted with something which looked like guilt. Now, why was that? he wondered.

'Renzo!' she exclaimed, raking a handful of bouncing red curls away from her forehead and giving him an uncertain smile. 'I wasn't expecting you.'

'So I see.' He put his briefcase on the hall table. 'Who was the man I saw leaving?'

'The man?' she questioned, but he could hear the sudden quaver in her voice.

Definitely guilt, he thought grimly.

'The man I met coming down in the elevator. Bad skin. Bad smell. Who was he, Darcy?'

Darcy met the cool accusation in Renzo's eyes and knew she had run out of reasons not to tell him.

'I need to talk to you,' she said.

He didn't respond straight away, just walked into the sitting room leaving her to follow him, her senses alerted to the sudden tension in his body and the forbidding set of his shoulders. Usually, he pulled her into his arms and kissed all the breath out of her when he arrived home but today he hadn't even touched her. And when he turned around, Darcy was shocked by the cold expression on his face.

'So talk,' he said.

She felt like someone who'd been put on stage in front of a vast audience and told to play a part she hadn't learnt. Because she'd never spoken about this before, not to anyone. She'd buried it so deep it was almost inaccessible. But she needed to access it now, before his irritation grew any deeper.

'He's someone I was in care with.'

'In care?'

She nodded. 'That's what they call it in England, although it's a bit of a misnomer because you don't actually get much in the way of care. I lived in a children's home in the north for most of my childhood.'

His black eyes narrowed. 'What happened to your parents?'

Darcy could feel a bead of sweat trickling its way down her back. Here it was. The question which separated most normal people from the unlucky few. The question which made you feel a freak no matter which way you answered it. Was it any wonder she'd spent her life trying to avoid having to do so?

And yet didn't it demonstrate the shallowness of her relationship with Renzo that in all the time she'd known him—this was the first time he'd actually asked? Dead parents had been more than enough information for him. He hadn't been the type of person to quiz her about her favourite memory or how she'd spent her long-ago Christmases.

'I'm illegitimate,' she said baldly. 'I don't know who my father was and neither did my mother. And she… Well, for a lot of my childhood, she wasn't considered fit to be able to take care of me.'

'Why not?'

'She had…' She hesitated. 'She had a drug problem. She was a junkie.'

He let out a long breath and Darcy found herself searching his face for some kind of understanding, some shred of compassion for a situation which had been out of her control. But his expression remained like ice. His black eyes were stony as they skimmed over her, looking at her as if it was the first time he'd seen her and not liking what they saw.

'Why didn't you tell me any of this before?'

'Because you didn't ask. And you didn't ask because you didn't want to know!' she exclaimed. 'You made that very clear. We haven't had the kind of relationship where we talked about stuff like this. You just wanted…sex.'

She waited for him to deny it. To tell her that there had been more to it than that—and Darcy realised she was already thinking of their relationship in the past tense. But he didn't deny it. His sudden closed look made his features appear shuttered as he walked over to the table near where he'd undressed her last night and her heart missed a beat as she saw him looking down at the polished surface, on which stood a lamp and nothing else.

Nothing else.

It took a moment for her to register the significance of this and that moment came when he lifted his black gaze to hers and slanted her an unfathomable look. 'Where's the necklace?' he questioned softly.

Darcy's mind raced. In the heat of everything that had happened, she'd forgotten about the diamond necklace he'd bought last night for her at the auction. She vaguely remembered the dazzle of the costly gems as he'd dropped them onto the table, but his hands had been all over her at the time and it had blotted out everything except the magic of his touch. Had she absent-mindedly tidied it away when she was picking up her clothes this morning? No. It had definitely been there when…

Fear and horror clamped themselves around her suddenly racing heart.

When…

Drake! Her throat dried as she remembered leaving him alone in the room while she went to fetch him a beer. Remembered the way he'd hurriedly left after his half-hearted attempt at blackmail. Had Drake stolen the necklace?

Of course he had.

'I don't—'

His voice was like steel. 'Did your friend take it?'

'He's not—'

'What's the matter, Darcy?' Contemptuously, he

cut through her protest. 'Did I arrive home unexpectedly and spoil your little plan?'

'What *plan*?'

'Oh, come on. Isn't this what's known in the trade
as a scam? To rob me. To cheat on me.'

Darcy stared at him in disbelief. 'You can't honestly believe that?'

'Can't I? Perhaps it's the first clear-headed thought
I've had in a long time, now that I'm no longer completely mesmerised by your pale skin and witchy
eyes.' He shook his head like a man who was emerging from a deep coma. 'Now I'm beginning to wonder whether something like this was in your sights
all along.'

Darcy felt foreboding icing her skin. 'What are
you talking about?' she whispered.

'I've often wondered,' he said harshly, 'what you
might give a man who has everything. Another house,
or a faster car?' He shook his head. 'No. Material
wealth means nothing when you have plenty. But innocence—ah! Now that is a very different thing.'

'You're not making sense.'

'Think about it. What is a woman's most prized
possession, *cara mia*?' The Italian words of endearment dripped like venom from his lips. '*Sì*. I can see
from your growing look of comprehension that you
are beginning to understand. Her virginity. Precious
and priceless and the biggest bartering tool in the
market. And hasn't it always been that way?'

'Renzo.' She could hear the desperation in her
voice now but she couldn't seem to keep it at bay.
'You don't mean that.'

'Sometimes I would ask myself,' he continued,

still in that same flat tone, 'why someone as beautiful and sensual as you—someone hard-up and working in a dead-end job—hadn't taken a rich lover to catapult herself out of her poverty before I came along.'

Desperation morphed into indignation. 'You mean…use a man as a meal ticket?'

'Why are you looking so shocked—or is that simply an expression you've managed to perfect over the years? Isn't that what every woman does ultimately—feed like a leech off a man?' His black gaze roved over her. 'But not you. At least, not initially. Did you decide to deny yourself pleasure—to look at the long game rather than the lure of instant gratification? To hold out for the richest man available, who just happened to be me—someone who was blown away by your extraordinary beauty coupled with an innocence I'd never experienced before?' He gave a cynical smile. 'But you were cunning, too. I see that now. For a cynic like me, a spirited show of independence was pretty much guaranteed to wear me down. So you refused my gifts. You bought cheap clothes and budget airline tickets while valiantly offering me the money you'd saved. What a touching gesture—the hard-up waitress offering the jaded architect a handful of cash. And I fell for it—hook, line and sinker! I was sucked in by your stubbornness and your pride.'

'It wasn't like that!' she defended fiercely.

'You must have thought you'd hit the jackpot when I gave you the key to my flat and bought you a diamond necklace,' he bit out. 'Just as I did when you gave yourself so willingly to me and I discovered you were a virgin. I allowed my ego to be flattered and to blind myself to the truth. How could I have *been* so blind?'

Darcy felt her head spin and that horrible queasy feeling came washing over her again, in giant waves. This couldn't be happening. In a minute she would wake up and the nightmare would be over. But it wouldn't, would it? She was living her nightmare and the proof was right in front of her eyes. In the midst of her confusion and hurt she saw the look of something like satisfaction on Renzo's face. She remembered him mentioning his parents' divorce and how bitterly he'd said that women could never be trusted. Was he somehow pleased that his prejudices had been reinforced and he could continue thinking that way? Yes, he was, she realised. He *wanted* to believe badly of her.

She made one last attempt because wasn't there still some tiny spark of hope which existed—a part which didn't want to let him go? 'None of that—'

'Save your lying words because I don't want to hear them. You're only upset because I came home early and found you out. How were you going to explain the absence of the necklace, Darcy?' he bit out. 'A "burglary" while you were out shopping? Shifting the blame onto one of the people who service these apartments?'

'You think I'd be capable of that?'

'I don't know what you're capable of, do I?' he said coldly. 'I just want you to listen to what I'm going to say. I'm going out and by the time I get back I want you out of here. Every last trace of you. I don't ever want to see your face again. Understand? And for what it's worth—and I'm sure you realise it's a lot— you can keep the damned necklace.'

'You're not going to go to the police?'

'And advertise exactly what kind of woman my girlfriend really is and the kind of low-life company she keeps? That wouldn't exactly do wonders for my reputation, would it? Do whatever you'd planned to do with it all along.' He paused and his mouth tightened as his black gaze swept down over her body. 'Think of it as payment for services rendered. A clean-break pay-off, if you like.'

It was the final straw. Nausea engulfed her. She could feel her knees buckling and a strange roaring in her head. Her hand reached out to grab at the nearest chair but she missed and Darcy felt herself sliding helplessly to the ground, until her cheek was resting on the smooth silk of the Persian rug and her eyes were level with his ankles and the handmade Italian shoes which swum in and out of focus.

His voice seemed to come from a long way off. 'And you can spare me the histrionics, Darcy. They won't make me change my mind.'

'Who's asking you to change your mind?' she managed, from beneath gritted teeth.

She saw his shadow move as he stepped over her and a minute later she heard the sound of the front door slamming shut.

And after that, thankfully, she passed out.

CHAPTER SIX

'You can't go on like this, Darcy, you really can't.'

The midwife sounded both kind and stern and Darcy was finding it difficult keeping her lips from wobbling. Because stern she could handle. Stern was something she was used to. It was the kindness which got to her every time, which made her want to cover her face with her hands and howl like a wounded animal. And she couldn't afford to break down, because if she did—she might never put herself back together again.

Her hand slipped down to her belly. 'You're sure my baby's okay?' she questioned for the fourth time.

'Your baby's fine. Take a look at the scan and see. A little bit on the small side perhaps, but thriving. Unlike you. You're wearing yourself out,' continued the midwife, a frown creasing her plump face. 'You're working too hard and not eating properly, by the look of you.'

'Honestly, I'll try harder. I'll…I'll cut down on my hours at work and start eating more vegetables,' said Darcy as she rolled up her sleeve. And she would. She would do whatever it took because all she could think about was that her baby was safe. *Safe*. Relief washed over her in almost tangible waves as the terror she'd experienced during that noisy ambulance ride began to recede. 'Does that mean I can go home?'

'I wanted to talk to you about that. I'm not very happy about letting you go anywhere,' said the midwife. 'Unless you've got somebody who can be there for you.'

Darcy tried not to flinch. She supposed she could pretend she had a caring mother or protective sister or even—ha, ha, ha—a loving husband. But that would be irresponsible. Because it wasn't just her she was looking out for any more. There was a baby growing inside her. Her throat constricted. Renzo's baby.

She tried not to tense up as the midwife began to measure her blood pressure. Things hadn't been easy since Renzo had left her lying on the floor of his Belgravia apartment, accusing her of histrionics before slamming the door behind him. But Darcy's unexpected faint hadn't been caused by grief or anger, though it had taken a couple of weeks more to realise why a normally healthy young woman should have passed out for no apparent reason. It was when she'd found herself retching in the bathroom that she'd worked it out for herself. And then, of course, she wondered how she could have been so stupid to have not seen it before. It all added up. But her general queasiness and lack of appetite—even the lateness of her period—had been easy to overlook after Renzo had dumped her.

Of course she'd hoped. Hoped like mad she'd somehow got her dates muddled, but deep down she'd known she hadn't because the brand-new aching in her breasts had told her so. She'd gone out to buy a pregnancy kit and the result had come as a shock but no great surprise. Heart racing, she'd sat on the floor of her bathroom in Norfolk staring at the blue line, wondering who to tell. But even if she *had* made some friends in her new home town, she knew there was only one person she *could* tell. Tears of injustice had stung her eyes. The man who thought she was a thief and a con woman. Who had looked at her with utter contempt in his eyes. But that was irrelevant. Renzo's opinion of her didn't really matter—all that mattered was that she let him know he was going to be a father.

If only it had been that easy. Every call she'd made had gone straight through to voicemail and she'd been reluctant to leave him her news in a message. So she'd telephoned his office and been put through to one of his secretaries for another humiliating experience. She'd felt as if the woman was reading from a script as she'd politely told her that Signor Sabatini was un-available for the foreseeable future. She remembered the beads of sweat which had broken out on her fore-head as she'd asked his secretary to have him ring her back. And her lack of surprise when he hadn't.

'Why…?' Her voice faltered as she looked up into the midwife's lined face. 'Why do I have to have someone at home with me?'

'Because twenty-eight weeks is a critical time in a woman's pregnancy and you need to take extra care. Surely there must be someone you could ask. Who's the baby's father, Darcy?'

Briefly, Darcy closed her eyes. So this was it. The point where she really needed to be self-sacrificing and ignore pride and ego and instinct. For the first time in a long time images of Renzo's darkly rugged face swam into her mind, because she'd been trying her best not to think about him. To forget that chiselled jaw and lean body and the way he used to put on those sexy, dark-rimmed glasses while he was working on plans for one of his buildings. To a large extent she had succeeded in forgetting him, banishing memories of how it used to feel to wake up in his arms, as she concentrated on her new job at the local café.

But now she must appeal for help from the man who had made her feel so worthless—whose final gesture had taken her back to those days when people used to look down their noses at her and not believe a word she said. She told herself it didn't matter what Renzo thought when the hospital phoned him. That she didn't care if he considered her a no-good thief because she knew the truth and that was all that mattered. Her hand reached down to lie protectively over her belly, her fingers curving over its hard swell. She would do anything to protect the life of this unborn child.

Anything.

And right at the top of that list was the need to be strong. She'd been strong at the beginning of the affair and it had protected her against pain. She'd done her usual thing of keeping her emotions on ice and had felt good about herself. Even during that weekend when he'd taken her to Tuscany and hinted at his trust issues and the fickleness of women, she had still kept her feelings buried deep. She hadn't expected anything—which was why it had come as such a surprise to her when they'd got back to England and he'd offered her the key to his apartment.

Had that been when she'd first let her guard down

and her feelings had started to change? Or had she just got carried away with her new position in life? Her plans to move to Norfolk had been quietly shelved because she'd enjoyed being his mistress, hadn't she? She'd enjoyed going to that fancy ball with him, when—after her initial flurry of nerves—she'd waltzed in that cherry blossom–filled ballroom in his arms. And if things hadn't gone so badly wrong and Drake hadn't turned up, it probably wouldn't have taken long for her to get used to wearing Renzo's jewels either.

She'd been a fool and it was time to stop acting like a fool.

Never again would she be whimpering Darcy Denton, pleading with her cruel Italian lover to believe her. He could think what the hell he liked as long as he helped take care of her baby.

She opened her eyes and met the questioning look in the midwife's eyes.

'His name is Renzo Sabatini,' she said.

Feeling more impotent than he'd felt in years, Renzo paced up and down the sterile hospital corridor, oblivious to the surreptitious looks from the passing nurses. For a man unused to waiting, he couldn't believe he was being forced to bide his time until the ward's official visiting hours and he got the distinct impression that any further pleas to be admitted early would by vetoed by the dragon-like midwife he'd spoken to earlier, who had made no secret of her disapproval. With a frown on her face she'd told him that his girlfriend was overworked and underfed and clearly on the breadline. Her gaze had swept over him, taking in his dark suit, silk tie and handmade Italian shoes and he could see from her eyes that she was sizing up his worth. He was being judged, he realised—and he didn't like to be judged. Nor put in the role of an absentee father-to-be who refused to accept his responsibilities.

But amid all this confusion was a shimmering of something he couldn't understand, an emotion which licked like fire over his cold heart and was confusing the life out of him. Furiously, he forced himself to concentrate on facts. To get his head around the reason he was here—why he'd been driven to some remote area of Norfolk on what had felt like the longest journey of his life. And then he needed to decide what he was going to do about it. His head spun as his mind went over and over the unbelievable fact.

Darcy was going to have a baby.

His baby.

His mouth thinned.

Or so she said.

Eventually he was shown into the side room of a ward where she lay on a narrow hospital bed—her bright hair the only thing of colour in an all-white environment. Her face was as bleached as the bed sheets and her eyes were both wary and hostile as she looked at him. He remembered the last time he'd seen her. When she'd slid to the floor and he had just let her lie there and now his heart clenched with guilt because she looked so damned fragile lying propped up against that great bank of pillows.

'Darcy,' he said carefully.

She looked as if she had been sucking on a lemon as she spoke. 'You came.'

'I had no choice.'

'Don't lie,' she snapped. 'Of course you did! You could have just ignored the call from the hospital, just like you've ignored all my other calls up until now.'

He wanted to deny it but how could he when it was true? 'Yes,' he said flatly. 'I could.'

'You let my calls go through to voicemail,' she accused.

Letting out a breath, Renzo slowly nodded. At the time it had seemed the only sane solution. He hadn't wanted to risk speaking to her, because hadn't he worried he would cave in and take her back, even if it was for only one night? Because after she'd gone he hadn't been able to forget her as easily as he'd imagined, even though she had betrayed his trust in her. Even when he thought about the missing diamonds and the way she'd allowed that creep to enter his home—that still didn't erase her from his mind. He'd started to wonder whether he'd made a big mistake and whether he should give her another chance, but pride and a tendency to think the worst about women had stopped him acting on it. He'd known that 50 per cent of relationships didn't survive—so why go for one which had the odds stacked against it from the start? Yet she'd flitted in and out of his mind in a way which no amount of hard work or travelling had been able to fix.

'Guilty as charged,' he said evenly.

'And you told your secretary not to put me through to you.'

'She certainly would have put you through if she'd known the reason you were ringing. Why the hell didn't you tell her?'

'Are you out of your mind? Is that how you like to see your women, Renzo?' she demanded. 'To have them plead and beg and humiliate themselves? *Yes, I know he doesn't want to speak to me, but could you please tell him I'm expecting his baby?* Or would you rather I had hung around outside the Sabatini building, waiting for the big boss to leave work so I could grab your elbow and break my news to you on a busy London street? Maybe I should have gone to the papers and sold them a story saying that my billionaire boyfriend was denying paternity!'

'Darcy,' he said, and now his voice had gentled. 'I'm sorry I accused you of stealing the necklace.'

Belligerently, she raised her chin. 'Just not sorry enough to seek me out to tell me that before?'

He thought how tough she was—with a sudden inner steeliness which seemed so at odds with her fragile exterior. 'I jumped to the wrong conclusions,' he said slowly, 'because I'm very territorial about my space.' But he had been territorial about her, too, hadn't he? And old-fashioned enough to want to haul that complete stranger up against the wall and demand to know what he'd been doing alone with her. 'Look, this isn't getting us anywhere. You shouldn't be getting distressed.'

'What, in my *condition*?'

'Yes. Exactly that. In your condition. You're pregnant.' The unfamiliar word sounded foreign on his lips and once again he felt the lick of something painful in his heart. She looked so damned vulnerable lying there that his instinct was to take her in his arms and cradle her—if the emerald blaze in her eyes weren't defying him to dare try. 'The midwife says you need somebody to take care of you.'

Darcy started biting her lip, terrified that the stupid tears pricking at the backs of her eyes would start pouring down her cheeks. She hated the way this newfound state of hers was making her emotions zigzag all over the place, so she hardly recognised herself any more. She was supposed to be staying strong only it wasn't easy when Renzo was sounding so…*protective*. His words were making her yearn for something she'd never had, nor expected to have. She found herself looking up into his darkly handsome face and a wave of longing swept over her. She wanted to reach out her arms and ask him to hold her. She wanted him to keep her safe.

And she had to stop thinking that way. It wasn't a big deal that he'd apologised for something he needed to apologise for. She needed to remind herself that Renzo Sabatini wouldn't even *be* here if it weren't for the baby.

'It's the unborn child which needs taking care of,' she said coldly. 'Not me.'

His gaze drifted down to the black-and-white image which was lying on top of the locker. 'May I?'

She shrugged, trying to ignore the tug at her heart as he picked it up to study it, as engrossed as she had ever seen him. 'Suit yourself.'

And when at last he raised his head and looked at her, there was a look on his face she'd never seen before. Was that wonder or joy which had transformed his dark and shuttered features?

'It's a boy,' he said slowly.

She'd forgotten about his precise eye and attention

to detail, instantly able to determine the sex of the baby where most men might have seen nothing but a confusing composition of black and white.

'It is,' she agreed.

'A son,' he said, looking down at it again.

The possessive way his voice curled round the word scared her. It took her back to the days when she'd been hauled in front of social services who'd been trying to place her in a stable home. Futile attempts which had lasted only as long as it took her mother to discover her new address and turn up on the doorstep at midnight, high on drugs and demanding money in 'payment' for her daughter. What had those interviews taught her? That you should confront the great big elephant in the room, instead of letting it trample over you when you weren't looking.

'Aren't you going to ask whether it's yours?' she said. 'Isn't that what usually happens in this situation?'

He lifted his gaze and now his eyes were flinty. 'Is it?'

Angered by the fact he'd actually *asked* despite her having pushed him into it, Darcy hesitated—tempted by a possibility which lay before her. If she told him he wasn't the father would he disappear and let her get on with the rest of her life? No, of course not. Renzo might suffer from arrogance and an innate sense of entitlement but he wasn't stupid. She'd been a virgin when she met him and the most enthusiastic of lovers during their time together. He must realise he was the father.

'Of course it's yours,' she snapped. 'And this baby will be growing up with me as its mother, no matter how hard you try to take him away!'

As he put the photo back down with a shaking hand she saw a flash of anger in his eyes. 'Do you really think I would try to take a child away from its mother?'

'How should I know what you would or wouldn't do?' Her voice was really shaking now. 'You're a stranger to me now, Renzo—or maybe you always were. So eager to think badly of someone. So quick to apportion blame.'

'And what conclusion would you have come to,' he demanded, 'if you'd arrived home to find a seedy stranger leaving and a costly piece of jewellery missing?'

'I might have stopped to ask questions before I started accusing.'

'Okay. I'll ask them now. What was he doing there?'

'He turned up out of the blue.' She pushed away a sweat-damp curl which was sticking to her clammy cheek. 'He'd seen a photo of me at the ball. He was the last person I expected or wanted to see.'

'Yet you offered him a beer.'

Because she'd been afraid. Afraid of the damage Drake could inflict if he got to Renzo before she did because she hadn't wanted her golden present to come tumbling down around her ears. But it had come tumbling down anyway, hadn't it?

'I thought he would blackmail me by telling you about my mother,' she said at last, in a low voice. 'Only now you know all my secrets.'

'Do I?' he questioned coolly.

She didn't flinch beneath that quizzical black gaze. She kept her face bland as her old habit for self-preservation kept her lips tightly sealed. He knew her mother had been a drug addict and that was bad enough, but what if she explained how she had funded her habit? Darcy could imagine only too well how that contemptuous look would deepen. Something told her there were things this proud man would find intolerable and her mother's profession was one of them. Who knew how he might try to use it against her?

Suddenly, she realised she would put nothing past him. He had accused her of all kinds of things—including using her virginity as some kind of bartering tool. Why shouldn't she keep secrets from him when he had such a brutal opinion of her?

'Of course you do. I'm the illegitimate daughter of a junkie—how much worse could it be?' She sucked in a deep breath and willed herself to keep her nerve. 'Look, Renzo, I know I'm expecting your baby and it must be the last thing you want but maybe we can work something out to our mutual satisfaction. I don't imagine you'll want anything more to do with me but I shan't make any attempt to stop you from having regular contact with your son. In fact, I'll do everything in my power to accommodate access to him.' She forced a smile. 'Every child should have a father.'

'That's good of you,' he said softly before elevating his dark eyebrows enquiringly. 'So what do you propose we do, Darcy? Perhaps you'd like me to start making regular payments until the baby is born? That way you could give up work and not have to worry.'

Hardly able to believe he was being so acquiescent, Darcy sat up in bed a little, nervously smoothing the thin sheet with her hand. 'That's a very generous offer,' she said cautiously.

'And in the meantime you could look for a nice house to live in for when our son arrives—budget no obstacle, obviously. In the country of your choice—that, too, goes without saying.'

She flashed him an uncertain smile. 'That's… that's unbelievably kind of you, Renzo.'

'And perhaps we could find you a street paved with gold while we're at it? That way you could bypass me completely and simply help yourself to whatever it was you wanted?'

It took a moment or two for her to realise he was being sarcastic but the darkly sardonic look on his face left her in no doubt. 'You were joking,' she said woodenly.

'Yes, I was *joking*,' he bit back. 'Unless you think I'm gullible enough to write you an open cheque so you can go away and bring up my son in whatever chaotic state you choose? Is that your dream scenario? Setting yourself up for life with a rich but absent babyfather?'

'As if,' she returned, her fingers digging into the thin hospital sheet. 'If I had gone looking for a wealthy sperm donor, I'd have chosen someone with a little more heart than you!'

Her words were forceful but as Renzo absorbed her defiant response he noticed that her face had gone as white as the sheet she was clutching. 'I don't want to hurt you, Darcy,' he said, self-reproach suddenly rippling through him.

'Being able to hurt me would imply I cared.' Her mouth barely moved as she spoke. 'And I don't. At least, not about you—only about our baby.'

Her fingers fluttered over the swell of her belly

and Renzo's heart gave a sudden leap as he allowed his gaze to rest on it. 'I am prepared to support you both.' His voice thickened and deepened. 'But on one condition.'

'Let me guess. Sole custody for you, I suppose? With the occasional access visit for me, probably accompanied by some ghastly nanny of your choice?'

'I'm hoping it won't come to that,' he said evenly. 'But I will not have a Sabatini heir growing up illegitimately.' He walked over to the window and stared out at the heavy winter clouds before turning back again. 'This child stands to inherit my empire, but only if he or she bears my name. So yes, I will support you, Darcy—but it will be on my terms. And the first, non-negotiable one is that you marry me.'

She stared at him. 'You have to be out of your mind,' she whispered.

'I was about to say that you have no choice but it seems to me you do. But be warned that if you refuse me and continue to live like this—patently unable to cope and putting our child at risk—I will be on my lawyers so fast you won't believe it. And I will instruct them to do everything in their power to prove you are an unfit mother.'

Darcy shivered as she heard the dark determination in his voice. Because wouldn't that bit be easy? If that situation arose he would start digging around in her past—and what a bonanza of further unsavoury facts he would discover. The drug addict bit was bad enough, but would the courts look favourably on the child of a prostitute without a single qualification to her name, one who was struggling to make ends meet and who had been admitted to hospital with severe exhaustion? Of course they wouldn't. Not when she was up against a world-famous architect with more money than he knew what to do with.

She licked her lips, naked appeal in her eyes. 'And if the marriage is unbearable, what then? If I *do* want a divorce sometime in the future, does that mean you won't give me one?'

He shook his head. 'I'm not going to keep you a prisoner, Darcy—you have my word on that. Perhaps we could surprise ourselves by negotiating a relationship that works. But that isn't something we need to think about today. My priority is to get you out of here and into a more favourable environment, if you agree to my terms.' His gaze swept over her, settling at last on her face so that she was captured by the dark intensity of that look. 'So...do I have your consent? Will you be my wife?'

A hundred reasons to refuse flooded into her mind but at that precise moment Darcy felt her son kicking. The unmistakable shape of a tiny heel skimmed beneath the surface of her belly and a powerful wave of emotion flooded over her. All she wanted was the best for her child, so how could she possibly subject him to a life like the one she had known? A life of uncertainty, with the gnawing sense of hunger. A life spent living on the margins of society with all the dangers that entailed. Secondhand clothes and having to make do. Free meals at school and charity trips to the seaside. Did she want all that for her little boy?

Of course she didn't.

She stared into Renzo's face—at all the unshakable confidence she saw written on his shuttered features. It would be easier if she felt nothing for him but she wasn't self-deluding enough to believe that. She thought how infuriating it was that, despite his arrogance and determination to get his own way, she should still want him. But she did. Her mind might not be willing but her flesh was very weak. Even though he'd wounded her with his words and was blackmailing her into marriage—she couldn't deny the quiver of heat low in her belly whenever he looked at her.

But sex was dangerous. Already she was vulnerable and if she fell into Renzo's arms and let him seduce her, wouldn't that make her weaker still? Once their relationship had been about passion but now it was all about possession and ownership. And power, of course—cold, economic power.

But a heady resolve flooded through her as she reminded herself that she'd coped with situations far worse than this. She'd cowered in cupboards and listened to sounds no child should ever have had to hear. She'd stood in courtrooms where people had talked about her future as if she weren't there, and she'd come through the other side. What was so different this time?

She nodded. 'Yes, Renzo,' she said, with a bland and meaningless smile. 'I will marry you.'

CHAPTER SEVEN

DARCY ALMOST LAUGHED at the pale-faced stranger in the mirror. What would the child she'd once been have thought about the woman whose reflection stared back at her? A woman dressed in clothes which still made her shudder when she thought about the price tag.

Her floaty, cream wedding gown had been purchased from one of Nicoletta's boutiques in Rome and the dress cleverly modified to conceal her baby bump but nonetheless, Darcy still felt like a ship in full sail. Her curls had been tied and tamed by the hairdresser who'd arrived at the Tuscan villa they were renting now that Vallombrosa had been sold, and from which they had been married that very morning. Darcy had wanted to wear normal clothes for her marriage to Renzo, as if to reinforce that it was merely a formality she was being forced to endure, but her prospective husband had put his foot down and insisted that she at least *looked* like a real bride…

'What difference does it make whether I wear a white dress or not?' she'd questioned sulkily.

'The difference is that it will feel more real if you wear white and carry flowers. You are a very beautiful woman, *cara*—and you will make a very beautiful bride.'

But Darcy had not felt at all real as she'd walked downstairs—though she couldn't deny that the dark blaze in Renzo's eyes *had* made her feel briefly beautiful. He had insisted they marry in Italy, presumably on the advice of his lawyers, who seemed to be running the whole show. But that part Darcy didn't mind. A wedding in Italy was bound to be more low-key than a wedding in England, where the press were much more curious and there was the possibility of someone from her past getting wind of it. With all the necessary paperwork in place, they had appeared before the civil registrar in the beautiful medieval town of Barga, with just Gisella and Pasquale as their witnesses. And just four days later they had been legally allowed to wed.

It had been the smallest and most formal of ceremonies in an ancient room with a high, beamed ceiling and although Gisella had voiced a slight wistfulness that they weren't having a religious service, Darcy, for one, was glad. It was bad enough having to go through something you knew was doomed, without having to do so before the eyes of the church.

But there had been a point when her heart had turned over and she'd started wishing it *were* real and that had been when Renzo had smiled at her once they'd been legally declared man and wife— his black eyes crinkling with a smile which had reminded her of the first time she'd met him. With his dark suit echoing the raven hue of his hair he'd made a sensational groom. And when he'd looked at her that way, he'd looked as if he actually *cared*—and she'd had to keep reminding herself that he didn't. It had all been an act for the benefit of those around them. She was here because she carried his child and for no other reason. But it had been difficult to remember that when he'd pulled her into his arms in full view of everyone.

She'd felt so torn right then. Her instinctive response had been to hug him back because that was how she always responded and they hadn't touched one another in any way since he'd turned up at the hospital with his ultimatum of a marriage proposal. But too much had happened for her to ever go back to that easy intimacy. How could she possibly lie in his arms and let him kiss her after all the cruel and bitter things which had been done and said? How could she bear to feel him deep inside her body when he'd been so eager to think badly of her?

She remembered freezing as his hands went to her expanded waist, feeling as if her body had suddenly turned to marble. 'Please, Renzo,' she'd whispered, her words a soft protest, not a plea.

But he hadn't let her go or changed his position. He'd dipped his head and spoke to her in low and rapid English, his fingers spanning the delicate fabric of the dress and increasing the points at which he'd been in contact with her.

'You are dressed to play the part of my bride and therefore you will act the part of my bride,' he'd said softly. 'Let's show the world that I have married a flesh-and-blood woman and not some pale-faced doll.'

It was then that he'd bent his head to claim her lips and it had been the weirdest kiss of her life. At

first her determination had made it easy not to respond, but the sensation of his lips on hers had soon
melted away her reservations and she'd sunk into
that kiss with an eagerness she hadn't been able to
disguise. She'd felt powerless beneath that brief but
thorough exploration. She hadn't been able to hold
back her gasp as she'd felt that first sweet invasion
of his tongue. Heat had flooded over her. Her hands
had reached up to hold on to him as the beat of her
heart had become erratic but suddenly the movement
had become about so much more than support. Suddenly she'd been clinging to him and revelling in the
feel of all that rock-hard flesh beneath her fingertips. She'd wanted him so much that she hadn't even
cared about his triumphant laugh of pleasure as he'd
drawn his lips away because it had felt like for ever
since he'd kissed her and it had tasted as delicious as
having a drink after a dusty walk. Like the first hint
of sweetness on your tongue when you badly needed
the boost of sugar.

A kiss like that was the inevitable forerunner of
intimacy and she must not let it happen again. She
dared not…

'You look miles away.' Renzo's low drawl broke
into Darcy's reverie and she watched his reflected
body as he strolled in from the en-suite bathroom of
their honeymoon suite, wearing nothing but a too-
small white towel slung low over his hips. Crystalline
droplets of water glittered like diamonds in his ebony
hair and, despite knowing she shouldn't be affected
by his near-nakedness, Darcy's brain was refusing to
listen to reason and instead was sending out frantic
messages to her pulse points.

It was the first time she'd seen him in a state of undress since the night of the ball, when they'd come home and he'd made rapturous love to her. The night before Drake had visited and the necklace had disappeared and her whole world had come crashing down around her. A necklace Renzo had been prepared to write off in his eagerness to be rid of her. It all seemed like a dream now and yet suddenly all that honed silken flesh was haunting her with everything she'd been missing.

'So why,' he questioned, his voice growing sultry as he walked over and stood behind her and wound one long finger around an errant curl, 'did you let them put your hair up like that?'

Darcy swallowed because, from this position, far too much of his flesh was on show and his skin was still damp and soap-scented from the shower. 'The hairdresser said loose hair would look untidy.'

'But perhaps your husband doesn't like it to look *tidy*,' he mocked, pulling out one pearl-topped pin quickly followed by another. 'He likes it to look wild and free.'

'Which is slightly ironic given that you're the most precise and ordered man on the planet. And I don't remember giving you permission to do that,' she protested as he continued to remove them.

'I'm your husband now, Darcy. Surely I don't have to ask permission to take your hair down?'

Glad for the tumble of curls concealing the reluctant lust which was making her cheeks grow so pink, Darcy stared down at her lap. 'You're my husband in name only,' she said quietly.

'So you keep saying. But since we're sharing a room and a bed—'

'Yes, I wanted to talk to you about that. Tell me again *why* we're sharing a bed.'

'Because I need to keep an eye on you. I promised the midwife and the doctor.' His black eyes glittered. 'And that being the case—just how long do you think you can hold off from letting me make love to you when you're as jumpy as a scalded cat whenever I come near?'

'I think *making love* a rather inaccurate way to describe what we do,' she said, sighing as the last curl tumbled free and he added the final pearl pin to the neat little line he'd assembled on the dressing table. 'I wish we didn't have this wedding party tonight.'

'I know. You'd much rather be alone with me.'

'I didn't say that.'

'I know you didn't.' His dark gaze was full of mockery. 'But a wedding is a wedding and it is fitting to celebrate such a momentous occasion with friends. We don't want them thinking our union is in name only, do we?'

'Even if it is?'

'Even if it is. So why not try playing your part with enthusiasm? Who knows? Sooner or later you might find the feelings have rubbed off.' He stroked her hair. 'You won't have anything to do, if that's what's worrying you. The food, the wine and the guests have all been taken care of.'

'And in the meantime I'm to be brought down and paraded around in my white dress like a cow in the marketplace?'

He gave a soft laugh. 'Looking at you now, that's

the very last image which springs to mind.' He leaned forward, his hands on her shoulders, his mouth so close that she could feel his warm breath fanning the curls at the back of her neck. And suddenly his voice was urgent. 'Listen to me, Darcy. Neither of us wanted this to happen but it's what we've ended up with. I didn't want to get married and I certainly didn't plan to be a parent and neither, presumably, did you.'

Her lips folded in on themselves. 'No.'

In the reflection of the glass their eyes met and Renzo wondered why, even in the midst of all this unwanted emotional drama, their chemistry should be as powerful as ever. Did she feel it too? She must.

He could see her nipples pushing against the silk of her wedding gown and the darkening of her emerald eyes, but the tight set of her shoulders and her unsmiling lips were telling him quite clearly to stay away. Once he had known her body completely, but not any more. Her bulky shape was unfamiliar now, just as she was. She was spiky, different, wary. It was difficult being around her without being able to touch her and, oh, how he wanted to touch her. That had not changed, despite everything which had happened. Her skin was luminous, her eyes bright, and the rampant red curls even more lustrous than before. Didn't people say that a woman with child developed a glowing beauty all of her own? He'd never really thought about it before now—why would he?—but suddenly he knew exactly what they meant. He noticed the way she kept moving her hand to her growing bump, as if she were in possession of the world's greatest secret.

Pregnant.

His mouth dried. It was still hard for him to get his head around that. To believe that a whole new life was about to begin and he must be responsible for it. He'd meant it when he told her he never wanted a family and not just because he recognised all the potential for pain which a family could bring. He had liked his life the way it was. He liked having to answer to no one except himself. And if every female who'd fallen into his arms had thought they'd be the one to change his mind, they had been wrong. He'd managed to get to the age of thirty-five without having to make any kind of commitment.

Had Darcy done what nobody else had been able to do—and deliberately got herself pregnant? But if that had been the case then he must take his share of the blame. He'd been so blown away by discovering she was a virgin that he couldn't wait for her to go on the pill. He remembered the first time he'd entered her without wearing a condom and the indescribable pleasure he'd felt. It had been primitive, powerful and overwhelming but it hadn't been wise. He had allowed sexual hunger to blind him to reason. He'd allowed her to take sole responsibility for birth control and look what had happened. His heart clenched tightly with an emotion he didn't recognise as he stared into her green eyes.

'Did you mean to get pregnant?' he demanded.

He saw her flinch and compose herself before answering.

'No,' she answered quietly. 'I had some sort of bug just before we went to Tuscany and I didn't realise...'

'That sickness would stop the pill from working?'

'Apparently.'

He raised his eyebrows. 'You weren't warned that could happen?'

'Probably—but with all the excitement about the holiday, I forgot all about it. It wasn't deliberate, Renzo—if that's what you're thinking.' She gave a wry smile. 'No woman in her right mind would want to tie herself to a man with ice for a heart, no matter how rich or well-connected he might be.'

And he believed her. He might wish he didn't but he did. His pale-faced bride in the floaty dress was telling the truth. 'So it seems we have a choice,' he said. 'We can go downstairs to our guests with good grace or I can take you kicking and screaming every inch of the way.'

'I won't embarrass you, if that's what you're worried about. I have no desire to make this any more difficult than it already is.'

'Good.'

Turning away, he dropped the towel and Darcy was treated to the distracting sight of his bare buttocks— each hard globe a paler colour than the dark olive of his back. She could see the hair-roughened power of those thighs and hated the way her stomach automatically turned over when she was doing everything in her power to fight her attraction.

'Tempted?' His voice was full of sensual mockery—as if he had the ability to read her expression even with his back turned. And she mustn't let him realise the accuracy of his taunt. If she wanted to protect herself, she mustn't let him get close to her—not in any way.

'Tempted by what—our wedding feast?' she questioned, sniffing at the air as if trying to detect the rich scents of cooking which had been drifting through the downstairs of the house all morning. 'Absolutely! To be honest, I do have a little of my appetite back. I could eat a horse.'

He gave a low laugh as Darcy scuttled into the bathroom where she spent a long time fiddling with her hair, and when she returned to the bedroom it was to find him dressed in that head-turning way which only Italian men seemed able to pull off. His dark suit emphasised his broad shoulders and powerful physique and he'd left his silk shirt open at the neck to reveal a sexy smattering of dark hair.

Uncertainly, she skimmed her hand down over her dress. 'Won't I look a little overdressed?'

'Undoubtedly,' he said drily. 'But probably not in the way you imagine.'

Her cheeks were still pink by the time they walked into the formal salon, which had been transformed with bridal finery by Gisella and a team of helpers from the nearby village. The cold winter weather meant they couldn't venture out into the huge grounds, but instead enormous fires were blazing and dark greenery festooned the staircases and fireplace. There were white flowers, white ribbons and sugar-dusted bonbons heaped on little glass dishes. A towering *croquembouche* wedding cake took pride of place in the dining room and on a table at the far end of the room—a pile of beautifully wrapped presents which they'd expressly stated they didn't want!

A loud burst of applause reached them as they walked in, along with cries of *'Congratulazioni!'* and *'Ben fatto, Renzo!'* The guests were all Renzo's friends, and although he'd told her he would pay for anyone she wanted to fly out to Tuscany for the celebration, Darcy hadn't taken him up on his offer. Because who could she invite when she'd lived her life a loner—terrified of forming any lasting commitments because of her past and the very real fear of rejection?

But she was pleased to see Nicoletta and not just because the glamourous Italian had helped with her trousseau. She'd realised that Renzo no longer had any lingering feelings about the woman he'd once had a 'thing' with. Darcy might have had an innate lack of self-confidence brought about by years of neglect, but even she couldn't fail to see the way her husband was looking at her tonight—a sentiment echoed by Nicoletta.

'I have never seen Renzo this way before,' she confided as Darcy sucked *limonata* through a straw. 'He can barely tear his eyes away from you.'

Darcy put her glass down. Because he was one of life's winners, that was why. He would want his marriage to succeed in the way that his business had succeeded and because his own parents' marriage had failed. That was why he was suddenly being so nice to her. And that scared her. It made her want to fight her instinctive attraction and to pull away from him. She didn't dare sink into a false state of security which would leave her raw and hurting when their marriage hit the skids. Because it would. Of course it would. How long would it take before her brilliant husband tired of her once reality kicked in? Had he even stopped to consider how a wife at the mercy of fluctuating hormones might fit into his calm and ordered life, let alone all the change which a new baby would bring?

But the evening fared better than she would have imagined. Renzo's obvious appreciation—whether faked or not—seemed to make everyone eager to welcome her into their midst. His friends were daunting, but essentially kind. She met lawyers, bankers and an eminent heart surgeon and although each and every one of them spoke to her in perfect English, she vowed to learn Renzo's native tongue. Because suddenly, she caught a glimpse of what the future could be like if she wasn't careful. Of Renzo and their son speaking a language which the new *mamma* couldn't understand, with her inevitably being cast into the role of outsider.

And that could also be dangerous. Renzo had been reasonable before the marriage, but now she had his ring on her finger there was no longer any need for him to be. If she didn't watch her back she would become irrelevant. She looked around at the elegant room her new husband was renting for what she considered an extortionate amount of money. Could she really envisage their son willingly accompanying her back to an unknown England and an uncertain future if the marriage became unbearable, and leaving all this privilege and beauty behind?

But she ate, chatted and drank her *limonata*, waiting until the last of their guests had gone before following Renzo up to their suite, her heart rattling loudly beneath her ribcage. She undressed in the bathroom, emerging wearing a nightgown Nicoletta had insisted on gifting her. It was an exquisite piece for a new bride to wear and one designed to be removed almost as soon as it had been put on. Despite the hard curve of her baby bump, the ivory silk-satin coated her body as flatteringly as a second skin. Edged with ivory lace, the delicate fabric framed the skin above her engorged breasts and the moment she walked into the bedroom Darcy saw Renzo's eyes darken.

Her own answering tug of lust made her reconsider her decision to distance herself from him, because surely physical intimacy would provide some kind of release and lessen the unmistakable tension which had sprung up between them. But sexual intimacy could also be dangerous, especially in their situation. Something was growing inside her which was part of him and how could she bear to cheapen that by having sex which was nothing but a physical *release*?

She sat down heavily on the side of the bed, not realising that she'd given a little groan until he glanced across at her.

'You must be tired.'

She nodded, suddenly feeling as if all the stuffing had been knocked out of her. 'I am. But I need to talk to you.'

'About…?'

'Stuff.'

His smile was slow, almost wolfish. 'Be a little bit more explicit, Darcy. What kind of stuff?'

She shrugged. 'Where we're going to live. Practicalities. That kind of thing. And we need to decide soon because I won't be allowed to fly once I'm past thirty-six weeks.'

His self-assured shake of his head was tinged with the arrogant sense of certainty which was so much a part of him. 'I have my own jet, Darcy. We can fly when the hell we like, provided we take medical support with us.'

She nodded as she pulled back the covers and got into the king-size bed, rolling over as far as possible until she had commandeered one side of it. 'Whatever,' she said. 'But we still need to discuss it.'

'Just not tonight,' he said, the bed dipping beneath his weight as he joined her. 'You're much too tired. We'll talk in the morning. And—just for the record— if you lie much closer to the edge, you're going to fall off it in the middle of the night and, apart from the obvious danger to yourself, you might just wake me up.' She heard the clatter as he removed his wristwatch and put it on the bedside table. 'Don't worry, Darcy, I'm reading your body language loud and clear and I have no intention of trying to persuade a woman to make love if she has set her mind against it.'

'Something which has never happened to you before, I suppose?' she questioned waspishly.

'As it happens, no,' he drawled. He snapped off the light. 'Usually I have to fight them off.'

Darcy's skin stung with furious heat. It was a lesson to never ask questions unless you were prepared to be stupidly hurt by the answer you might receive. Lying open-eyed in the darkness, almost immediately she heard the sounds of Renzo's deep and steady breathing and fearfully she foresaw a restless night ahead, plagued by troubled thoughts about the future. But to her surprise she felt warm and cosseted in that big bed with a brand-new wedding ring on her finger. And, yes, even a little bit *safe*.

As the keen Tuscan wind howled outside the ancient house Darcy snuggled down into her pillow and, for the first time in a long time, slept soundly.

CHAPTER EIGHT

RENZO INSISTED ON a honeymoon—cutting through Darcy's automatic protests when she went downstairs the following morning to find him in the throes of planning it. As she glanced at the road map he'd spread out on the dining-room table, she told him it would be hypocritical; he said he didn't care.

'Maybe you're just doing it to make the marriage look more authentic than it really is,' she observed, once she had selected a slice of warm bread from the basket. 'Since we haven't actually consummated it.'

'Maybe I am,' he agreed evenly. 'Or maybe it's because I want to show you a little of my country and to see you relax some more. You slept well last night, Darcy.' His black eyes gleamed but that was the only reference he made to their chaste wedding night, though she felt a little flustered as his gaze lingered on the swell of her breasts for slightly longer than was necessary. 'And we can consummate it anytime you like,' he said softly. 'You do realise that, don't you?'

She didn't trust herself to answer, though her burning cheeks must have given away the fact that the subject was very much on her mind. Sharing a bed so he could keep an eye on her was more straightforward in theory than in practice. Because a bed was a bed, no matter how big it was. And wasn't it true that at one point during the night her foot had encountered one of her new husband's shins and she'd instinctively wanted to rub her toes up and down his leg, before hastily rolling away as if her skin had been scorched?

She told herself their situation was crazy enough but at least she was in full control of her senses—and if she had sex with him, she wouldn't be. And she was afraid. Afraid that the pregnancy was making her prone to waves of vulnerability she was supposed to have left behind. Afraid he would hurt her if he saw through to the darkness at the very core of her. Because something had changed, she recognised that. He was being *gentle* with her in a way he'd never been before. She knew it was because she was carrying his baby but even so… It was intoxicating behaviour coming from such an intrinsically cold man and Darcy might have been bewitched by such a transformation, had she not instinctively mistrusted any type of kindness.

But she couldn't get out of the 'honeymoon' he was planning and perhaps that was a good thing. It would be distracting. There would be things to occupy them other than prowling around their beautiful rented villa like two wary, circling tigers, with her terrified to even meet those brilliantine black eyes for fear he would read the lust in hers and act on it…

So she packed her suitcase with the warm clothes which had also been purchased from Nicoletta's boutique and Renzo loaded it into the back of his sports car. The air was crisp as they drove through the mountains towards Italy's capital, the hills softly green against the ice-blue sky as the powerful car swallowed up the miles. They stopped in a small, hilltop town for an early lunch of truffled pasta followed by *torta della nonna* and afterwards walked through narrow cobbled streets to the viewpoint at the very top, looking down on the landscape below, which was spread out like a chequered tablecloth of green and gold.

Darcy gave a long sigh as her elbows rested on the balustrade and Renzo turned to look at her.

'Like it?' he questioned.

'It's beautiful. So beautiful it seems almost unreal.'

'But there are many beautiful parts of England.'

She shrugged, her eyes fixed on some unseen spot in the distance. 'Not where I grew up. Oh, there were lots of lovely spaces in the surrounding countryside, but unless they're on your doorstep you need funds to access them.'

'Was it awful?' he questioned suddenly.

She didn't answer immediately. 'Yes,' she said, at last.

He heard the sadness in that single word and saw the way her teeth chewed on her bottom lip and he broke the silence which followed with a light touch to her arm. 'Come on. Let's try and get there before it gets dark.'

She fell asleep almost as soon as she got in the car and as Renzo waited in line at a toll gate, he found himself studying that pale face with its upturned freckled nose. Her red curls hung over one shoulder in the loose plait she sometimes wore and he thought that today she looked almost like a teenager, in jeans and a soft grey sweater. Only the bump reminded him that she was nearly twenty-five and soon going to have his baby.

Could they make it work? His leather-gloved fingers gripped the steering wheel as they moved forward. They *had* to make it work. There was no other choice, for he would not replicate his own bleak and fatherless childhood. He realised how little she'd actually told him about her own upbringing, yet, uncharacteristically, she had mentioned it today. And even though that haunted look had come over her face, he had found himself wanting to know more.

Wasn't that his role now, as husband and prospective father—to break the ingrained rules of a lifetime and find out as much about Darcy as possible? And wasn't the best way to do that to tell her something about *him*—the kind of stuff women had quizzed him about over years, to no effect. Because communication was a two-way street, wasn't it? At least, that was what that therapist had told him once. Not that he'd been seeing her professionally. To him she was just a gorgeous brunette he'd been enjoying a very physical relationship with when she'd freaked him out by telling him that she specialised in 'family therapy' and he could confide in her anytime she liked. His mouth thinned. Maybe he should have taken her up on her offer and gathered tips about how to deal with his current situation.

Darcy woke as they drove into the darkening city whose ancient streets were deeply familiar to him from his own childhood. Taking a circuitous route, Renzo found himself enjoying her murmured appreciation of the Campidoglio, the Coliseum and other famous monuments, but he saw her jaw drop in amazement when he stopped outside the sixteenth-century *palazzo* on the Via Condotti, just five minutes from the Spanish Steps.

'This isn't yours?' she questioned faintly, after he'd parked the car and they'd travelled up to the third floor.

'It is now. I bought it a couple of years ago,' he replied, throwing open the double doors into the main salon, with its high ceilings, gilded furniture and matchless views over the ancient city. 'Although the Emperor Napoleon III happened to live here in 1830.'

'Here? Good grief, Renzo.' She stood in the centre of the room, looking around. 'It's gorgeous. Like… well, like something you might see in a book. Why don't you live here? I mean, why London?'

'Because my work is international and I wanted to establish a base in London and the only way to do that properly is to be permanently on-site. I don't come back here as often as I should, but maybe some day.'

'Renzo—'

But he cut her off with a shake of his head. 'I know. You want to talk—but first you should unpack. Get comfortable. We need to think about dinner but first I need to do a little work.'

'Of course,' she said stiffly.

'Come with me and I'll show you where the main bedroom is.'

Down a high-ceilinged corridor she followed him to yet another room which defied expectation. The enormous wooden bed had a huge oil painting on the wall behind it, with elaborate silk drapes on either side, which made it seem as if you were looking out of a window onto mountains and trees. Darcy blinked as she stared at it. *How am I even* here? she wondered as she unwound the soft blue scarf which was knotted around her neck. She looked around the room, taking in the antique furniture, the silken rugs and the price-less artwork. Yet this staggering display of a wealth which many people would covet had little meaning for her. She didn't want *things*—no matter how ex-quisite they were. She wanted something which was much harder to pin down and which she suspected would always elude her.

She showered and changed into a cashmere tunic with leggings, padding barefoot into the salon to see her new husband at his computer, the familiar sight of one of his spectacular designs dominating the screen. But despite her noiseless entrance he must have heard her because he turned round, those dark-rimmed spectacles on his nose giving him that sexy, geeky look which used to make her heart turn over.

Still did, if she was being honest.

'Room to your satisfaction?' he questioned.

'Bit cramped, actually.'

He gave the glimmer of a smile. 'I know. Makes you claustrophobic. Hungry?'

'After that enormous lunch?' She wrinkled her nose. 'Funnily enough, I am.'

'Good.' His gaze roved over her, black eyes gleam-ing as they lingered a little too long. 'Looks like you have some catching up to do. You need to put some meat on those bones.'

She didn't reply to that. She wasn't going to tell him that she felt all breasts and bump. She wanted to tell him not to look at her body any more than was absolutely necessary.

And yet she wanted him to feast his eyes on it all day and make her glow inside.

'We could eat out,' he continued. 'I could take you to Trastevere, where you can eat some real Italian food and not something designed to try to appeal to an international palate. Or...'

She raised her eyebrows questioningly. 'Or?'

'We could order in pizza.'

'Here?'

'Why not?'

She shrugged as she stared through an arch to see a long, softly polished dining table set with tall silver candelabra. 'It seems way too grand.'

'A table is there to be used, Darcy, no matter what you're eating.'

It seemed decadent to find themselves there an hour later sitting on ormolu chairs, eating pizza with their fingers. As if they had broken into a museum and had temporarily set up home for the night.

'Good?' questioned Renzo as she popped the last piece of anchovy in her mouth and licked bright orange oil from her fingers.

'Heaven,' she sighed.

But it still seemed like a dream—as if it were happening to someone else—until they returned to the main salon and he asked her if she wanted mint tea. She didn't know what made her ask if he had hot chocolate and was surprised when he said he'd find out—and even more surprised when he returned a few minutes later with a creamy concoction in a tall mug. A potent memory squeezed at her heart as she took the drink from him—perhaps it was the sweet smell of the chocolate which made the words slip out before she could stop them.

'Wow! I haven't had this since…'

She caught herself on but it was too late.

'Since when?'

She kept her voice airy. 'Oh, nothing to interest you.'

'I'm interested,' he persisted.

She wondered if the shaky way she put the mug down gave away her sudden nerves. 'You've never been interested before.'

'True,' he agreed drily. 'But you're carrying my baby now and maybe I need to understand the mother of my child.'

And Darcy knew she couldn't keep avoiding the issue—just as she knew that to do so would probably intrigue him. Even worse—it might make him start to do his own investigative work and *then* what might he discover? Her heart sank. She knew exactly what he would discover. He would discover the reason for the deep dark shame which still festered inside her. She stared at the cooling chocolate, wishing she could turn back time and that this time he wouldn't ask. But you couldn't turn back time. Just as you couldn't hide everything from a man who was determined to find out.

'It sounds so stupid—'

'Darcy,' he said, and his voice sounded almost *gentle*.

She shrugged. 'The chocolate reminded me of going out to a café when I was a little girl. Going to meet some prospective new foster parents.'

The image came back to her, unbearably sharp and

achingly clear. She remembered strawberry-covered cakes gleaming behind glass frontage and the waitresses with their starched aprons. It had been one of those awkward but hopeful meetings, with Darcy's social worker the referee—observing the interaction between a little girl who badly needed a home and two adults who wanted to give her one. They'd bought her hot chocolate in a glass mug, topped with a hillock of whipped cream and a shiny cherry on top. She'd stared at it for a long time before she could bear to disturb its perfection and when she'd drunk from it at last, the cream had coated her upper lip with a white moustache and made everyone laugh. The laughter was what she remembered most.

'Foster parents?' prompted Renzo, his deep voice dissolving the image.

'I didn't have the most…stable of childhoods. My mother was seventeen when she was orphaned. The roads were icy and her father took the bend too fast. They said he'd been…drinking. The police knocked at her door on Christmas Eve and said she'd better sit down. She once told me that after they'd gone she looked at the Christmas tree and all the presents underneath it. Presents which would never be opened…' Her voice trailed off. It had been a rare moment of insight and clarity from a woman whose life had been lived in pursuit of a constant chemical high. 'And it… Well, it freaked her out.'

'I'm not surprised. Did she have any relatives?'

Darcy shook her head. 'No. Well, there were some on the west coast of Ireland but it was too late for her to get there in time for the holiday. And she couldn't face intruding on someone else's Christmas. Being the spectre at the feast. Being pitied. So she spent the holiday on her own and soon after she went to Manchester with the money she'd inherited from her parents but no real idea about a career. In fact, she had nothing to commend her but her looks and her newfound ability to party.'

'Did she look like you?' he questioned suddenly.

'Yes. At least, at the beginning she did.' Darcy closed her eyes. She'd seen pictures of a feisty-looking redhead with green eyes so like her own. Seen her tentative smile as that young woman cradled the infant Darcy in her arms. She didn't want to tell Renzo what had happened to those looks—not when she couldn't bear to think about it herself. 'Before the drugs took hold. I was first taken into care at the age of two and I stayed there until I was eight, when my mother went to the courts to try to "win" me back, as she put it.'

'And did she succeed?'

'She did. She could put on a good performance when the need arose.'

'And what was that like—being back with her?'

Darcy swallowed. How much could she tell him? How much before a look of disgust crossed his face and he started to worry whether she might have inherited some of her poor mother's addictive traits—or the other, even more unpalatable ones? 'I'll leave that to your imagination,' she said, her voice faltering a little. 'She used me to interact with her dealer, or to answer the door when people she owed money to came knocking. There's nothing quite like a child in an adult's world for throwing things off balance.'

'And were you *safe*?' he demanded.

'I was lucky,' she said simply. 'Lucky that some kind social worker went over and above the call of duty and got me out of there. After that I went to the children's home—and, to be honest, I felt glad to be there.'

Not safe. Never really safe. But *safer*.

'And what did you do when you left there?'

'I came to London. Went to night school and caught up with some of the education I'd missed. It's why I ended up waitressing—nobody really cares if you've got a GCSE in Maths if you can carry a tray of drinks without spilling any.'

There was no sound in the room, other than the ticking of some beautiful freestanding clock which Darcy suspected might have been in place when Napoleon himself was living there.

'So...' His voice was thoughtful now; his black eyes hooded. 'Seeing as so much of your childhood was spent with people making decisions for you, where would *you* like to live when our baby is born, Darcy?'

Not only was it not the reaction she'd been expecting, it was also the most considerate question anyone had ever asked her and Darcy was terrified she was going to start blubbing—an over-the-top response from someone who'd experienced little real kindness in her life. But she needed to keep it together. She'd been given enough false hope in life to build Renzo's offer up into something it wasn't.

'I would prefer to be in England,' she said slowly. 'Italy is very beautiful and I love it here but I feel like a foreigner.' She forced a laugh. 'Probably because I am.'

'My apartment in Belgravia, then?'

She shook her head. 'No. That won't do. I don't really want to go back there.'

He looked faintly surprised, as she supposed anyone might be if their new wife had just rejected a luxury apartment worth millions of pounds. 'Because?'

Should she tell him that she felt as if she'd lived another life there? She'd behaved like someone she no longer recognised—with her balcony bras and her tiny panties. She'd been nothing but his plaything, his always-up-for-it lover who was supposed to have been expendable before all this happened. How could she possibly reconcile that Darcy with the woman she was now and the mother she was preparing to be? How could she bear to keep reminding herself that he'd never planned for her to become a permanent fixture in his life? 'It's not a place for a baby.'

He raised his dark eyebrows. 'You're not suggesting we decamp to that tiny cottage you were renting in Norfolk?'

'Of course not,' she said stiffly. 'I think we both know that wouldn't work. But I would like to bring up the baby away from the city.' She licked her lips and her tongue came away with the salty flavour of capers. 'Somewhere with grass and flowers and a park nearby. Somewhere you can work from, so it doesn't necessarily have to be a long way out of London, just so long as it's *green*.'

He nodded and gave a small smile. 'I think we can manage that.'

'Thank you.'

Hearing her voice tremble, Renzo frowned. 'And you need to get to bed. Now. You look washed out.'

'Yes.' Awkwardly, she rose to her feet and walked across the room, feeling the soft silk of a Persian rug beneath her bare feet. But despite her initial reservations at having told him more than she'd ever told anyone, Darcy was amazed by how much *lighter* she felt. And she was grateful to him, too—stupidly relieved he'd managed to keep his shock and disgust to himself because most people weren't that diplomatic. All she wanted now was to climb into bed and have him put his arms round her and hold her very tight and tell her it was going to be all right. She closed her eyes. Actually, she wanted more than that. Could they be intimate again? Could they? Hadn't that book on pregnancy explained that sex in the latter stages was perfectly acceptable, just as long as you didn't try anything too adventurous?

For the first time in a long time, she felt the faint whisper of hope as she brushed her teeth, her hands wavering as she picked up the exquisite silk nightgown she'd worn on her wedding night, feeling the slippery fabric sliding between her fingers. It was beautiful but it made her feel like someone she wasn't. Or rather, somebody she no longer was. Wouldn't it be better to be less *obvious* if she wanted them relaxed enough to get to know one another again? Shouldn't it be a slow rediscovery rather than a sudden whambam, especially given the circumstances in which they found themselves?

Pulling on one of Renzo's T-shirts, which came to halfway down her thighs, she crept beneath the duvet and waited for him to come to bed.

But he didn't.

She tried to block the thoughts which were buzzing in her mind like a mosquito in a darkened room, but some thoughts just wouldn't go away. Because apart from that very public kiss when he'd claimed her as his bride, he hadn't come near her, had he? And something else occurred to her, something which perhaps *she* had been too arrogant to take into account. What if he no longer wanted her? If he no longer desired her as a man was supposed to desire a woman.

Tossing and turning in those fine cotton sheets, she watched the hand of the clock slowly moving. Soon her heart rate overtook the rhythmical ticking. Eleven o'clock. Then twelve. Shortly before one she gave in to the exhaustion which was threatening to crush her and Darcy never knew what time Renzo came to bed that night, because she didn't hear him.

CHAPTER NINE

'So… What do you think? Does it meet with your approval?' Renzo's eyes didn't leave Darcy's profile as they stood in the grounds of the imposing manor house. A seagull heading for the nearby coast gave a squawk as it flew overhead and he could definitely detect the faint tang of salt in the air. A light breeze was ruffling his wife's red curls, making them gleam brightly in the sunshine. How beautiful she looked, he thought—and how utterly unapproachable. And how ironic that the woman he'd spent more time with than anyone else should remain the most enigmatic woman of them all. 'You haven't changed your mind about living here now that it's actually yours?'

Slowly she turned her head and returned his gaze, those glittering emerald eyes filled with emotions he couldn't begin to understand.

'Ours, you mean?' she said. 'Our first marital home.'

He shook his head. 'No. Not mine. I've spoken with my lawyers and the deeds have been made over to you. This is yours, Darcy. Completely yours.'

There was a moment of silence before she frowned and blinked at him. 'But I don't understand. We talked about it in Rome and I thought we'd agreed that a house in England was going to be the best thing for us.' She touched the ever-increasing girth of her belly. 'All of us.'

Was she being deliberately naïve, he wondered—or just exceptionally clever? Did she know she had him twisted up in knots and he didn't have a damned clue how to handle her? Because he was starting to realise that, despite his experience with women, he had no idea how to sustain a long-term relationship. He'd never had to try before. In the past he had always just walked away—usually because boredom had set in and he'd found the increasing demands tedious. But with Darcy he couldn't do that. Furthermore, he didn't want to. He wanted this baby so badly. It scared him just how badly. For a man who'd spent his life building things for other people—someone who considered himself urbane, sophisticated and cool—he hadn't reckoned on the fierce and primitive pride he felt at having created the most precious thing of all.

Life.

But Darcy remained a mystery he couldn't solve. She'd closed herself off to him since that night in Rome. She'd told him more about what he'd already known and the brutal facts had horrified him when he'd thought how tough her childhood must have been. He'd sat up for a long time that night after she'd rushed off to bed, drinking whisky until it had tasted stale in his mouth and gazing into space as he'd wondered how best to deal with the information. But he had dealt with it in the same way he dealt with anything emotional. He'd compartmentalised it. Filed it away, meaning to do something about it sometime but never getting round to it. She'd been asleep by the time he'd slid into bed beside her, her fecund body covered in one of his oversized T-shirts, sending out a silent signal to stay the hell away from her. He remembered waking up to a beautiful Roman morning with the air all clear and blue. They'd gone out for coffee and *cornetti* and he hadn't said a word about her revelations and neither had she. She'd closed herself off from him again and he sensed that he could frighten her away if he didn't let her take this thing at her own pace.

But it hadn't worked.

Because now she looked at him so warily by day, while at night she still wore those infernal all-enveloping T-shirts and lay there quietly, holding her breath—as if daring him to come near. Had he handled it badly? If it had been any other woman he would have pulled her into his arms and kissed her until she was wet and horny—reaching for him eagerly, the way she used to.

But she was not *any other woman*. She was his wife. His pregnant wife. How could he possibly ravish her when she was both bulky and yet impossibly fragile? Her skin looked so delicate—the blue tracery of her veins visible beneath its porcelain fragility—as if to even breathe on her might leave some kind of mark. And against her tiny frame, the baby looked huge—as if what her body had achieved was defying both gravity and logic, something which continued to amaze him. He'd even taken to working solely from home these past weeks, cancelling a trip to New York and another to Paris, terrified she was

going to go into labour early even though there were
still three weeks to go.

'Let's get inside,' he said abruptly. He unlocked
their new front door and stood back to let her pass
and their footsteps sounded loud in a house which was
still largely empty, save for the few pieces of furniture which had already been delivered. But at least it
wasn't cold. Despite the bite of early spring, the estate
agent must have put on the heating—knowing that
today was their first visit as official owners. The door
swung closed behind them and he realised that she
was still looking at him with confusion in her eyes.

'Why have you put the house in my name, Renzo?
I don't understand.'

'Because you need to have some kind of insurance
policy. Somewhere to call home if—'

'If the marriage doesn't work out?'

'That's right.'

She nodded as if she understood at last for her
face had whitened, her eyes appearing darkly emerald against her pale skin.

'But you said—'

'I know what I said,' he interrupted. 'But I didn't
factor in that the situation might prove more difficult
than I'd anticipated.'

'You mean, my company?'

'No, not your *company*,' he negated impatiently,
and then suddenly the words came bubbling out of
nowhere, even though he hadn't intended to say them.
'I mean the fact that I want you so damned much and
you don't seem to want me any more. The fact that
you're always just out of reach.'

Shocked, Darcy stared at him. So she *hadn't* been

imagining it. It *had* been lust she'd seen in his eyes and sexual hunger which made his body grow tense whenever she walked in the room. So why hadn't he touched her? Why did he keep coming to bed later and later while keeping their days ultrabusy by whisking her from property to property until at last she'd fallen in love with this East Sussex house which was only eight miles from the sea?

The truth was that he hadn't come near her since that night in Rome, when she'd told him everything about her mother. She felt her stomach clench. Actually, not quite everything—and hadn't she been thankful afterwards that she hadn't blurted out the whole truth? Imagine his reaction if she'd told him *that*, when he was already repulsed by what he knew, even though he'd done his best to hide it. And it was funny how the distance between a couple could grow almost without you realising. They'd been wary in each other's company. As the space between them had increased, she'd found the presence of her Italian husband almost... *forbidding*.

But if she had read it all wrong, then where did that leave her? If he hadn't been making value judgments about her, then why was she being so passive—always waiting for Renzo to make the first move? Yes, he was an alpha man with an instinctive need to dominate but it wasn't beyond the realms of possibility that he was simply being cautious around the baby she carried in her belly. He'd never had a pregnant lover before. He had taught her so much—wasn't this her chance to teach *him* something?

She walked over to him and, without warning, raised herself up on tiptoe to press her lips against his—feeling him jerk with surprise before sliding his arms around her waist to support her. Their tongues met as he instantly deepened the kiss but although Darcy could feel herself begin to melt, she forced herself to pull away.

'No,' she whispered. 'Not here. Not like this. Let's go upstairs. I need to lie down.'

'To bed?'

She took his hand and began to walk towards the stairs. 'Why not? It just happens to be about the only piece of furniture we have.'

An old-fashioned boat bed had been delivered to the master bedroom, her only instruction to the removal men being that the thick plastic covering the mattress should be taken away and disposed of. The wooden-framed structure dominated an otherwise empty room and on its king-size surface lay the embroidered coverlet she'd found when she and Renzo had been rooting around in one of Rome's antiques markets. She hadn't asked for it to be placed there but now it seemed like a sign that this had been meant to happen.

'Get undressed,' she whispered as she pulled off her overcoat and dropped it to the ground.

His eyes were fixed on hers as he removed his jacket, his sweater and trousers. Soon their discarded clothes were mingled in a heap beside the bed and at last Darcy stood in front of him. She was naked and heavily pregnant and feeling more than a little awkward, yet the look of desire in his eyes was melting away any last trace of shyness.

'I feel...bulky,' she said.

'Not bulky,' he corrected, his voice husky. 'Beautiful. Luscious and rounded—like the ripest of fruits about to fall from the tree.'

She shivered as he spoke and he took her into his arms.

'You're cold,' he observed.

She shook her head, still reeling from his words and the way he'd looked at her as he said them. 'No, not cold. Excited.'

'Me, too.' He gave a low laugh as he unfolded the coverlet and shook it out over the mattress.

'It almost looks as if we're planning on a picnic,' she said, her voice suddenly betraying a hint of uncertainty.

'That's exactly what I'm planning. I'm going to feast on you, *mia bella*.' But his face suddenly darkened as he pulled her into his arms and their bare flesh met for the first time in so long. 'I'm out of my depth here, Darcy,' he groaned. 'I've never made love to a pregnant woman before and I'm scared I'm going to hurt you. Tell me what you want me to do.'

'Just kiss me,' she whispered as they sank down onto the mattress. 'And we'll make it up as we go along.'

He kissed her for a long time. Tiny, brushing kisses at first and then deeper ones. And for a while, there were hard kisses which felt almost angry—as if he was punishing her for having kept him away for so long. But his anger soon passed and the kisses became exploratory as he licked his way inside her mouth and they began to play a silent and erotic game of tongues.

And then he started to touch her as Darcy had ached for him to touch her night after lonely night, waiting in vain for him to come to bed. At first he simply skated the palms of his hands down over her, as if discovering all the different contours and curves which had grown since last time they'd been intimate. No area of skin escaped the light whisper of his fingertips and she could feel every nerve ending growing acutely sensitised. Slowly, he circled each breast with his thumb, focussing his attention on each peaking nipple and putting his mouth there to lick luxuriously until she was squirming with frustrated longing. She wanted him to hurry yet she wanted him to take all day. But the rhythmical movements of his hand relaxed her completely, so that she was more than ready for his leisurely exploration of her belly when it came.

Their gazes met as his fingers splayed over the tight drum, his black eyes filled with question. 'This is okay?' he breathed.

'This is more than okay,' she managed, her voice growing unsteady as he slipped his hand down beyond to the silky triangle of hair, fingering her honeyed flesh so that she gasped with pleasure and the scent of her sex filled the air.

She reached for him, her pleasure already so intense that she could barely think straight as she tangled her fingers through his thick black hair, before hungrily reacquainting herself with the hard planes of his body. His shoulders were so broad and powerful; his pecs iron-hard. She loved the smattering of hair which roughened the rocky torso. Her fingertips skated lightly over his chest, feeling the rock-like definition of his abs. She thought his skin felt like oiled silk and she traced a lingering path over the dip of his belly before her fingers curled around the hardness of his erection, but he shook a cautionary head and pulled her hand away.

'It's been too long,' he said unevenly.

'You're telling me!'

'And I need to do it to you right now before I go out of my mind—the only question is, how?'

In answer, Darcy turned onto her side, wiggling her bottom against his groin in blatant invitation. 'Like this, I think.'

'But I can't see you.'

'Doesn't matter. And it never used to bother you. Go on.' She wiggled again and he groaned and she could feel how big he was as his moist tip positioned enticingly against her wet heat. 'You can feel me now and look at me later.'

He gave a low laugh and said something softly profound in Italian as he eased inside her. But the moan he gave was long and Darcy thought she'd never heard such an exultant sound before.

'Okay?' he bit out, holding himself perfectly still.

'More than okay,' she gasped.

'I'm not hurting you?'

'No, Renzo, but you're frustrating the hell out of me.'

His laugh sounded edgy but he began to move. In slow motion, he stroked himself in and out of her, his palms cupping her heavy breasts, his lips on her neck—kissing her through the thick curtain of curls. Darcy closed her eyes as she gave into sensation, forgetting that this was the only time they ever seemed truly equal. Forgetting everything except for the pulse points of pleasure throbbing throughout her body and the inexorable building of her orgasm as Renzo made love to her. Insistent heat pushed towards her. She could feel it coming—as inevitable as a train hurtling along the track—and part of her wanted to keep it at bay, to revel in that sweet expectation for as long as possible. But Renzo was close, as well—she could sense that, too. She'd had him come inside her too many times not to realise when he was near the edge. So she let go. Let pleasure wash over her—wave after sweet wave of it—until his movements suddenly quickened. He thrust into her with a deeper sense of urgency until at last he quivered and jerked and she felt the burst of his seed flooding into her.

Afterwards he lay exactly where he was and so did she. His skin was joined to hers, his body, too. It felt warm and sticky and intimate. Darcy just wanted to savour the moment and her deep sense of contentment as she waited for his verdict on that deeply satisfying interlude. Still remembering the dreamy things he'd murmured when they'd started to make love, part of her anticipating just what his next words might be. But when they came, it felt as if someone had ripped through that lazy contentment like a knife ripping through delicate silk.

'So... Was that my reward, I wonder, *cara mia*?' he questioned softly.

She pulled away from him, aware of the sudden pounding of her heart and the general indignity of turning to face a man when any kind of action was proving laborious. Especially when you were completely naked beneath the gaze of a pair of eyes which looked suddenly distant. She told herself not to read unnecessary stuff into his words—not to always imagine the worst. *He told you he wanted you and that he's been lusting after you...so go with that.*

'I'm afraid I'm not with you,' she said lightly.

'No?' He turned onto his back and yawned. 'You mean that wasn't your way of thanking me for buying you a home of your own? For finally getting the independence you must have craved for all these years?'

Darcy froze as the meaning of his words sank in and suddenly all that vulnerability which was never far from the surface began to rise in a dark unwanted tide. Groping down over the side of the bed, she managed to retrieve her overcoat and slung it over herself to cover her nakedness.

'Let's just get this straight.' Her voice was trembling. 'You think I had sex with you because you made me an overgenerous offer I hadn't actually asked for?'

'I don't know, Darcy.' His tone had changed. It rang out, iron-hard—like the sound of a hammer hitting against a nail. And when he turned his head to look at her, his eyes were icy. Like the black ice you sometimes saw when you were out on the roads in winter. Or didn't see until it was too late. 'I just don't get it with you. Sometimes I think I know you and other times I think I don't know you at all.'

'But aren't all relationships like that?' she questioned, swallowing down her fear. 'Didn't some songwriter say that if our thoughts could be seen, they'd probably put our heads in a guillotine?'

His eyes were narrowed as they studied her. 'And if I promised to grant you leniency, would you give me access to your thoughts right now?'

Darcy didn't react. She could tell him the rest of

her story—and maybe if it had been any other man than Renzo she would have done so. But he had already insulted her by thinking she'd had sex with him just because he'd bought her this house. To him, it all boiled down to a transaction and he didn't really trust himself to believe anything different. He thought of everything in terms of barter between the sexes because he didn't really *like* women, did he? He'd told her that a long time ago. He might want her but he didn't trust her and even though she could try to gain that trust by confessing her biggest secret, surely it was too big a gamble?

'I'm just wondering why you seem determined to wreck what chance we have of happiness,' she said, in a low voice. 'We have a lovely new home and a baby on the way. We're both healthy and we fancy each other like crazy. We've just had amazing sex—can't we just enjoy that?'

Black eyes seared into her for a long moment until eventually he nodded, his hand snaking around her waist and pulling her closer so that she could feel the powerful beat of his heart.

'Okay,' he said as he stroked her hair. 'Let's do that. I'm sorry. I shouldn't have said that. It's just all very new to me and I don't do trust very easily.'

Silently, she nodded, willing the guilt and the tears to go away. All she wanted was to live a decent life with her husband and child. She wanted what she'd never had—was that really too much to ask? She relaxed a little as his hand moved from her hair to her back, his fingertips skating a light path down her spine. Couldn't she be the best kind of wife to him, to demonstrate her commitment through her actions rather than her words?

He leaned over her, black fire blazing as he bent his face close. 'Are you tired?'

She shook her head. 'Not a bit. Why?'

His thumb grazed the surface of her bottom lip and she could feel his body hardening against her as he gave a rueful smile. 'Because I want you again,' he said.

CHAPTER TEN

DARCY'S FIRST INKLING that something was wrong
came on a Monday morning. At first she thought it
was nothing—like looking up at the sky and thinking
you'd imagined that first heavy drop of rain which
heralded the storm.

Renzo was in London unveiling his design for the
Tokyo art gallery at a press conference—having left
the house at the crack of dawn. He'd asked if she'd
wanted to accompany him but she'd opted to stay, and
was in the garden pegging out washing when the call
came from one of his assistants, asking if she was
planning to be at home at lunchtime.

Darcy frowned. It struck her as a rather strange
question. Even if she wasn't home, Renzo knew she
wouldn't have strayed much further than the local
village—or, at a pinch, the nearby seaside town of
Brighton. All that stuff they said about pregnant
women wanting to nest was completely true and she'd
built a domestic idyll here while awaiting the birth
of their baby. And hadn't that nesting instinct made
her feel as though life was good—or as good as it
could be? Even if sometimes she felt guilt clench at
her heart unexpectedly, knowing that her husband

remained ignorant of her biggest, darkest secret. But why rock the boat by telling him? Why spoil something which was good by making him pity her and perhaps despise her?

Placing the palm of her hand over the tight drum of her belly, she considered his assistant's question. 'Yes, I'm going to be here at lunchtime. Why?'

'Signor Sabatini just asked me to make sure.'

Darcy frowned. 'Is something wrong? Is Renzo around—can I speak to him, please?'

The assistant's voice was smooth but firm. 'I'm afraid that won't be possible. He's in a meeting. He said to tell you he'll be with you soon after noon.'

Darcy replaced the receiver, trying to lose the sudden feeling of apprehension which had crept over her, telling herself it was only because that fractured phone call felt a little like history repeating itself which had made her nervous. At least it hadn't been the same assistant who had stonewalled her attempts to get through to Renzo to tell him she was pregnant. That assistant had suddenly been offered a higher position in a rival company, something which Darcy suspected Renzo had masterminded himself. He'd seemed to want to put the past behind them as much as she did. *So stop imagining trouble where there isn't any.*

But it didn't matter how much she tried to stay positive, she couldn't seem to shake off the growing sense of dread which had taken root inside her. She went inside and put away the remaining clothes pegs—something her billionaire husband often teased her about. He told her that hanging out washing was suburban; she told him she didn't care. She knew he wanted to employ a cleaner and a housekeeper, and to keep a driver on tap instead of driving herself— in the fairly ordinary family car she'd chosen, which wasn't Renzo's usual style at all. The private mid- wife who lived locally and could be called upon at any time had been her only concession to being mar- ried to a billionaire.

But she wanted to keep it real, because reality was her only anchor. Despite Renzo's enormous power and wealth, she wanted theirs to be as normal a family as it was possible to be. And despite what she'd said when he'd railroaded her into the marriage, she badly wanted it to work. Not just because of their baby or because of their unhappy childhoods. She looked out the window, where her silk shirt was blowing wildly in the breeze. She wanted it to work because she had realised she loved him.

She swallowed.

She loved him.

It had dawned on her one morning when she'd woken to find him still sleeping beside her. In sleep he looked far less forbidding but no less beautiful. His shadowed features were softened; the sensual lips relaxed. Two dark arcs of eyelashes feathered onto his olive skin and his hair was ruffled from where she'd run her hungry fingers through it sometime dur- ing the night. She remembered the powerful feeling which had welled up inside her as the full force of her feelings had hit her and she wondered how she could have failed to recognise it before.

Of course she loved him. She'd been swept away by him from the moment she'd looked across a crowded nightclub and seen a man who had only had eyes for her. A once-in-a-lifetime man who'd made her feel a once-in-a-lifetime passion, despite the fact that he could be arrogant, tricky and, at times, downright difficult. And if fate—or rather pregnancy—had given her the opportunity to capitalise on those feelings and for passion to evolve into love, then she had to make the most of it. He might not feel the same way about her but she told herself that didn't matter because she had more than enough love to go round. She planned to make herself indispensable—not just as the mother of his child, but as his partner. To concentrate on friendship, respect and passion and reassure herself that maybe it could be enough. And if sometimes she found herself yearning for something more—well, maybe she needed to learn to appreciate what she had and stop chasing fantasy.

She spent the next hour crushing basil leaves and mashing garlic, trying to perfect a pesto sauce as good as the one they'd eaten in Rome on the last evening of their honeymoon. Then she picked a handful of daffodils and put them in a vase and had just sat down with a cup of tea to admire their yellow frilliness, when she heard the front door slam.

'I'm in here!' she called. She looked up to see Renzo framed in the doorway, her smile and words of welcome dying on her lips when she saw the darkness on his face. She put the cup down with a suddenly shaking hand. 'Is something wrong?'

He didn't answer and that only increased her fear. His hands were white-knuckled and a pulse was beating fast at his temple, just below a wayward strand of jet-black hair. She could sense an almost palpable tension about him—as if he was only just clinging on to his temper by a shred.

'Renzo! What's wrong?'

He fixed her with a gaze which was cold and hard. 'You tell me,' he said.

'Renzo, you're scaring me now. What is it? I don't understand.'

'Neither did I.' He gave a harsh and bitter laugh. 'But suddenly I do.'

From his pocket he took out an envelope and slapped it onto the table. It was creased—as if somebody had crushed it in the palm of their hand and then changed their mind and flattened it out again. On the cheap paper Renzo's name had been printed—and whoever had written it had spelt his surname wrong, she noted automatically.

His lip curved. 'It's a letter from your friend.'

'Which *friend*?'

'Shouldn't take you long to work that one out, Darcy. I mean, it isn't like you have a lot of friends, is it?' His mouth twisted. 'I never really understood why before. But suddenly I do.'

She knew then. She'd seen the look often enough in the past not to be able to recognise it. She could feel the stab of pain to her heart and the sickening certainty that her flirtation with a normal life was over.

'What does it say?'

'What do you think it says?'

'I'd like to hear it.' Was she hoping for some sort of reprieve? For someone to be writing to tell him that she'd once told a policewoman a lie—or that she'd missed school for a whole three months while her mother kept her at home? She licked her lips and looked at him. 'Please.'

With another contemptuous twist of his lips he pulled out the lined paper and began to read from it, though something told her he already knew the words by heart.

"'Did you know that Pammie Denton was a whore? Biggest hooker in all of Manchester. Ask your wife about her mam.'"

He put the note down. 'It's pointless asking if you recognise the writing, since it's printed in crude capitals, but I imagine Drake Bradley must be the perpetrator and that this is the beginning of some clumsy attempt at blackmail. Don't you agree?' he added coolly.

Her normal reaction would have been to shut right down and say she didn't want to talk about it because that had been the only way she'd been able to cope with the shame in the past, but this was different. Renzo was her husband. He was the father of her unborn baby. She couldn't just brush all the dirty facts under the carpet and hope they would go away.

And maybe it was time to stop running from the truth. To have the courage to be the person she was today, rather than the person forged from the sins of yesterday. Her heart pounded and her mouth grew suddenly dry. To have the courage to tell him what maybe she should have told him a long time ago.

'I'd like to explain,' she said, drawing in a deep breath.

He gave her another unfathomable look as he

opened up the refrigerator and took out a beer and Darcy blinked at him in consternation because cool and controlled Renzo Sabatini never drank during the day.

'Feel free,' he said, flipping the lid and pouring it into a glass. But he left the drink untouched, putting it down on the table and leaning against the window sill as he fixed her with that same cold and flinty stare. 'Explain away.'

In a way it would have been easier if he'd been angry. If he'd been hurling accusations at her she could have met those accusations head-on. She could have countered his rage with, not exactly *reason*— but surely some kind of heartfelt appeal, asking him to put himself in her situation. But this wasn't easy. Not when he was looking at her like that. It was like trying to hold a conversation with a piece of stone.

'My mother was a prostitute.'

'I think we've already established that fact and I think I know how prostitution works,' he said. 'So what exactly was it you wanted to *explain*, Darcy?'

It was worse than she'd thought because there *was* anger, only it was quiet and it was brooding and it was somehow terrifying. Because this was a man she scarcely recognised. It was as if his body had become encased in a thick layer of frost. As if liquid ice were running through his veins instead of blood.

She looked at him, wanting to convey a sense of what it had been like, trying to cling on to the certainty that there *was* something between her and Renzo—something which was worth fighting for. There had to be. He might take his parental responsibilities very seriously but deep down she knew he wouldn't have married her or contemplated staying with her unless they had *something* in common. 'She was an addict. Well, you know that bit. Only… Well, drugs are expensive—'

'And a woman can always sell her body?' he interposed acidly.

She nodded, knowing this time there was no going back. That she needed to tell him the truth. The cruel, unedited version she'd never even been able to admit to herself before, let alone somebody else.

'She can,' she said. 'Until her looks start to go—and that tends to happen sooner rather than later where addicts are concerned. My mother had once been beautiful but her looks deserted her pretty quickly. Her…her hair fell out and then…'

She flushed with shame as she remembered the kids at school taunting her and she remembered that she'd once thought she would never tell him this bit, but she knew she had to. Because why was she trying to protect her mother's memory, when she had uncaringly gone out and wrecked as many lives as it took to get that hypodermic syringe plunging into her arm?

'Then her teeth,' she whispered, staring down at the fingers which were knotted together in her lap. 'And that was the beginning of the end, because she kept losing her dentures whenever she got stoned. She was still able to get clients—only the standard of client went rapidly downhill, as I'm sure you can imagine, and so did the amount of money she was able to charge.'

And that had been when it had got really scary. When she hadn't wanted to go home from school at night—even though she was so stressed that learning had become impossible. She'd never know what she'd find when she got there—what kind of lowlife would be leering at her mother, but, worse, leering at *her*. That had been where her mistrust of men had started and if that kindly social worker hadn't stepped in, she didn't know what would have happened. To most people, going back to the children's home would have seemed like the end of the road—but to her it had felt like salvation.

'It sounds a nightmare,' he said flatly.

Sensing a sea change in his mood, Darcy looked up but the hope in her heart withered immediately when she saw that his stony expression was unchanged. 'It was. I just want you to understand—'

'No,' he said suddenly, cutting across her words. 'I'm not interested in understanding, Darcy. Not any more. I want you to know that something was destroyed when I received this letter.'

'I realise it was shocking—'

He shook his head. 'No. You're missing the point. I'm not talking about *shocking*. Human behaviour has always been shocking. I'm talking about trust.'

'T-trust?'

'Yes. I can see the bewilderment on your face. Is that word such an alien concept to you?' His mouth twisted. 'I guess it must be. Because I asked you, didn't I, Darcy? I asked you not once, but twice, whether you were keeping anything else from me. I thought we were supposed to be embracing a new openness—an honest environment in which to bring up our child, not one which was tainted by lies.'

She licked her lips. 'But surely you can understand why I didn't tell you?'

'No,' he snapped. 'I can't. I knew about your mother's addiction. Did you expect me to judge you when I found out how she paid for that addiction?'

'Yes,' she said helplessly. 'Of course I did. Because I've been judged by every person who ever knew about it. Being the daughter of Manchester's biggest hooker tends to saddle you with a certain reputation. People used to sneer at me. I could hear them laughing behind my back. And even though my social worker said it was because I was attractive and people would try to bring me down by exploiting my vulnerability, that didn't stop the hurt. It's why I left and came to London. It's why I never was intimate with a man before I met you.'

'Why you never accepted the gifts I tried to give you,' he said slowly.

'Yes!' she answered, desperately searching for a chink in the dark armour which made him look so impenetrable. Searching for the light of understanding in his eyes which might give her hope.

But there was none.

'You do realise, Darcy,' he questioned, 'that I can't live with secrets?'

'But there aren't any—not any more. Now you know everything about me.' Her heart was crashing wildly against her ribcage as she pleaded her case like a prisoner in the dock. 'And I need never lie to you again.'

He shook his head. 'You just don't get it, do you?' he said and his voice sounded tired. 'You knew that my childhood was tainted with secrets and lies. I told you a long time ago that I had trust issues and I meant it. How the hell can I ever trust you again? The truth is that I can't.' He gave a bitter laugh. 'And the even bigger truth is that I don't even want to.'

She was about to accuse him back. To tell him that he'd never trusted her in the first place. Look how he'd reacted when he'd discovered she was pregnant—showering her with suspicious questions when she'd lain in her hospital bed. He'd even thought she'd had wild sex with him just because he'd bought her a house. But her accusations remained unspoken because what was the point? No matter what she did or said, something in him had died—she could tell that from the emptiness in his eyes when he looked at her.

She nodded. 'So what do you want to do?'

He lifted the glass of beer now and drank it down in a draught, before slowly putting the empty glass back down on the table. 'I'm going back to London,' he said and Darcy could hear the bitterness in his tone. 'Because I can't bear to be around you right now.'

'Renzo—'

'No, please. Let's keep this dignified, shall we? Don't let's either of us say anything we might later regret, because we're still going to have to co-parent. We'll obviously need to come to some sort of formal agreement about that but it isn't something we need to discuss right now. I think you know me well enough to know that I won't be unreasonable.'

She nearly broke then—and what made it worse was the sudden crack in his voice as he said those words. As if he was hurting as much as she was. But he wasn't, was he? He couldn't be. Because nobody could possibly share this terrible pain which was searing through her heart and making it feel as if it had exploded into a million little pieces.

'You have the services of the midwife I've employed,' he continued. 'I spoke to her from the car on the way here and explained the circumstances and she has offered to move into the annex if that would make you feel more secure.'

'No, it would not make me feel more secure!' Darcy burst out. 'I don't want a total stranger living here with me.'

He gave a short, sarcastic laugh. 'No. I can't imagine you do. Living with a stranger isn't something I'd particularly recommend.'

And then he turned his back on her and walked out, closing the door with a click behind him. Darcy struggled to her feet to watch him walking down the garden path, past the washing line. The wind was blowing the sleeves of her shirt so that they flapped towards him, as if they were trying to pull him back, and how she wished they could. She considered rushing down the path after him, cumbersome in her late pregnancy, grabbing the sleeve of his handmade Italian suit and begging him to give her another chance. To stay.

But dignity was the one thing she had—maybe the only thing she had left.

So she watched him go. Watched him get into the back of the luxury car with the sunlight glinting off dark hair as blue-black as a raven's wing. His jaw set, he kept his gaze fixed straight ahead, not turning round as the powerful vehicle pulled away. There was no last, lingering look. No opportunity for her eyes to silently beseech him to stay.

The only thing she saw was his forbidding profile as Renzo Sabatini drove out of her life.

CHAPTER ELEVEN

AFTER HE'D GONE, a wave of desolation swept over Darcy—a desolation so bleak that it felt as if she were standing on the seashore in the depths of winter, being buffeted by the lashing sea. As his car disappeared from view she stumbled away from the window, trying to keep her wits about her, telling herself that her baby was her primary focus—her *only* focus—and she needed to protect the innocent life inside her. Briefly she closed her eyes as she thought about what Renzo had just found out—the shameful truth about her mother being a common prostitute. Would she be forced to tell her son about the kind of woman his grandmother had been? Yet surely if there was enough love and trust between her and her little boy, then anything was possible.

She swallowed because nothing seemed certain—not any more. She could understand her husband's anger but it had been impossible to penetrate. It had been a controlled reaction which shouldn't have surprised her—but another aspect of it had and that was what was confusing her. Because he hadn't threatened her with the full force of his wealth and power after making his sordid discovery, had he? Wouldn't another man—a more ruthless man—have pressured her with exposure if she didn't relinquish her role as primary carer to their baby?

Brushing away the sweat which was beading her brow, she knew she ought to sit down but she couldn't stop pacing the room as her jumbled thoughts tried to assemble themselves into something approaching clarity. His voice had been bitter when he'd spoken to her—almost as if he'd been hurt. But Renzo didn't *do* hurt, did he? Just as he didn't do emotion.

Surely he must recognise why she'd kept her terrible secret to herself—why the shame of the past had left her unable to trust anyone, just as *he* had been unable to trust anyone.

But Renzo had trusted *her*, hadn't he?

The thought hit her hard.

How many times had he trusted her?

He'd trusted her to take the pill and, even though that method of birth control had failed, he'd trusted her enough to believe her explanation.

He'd trusted her enough to confide in her when he first took her out to Tuscany and told her things he need never have said. And then, when they'd got back to England, he'd trusted her enough to give her the key to his apartment. He might not have wooed her with words but words were cheap, weren't they? Anyone could say stuff to please a woman and not mean it. But Renzo's actions had demonstrated trust and regard and that was pretty amazing. It might not have been love but it came a pretty close second. And she had blown it.

Tears welled up in her eyes as she stared at the yellow blur of daffodils in the vase. She had blown it by refusing to trust *him*—by not lowering the defences she'd erected all those years ago, when the police had asked her questions and she'd been too frightened to tell the truth, for fear her mother would go to jail. Renzo hadn't judged her because her mother had been an addict and he wouldn't have judged her because she'd been a prostitute—what had made him turn away with that tight-lipped face was the fact that she'd lied to him. Again and again, she'd kept her secrets to herself.

So what was she going to do about it? She looked at the bright blue sky outside, which seemed to mock her. Stay here with the midwife on standby, while she waited for the baby to arrive? Day following day with remorse and regret and the feeling that she'd just thrown away the best thing which had ever happened to her? Or have the courage to go to Renzo. Not to plead or beg but to put her feelings on the line and tell him what she should have told him a long time ago. It might be too late for him to take her back, but surely he could find it in his heart to forgive her?

Picking up the car keys, she went to the garage and manoeuvred the car out on the lane, sucking in lots of deep and calming breaths just as they'd taught her in the prenatal relaxation classes. Because she had a very precious passenger on board and there was no way she should attempt to drive to London if she was going to drive badly.

She let out the clutch and pulled away, thinking that she should have been scared but she'd never felt so strong or so focussed. She kept her mind fixed firmly on the traffic as the country roads gave way to the city and she entered the busy streets of London, glad she was able to follow the robotic instructions of the satnav. But her hands were shaking as eventually she drew up outside the towering skyscraper headquarters of Sabatini International. She left the car by the kerb and walked into the foyer, where a security guard bustled up importantly, barring her way.

'I'm afraid you can't park there, miss.'

'Oh, yes, I can. And it's Mrs, actually—or Signora, if you prefer. My husband owns this building. So if you wouldn't mind?' Giving a tight smile at his goggle-eyed expression, she handed him her car keys. 'Doing something with my car? I'd hate Renzo to get a ticket.'

She was aware of people staring at her as she headed for the penthouse lift but maybe that wasn't surprising. Among the cool and geeky workers milling around, she guessed a heavily pregnant woman with untidy hair would be a bit of a talking point. The elevator zoomed her straight up to the thirty-second floor, where one of Renzo's assistants must have been forewarned because she stood directly in Darcy's path, her fixed smile not quite meeting her eyes.

'Mrs Sabatini.' She inclined her head. 'I can't let you disturb him. I'm afraid your husband is tied up right now.'

Suddenly tempted by a wild impulse to ask whether Renzo had suddenly been converted to the pleasures of bondage, Darcy looked at her and nodded, but she didn't feel anger or irritation. The woman was only doing her job, after all. In the past she might have crumbled—gone scuttling back downstairs with a request that Renzo contact her when he had a free moment. But that was then and this was now. She'd overcome so much in her life. Seen stuff no child should ever see. She'd come through the other side of all that and yet...

Yet she had still let it define her, hadn't she? Instead of shutting the door on the past and walking away from it, she had let it influence her life.

Well, not any more.

'Watch me,' Darcy said as she walked across the carpeted office towards Renzo's office, ignoring the woman's raised voice of protest.

She pushed open the door to see Renzo seated at the top of a long boardroom table with six other people listening to what he was saying, but his words died away the moment he glanced up and saw her. Comically, every head swivelled in her direction but Darcy didn't pay them any attention; she was too busy gazing into the eyes of her husband and finding nothing in their ebony depths but ice. But she was going to be strong. As strong as she knew she could be.

'Darcy,' he said, his eyes narrowing.

'I know this isn't a convenient time,' she said, preempting his dismissal and drawing herself up as tall as she could. 'But I really do need to speak to you, Renzo. So if you people wouldn't mind giving us five, we'll make sure this meeting is rescheduled.'

Almost as if they were being controlled by some unseen puppet master, six heads turned to Renzo for affirmation.

He shrugged. 'You heard what the lady said.'

Darcy's heart was pounding as they all trooped out, shooting her curious looks on their way, but Renzo still hadn't moved. His expression remained completely impassive and only the sudden movement of his fingers as he slammed his pen onto the table gave any indication that he might be angry at her interruption.

'So what are you doing here?' he questioned coolly. 'I thought we'd said everything there is to say.'

She shook her head. 'But we haven't. Or rather, I haven't. You did a lot of talking earlier only I was too shocked and upset to answer.'

'Don't bother,' he said, sounding almost…*bored*. 'I don't want to hear any more of your lies. You want to hold on to your precious secrets, Darcy? Then go right ahead! Or maybe find a man you trust enough to tell the truth.'

She let out a shuddered breath, struggling to get out the words she knew she needed to say. 'I trust you, Renzo. It's taken me this long to dare admit it, but I do. I trust you enough to tell you that I've been scared…and I've been stupid. You see, I couldn't believe someone as good as you could ever be part of my life and I thought…' Her voice stumbled but somehow she kept the tears at bay. 'I thought the only way I could hold on to it was to be the person I thought you'd want me to be. I was terrified that if you knew who I really was, that you would send me away— baby or no baby—'

'You can't—'

'No,' she said fiercely, and now the tears *had* started and she scrubbed them away furiously with the back of her fist. 'Let me finish. I should have celebrated my freedom from the kind of life I'd grown up in. I should have rejoiced that I had found a man who was prepared to care for me, and to care for our baby. I should have realised that it was a pretty big deal for you to tell me stuff about your past and give me a key to your apartment. I should have looked for the meaning behind those gestures instead of being too blind and too scared to dare. And rather than keeping my feelings locked away, I should have told you the biggest secret of all.'

He froze. 'Not another one?'

'Yes,' she whispered. 'The final one—and I'm about to let you in on it. Not because I want something in return or because I'm expecting something back, but because you need to know.' Her voice trembled but she didn't care. This was her chance to put something right but it was also the truth—shining, bold and very certain, no matter the consequences. 'I love you, Renzo. I've loved you from the first moment I saw you, when the thunderbolt hit me, too. Because that feeling never went away. It just grew and grew. When we made love that first time, it was so powerful—it blew me away. I've never wanted to be intimate with a man before you and I know that, if you don't want me, I won't ever find somebody who makes me feel the way you do.'

There was a silence when all Darcy could hear was the fierce pounding of her heart and she could hardly bear to look at him for fear that she might read rejection in his face. But she had to look at him. If she had learned anything it was that she had to face up to the truth, no matter how painful that might be.

'How did you get here?' he demanded.

She blinked at him in confusion. 'I...drove.'

He nodded. 'You parked your car in the middle of the city when you've only recently passed your test?'

'I gave the keys to the security guard.' She licked her lips. 'I told him I was your wife.'

'So you thought you'd just drive up here and burst into my building and disrupt my meeting with a few pretty words and make it all better?'

'I did...' She drew in a deep breath. 'I did what I thought was best.'

'Best for you, you mean?'

'Renzo—'

'No!' he interrupted savagely and now all the coldness had gone—to be replaced with a flickering fire and fury which burned in the depths of his black eyes. 'I don't want this. *Capisci?* I meant what I said, Darcy. I don't want to live this way, wondering what the hell I'm going to find out about you next. Never knowing what you're hiding from me, what secrets you're concealing behind those witchy green eyes.'

She searched his face for some kind of softening but there was none. And who could blame him? She'd known about his trust issues and she'd tested those issues to the limit. Broken them beyond repair so that they lay in shattered ruins between them. The hope which had been building inside her withered and died. Her lips pressed in on themselves but she would not cry. *She would not cry.*

She nodded. 'Then there's nothing more to be said, is there? I'll leave you so that you can get on with your meeting. You're right. I should have rung ahead beforehand, but I was afraid you wouldn't see me. I guess I would have been right.' She swallowed. 'Still, I'm sure we can work something out. The best and most amicable deal for our baby. I'm sure we both want that.' There was a pause as she took one long last look at him, drinking in the carved olive features, the sensual lips and the gleam of his black eyes. 'Goodbye, Renzo. Take…take good care of yourself.'

And then, with her head held very high, she walked out of his office.

Renzo stared at her retreating form, his mind spinning, aware of the door closing before opening again and his assistant rushing in.

'I'm sorry about that, Renzo—'

But he waved an impatient hand of dismissal until the woman left him alone again. He paced the floor space of his vast office, trying to concentrate on his latest project, but all he could think about was the luminous light of Darcy's green eyes and the brimming suggestion of unshed tears. And suddenly he found himself imagining what her life must have been like. How unbearable it must have been. All the sordid things she must have witnessed—and yet she had come through it all, hadn't she? He thought how she'd overcome her humble circumstances and what she had achieved. Not in some majorly highpowered capacity—she'd ended up waitressing rather than sitting on the board of some big company. But she'd done it with integrity. She'd financed her studies and read lots of novels while working two jobs— yet even when she'd been poured into that tight satin cocktail dress she had demonstrated a fierce kind of pride and independence. She'd never wanted to take a single thing from him, had she? She'd refused much more than she'd accepted and it hadn't been an act, had it? It had been genuine. From the heart. A big heart, which she'd been scared to expose for fear that she'd be knocked back, just as she must have been knocked back so many times before.

And he had done that to her. Knocked her back and let her go, right after she'd fiercely declared her love for him.

Her *love* for him.

He was prepared to give up that, along with her beauty and her energy, and for what?

For *what*?

A cold dread iced his skin as swiftly he left his office, passing his assistant's desk without saying a word as he urgently punched the button of the elevator. But the journey down to the basement seemed to take for ever, and Renzo's fist clenched as he glanced at his watch, because surely she would have left by now.

It took a moment for his eyes to focus in the gloomy light of the subterranean car park but he couldn't see her. Only now it wasn't his fist which clenched but his heart—a tight spear of pain which made him feel momentarily winded. What if she'd driven off after his callous rejection and was negotiating the busy roads to Brighton as she made her way back towards an empty house?

Pain and guilt washed over him as his eyes continued to scan the rows of cars and hope withered away inside him. And then he saw her on the other side of the car park in the ridiculously modest vehicle she'd insisted she wanted, in that stubborn way which often infuriated him but more often made his blood sing. He weaved his way through the cars, seeing her white face looking up at him as he placed the palm of his hand against the glass of the windscreen.

'I'm sorry,' he mouthed, but she shook her head.

'Let me in,' he said, but she shook her head again and began putting the key in the ignition with shaking fingers.

He didn't move, but placed his face closer to the window, barely noticing that someone from the IT department had just got out of the lift and was staring at him in open-mouthed disbelief. 'Open the door,' he said loudly. 'Or I'll rip the damned thing off its hinges.'

She must have believed him because the lock clicked and he opened the door and sat in the passenger seat before she could change her mind. 'Darcy,' he said.

'Whatever it is you want to say,' she declared fiercely, 'I don't want to hear it. Not right now.'

She'd been crying. Her face was blotchy and her eyes red-rimmed and he realised that he'd never seen her cry—not once—she, who probably had more reason to cry than any other woman he'd known.

He wanted to take her in his arms. To feel her warmth and her connection. To kiss away those drying tears as their flesh melted against each other as it had done so many times in the past. But touching was cheating—it was avoiding the main issue and he needed to address that. To face up to what else was wrong. Not in her, but in him. Because how could she have ever trusted him completely when he kept so much of himself locked away?

'Just hear me out,' he said, in a low voice. 'And let me tell you what I should have told you a long time ago. Which is that you've transformed my life in every which way. You've made me feel stuff I never thought I'd feel. Stuff I didn't want to feel, because I was scared of what it might do to me, because I'd seen hurt and I'd seen pain in relationships and I didn't want any part of that. Only I've just realised...' He drew in a deep breath and maybe she thought he wasn't going to continue, because her eyes had narrowed.

'Realised what?' she questioned cautiously.

'That the worst pain of all is the pain of not having you in my life. When you walked out of my office just now I got a glimpse of just what that could be like—and it felt like the sun had been blotted from the sky.'

'Very poetic,' she said sarcastically. 'Maybe your next girlfriend will hear it before it's too late.'

She wasn't budging an inch but he respected her for that, too. If it had been anyone else he wouldn't have stayed or persisted or cared. But he was fighting for something here. Something he'd never really thought about in concrete terms before.

His future.

'And there's something else you need to know,' he said softly. 'And before you look at me in that stubborn way, just listen. All those things I did for you, things I've never done for anyone else—why do you think they happened? Because those thunderbolt feelings never left me either, no matter how much I sometimes wished they would. Because I wanted our baby and I wanted you. I like being with you. Being married to you. Waking up to you each morning and kissing you to sleep every night. And I love you,' he finished simply. 'I love you so much, Darcy. Choose what you do or don't believe, but please believe that.'

As she listened to his low declaration of love,

Darcy started to cry. At first it was the trickle of a solitary tear which streaked down her cheek and ended up in a salty drip at the corner of her mouth. She licked it away but then more came, until suddenly they were streaming her face but the crazy thing was that she didn't care.

In the close confines of the car she stared at him through blurry vision and as that vision cleared the dark beauty of his face no longer seemed shuttered. It seemed open and alight with a look she'd always longed to see there, but never thought she would. It was shining from his eyes as a lighthouse shone out to all the nearby ships on the darkest of nights. 'Yes, I believe you,' she whispered. 'And now you need to hold me very tightly—just to convince me I'm not dreaming.'

With a soft and exultant laugh Renzo pulled her into his arms, smoothing away the tangle of curls before bending his head to kiss away the tears which had made her cheeks so wet. She clung to him as their mouths groped blindly together and kissed as they'd never really kissed before. It was passionate and it was emotional—but it was superseded by a feeling so powerful that Darcy's heart felt as if it were going to spill over with joy, until she suddenly jerked away—tossing her head back like a startled horse.

'Oh, I love you, my beautiful little firecracker,' he murmured as she dug her fingers into his arms.

'The feeling is mutual,' she said urgently. 'Only we have to get out of here.'

He frowned. 'You want to go back to Sussex?'

She flinched and closed her eyes as another fierce contraction gripped her and she shook her head. 'I don't think we're going to make it as far as Sussex. I know it's another two weeks away, but I think I'm going into labour.'

It was a quick and easy birth—well, that was what the cooing midwives told her, though Darcy would never have described such a seismic experience as *easy*. But she had Renzo beside her every step along the way. Renzo holding her hand and mopping her brow and whispering things to her in Italian which— in her more lucid moments—she knew she shouldn't understand, but somehow she did. Because the words of love were universal. People could say them and not mean them. But they could also say them in a foreign language and you knew—you just *knew*—what they meant and that they were true.

It was an emotional moment when they put Luca Lorenzo Sabatini to her breast and he began to suckle eagerly, gazing up at her with black eyes so like his daddy's. And when the midwives and the doctor had all left them, she glanced up into Renzo's face and saw that his own eyes were unusually bright. She lifted her hand to the dark shadow of growth at his unshaven jaw and he met her wondering gaze with a shrug of his powerful shoulders. Was he *crying*?

'*Scusi,*' he murmured, bending down to drop a kiss on his son's downy black head before briefly brushing his lips over Darcy's. 'I'm not going to be a lot of use to you, am I—if I start letting emotion get the better of me?'

And Darcy smiled as she shook her head. 'Bring it on,' she said softly. 'I like seeing my strong and powerful man reduced to putty by the sight of his newborn baby.'

'It seems as if my son has the same power over me as his mother,' Renzo responded drily. He smoothed back her wild red curls. 'Now. Do you want me to leave and let you get some rest?'

'No way,' she said firmly, shifting across to make space for him, her heart thudding as he manoeuvred his powerful frame onto the narrow hospital bed. And Darcy felt as if she'd never known such joy as when Renzo put his arm around her and hugged her and Luca close. As if she'd spent her life walking along a path—much of the time in darkness—only to emerge into a place full of beautiful light.

'It's not the most comfortable bed in the world, but there's room on it for the three of us. And I want you beside me, Renzo. Here with me and here with Luca.' And that was when her voice cracked with the emotion which had been building up inside her since he'd told her he loved her. 'In fact, we're never going to let you go.'

EPILOGUE

KICKING OFF HER shoes and flopping onto the sofa with a grateful sigh, Darcy frowned as Renzo handed her a slim leather box. 'What's this?' she questioned.

He raised his brows. 'Isn't the whole point of presents that they're supposed to be a surprise?'

'But it isn't my birthday.'

'No,' he said steadily. 'But it's Luca's.'

'Yes.' The box momentarily forgotten, Darcy looked into her husband's ebony eyes and beamed. Hard to believe that their beautiful son had just celebrated his first birthday. A year during which he'd captivated everyone around him with his bright and inquisitive nature, which at times showed more than a glimpse of his mother's natural stubbornness.

Today, with streamers and balloons and a bit too much cake, they'd held a party for all his little friends in Sussex—while the mothers had each sipped a glass of pink champagne. Confident in her husband's love, and freed from the shame of the past, Darcy had started to get to know people—both here in Sussex and in their London house, as well as the beautiful Tuscan villa where they spent as many holidays as they could. Invitations had started to arrive as, for the first time in

her life, she'd begun to make friends. Real friends—
though her best friend was and always would be her
husband. She looked at him now with bemusement.

'Open it,' he said softly.

She unclipped the clasp and stared down at the
necklace. A triple row of square-cut emeralds gleamed
greenly against the dark velvet and there was a moment of confusion before she lifted her eyes to his. She
remembered how, just after Luca's birth, he'd gone to
see Drake Bradley and persuaded the blackmailer to
tell him where he'd pawned the diamond necklace.
He'd got Drake's confession on tape of course and,
with the threat of prosecution and prison very real,
Renzo had surprised everyone by refusing to turn him
in to the police. Instead, he'd given Drake a chance—
offering him a job working on the site clearance of one
of his new projects in England. Employment Drake
had eagerly accepted—possibly his first ever legiti-
mate job and one which, against all the odds, he ex-
celled at. For ever after, he treated Renzo with the
dedication and loyalty a badly beaten dog might display towards the man who had rescued him.

Keep your friends close... Renzo had whispered to
her on the night when the diamond necklace was back
in his possession, after she'd finished remonstrating
with him for putting himself in possible danger. But his
expression had been rueful as she had held the dazzling
diamond neckpiece as if it were an unexploded bomb.

'I guess you wouldn't get a lot of pleasure out of
wearing this now?'

Darcy had shaken her head. 'Nope. Too much bad
history. And I'm no big fan of diamonds, you know
that.'

The next day Renzo had returned the piece to the charity, telling them to auction it again. And he hadn't mentioned jewellery since.

Until now.

'Renzo,' Darcy whispered, her gaze dazzled by the vivid green fire of the emeralds. 'This is too much.'

'No,' he said fiercely. 'It isn't. Not nearly enough. If I bought up the contents of every jewellery shop in the world, it still wouldn't be enough. Because I love you, Darcy. I love what you've given and shown me. How you've made me the man I am today, and I like that man much better than the one I was before.' His voice dipped, his gaze dark as the night as it blazed over her. 'And didn't I always say you should have emeralds to match your eyes?'

Very wet eyes now, she thought, but she nodded as he kissed away her tears. And the jewels were suddenly forgotten because, when it boiled down to it, they were just pretty pieces of stone. The most precious thing Darcy had was her love—for her son and for her husband. And the chance to live her life without shame and without secrets.

'Come here, *mia caro*,' she whispered, practising her ever-increasing Italian vocabulary as she pulled him down onto the sofa next to her.

'What did you have in mind?'

'I just want to show you...' she smiled as her fingertip stroked his cheek until she reached the outline of his sensual mouth, which softened as she edged her own lips towards it '...how very much I love you.'

* * * * *

ENGAGED FOR HER ENEMY'S HEIR

KATE HEWITT

To my lovely editor, Victoria.
Thank you for all your help with this one!

CHAPTER ONE

IT SEEMED AS if a funeral was just a chance for people to get drunk. Not that Allegra Wells had personal experience of such a thing. She'd stuck to sparkling water all evening and now stood on the sidelines of the opulent hotel ballroom in Rome where her father's wake was being held and watched people booze it up. She could have felt bitter, or at least cynical, but all she could dredge up was a bone-aching, heart-deep weariness.

It shouldn't be this way.

Fifteen years ago it wouldn't have been.

She took a slug of water, half wishing it was alcohol that would burn its way down to her belly and make her finally feel something. Melt the ice she'd encased herself in for so long, so that numbness had become familiar, comforting. She didn't even notice it most of the time, content with her life back in New York, small as it was. It was only now, surrounded by strangers and with her father dead, that she felt painfully conscious of her isolation in the world she'd always viewed at a safe distance. The father who had turned his back on her without a thought.

Her father's second wife and stepdaughter Allegra knew, at least by sight. She'd never met them but she'd seen photos when, in moments of emotional weakness, she'd done an Internet search on her father. Alberto Man-

cini, CEO of Mancini Technologies. He was in the online tabloids often enough, because his second wife was
young and socially ambitious—at least she seemed to
be, from everything Allegra had seen and read online.

Her behaviour at the funeral, wearing black lace and
dabbing her eyes with artful elegance, didn't make Allegra think otherwise. She hadn't spared Allegra so much
as a glance, but then why would she? No one knew who
Allegra was; she'd only known about the funeral because
her father's lawyer had contacted her.

Around her people swirled and chatted, caught up
in their own intricate dance of social niceties. Allegra
wondered why she stayed. What she was hoping to find
here? What did she think she could gain? Her father was
dead, but he'd been dead to her for fifteen years, or at
least she'd been dead to him. No messages, no letters or
texts or calls in all that time. Nothing, and that was what
she grieved for now, not the man himself.

The father she'd lost a long time ago, whose death now
made her remember and ache for all she'd missed out on
over the years. Was that why she'd come? To find some
sort of closure? To make sense of all the pain?

Allegra's mother had been furious that she'd been at-
tending, had seen it as a deep and personal betrayal.
Just remembering Jennifer Wells's icy silence made
Allegra's stomach cramp. Interactions with her mother
were fraught at the best of times. Jennifer had never recovered from the way her husband had cut both her and
Allegra out of his life, as neatly and completely as if he'd
been wielding scissors. Although it hadn't felt neat. It had
felt bloody and agonising, thrust from a life of luxury
and indulgence into one of deprivation and loneliness,
trying to make sense of the sudden changes, her father's

absence, her mother's tight-lipped explanations that had actually explained nothing.

'Your father decided our marriage was over. There's nothing I could do. He wants nothing to do with either of us any more. He won't give us a penny.'

Just like that? Allegra had barely been able to believe it. Her father loved her. He swooped her up in her arms, he tickled her, called her his little flower. For years she had waited for him to call, text, write, anything. All she'd got, on and on, was silence.

And now she was here, and what was the point? Her father was gone, and no one here even knew who she was, or what she'd once been to him.

From across the room Allegra saw a flash of amber eyes, a wing of ink-black hair. A man was standing on the sidelines just as she was, on the other side of the room. Like her he was watching the crowds, and the look of contained emotion on his face echoed through Allegra, ringing a true, clear note.

She didn't recognise him, had no idea what he'd been to her father or why he was there—yet something in him, the way he held himself apart, the guarded look in his eyes, resonated with her. Made her wonder. Of course, she wouldn't talk to him. She'd always been shy, and her parents' divorce had made it worse. Chatting up a stranger at the best of times verged on impossible.

Still she watched him, covertly, although she doubted he noticed her all the way across the room, a pale, drab young woman dressed in fusty black with too much curly red hair. He, she realised, was definitely noticeable, and many women in the room were, like her, shooting him co-vert—and covetous—looks. He was devastatingly attrac-tive, almost inappropriately masculine, his tall, muscular form radiating energy and virility in a way that seemed wrong at a funeral, and yet was seductively compelling.

They were here to commemorate death, and he was all life, from the blaze of his tawny eyes to the restless energy she felt in his form, the loosely clenched fists, the way he shifted his weight, like a boxer readying for a fight. She was drawn not just to his beauty but to his vitality, feeling the lack of it in herself. She felt drained and empty, had for a long time, and as for him…?

Who was he? And why was he here?

Taking a deep breath, Allegra turned and headed for the bar. Maybe she would have that drink after all. And then she would go back to the *pensione* where she'd booked a small room, and then to the reading of her father's will tomorrow, although she hardly thought he'd leave her anything. Then home to New York, and she'd finally put this whole sorry mess behind her. Move on in a way she only now realised she hadn't been able to.

She ordered a glass of red wine and retreated to a private alcove off the main reception room, wanting to absent herself as much as she could without actually leaving.

She took a sip of wine, enjoying the velvety liquid and the way it slipped down her throat, coating all the jagged edges she felt inside.

'Are you hiding?'

The voice, low, melodious, masculine, had her tensing. She flicked her gaze up from the depths of her glass and her eyes widened in shock at the sight of the man in front of her. *Him.*

It was as if she'd magicked him from her mind, teleported him across the room to stand here like a handsome prince from a fairy-tale, except there was something a little too wicked about the glint in his eye, something too hard about the set of his mouth, for him to be the prince of a story.

Was he the villain?

Too stunned to form a coherent response, or one of any kind, Allegra simply stared. He really was amazingly good-looking—dark hair cut slightly, rakishly long, those glinting, amber eyes, and a strong jaw with a hint of sexy stubble. He was dressed in a dark grey suit with a darker shirt and a silver-grey tie, and he looked a little bit like Allegra imagined Mephistopheles would look, all dark, barely leashed power, the energy she'd felt from across the room even more forceful now, and twice as compelling.

'Well?' The lilt in his voice was playful, yet with a dark undercurrent that snaked its way inside Allegra like a river of chocolate, pure sensual indulgence. 'Are you?'

Was she what? She was gaping, that much was certain. Allegra snapped her mouth closed and forced her expression into something suitably composed. She hoped.

'As a matter of fact, I am. Hiding, that is. I don't know anyone here.' She took a sip of wine, needing the fortification as well as the second's respite.

'Do you make a habit of crashing funerals?' he asked lightly, and she tensed, not wanting to admit who she was…the rejected daughter, the cast-off child, coming back for scraps.

"Not unless there's an open bar," she joked, hefting her glass, and the man eyed her thoughtfully. Did he believe her? She couldn't tell. 'Did you know him?' she asked. 'Alberto Mancini?' The name stuck in her throat, and she saw a flash in the stranger's eyes, a single blaze of feeling that she couldn't identify but which still jolted her like lightning.

'Not directly. My father did business with him, a long time ago. I wanted to…pay my respects.'

'I see.' She tried to gather her scattered wits. The look of sleepy speculation in the man's eyes made her skin prickle. His gaze was like a caress, invisible fingertips trailing on her heated skin. She'd never reacted to someone so viscerally before, so immediately. Maybe it was simply because her emotions were raw, everything too near the surface. She certainly couldn't ever recall feeling this way before. 'That's very kind of you.' He smiled and said nothing. 'What did you say your name was?'

'I didn't.' His gaze swooped over her again, like a hawk looking for its prey. 'But it's Rafael.'

Rafael Vitali didn't know who this beguiling woman was, but he was captivated by her cloud of Titian curls, the wide, grey eyes that were as clear as mirrors, reflecting her emotions so he could read them from across the room. Weariness. Sorrow. *Grief.*

Who was she? And what was her relationship to Mancini? It didn't really matter, not now his business was done, justice finally satisfied, but he was still curious. A family friend—or something less innocuous? A lover? A mistress? She hadn't come just for the bar, of that he was certain. So what was she hiding?

Rafael took a sip of his drink, watching the emotions play across her face like ripples in water. Confusion, hope, sadness. A lover, he decided, although she was surely young enough to be his daughter. Mancini's wife and daughter were across the room, looking sulky and even bored. Rafael would have spared a second of sympathy for the man's widow if he hadn't known how she'd raced through his money. And tomorrow she would discover how little there was left…perfect justice, considering how Mancini had done the same to his mother, leaving her with nothing.

And as for his father…

He braced himself for the flash of pain, the memories he closed off as a matter of self-protection, of sanity. He never let himself think about his father, couldn't go to that dark, closed-off place, and yet for some reason Mancini's death had pried open that long-locked door, and now he was feeling flickers of the old pain, as raw as ever, like flashes of lightning inside him, a storm of emotion he needed to control.

'Take care of them for me, Rafael. You're the man of the house now. You must protect your mother and sister. No matter what…'

But, no. He needed to slam that door shut once more, and right now he knew the perfect way to do it…with this beguiling woman by his side.

'I hope the bar is worth enduring a wake for,' he said lightly, and she grimaced.

'I'm not really here for the bar.'

'I thought not.' He braced a shoulder against the wall so he was closer to her, inhaling her light, floral scent. A flyaway strand of coppery hair brushed his shoulder. She was utterly lovely, from her silver-grey eyes to her pert nose and lush mouth, her skin pale and creamy with a scattering of red-gold freckles. 'So how did you know him?' he asked.

She shrugged, her gaze sliding away. 'I knew him a long time ago. I'm not even sure he'd have remembered me, to be honest.' She let out a wavering laugh that sounded a little too sad, and Rafael resisted the tug of sympathy he felt for her. He didn't want to feel sorry for her, not now. Not when he'd already decided to sleep with her. Besides, she was no doubt been one of Mancini's cast-off mistresses, a gold-digger in it for the money and baubles. Why feel sorry for such a woman?

And yet he couldn't help but notice how fragile she looked, as if a breath might blow her away. There were violent smudges like bruises under her eyes, and her face was pale underneath the gold dust scattering of freckles. The figure underneath the rather shapeless black dress looked slender and willowy, with a hint of intriguing curves. 'I can't believe anyone would forget you,' he said, and was amused to see her cheeks turn pink, her pupils flare, as if she were an innocent unused to compliments.

'Well…you'd be surprised,' she returned with an uncertain laugh. 'What business did your father have with my—with him?'

'A new technology for mobile phones.' He didn't want to talk about the past. 'At least new at the time. The industry has moved on quite a bit since then.' But the technology would have made his father a lot of money, if Mancini hadn't cut him off. If he'd lived.

'I wouldn't know. I'm rather useless with technology. I can barely manage my own phone.' She took a sip of wine, golden-red lashes sweeping down onto her porcelain cheeks. Rafael had the desire, unsettlingly strong, to sweep his thumb along her cheek and see if her pale skin felt as creamily soft as it looked.

'What do you do, then?' he asked. 'For a living?' He reckoned she must be in her late twenties. Had she found a new sugar daddy?

'I work at a café, in Greenwich Village. It's a music café.'

'A music café? I've never heard of such a thing.'

'It's a shop for instruments and libretto,' Allegra explained. 'As well as a café. But it's so much more than that—it hosts concerts for aspiring musicians, and offers lessons to all sorts of people. It's a bit of a community hub, for music-lovers at least.'

'And you are one, I gather?'

'Yes.' Her voice was quiet and heartfelt, as well as a little bit sad. 'Yes, music is very important to me.'

Rafael watched her, disconcerted by this shy admission, by the genuineness of it, of her. He didn't want to confuse or complicate his feelings, had no intention of deepening what would be a shallow but satisfying sexual transaction.

'I suppose I should leave,' Allegra said slowly. 'I don't really have a reason to stay.' She sounded reluctant, and when she looked up at him her eyes were full of mute appeal, wanting him to stop her. And stop her he would.

'It's still early,' he said as he angled his body closer to her, his shoulder brushing hers, letting her feel both his heat and intent. Her eyes widened, and her tongue darted out to touch her lips. Primal need blazed through him. She was either artless or very, very experienced— he couldn't tell which, but either way she enflamed him. 'But we don't have to stay here. Tell me what your favourite piece of music is.'

'Oh…' She looked surprised, and then shyly pleased. 'I don't think you'd know it.'

'Try me.'

'All right.' She smiled, and it felt like a ray of sunlight on his soul, disconcertingly bright, reaching too many dark corners. It was just a *smile*. 'It's the third movement of the Cello Sonata by Shostakovich. Do you know it?'

'No, but I wish I did. I wish I could hear it.'

'He's not one of the most well-known composers, but his music is so emotional.' Her grey eyes developed a pearly sheen; she looked almost tearful. 'It moves me like nothing else does.'

'Now I really wish I could hear it.' The look of naked emotion on her face caught at him unexpectedly. He'd started the conversation about music as a way to invite

her up to his suite, but now he found he genuinely wanted
to hear the piece. 'I have a suite in this hotel,' he said.
'With an amazing sound system. Why don't you come
upstairs and listen to the piece with me?'

Allegra's eyes widened with stunned comprehension.
'Oh, but…'

'We can have a proper drink at the same time. The
bar up there is much better than the plonk they're serving down here.' He whisked her glass from her fingertips
and deposited it on the tray of a hovering waiter. 'Come.'
He held out his hand, willing her to agree. The evening
couldn't end here, unsettled, unsated. He needed more.
He craved the connection and satisfaction he knew he'd
find with her, however brief.

Allegra stared at his outstretched hand, her eyes wide,
her fingers knotted together. 'I'm not…' she began, and
then trailed off, looking endearingly uncertain. Was it
an act? Or was she really reluctant?

He didn't want her reluctant. 'I am,' he said, and
reached for her hand, pulling her gently towards him.
She came slowly, with hesitant steps, her wide-eyed gaze
searching his face, looking for reassurance.

And he gave it as his fingers closed around hers, encasing the spark that had leapt between them at the first
brush of skin. He drew her by the hand, away from the
circulating crowds. A few people gave them curious
looks, a veiled glance of envy that Rafael ignored, just
as he'd ignored the subtle and not so subtle come-ons of
the various women there. There was only one he wanted,
and he was holding her hand.

They walked hand in hand out of the room, across the
foyer, and then to the bank of gleaming lifts. Rafael's
heart started to race in expectation. He was looking for-

ward to this more than he'd looked forward to anything
in a long time.

He pressed the button for the lift, holding his breath,
not wanting to break the fragile spell that was weaving
its way around both of them. Not wanting to let her entertain second thoughts.

The doors opened and they stepped inside, the lift
thankfully empty. As the doors closed Rafael turned to
her. 'You have the most enchanting smile.'

She looked completely surprised. 'Do I?' she asked,
and he nodded, meaning it, because her smile *was* lovely,
a shy, slow unfurling, like the petals of a flower. More
and more he was thinking she was genuine, that her air
of innocence and uncertainty wasn't an act. At least,
not that much of an act. She must have had some experience, to be mourning Mancini, and yet she almost
seemed untouched.

'You do. And I think it is a rare but precious thing.'
He leaned back against the wall of the lift and tugged
her gently towards him, close enough so their hips
nudged each other's and heat flared, a spreading, honeyed warmth that left him craving more. 'I would like
to see it more often.'

'We have been at a funeral,' Allegra murmured, her
gaze sweeping downwards. 'There hasn't been much
cause to smile.'

The doors pinged open before Rafael had to come up
with a response to that thorny statement. He stepped out,
directly into the penthouse suite he'd booked. Allegra
looked around the soaring, open space, her eyes wide.

'This is amazing...'

Was she not used to such things? Rafael shrugged the
question aside, drawing her deeper into the room. The
doors to the lift closed. At last they were alone.

CHAPTER TWO

WHAT WAS SHE DOING? Allegra felt as if she'd stumbled into an alternate reality. What kind of woman followed a strange, sexy man up to his penthouse suite? What kind of woman fell headlong under his magnetic spell?

Certainly not her. She didn't do anything unexpected or impetuous. She lived a quiet life, working at the café, her closest friend its owner, an eighty-year-old man who treated her like a granddaughter. Her life was small and safe, which was how she wanted it. And yet from the moment Rafael's hand had touched hers she'd been lost, or perhaps found. She felt as she'd been wired into a circuit board she'd had no idea existed, nerves and sensations springing to life, making her entire body tingle.

She *felt*, and after the numbness she'd encased herself in that was both good and painful, a necessary jolt, waking her up, reminding her she was alive and someone, *someone* was looking at her with warmth and even desire, wanting her to be there. The knowledge was intoxicating, overwhelming.

Rafael was still holding her hand, his warm, amber eyes on hers, his smile as slow and sensual as a river of honey trickling through her.

It was dangerous, letting herself be looked at like that. Dangerous and far too easy to float down that river, see where its seductive current took her. They were here to listen to music, but Allegra wasn't so naïve and inexperienced not to realise what that meant. Why Rafael had really asked her up here.

Nervous and unsettled by her spiralling thoughts, Allegra tugged her hand from Rafael's and walked around the suite, taking in all the luxurious details, soaring ceilings and marble floors, ornate woodwork and silk and satin cushions on the many sofas scattered around the large living area.

'This place really is incredible,' she said. Her voice sounded high and thin. 'What a view.' Floor-to-ceiling windows framed a spectacular view of the city on three sides. 'Is that the Coloseum?' She pointed blindly, and then felt Rafael come to stand behind her, his body so close she could feel his heat. If she stepped backwards so much as an inch she'd be touching him, burned by him. She wanted it, and yet she was afraid. This was entirely new, and new meant unfamiliar. Strange. *Dangerous.*

Except…what, really, did she need to be afraid of? Rafael couldn't hurt her, not in the way she'd been hurt before, soul deep, heart shattered. She wouldn't let him. She was nervous, yes, because this was strange and new, but she didn't have to be *afraid*. She took a deep breath, the realisation calming her. She could be in control of this situation.

'Yes, it's the Coliseum.' His hands rested lightly on her shoulders, and a slight shudder went through her, which she knew he felt. Daring now to prolong the moment, to up the ante, she leaned back so she was resting lightly against him. The feel of his chest, hard and warm, against her back was a comforting, solid weight, grounding her in a way she hadn't expected. Making her want to stay there.

Rafael's hands tightened on her shoulders and they stood there for a moment, her back against his chest so they could feel each other's heartbeats. Allegra closed her eyes, savouring the moment, the connection. Because that's what she wanted, what she needed now…to feel connected to someone. To feel alive.

So much of her life had been lived alone, since she was too shy to make friends at school, too confused and hurt to reach out to her mother, too wounded and wary to seek love from the handful of dates she'd had over the years. But *this*…one single, blazing connection, to remind her she was alive and worth knowing…and then to walk away, unhurt, still safe.

'Shall we have champagne?' Rafael's voice was soft, melodious, and Allegra nodded. She wasn't much of a drinker, but she wanted to celebrate. Wanted to feel this was something worth celebrating.

'That sounds lovely.'

He moved away and she turned, wishing she could get hold of her galloping emotions, her racing pulse. Feeling this alive was both exquisite and painful. What was it about this man that made her want to take a step closer, instead of away? That made her want to risk after all this time?

The pop of a cork echoed through the room, making Allegra start. Rafael poured two glasses, careless of the bubbles that foamed onto the floor. *'Cin-cin,'* he murmured, a lazy look in his eyes, and he handed her a glass.

'Cin-cin,' Allegra returned. She hadn't spoken the informal Italian toast since she was twelve years old, and the memory was bitter-sweet. New Year's Eve at her family home, an estate in Abruzzi, snow-capped mountains ringing the property. Her father had given her her first taste of champagne, the crisp bubbles tart and surpris-

ing on her tongue. The sense of happiness, like a bubble inside her, at being with her family, safe, secure, loved.

Had it all been a mirage? A lie? It must have been. Or perhaps she was remembering the moment differently, rose-tinted with the innocence of childhood, the longing of grief. Perhaps her father hadn't been as doting as she remembered; perhaps he'd taken a call moments after the toast, left her alone. How could she ever know? She couldn't even trust her memories.

'Are you going to drink?' Rafael asked, and Allegra blinked, startled out of her thoughts.

'Yes, of course.' She took a sip, and the taste was as crisp and delicious as she remembered. She blinked rapidly, wanting to clear the cobwebs of memory from her already overloaded mind. She didn't want to get emotional in front of a near-stranger.

'Tell me about yourself,' she said when she trusted herself to sound normal. 'What do you do?'

'I run my own company.'

She raised her eyebrows. 'What kind of company?'

'Property. Mainly commercial property, hotels, resorts, that sort of thing.'

He was rich, then, probably very rich. She should have guessed, based simply on his presence, his confidence. Even his cologne, with the dark, sensual notes of saffron, smelled expensive. Privileged. She'd been privileged once too, before her parents' divorce. More privileged and even spoiled than she'd ever realised, until it had all been taken away.

Not that she'd been focused on her father's money. Although her mother complained bitterly that after the divorce she'd got nothing, that she'd had to scrounge and beg and pawn what jewellery she'd managed to keep, Allegra hadn't really cared about any of it. Yes, it had been a huge step down—from an enormous villa to a two-bedroom apartment too far uptown to be trendy, public school, no holidays, often living off the generosity of her mother's occasional boyfriends, a parade of suited men who came in and out of her mother's life, men Allegra had tried her best to avoid.

All of it had made her mother bitter and angry, but Allegra had missed her father's love more than any riches or luxuries. And at the same time she'd become determined never to rely on anyone for love or anything else ever again. People let you down, even, especially, the people closest to you. That was a lesson she didn't need to learn twice.

'And you enjoy what you do?' she asked Rafael. She felt the need to keep the conversation going, to avoid the look of blatant, sensual intent in his eyes. She wasn't ready to follow that look and see where it led, not yet, and Rafael seemed content to simply sip and watch her with a sleepy, heavy-lidded gaze.

'Very much so.' He put his half-full glass on a table and moved towards the complicated and expensive-looking sound system by the marble fireplace. 'Why don't we listen to your music? Shostakovich, you said, the third movement of the cello sonata?'

'Yes...' She was touched he'd remembered. 'But surely you don't have it on CD?'

He laughed softly. 'No, I'm afraid not. But the sound system is connected to the Internet.'

'Oh, right.' She laughed, embarrassed. 'Like I said, I'm not good with technology.'

'You can leave that to me. I can find it easily enough.' And he did, for within seconds the first melancholy strains of the music were floating through the room. Rafael turned to her, one hand outstretched, just as it had been before. 'Come.'

The music was already working its way into her soul, the soft strains winding around her, touching a place inside her no person ever accessed. Music was her friend, her father, her lover. She'd given it the place meant for people, for relationships, and she'd done that deliberately. Music didn't hurt you. It didn't walk away.

She took Rafael's hand, the sorrowful emotion of the cello resonating deep within her. Rafael drew her down onto the sumptuous leather sofa, wrapping one arm around her shoulders so she was leaning into him, breathing in his scent, her body nestled against his.

It was the closest she'd ever been to a man, and yet bizarrely the intimacy felt right, a natural extension of the music, the moment, both of them silent as the cello and piano built in sound and power.

Then Rafael drew her against him even more tightly, so her cheek was pressed against his chest, her body pressed against his, and Allegra closed her eyes, letting the music wash over her. She needed this. She closed her eyes, the music and Rafael and the champagne all combining to overwhelm her senses even as it made her want more, to let herself be swept away on this tide of emotion and see where it took her.

Underneath her cheek Rafael's chest rose and fell in steady, comforting breaths. His fingers stroked her arm and his breath feathered her hair. Everything about the moment felt incredibly intimate, more so than anything Allegra had ever experienced before. If only they could go on like this for ever, feeling each other's breaths, each beat of their hearts.

The music built to its desperate, haunting crescendo and then the strains fell away into silence. It had been, Allegra knew from having listened to the piece many times, just over eight minutes, and yet it felt like a lifetime. She felt both drained and intensely alive at the same time, and in the ensuing stillness neither of them moved or spoke.

'Do you know,' Allegra finally said softly, 'the cello is closest instrument to the human voice? I think that's why it affects me so much.' She let out a shaky laugh, conscious of the tears on her cheeks, the rawness of the moment. The music had affected her more now than it ever had before.

'It is a stunning piece of music,' Rafael said quietly. His thumb found her tear and gently swept it away, stealing her breath, making her ache. 'It causes me to both yearn and mourn.'

'Yes...' The sensitive, sincerely spoken observation pierced her to her core. *This* was the connection she craved, and unthinkingly she twisted in his arms, smiling through her tears, her face tilted up to his. Then she caught the blazing look in his eyes, felt its answer in the sudden, desperate thrill that rippled through her body. And this connection, even sweeter and more powerful than the last...

He dipped his head and she held her breath, the whole world suspended, expectant—and then his mouth was covering hers in a kiss that felt like both a question and an answer, a need both sating and sparking to life. It was enough, and yet it made her want so much more.

Allegra's hands clenched on the crisp cotton of his shirt as his mouth moved with thorough and expert persuasion on hers, gentle and yet so sure. She'd never known a kiss could be like this, touching her to her very core, piercing her right through, *knowing* her. And right now she wanted to be known.

And then it became wonderfully, thrillingly more. In

one easy movement Rafael swept her up and across the room and she found herself lying down on the soft leather cushions, his face flushed and his eyes jewel-bright as he looked down at her.

'You are so beautiful. So lovely.' With gentle hands he pushed her disordered curls away from her face, his fingers skimming across her skin, exploring her features. Allegra closed her eyes, submitting to his touch, revelling in it. The feel of his fingers on her face felt as intimate as the kiss, his touch so gentle and reverent it made her ache in an entirely new way.

He slid his hands lower, each touch a question, his fingers feeling her collarbone and then his palm moulding to the curve of her breast.

'A different kind of music,' he murmured, his mouth following the trail of his hand, and she laughed, the sound shaky and breathless. Yes, this was new music, and he was teaching her its breathtaking melody. She'd thought, in this moment, that she might feel fear, or at least uncertainty, but she didn't.

She felt wonderful, and she wanted to keep feeling wonderful, to come alive under someone's hands, feel as close to another person as she could. For one night. One moment. When would she ever get a chance like this again?

Somehow Rafael had managed to slip her dress from her shoulders, and now her upper half was bare to him. He bent his head, nudging aside her bra with his tongue, and she gasped aloud, the feel of him against her sensitised flesh a jolt to her whole body.

'Oh...' The single syllable held a world of newly gained knowledge as pleasure pierced her with sweet arrows. Her hands roved over his back, drawing him closer to her, desire an insistent pulse inside her.

Of their own accord her hips rose, welcoming the knowing touch of his hand. His fingers brushed her underwear and she bit off a gasp. *She'd had no idea...*

Rafael lifted his head, his gaze glittering as he looked down at her, his breathing as ragged as her own. The obvious fact that he wanted her as much as he wanted him solidified her certainty that this was what she wanted. What she needed. A connection, pure and true.

'Will you come into the bedroom with me?'

She nodded wordlessly, knowing there was only one answer her aching body and heart could give.

'Yes.'

In one fluid movement Rafael rose from the sofa and drew her towards the bedroom. Allegra followed, barely conscious of her rucked-up dress, her tangled hair.

The bedroom was as elegant and luxurious as the living area, and Allegra glanced at the massive king-sized bed, standing on its own dais and covered in a navy satin duvet. Rafael turned her to face him, framing her face with his hands as he kissed her again, even more deeply, and she responded, his kiss drawing a deep, pure note from her soul.

Rafael tugged the zip down the back of her dress so the black silk fell away, leaving her in nothing but her bra and pants, both simple and black, hardly sexy, and yet his gaze gleamed with approval as he looked at her, and her heart swelled. She had never realised how wonderful it felt, to have a man look at her like that. Want her like that. He drew her towards him, her breasts brushing against his chest, her hips nudging his so she could feel the hard length of his arousal against her stomach.

'Cold?' he whispered, and she shook her head.

No, she was not cold. It was a balmy spring evening,

and the hotel suite was warm. The shiver was because of him, and he knew it, and she didn't care.

He kissed her again, working his way down her jaw and collar bone to press his lips against the V between her breasts. She threaded her fingers through his hair, anchoring herself to him. She felt adrift in sensation, and his touch was the only thing that tethered her to earth.

Then he was moving his mouth lower, peeling away her bra and pants with his hands, sinking down onto his knees in front of her so Allegra swayed, shocked and overwhelmed by the feel of his hands on her hips, his *mouth…*

'Oh…' Her breath came out in shattered gasps. It was so unbearably intimate, to have him looking at the very essence of her, revering her in an act so selfless and giving and… *'Oh.'*

Rafael's dark chuckle reverberated through her bones as her body trembled on the precipice of an orgasm that felt like an explosion. He rose again and drew her to the bed, leaving her trembling and aching and wanting more.

She watched, dazed, as he shucked off his clothes, revealing a bronzed torso, the muscles of his abdomen scored into hard, perfect ridges. His legs were long and powerful, and as for the most male part of him…

He was a work of beauty.

'You may look,' Rafael said as he covered her body with his. 'And you may also touch.' And then he was kissing her again, his arousal pressing into her with thrilling insistence, and that restless ache became an overwhelming clamour in her body, drowning out all thought, all doubt.

She gasped out loud as his fingers touched her in her most intimate and feminine places, teasing, toying, exploring, *knowing.* Her fingernails dug into the satiny skin of his shoulders as her body strained for the glittering apex she felt, just out of her reach, a pinnacle she needed to find, that she wanted them to ascend together.

And then, finally, he was sliding inside her, his breathing harsh and ragged as he filled her up, the momentary twinge of pain lost in the utter rightness of the sensation, the union complete and total.

He stopped, swearing under his breath, and, lost in a haze of need, Allegra stilled underneath him.

'Rafael…?'

'You are *vergine*?' he demanded, and she gulped.

'Yes…'

He swore again, his forehead pressed to hers. 'I had no idea…'

'Why would you?' she managed, and he let out a shudder, his eyes clenched closed.

'You should have told me.'

'Rafael…' She arched her hips upwards, letting her body plead in a way her words could not. She couldn't let him stop now, not when everything in her was aching and demanding. With a groan he kept moving, the delicious slide of his body in hers making Allegra forget that tense moment as she gave herself up to the sensations cascading through her, building in a beautiful crescendo, and then the glittering apex burst into crystalline shards of pleasure around her as she let out a cry that rent the still air and then fell away like the most sacred note of music she'd ever heard.

Rafael rolled off Allegra, managing to suppress the curse that sprang to his lips once more. She'd been a *virgin*. He hadn't expected that, not even when he'd decided she was artless and genuine, and guilt soured like acid in his stomach. He'd stolen someone's innocence. He'd used someone who should have been protected, cared for. He'd done something he'd sworn he would never do again. Break a sacred trust.

He'd assumed she was a woman of some experience, even if she'd seemed a little shy. He never would have brought her upstairs otherwise. He never would have gone ahead with his seduction.

And yet…the music, the mood, the way Allegra had looked at him with hungry hope…all of it had made him yearn in a way that now left him feeling deeply uneasy. Sex was a transaction, nothing more, pleasurable and easy as it was. He didn't ever let it mean anything, and he hoped like hell Allegra wasn't imbuing it with some kind of emotion he would never let himself feel.

And yet it had been the innocent purity of her response that had been his undoing. *He hadn't even used birth control.* The realisation crystallised like ice inside him. He'd meant to reach for a condom, but in the moment he'd completely forgotten. He'd lost his head. He'd certainly lost control of his body.

Next to him Allegra was still, a rosy flush covering her pale, porcelain body, the perfect foil for the creaminess of her skin. Her hair was spread across the pillow in a tangle of red-gold curls, making him want to thread his fingers through them even now, and pull her towards him for an open-mouthed kiss. Even now, with his climax still thudding through him, knowing how innocent she'd been, he wanted her. He'd never wanted a woman so quickly, or so much.

Allegra rolled on her side, curling into him, her arms wrapped around his chest. Rafael froze, confusion colliding with alarm, irritation with guilt. He didn't do pillow talk. Ever. All of his bed partners knew what he expected in bed, and what he definitely didn't want. He made it very clear from the beginning that emotional attachments were a no-go zone, except Allegra, of course, hadn't received that memo. And as a virgin she would no doubt expect some intimacy now, some soft talk that he knew he was utterly incapable of. He didn't let people get close. People he could hurt. People he could fail.

As he'd already hurt Allegra, deflowering her in what amounted to a tawdry one-night stand.

Her leg found its way between his, her damp cheek pressed to his chest. She let out a shuddering sigh.

'I miss him,' she whispered, her voice sounding broken. 'I miss him so much.'

Shock had Rafael stilling. *What the hell...?* 'Miss him?' he repeated tonelessly.

'I know I shouldn't, there's nothing to miss,' she continued softly. 'I hadn't even seen him in fifteen years. But I do miss him. I miss what we once had, what I thought we had. That's why I came tonight, I think. Because I was looking for something, some kind of closure...'

She was talking about Mancini. But *fifteen years...* She couldn't have been his mistress. She was in her late twenties at most.

'Allegra,' Rafael asked hoarsely, turning to stare down into her pale, lovely face. 'Who are you?'

She looked up at him with tear-drenched eyes. 'I'm his daughter,' she said simply, and Rafael bit down on the curse that sprang to his lips.

Allegra was Alberto Mancini's *daughter*. The daughter of his enemy, his nemesis, was lying in his arms, seeking his comfort, because her dear father, the man who had as good as murdered his own, was dead.

His stomach heaved. He felt a thousand different emotions—fury and guilt, disgust and alarm, regret and sorrow. He was sickened by his own part in this unexpected drama, taking a woman's innocence, a woman who he should, by rights, have nothing to do with. He'd hated the Mancinis for so long, had wanted only justice…but what was this? What was *he*? Allegra was looking for comfort and he had none to give.

He rolled away from her and out of bed, grabbing his boxers and slipping them on in one jerky movement. From behind him he heard Allegra shift in bed, and then her voice, trembling, uncertain.

'Rafael?'

'You should go.' His voice was brusque; he didn't think he could have gentled it if he'd tried. Anger was coursing through him now, a pure, clean rage. Mancini's *daughter*. Did she know what her father had done? Did she realise the blood he had on his hands? Reasonably he knew she couldn't; she must have been a child when his own father had died.

And yet…she was a Mancini. She missed her father, a man he'd hated. She'd been innocent, and he'd abused it. His feelings were a confused tangle of guilt and anger, shame and frustration. It was all too much to deal with. He needed her out of his life. Immediately.

'You…you want me to go?' Her voice was a trembling breath of uncertainty.

'I'll call you a cab.' He reached for his trousers and pulled them on. Then, because she still wasn't moving, he grabbed her dress and tossed it to her. It fell on her lap; she didn't even reach for it.

She looked gorgeous and shocked, sitting in his bed, the navy sheet drawn up to her breasts, her hair tumbling about her shoulders, her eyes heartbreakingly wide.

'But… I don't understand.'

'What is there to understand?' Each word was bitten off with impatience. Innocent she might might have

been, but surely she could figure out what was going on.
'We had a one-night stand. It's over.' He paused. 'If I'd
known you were a virgin, I would have done things a bit
differently. But as it was…' He shrugged. 'You seemed
happy enough with how things happened.'

She blinked as if she'd been slapped, and then she
lifted his chin, showing a sweet courage that made his
emotions go into even more of a tailspin.

'I *was*,' she agreed with emphasis. 'I may be innocent,
but even I can tell when an exit strategy needs some work.
And yours sucks.'

'Thanks for the tip, but the sentiment remains the
same.' Rafael folded his arms, a muscle pulsing in his
jaw. Too many emotions had been accessed tonight, too
many raw nerves twanging painfully. He couldn't take
any more. She had to *go*.

Allegra took a deep breath, lifting her chin, blinking back tears. 'Will you give me a moment of privacy
to dress?' she asked with stiff dignity, and although he
could have retorted that he'd already seen her naked,
Rafael didn't have it in him to be that cruel. Her fragile
courage touched him in a way he didn't like, and he gave
a terse nod before stalking from the room.

He needed a drink, something far stronger than champagne. This didn't feel at all like he'd expected it to,
needed it to. He'd been looking for satisfaction, and instead he felt more restless than ever. Restless and remembering.

*'All you have is your honour, Rafael. That's all that's
ever left. Your honour and your responsibilities as a
man.'*

But he had neither now.

The door to the bedroom opened just as Rafael poured
himself a generous measure of whisky. He forced him-

self not to turn as he heard Allegra's heels click across the marble floor of the living area. Remained with his back to her as she pressed the button for the lift and the doors pinged open.

'Goodbye,' she said, her voice soft and sad and proud all at once, and then she was gone.

Alone in his penthouse suite, Rafael raised the glass of whisky to his lips. He stared out at the unending night and then, instead of drinking, he threw the tumbler against the wall, where it shattered.

CHAPTER THREE

ALLEGRA SAT DOWN in the lawyer's office, her stomach seething with bitter memory as well as nerves. It was the day after her father's funeral, and also of the biggest mistake of her life. She'd left Rafael's hotel suite with her chin held high but her self-esteem, her whole self in tatters, everything in her reeling from his treatment of her.

He'd been so tender, and she'd felt so treasured. Had it all been a lie? *Again?* It seemed she did have to learn that lesson twice. People weren't what they seemed. They said and did what they liked to get what they wanted and then they walked away.

And she was the one left, alone and hurting.

Except, she'd told herself last night, staring gritty-eyed at the ceiling of her bedroom in the modest *pensione*, she didn't have to be hurt by this. Before it had begun she'd told herself she wouldn't be. What they'd done together might have seemed meaningful at the time, but he was still a stranger. A sexy, selfish, unfeeling stranger. It wasn't as if she'd loved him. She hadn't even known him.

She'd made a mistake, she told herself as she rose from bed that morning, body and heart aching with fatigue. A sad, sorry mistake, because she'd given a part of herself to someone who hadn't deserved it. She'd searched for comfort and affection from someone who had neither wanted nor offered neither. She'd survive, though. She had before.

She'd lost her father when she'd felt most vulnerable, had watched him walk away from her without a backward glance. She'd seen her mother withdraw into bitterness and desperation, and she'd fended for herself since she was eighteen. Over the years she'd lost plenty of dreams, and this didn't have to hurt nearly as much. She wouldn't let it.

Signor Fratelli had been insistent that she attend the meeting, although Allegra didn't know why. She doubted her father had left her or her mother anything; if he hadn't given her anything in life, why would he in death? She wasn't looking forward to the meeting, to sitting in a stuffy room with her father's second wife and stepdaughter, the family he'd chosen. Still, it would be a few minutes of discomfort and tension, and then she could return to New York. Act as if none of this had ever happened.

'Signorina Mancini.' The lawyer greeted her with a tense smile as Allegra was ushered into the stately room with its wood-panelled walls and leather club chairs. 'Thank you for coming.'

'It's Signorina Wells, actually,' Allegra said quietly. Her mother had reverted to her maiden name, as had Allegra, after the divorce. She glanced at Caterina Mancini, whose icy hauteur didn't thaw in the least as her arctic-blue eyes narrowed. Her gaze flicked away from Allegra and she didn't offer a greeting.

Next to her, her daughter Amalia, around the same age as Allegra, shifted uncomfortably, giving Allegra a quick, unhappy smile before looking away. Allegra felt too tired and on edge to return it. The other woman had her mother's cool blonde looks without the icy demeanour. In different circumstances, another life, Allegra might have considered getting to know her. Now she could barely summon the emotional energy to sit next to the two women who had taken her and her mother's places in her father's life.

Signor Fratelli began making some introductory remarks; through a haze of tiredness Allegra tried to focus on what he was saying.

'I am afraid, in recent weeks, there has been some change to Signor Mancini's financial situation.'

Caterina's gaze swung to pin the lawyer. 'What kind of change?' she demanded.

'Another corporation now has controlling shares in Mancini Technologies.'

Caterina gasped, but the words meant little to Allegra. She still didn't know why the lawyer had insisted she be there for such news.

'What do you mean, controlling shares?' Caterina asked, her voice high and shrill.

'Signor Vitali of V Property has secured controlling shares,' the lawyer explained. 'Only recently, but he is now essentially the CEO of Signor Mancini's company. And he will be here shortly to explain his intentions regarding its future.'

Allegra sat back and closed her eyes as Caterina's ranting went on. What did she care that some stranger now owned her father's company? None of this was relevant to her. She shouldn't have come. Not to the lawyer's, and not even to Italy.

'Ah, here he is,' Signor Fratelli said, and then the door to his office opened and Rafael appeared like a dark angel from her worst dreams.

Allegra stared at him in shock, too stunned to react other than to gape. He looked remote and professional and very intimidating in a navy blue suit, his eyes narrowed, his mouth a hard line. His cool gaze flicked to Allegra and then away again without revealing any emotion at all. Allegra shrank back into her chair, her mind spinning, her body already remembering the sweet feel of his hands... *What was he doing here?*

Signor Fratelli stood. 'Welcome, Signor Vitali.'

Maybe because she was so tired and overwhelmed, it took Allegra a few stunned seconds to realise what it all meant. Rafael was Signor Vitali of V Property. *He* owned her father's company. Had he known who she was last night? Was it some awful coincidence, or had *she* been part of his takeover? She pressed her hand to her mouth and took several deep, steadying breaths. The last thing she wanted to do was throw up all over Rafael Vitali's highly polished shoes.

She was so busy trying to keep down her breakfast that she missed the flurry of conversation that swirled around her. Distantly she registered Caterina's outraged exclamations, Rafael's bored look. Signor Fratelli was looking increasingly unhappy.

Allegra straightened in her chair, her hands gripping the armrests as she struggled to keep up with what was being said.

'You can't do this,' Caterina protested, her face pale with blotches of angry colour visible on each over-sculpted cheekbone.

'I can and I have,' Rafael returned in a drawl. 'Mancini Technologies will be dissolved immediately.'

Allegra stayed silent as Rafael outlined his plan to strip her father's company of its apparently meagre assets. Then Signor Fratelli chimed in with more devastating news—nearly all of her father's assets, including the estate in Abruzzi, had been tied up with the company.

The result, Allegra realised, was that her father had died virtually bankrupt.

'You killed him,' Caterina spat at Rafael. 'Do you know that? He died of a heart attack. It must have been the shock. *You killed him.*'

Rafael's expression did not change as he answered coldly, 'Then I am not the only one with blood on my hands.'

'What is that supposed to mean?' Caterina demanded, and Rafael didn't answer.

Numb and still reeling from it all, Allegra turned to Signor Fratelli. 'May I go?' She didn't think she could stand to be in the same room as Rafael much longer. He'd used her. More and more she was sure he'd known who she was, and had planned it. Had it amused him, to have the daughter of the man he'd ruined fall into his hands, melt like butter?

'There is something for you, *Signorina*,' the lawyer told her with a sad smile. 'Signor Mancini had a specific bequest for you.'

'He did?' Surprise rippled through her along with a fragile, bruised happiness, even in the midst of her shock and grief. Signor Fratelli withdrew a velvet pouch from his desk drawer and handed it to Allegra.

Caterina craned her neck and Rafael and Amalia both looked on as Allegra clasped the pouch. She didn't want to open it in front of them all, but it was clear everyone expected it. Caterina was bristling with outrage, seeming as if she wanted to snatch the precious bag from Allegra's hands.

Taking a deep breath, she opened the pouch and withdrew a stunning necklace of pearls, with a heart-shaped diamond-encrusted sapphire at its centre. She knew the piece; it had belonged to her father's mother, and her mother had loved to wear it. Tears pricked her eyes and she blinked them back. The value of the piece was not in its jewels but in the sheer, overwhelming fact that her father had remembered her. She clenched the necklace in her fist, gulping down the emotion, before she managed to give Signor Fratelli a quick nod.

'*Grazie,*' she whispered, the Italian springing naturally to her lips.

'There is a letter as well,' Signor Fratelli said.

'A letter?' Allegra took the envelope from the lawyer with burgeoning hope. Perhaps now she would finally understand her father's actions. His abandonment. 'Thank you.' The letter she refused to open here. She rose from her seat, making for the door.

As she brushed past Rafael she inhaled the saffron scent of his cologne and her stomach cramped as memories assailed her.

His hands touching her so tenderly. His body moving inside hers in what had been an act more intimate than anything Allegra had ever experienced or imagined. She'd understood all along that it had been a one-night stand; she'd known that they weren't building a relationship. And yet the reality had been both harsher and more intense than she'd ever expected—both the import of what she'd shared with Rafael and the cruelty of him kicking her out the door.

Now, on shaking legs, with her head held high, she walked past him and out the door. She'd just started down the steps when the door opened behind her and Rafael called her name.

Allegra hesitated for no more than a second before she kept walking.

'Allegra.' He strode easily to catch her, touching her lightly on the arm. Even the brush of his fingers on her wrist had her whole body tensing and yearning. Remembering. She shook him off.

'We have nothing to say to each other.'

'Actually, we do.' His voice was low and authoritative, commanding her to stop. She paused, half turning towards him, wanting to ignore how devastatingly attractive he looked even now.

'What,' she demanded in a shaking voice, 'could you possibly have to say to me now? You got your revenge.'

'Revenge?' His mouth firmed into a hard line. 'You mean justice.'

'Did you know I was his daughter last night?' Allegra demanded shakily. 'Did it…did it *amuse* you, having me fall all over you when you knew you were ruining him?'

'I didn't know you were Mancini's daughter, and if I had, I wouldn't have touched you. I want nothing to do with any Mancini, ever.' He spoke with a cold flatness that made Allegra recoil.

'Why? What had my father ever done to you?'

'That is irrelevant now.'

'Fine.' She wouldn't let herself care. She intended to forget Rafael Vitali ever existed from this moment on. 'Then we have nothing to say to each other.'

'On the contrary.' Once more Rafael stayed her with his hand. 'We didn't use birth control.'

Five simple words that had her stilling in frozen shock, dawning horror. She licked her lips, her mind spinning. She was so innocent, had felt so overwhelmed, that the fact they hadn't used birth control hadn't even crossed her mind. She was ashamed by her own obvious naiveté.

'If you are pregnant,' Rafael continued in a low, steady voice, 'then you will have to tell me.' His tone brooked no argument, no protest.

'Why?' Allegra demanded. 'You wanted to have nothing to do with me last night. Why would you want to deal with my child?'

'Our child,' Rafael corrected her swiftly. He handed her a business card, which Allegra took with numb fingers. 'Naturally I hope this will come to nothing. But if it does not, I am a man of honour.' Cold steel entered his voice, making Allegra flinch. 'I take care of what is mine.'

Come to nothing.

An appropriate term for the evening they'd shared, and any possibility emerging from it. Allegra longed to rip his business card into shreds, but the gesture seemed childish. She crumpled it in her fist instead.

'Suffice it to say,' she bit out, 'I have no desire ever to speak to you again, about anything.'

'I'm serious, Allegra.'

'So am I,' she choked, and then hurried down the stairs.

Back at the *pensione*, still trembling from her encounter with Rafael, Allegra finally opened the letter from her father.

Dear Allegra,
Forgive an old man the mistakes he made out of sorrow and fear. I cared more for my reputation than for your love, and for that I will always be sorry.

Your mother loved this necklace, but it belongs to you. Please keep it for yourself, and do not show it to her.

I don't expect you to understand, much less forgive me.
Your Papa.

Tears streaked silently down her face as she read the letter again and again, trying to make sense of it. He'd loved his reputation more than her? What did that even mean? The letter hadn't answered anything, only stirred up more questions.

And yet…he was sorry. He *had* loved her. But if that was the case, why had he been able to let her go?

Rafael sat in the lawyer's office, the acid of regret churning in his stomach. In his mind he could see Allegra's huge, silvery, tear-filled eyes, and another pang of guilt assailed him. He'd handled last night badly. He knew that, yet he also knew he couldn't have changed his reaction. Alberto Mancini had killed his father. What he'd done in exchange to Allegra—treating her harshly after a single night together—was negligible in comparison.

As for a possible pregnancy…he would provide for any child of his, absolutely. There was no question about that at all. But he hoped to heaven and back that Allegra was not carrying his baby. And he wished he'd been able to temper his actions last night, at least a little. Or, even better, that the whole night had never happened.

Yet even as the thought flitted through his mind he knew he was a liar. Last night had been incredible, explosive, the most intense sexual encounter of his life. He hadn't used birth control because he'd been so overcome with desire, with basic, blatant need. He'd wanted her last night and seeing her this morning, looking so pale and proud, he'd wanted her all over again, to his own shame.

'Signor Vitali? Is there anything left to say?'

Rafael blinked the lawyer back into focus, along with Mancini's widow and stepdaughter. He'd thought he'd enjoy seeing Caterina Mancini brought low but, despite the obvious fact that she was a gold-digger, he felt sorry for her. She'd had nothing to do with his father's down-fall, and right now his eye-for-an-eye justice tasted bitter.

And if she was right, and Mancini had died of a heart attack, of shock at having his business bought out from under him...

Then he'd killed Mancini just as Mancini had killed his father.

Uncertainty and guilt cramped his stomach. He didn't like either emotion, would not entertain them for a moment. If his actions had brought about Mancini's death, then so be it. Justice had finally, fully been served. He had to believe that.

Allegra travelled back to New York in a daze, sleeping nearly the entire flight, wanting only escape from the grief and memory and pain.

The world felt as if it had righted itself a little bit when she was back in her studio apartment in the East Village, enjoying the quiet, peaceful solitude of her own space, the sound of muted traffic barely audible from the sixth floor. She'd said hello to Anton, her boss and landlord, and then retreated upstairs. All she needed now was some music to help to soothe and restore her.

Allegra automatically reached for her favourite Shostakovich before her hand stilled, her stomach souring. Had Rafael ruined her favourite music for her for ever? Maybe. She chose some Elgar instead, and then curled up on her sofa, hugging a pillow to her chest, trying not to give in to tears.

A few minutes later her mobile rang, and Allegra's heart sank a little to see it was her mother.

'Well?' Jennifer demanded before Allegra had said so much as hello. 'Did you get anything? Did I?'

'It was a lovely funeral service,' Allegra said quietly,

and Jennifer merely snorted. Her mother held no love, or even any sentiment, for Alberto Mancini. 'We didn't get anything,' she said after a tiny pause. Although she didn't understand it, she would heed her father's advice not to tell her mother about the sapphire necklace. 'He didn't even have much to give.' She explained about Rafael Vitali and his takeover of Mancini Technologies, striving to keep her voice toneless, betraying none of the emotion still coursing through her at the memory of that one earth-shattering night. She'd forget it. She'd start forgetting it right then. She had to.

'Vitali?' Jennifer said sharply. 'He bought the company?'

'Yes.'

'Not that it has anything to do with us.'

'No,' Allegra agreed dourly. 'Although Caterina Mancini accused him of practically killing…' Even now she could not say Papa. He might have signed the letter as her *papa*, but he hadn't acted or felt like one since she'd been a child. 'Him. Because the heart attack might have been brought on by shock.' The thought that Rafael might have actually killed her father was like a stone inside her.

And she'd given herself to this man.

Jennifer was silent for a moment. 'It's over,' she said at last, and that knowledge rested in Allegra's stomach like lead. Yes, it was over. It was all over.

Over the next month Allegra did her best to move on with her life. She worked at the café, she chatted with customers, she walked in the park and tried to enjoy the small pleasures of her life, but after that one earth-shattering night with Rafael, everything felt dull and colourless.

It was foolish to miss him when he'd treated her so brutally, and yet Allegra felt like Sleeping Beauty who had been woken up. She couldn't go back to sleep again. Retreat was not an option, and yet it was the only one she'd ever known.

So she tried to forget about that evening entirely, but a month after she returned from Italy she threw up her breakfast. She passed it off as having had a dodgy take-away the night before, but when she threw up the next morning, realisation crept in, cold and unwelcome. The third morning she bought a pregnancy test.

She stared down at the two pink lines in shock, realisation coursing through her in an icy wave. It seemed too unfair that on top of having the misfortune to have slept with Rafael Vitali and then been brutally rejected by him, she now was carrying his baby. One night—and now this?

Her baby. Her child, living inside her, like a flower, waiting to unfurl. The maternal instinct was so strong it took her breath away. She hadn't expected it, had never even thought about having children, not seriously. After all, she was perennially single, with no one in the picture or even on the horizon.

And yet…*a baby.* Someone to love, someone to make a family with, a proper family. She would never abandon her baby the way her father had abandoned her. She'd never take out her frustration and bitterness on her child the way her mother had on her. She'd be the best mother she knew how to be, already loving this scrap of humanity with a fierceness that surprised and humbled her.

A baby. A new start, a second chance at love, at life, at happiness. Allegra placed one protective hand across her middle and closed her eyes.

CHAPTER FOUR

'CARO?'

The teasing, lilting voice of the woman Rafael had picked up in a bar only irritated him. He glanced across at her, noting the ruthlessly toned limbs, the well-endowed chest, the pouting mouth. None of it appealed to him. He couldn't even remember her name.

'You can go.'

Her lipsticked mouth dropped open in outrage and Rafael turned away, bored and disgusted. He hadn't even touched her, and he didn't want to. His libido had barely stirred once since Allegra had left his bed. He hadn't slept with anyone, had lost interest.

'Rafael…' She reached out her arms, her pout deepening, and impatience bit at him.

'Seriously. Go.' He gestured to the door of his penthouse suite. He was in Paris on business, and as the blonde beauty stalked towards the door, it occurred to Rafael that he was behaving just as he had before, throwing a woman out of his room.

Seemed he didn't have a great track record.

But, damn it, he'd expected her to call. A courtesy call, at least, to tell him she wasn't pregnant. Although why he should expect courtesy from her when he'd shown her so little he didn't know.

So she hadn't called. Obviously she wasn't pregnant, and he could move on with his life. He could forget Allegra Wells and the sweet purity of her smile, the tears that had streaked down her porcelain cheeks when she'd listened to that music, the way her body had yielded and curled into his, accepting him wholly in a way he'd never felt before. Complete. *Right*.

Idiot.

It had been a casual sexual encounter, one of many, nothing more. Allegra Wells was out of his life…for good. Which was just how he wanted it, because he was done with the Mancinis. He'd taken the man's business, dismantled the industry that had been built on his father's grave.

Justice had been served, and yet there was no one to share his victory. His mother and father were dead, and he didn't even know where Angelica was. The family he'd sworn to protect and provide for was scattered, destroyed. And Rafael still felt restless, vaguely guilty and unfulfilled, as if he was missing something…or someone.

'This might be a little cold.'

Allegra winced slightly at the feel of the cold gel on her tummy and then the insistent prodding of the ultrasound wand. It was her eighteen-week scan, and she couldn't wait to see her baby. She craned her neck to gaze in anxious curiosity at the black and white screen and the fuzzy image that suddenly appeared, along with the whooshing, galloping noise of her baby's heart.

Excitement leaped inside her as the figure gained definition and clarity—head, arms, legs, beating heart. Everything tucked up like a present waiting for her. Allegra let out a choked cry, smiling through her tears.

It hadn't been an easy pregnancy. It was over three

months since she'd made the decision to keep this baby, three months of debilitating morning sickness, throwing up nearly every morning and twice having to go to hospital to be treated for dehydration. She'd lost weight, struggled to work, and wondered how on earth she was going to manage as a single mother.

Because she intended to do this alone. She couldn't face telling Rafael about their baby. She couldn't face her child having a father like she'd had, one who would walk away when he felt like it. She still didn't understand what her father's note had meant, and she hadn't dared yet to ask her mother about it, but she'd experienced enough of Rafael Vitali to know she couldn't trust him to stick around.

Still she didn't know how she was going to manage, in a studio apartment with a low-paying job. She hadn't figured it out yet, but she would. Eventually. Now, however, her all of her fears fell away at the beautiful sight of her baby. *Her baby.*

The technician frowned and poked harder with the wand. Allegra winced. Then, more alarmingly, the technician put the instrument down and rose from her seat by the examining table where Allegra was lying.

'I'll be right back,' she murmured, and then left the room.

Allegra lay there, shivering from the cold gel, her gently rounded belly damp and exposed. Unease crept icy fingers along her spine. Technicians weren't supposed to leave in the middle of an appointment like that, surely?

She found out moments later when an important-looking doctor in a white lab coat followed the technician back into the room, frowning as she looked at the screen with the beautiful, fuzzy image of Allegra's child.

'What's going on?' Allegra asked, her voice high and strained with anxiety.

'Just a moment please, Miss… Wells.' The doctor glanced briefly at her file before turning her narrowed gaze back on the screen. Something was wrong. Allegra could feel it in her bones, in her frightened, hard-beating heart. Something had gone wrong with this pregnancy. With her baby.

She lay there, everything in her frozen and fearful, as the doctor took the wand and began to prod her belly once more, murmuring to the technician who murmured back, none of it audible to Allegra.

'Please,' she begged. 'Please, tell me what's going on.'

The technician gave her a smile of such sorrowful sympathy that Allegra wished she hadn't asked. Then she handed her a paper towel to wipe off the gel while the doctor continued to study the image on the screen—the image of her baby.

'Dr Stein will speak with you shortly,' the technician murmured.

Moments later Allegra had all the answers she didn't want. The words reverberated emptily through her, making horrible sense and sounding unintelligible, impossible, at the same time. Congenital heart defect were the three words that hurt the most.

'But what does that mean exactly?' she demanded, her voice shaking. She knew there were heart defects that were operable. There were even some that were asymptomatic, hardly worth mentioning. But looking at Dr Stein's compassionate face, she feared her baby didn't have one of those.

'The particular defect we're discussing is life-threatening,' Dr Stein said quietly. 'The baby wouldn't live past a few months of age, if that.' Allegra gaped and she continued, 'We'll order an amniocentesis as soon as possible, to know for sure what we'll dealing with. This may take up to three weeks, I'm afraid. Based on the ultrasound, it could be one of several heart defects, of varying seriousness.'

'But you think it's a more serious one?' Allegra whispered, and Dr Stein gave her an unhappy look.

'I'm afraid that, yes, it's looking like that, but we won't know until we get the results of the amniocentesis. It's difficult to diagnose this kind of condition from only a scan.'

Allegra walked home in a fog, barely aware of the steps that took her up to her sixth-floor studio. Anton poked his head out of his apartment to ask how she was, and Allegra didn't even know what she said. The world felt muted, as if everything was taking place far away, to other people. Nothing mattered. Nothing at all mattered any more.

She lay on her bed, one hand pressed against her middle. Already, she'd barely been coping, stumbling through each day, trying to survive the awful morning sickness that had exhausted her so utterly. She hadn't let herself think too much about the future, and now it looked like there might not be one. How was she going to wait three long weeks to find out?

And through the haze of her grief and fear, one fact kept coming back to torment her. *She should have told Rafael.* No matter how he had treated her, he should know she was pregnant with his child. He should be aware of what was happening.

Still she resisted. She didn't want to give him a chance to reject her all over again, along with their baby. She didn't want to face his accusations and anger, as he no doubt would be furious that she hadn't told him she was pregnant. She especially didn't want to open herself up to hurt.

Since Rome, she'd done her best to push all thoughts of Rafael out of her mind. She'd told herself there was still time to tell him about the baby, if she ended up deciding that was the best thing to do, which she wasn't at all sure it was. She just needed to feel better first, to find her feet. When she felt stronger, she could think about whether she wanted Rafael involved, even if everything in her had shied away from it.

But now? Now everything had sped up and become urgent. She had to make hard decisions, agonising choices. And Rafael deserved to be a part of that process, even if she dreaded talking to him again.

Allegra battled the possibilities in her mind as the date of her amniocentesis came closer. Finally, two days before the scheduled procedure, she took out the crisp white business card Rafael had handed her outside the lawyer's office. With trembling fingers she dialled the mobile number printed starkly on the card.

He answered after two rings. 'Yes?'

'It's Allegra.' Her voice was a thready whisper, and she straightened, determined to be strong. The silence on the end of the line stretched on for several seconds.

'Yes?' Rafael finally said again, his voice tense, guarded.

Allegra took a deep breath. 'I'm calling because something has happened.' Rafael didn't say anything and she forced herself to continue. 'I'm pregnant and—'

'You're pregnant?' His breath hissed sharply between his teeth. 'By *me*?'

'Yes, of course by you—'

'Then why are you telling me now? You must be halfway through your pregnancy.'

'Almost,' Allegra agreed.

'Then why—?'

'Rafael, please, just listen. I'm pregnant and I had an ultrasound and it looks like there is something wrong with the baby. Something serious.' Her voice caught and she dashed at her eyes with her hand. She couldn't break down now. She had to stay strong. The last person to look for comfort from was Rafael.

Rafael remained silent for a few taut seconds. 'What kind of thing are you talking about?' he finally asked.

'A congenital heart defect.' Allegra drew a ragged breath. 'I'm having an amniocentesis in two days' time to determine—'

'In New York?'

'Yes.'

'I'll be there.'

Shock had her mouth dropping open. '*Be* there? But—'

'Of course I'll be there,' Rafael said roughly. 'This is my child. Isn't it?'

'Of course it is.'

'Then I'll be there. I'll call again tomorrow to confirm the details.'

Allegra wasn't sure what she'd been expecting Rafael's response to be, but that wasn't it. As she hung up the phone she battled between trepidation at seeing him again and a treacherous relief that someone was going to walk through this with her. She was used to being alone, preferred it, but she didn't want to be alone in this.

And yet Rafael? She was, Allegra knew, going to have to be careful. With her baby, and with her heart.

Rafael drummed his fingers against the armrest as the limo cut smoothly through Manhattan's midtown traffic, heading towards Allegra's flat in the East Village. The shock and fury he'd felt that she'd hidden her pregnancy from him for so long had been replaced by a far greater fear for the health of their unborn child. He was going to have a *child*. Someone to protect and provide for, cherish and guard with his life. A life he would treasure, if he ever got the chance.

Rafael had never believed in the idea of atonement, and yet he thought of it now. Perhaps the sins of the past could be righted by this future...his child's future. Perhaps he would finally find the peace and satisfaction he craved, through the life of this innocent.

He'd deal with Allegra's wilful deception later; right now they needed to get through the current crisis...whatever happened. He'd let down those who'd depended on him before and he wouldn't do it again. He would not fail his child.

The limo pulled up in front of a tall brick building. Rafael's mouth thinned as he stepped out of the limo and scanned the names by the buzzers. His eyes narrowed as he saw that Allegra was on the sixth floor, and the building had no lift. She was walking up and down six flights of stairs every day? Surely that could not be good for her or their child.

He pressed the buzzer and her voice, sounding tired and wavering, came through the intercom.

'I'll be right down.'

Tense with anxiety, he shoved his hands in the pockets of his trousers and scanned the building again. It looked run-down and dangerous, a drift of takeaway menus littering the front step, the bins outside overflowing. This was no place for the mother of his child to live.

Moments later Allegra appeared in the doorway. As she opened the door, Rafael tried to hide his shock. She looked terrible—her face was pasty and pale, her hair lifeless and dull, and she'd lost far too much weight. The

T-shirt and light trousers she wore for a humid summer's day in the city hung on her like rags on a scarecrow.

Rafael stepped forward to take her arm. She recoiled slightly at his touch, but he held her arm anyway. 'You look as if a breath of wind might blow you away.'

'I've been ill.'

'You should have called me earlier.' He could not keep the recrimination from his voice.

'Please, let's not argue. It's taking all my strength to get through this day already.'

Rafael nodded tersely, knowing she was right. Every instinct in him clamoured to demand why she'd hidden the pregnancy from him when he'd been as clear as he could that he'd wanted to know. But now was not the time. Still, he determined grimly, the time would come. He'd make sure of it.

He helped Allegra into the car, noting the way she sank into the seat with a relieved sigh, resting her head against the leather cushions.

'What did you mean, you've been ill?' he asked as the limo pulled away from the kerb.

'Morning sickness,' she murmured. 'I've had it terribly. I've hardly been able to keep anything down.'

You should have told me. He bit back the words. 'Isn't there anything the doctors can do? Medication…?'

'I was prescribed something, but it didn't really help. It's started to get a little bit better recently, thank goodness, and my doctors think it might go away soon if…' She bit her lip, her eyes bright with tears.

Rafael could finish that awful sentence. If she continued with this pregnancy, if their baby was healthy. 'We need more information,' he said gruffly, 'before any decisions are made.' But already he'd made a decision. He wasn't leaving her, and she wasn't staying in a walk-up flat in a run-down neighbourhood. Her place, no matter what happened, was with him. He would protect her and their baby. He thought back to that terrible day, outside his father's study door. He'd failed in protecting those he loved that day. He'd been too weak, too slow to act, too naïve. But he would not fail again. The need to protect his ill-gotten family burned within him, brighter and fiercer than anything he'd ever felt before.

Allegra could feel the tension emanating from Rafael, but she didn't have the energy to wonder or worry about it. All her strength was taken up with preparing for what lay ahead.

She'd barely slept last night, too worried by both the procedure and its possible results. She hadn't even had time to think about Rafael and seeing him again.

And yet now that he was here…she inhaled the saffron scent of his aftershave, felt the coiled, restless power of him, just as she had before. It made her ache. It made her remember. Even now she felt a treacherous dart of desire. How stupid, considering their situation, and the way he'd treated her.

They didn't speak all the way to the hospital, but that was okay. Allegra didn't think she could manage chit-chat, and talking about what mattered felt too hard. The limo pulled up to the front of the hospital, and Rafael leapt out before Allegra could so much as reach for the handle.

He opened her door and with one arm around her shepherded her into the building. She wasn't that fragile, but she craved his protectiveness now. It felt strange, when she'd taught herself not to rely on anyone. Now she wanted to. She needed to.

Before long they were in a treatment room, with Allegra lying down on the examining table and Rafael sitting tensely on a chair next to her. A technician prepared her for the ultrasound, and the now-familiar whooshing sound of her baby's heart filled Allegra with both relief and joy.

She glanced across at Rafael, shocked and then touched by the look of tender wonder softening his face. His surprised gaze met hers and he gave her a smile that seemed almost tremulous. Another point of connection, as sweet as any they'd ever shared, and yet… Could she trust it? Dared she think about what happened next, or in the long term?

'Now this won't take long,' the doctor assured her. 'And it shouldn't hurt too much. I've given you a local anaesthetic to numb the area, but you might experience some minor discomfort and cramping.'

Allegra took in the size of the needle and instinctively reached for Rafael's hand. He encased her hand in his larger one, and she squeezed it hard as the needle went in. It didn't hurt, but it still scared her. Everything about this scared her.

In a few moments it was over, and the technician was wiping the gel off Allegra's stomach.

'Are you all right?' Rafael asked in a low voice, and Allegra nodded.

'Yes. I think so.' She felt shaky and a bit tearful, and she had some mild cramps, but nothing she couldn't deal with. She tried to shake his hand off, wanting to be strong, but he kept holding hers.

'You need to rest.'

'You should take the rest of the day off,' the doctor advised. 'Normal activity can be resumed tomorrow.'

Rafael frowned at that, but said nothing. Together they left the treatment room, and it wasn't until they were in the limo and Rafael was telling the address to the driver that Allegra realised he wasn't taking her home.

'Wait—where are we going?' she asked.

'To my hotel near Central Park.' Rafael sat back.

'But I want to go home,' Allegra said. She wanted her bed and her music and the comforts of the familiar.

Rafael glanced at her, his expression unreadable. 'That apartment is completely inappropriate for a woman in your condition.'

'You mean pregnant?' Allegra stared at him, surprised by his high-handedness even as she wondered why she should be. Rafael had been completely in control of every situation she'd seen him in.

'Climbing six sets of stairs to get to your home cannot be good for our baby,' Rafael stated.

'Plenty of women do that and more—'

'Yet you are the one I care about,' Rafael cut her off. 'And frankly you look terrible—tired, pale, drawn. You need proper rest.'

'Thanks very much,' Allegra snapped. Her feminine pride was hurt by his blunt assessment, even though she knew she didn't look good, and hadn't for a while.

'The reason I look tired, Rafael, is because I've had extreme morning sickness, not because I climb some stairs.'

'It can't help.'

'So what are you suggesting? That I move house?'

'Precisely,' Rafael answered in a clipped voice. 'You will live with me in my hotel suite until the results from the amniocentesis return.'

She stared at him in disbelief. She'd wanted someone to lean on, yes, for a little bit. But not someone to take over her life. Yet should she have expected anything else from this man? 'I can't live with you,' she protested. 'I don't want to live with you. I have a job—'

'Managing a café, on your feet all day? Take sick leave.'

'I can't—'

'Then I shall arrange it.'

Allegra simply stared, too shocked by his autocratic statements to frame a suitable reply. She should have expected this, but she'd been so tired and shaky and fearful, she'd just been glad to have someone to lean on for a little while. Now she was starting to wish she'd never called Rafael at all. 'This is ridiculous.'

'Even so.' Rafael was as unmovable as a brick wall, his expression obdurate. And meanwhile they were speeding towards Central Park, away from her flat, her job, her life.

'You can't just waltz into my life and make all these changes and demands,' Allegra persisted. 'I won't let you.'

Rafael raked a hand through his hair, taking a deep breath and letting it out slowly. Allegra had the strange sense that he was battling a deeper emotion than she understood. 'I realise you do not want me to tell you what to do,' he said evenly. 'But when you put your emotional reaction to that aside, you will surely realise that I am right.'

Allegra let out a huff of disbelieving laughter. 'What I *didn't* realise is how unbelievably arrogant you are.'

Rafael's mouth firmed. 'This isn't about arrogance. I'm not issuing orders simply to show who's in control.'

'Really?'

'I am considering your health, Allegra, as well as that of our child.'

'And if I refuse?' Allegra asked. 'What will you do?'

'Why would you refuse? You want what is best for our baby, do you not? As do I.'

A lump formed in her throat and her eyes burned. He dared to suggest she didn't care for their child? 'Of course I do.'

'Then surely rest and relaxation in a comfortable place is it? Why overtax and strain yourself when you don't have to? Why climb six sets of stairs when you don't have to?' He held up a hand to stem any protests she might have made. 'I understand that climbing the stairs might have no negative effect on your pregnancy. But what if there is the smallest chance that it did?' He leaned forward, his eyes burning bright. 'If you could turn back time, do things differently…' For a second his voice choked, and Allegra had the distinct feeling he was talking about something else.

'What would you change, Rafael?' she asked quietly. 'What would you do differently?'

He shook his head, the movement abrupt and dismissive. 'It is now that matters. Now you have the chance to make the best choice for your—our—baby.'

Allegra stared at him, both transfixed and uncertain. 'You can't keep me in some bubble. Pregnant women are able to live normally.'

'Two weeks is all I'm asking. Two weeks until we know what we're dealing with, and then we can reassess. Discuss.'

Discuss what was likely to be a life-threatening condition. The unshed tears that burned behind her lids threatened to fall. Suddenly it felt like too much; her resistance had been feeble but it was all she had. She couldn't fight any more, couldn't stay strong and remote as she always tried to.

'Fine.' She sagged against the seat as the limo pulled

up in front of one of the city's most luxurious hotels. 'You win.' Relief and triumph flashed in Rafael's amber eyes, and in that moment she wondered just how much she was conceding.

CHAPTER FIVE

ALLEGRA BLINKED SLEEPILY in the early evening gloom of the hotel suite's master bedroom. She'd fallen into a deep, dreamless sleep almost as soon as her head had touched the soft, feather down pillow, and judging by the twilight settling softly over the city sky she'd been asleep for several hours.

She stretched and then snuggled under the soft duvet, tempted to stay there for ever. When they'd arrived at the hotel suite, Rafael had been graciousness itself, insisting she take the master bedroom, ringing for some juice when she said she was thirsty, and telling her to sleep for as long as she'd liked.

When she'd crawled into the king-sized bed Allegra had realised just how exhausted she really was, and her last thought before she drifted off was that she was, in the end, glad Rafael had insisted she come here. Not that she intended on admitting as much to him.

Now, as she struggled to a sitting position with a wide yawn, she wondered what exactly she was supposed to do here. What *they* were supposed to do. An afternoon was one thing, but did Rafael really expect her to stay here for two weeks, kicking her heels, until the amnio results came back? And what was he going to do while she waited? How were they supposed to get along? Battling deeper unease, Allegra rose from the bed.

She treated herself to a long, lovely soak in the sunken marble tub and then dressed in her summery trousers and top before heading into the main living area of the suite in search of Rafael.

He was sitting at a desk in a study alcove off the sumptuous living room, frowning down at his laptop, but he looked up quickly as she stepped from the doorway of the bedroom.

His gaze scanned her searchingly from her damp hair curling about her face to her bare feet. 'You slept well?'

'Yes, very well. It's been ages.' It was, she'd seen as she'd dressed, nearly seven o'clock at night.

'Are you hungry?' Rafael rose from the desk. 'I ordered a variety of dishes from room service. I hoped something might appeal to you.'

'That's very kind of you.' After months of barely managing a mouthful, she knew she needed to eat more.

'Come into the dining room.'

Allegra followed him into the dining room that adjoined the kitchen, which was just as elegant as every other room in the suite. The place was twenty times the size of her studio, decorated with silks and satins, antiques and exquisite paintings. She felt almost as if she were in a museum—a very comfortable, luxurious museum.

'Wow,' Allegra managed, surprised and touched by the spread of food left in warming dishes on the table. She saw clear broths and simple pasta dishes, fresh fruit and half a dozen different salads. Amazingly, despite the constant nausea she'd been battling for the last few months, she felt a little hungry. 'This looks amazing.'

'Take whatever you like. We can eat out on the terrace.'

'Thank you.' He was being so kind, and yet she was afraid to trust it. Reluctant to start depending on his charity and consideration, when it all could change so suddenly...just as it had before.

Rafael handed her a plate and Allegra took it and began to serve herself from some of the dishes. 'How were you able to book the penthouse suite of this place?' she asked. 'I've heard it's booked months in advance.'

Rafael shrugged one powerful shoulder. 'Considering I own this hotel, it was not a problem.'

He *owned* this hotel? It was one of the city's best. Allegra had known Rafael was wealthy and powerful, but it was brought home to her yet again in that moment—along with the realisation of how he could wield that power, if he so chose. How he already had, taking over her father's business. This was man who was ruthless, brutal in his determination to get what he wanted...whatever that was. She needed to remember that.

Allegra finished filling her plate and then took it outside to the terrace overlooking Central Park. The air was a balmy caress, and the terrace was decorated with potted plants and fairy-lights, making it feel like a little bit of the park had been brought thirty floors up.

'This is lovely,' she said as she sat on a chaise and picked at a few mouthfuls of pasta salad. 'Thank you.'

Rafael sat across from her, his plate balanced on his lap. He was wearing the dark trousers and crisp white shirt he'd worn earlier, the shirt now opened at the collar, revealing the strong column of his throat. Stubble glinted on his jaw and the whiteness of the shirt was a perfect foil for his burnished, olive skin. He looked, Allegra acknowledged with a pang, as devastatingly attractive as he had that night in Rome. As irresistibly desirable...except, of course, she would resist him. She had to, because the situation was fraught enough, dangerous enough. She couldn't let herself depend on him any more than she already was. She certainly couldn't start to care for him.

'I've arranged for you to take the next two weeks off work,' Rafael stated as he forked a mouthful of pasta.

'What? How?'

'I spoke to your employer and landlord, Anton. He understands.'

Allegra's head was spinning. 'But you... Two weeks?' She blinked at him. 'But—'

'You have exhausted yourself, whether you realise it or not. You need a proper rest, both for your own health and our child's.'

Allegra couldn't deny that, but she still chafed against his commands. She was used to being independent. She needed to feel strong. 'That was not your call to make. This is my life, Rafael.'

'And as I said before, I know you want what is best for the baby.'

It was a trump card he could play every time, and there was nothing she could do about it, because he was right. She enjoyed her job, but it had been exhausting and she knew she couldn't keep it up for ever. A rest, even one that was enforced, had some merit, as reluctant as she was to admit it to him.

But a rest here with Rafael? Allegra still couldn't imagine spending the next two weeks with him. There was so much they hadn't discussed...his heartless dismissal of her after their night together, her hiding her pregnancy, even the business his father had had with hers. Her father's death. There was so much tension and latent anger and uncertainty—and now they were meant to get along?

And beyond that, she didn't even *know* Rafael. She'd intentionally tried not to think of him since they'd parted, wanting to forget about him completely. She's resisted doing Internet searches, even though she'd been tempted to know more about him.

And now here they were, sitting across from each other, their baby nestled inside her. Allegra didn't know what to think of any of it, how to respond, how to feel. Part of her was clamouring for retreat, while another part recognised that that was no longer an option, not with a child to think of. A child to love.

In any case, now certainly wasn't the time to tackle any of those difficult issues. They just needed to get through the next two weeks and see what the results of the amniocentesis were.

They spent the evening, incongruously, sitting next to each other on the sumptuous silk-covered sofa, watching TV on a huge flat screen that had been hidden behind an oil painting. After the first few tense minutes Allegra started to relax, enjoying being able to turn off her brain and watch reality TV fluff. And she enjoyed the feel of Rafael's strong body next to her, his thigh touching hers, his arm stretched along the back of the sofa. She could almost imagine this was normal, that she was normal, with a baby and a husband and a life like so many women wanted and had.

Which was a *very* dangerous way to think.

The next morning Rafael suggested they go to her flat to pick up her things, and they rode in silence down Park Avenue to her little studio. It felt strange to have Rafael in her personal space, his inscrutable gaze flicking over her belongings—her framed concert posters, her few personal photos—even the shelf of well-thumbed cookbooks in the tiny alcove kitchen felt revealing of her somehow.

'I didn't realise you actually played.' He nodded towards the cello on its stand in the corner.

'I don't, not really.' She looked away, not wanting to talk about her cello playing, or lack of it. She hadn't played since she was eighteen years old.

'Do you wish to bring it to the hotel?'

'No,' she said after a moment, her tone reluctant but firm. 'I won't play it.'

'Are you sure?'

'Yes.'

He stared at her for a moment, his gaze narrowed, as if he was trying to figure out what was going on in her head. Allegra looked away. She couldn't explain her complicated relationship to music, how much it meant to her, how it had provided something she knew instinctively people were meant to provide. She certainly didn't want to go into the reason why she'd stopped playing the cello, the dismal failure she'd been. Thankfully Rafael let the subject drop.

After gathering her clothes, books, and a few personal items, they headed back to the hotel. Allegra knew she couldn't put off something she'd been dreading—calling her mother.

Although they lived in the same city, she and Jennifer rarely saw each other. Her mother had her own life on the Upper East Side, tightly enfolded in a clique of aging socialites and impoverished divorcées, trying to live in the manner she preferred with the help of boyfriends and benefactors, and an endless diatribe of highstrung negativity.

Allegra understood the reason for it, knew her mother had never recovered from her father's divorce and abandonment, his decision to end their marriage so abruptly and cut them off with barely a cent, but it didn't make it any easier to deal with her.

Jennifer hadn't been much interested in Allegra's pregnancy so far, except to remind her repeatedly that single motherhood was no picnic, thereby launching down an endless memory lane trip of her own struggles and regrets until Allegra had tuned her mother out. But the mention of a wealthy father to her grandchild was sure to prick Jennifer's ears up and have her asking all sorts of questions. Questions Allegra didn't feel much up to answering right now.

After she'd unpacked in her room, and with Rafael installed in the study on his laptop, Allegra made the call.

'You're what?' Jennifer asked sharply when Allegra had explained she was staying at the hotel.

'Just for a little while.' Allegra took a deep breath. 'Rafael Vitali is…he's the father of my baby. We…we got together when I was in Italy.'

'Rafael Vitali? This is the son of Marco Vitali?'

Startled, Allegra said, 'I… I suppose so. I don't know. Why? Do you know his father?'

'Your father did business with him a long time ago,' Jennifer said after a pause. 'It didn't work out.'

Unease prickled along Allegra's spine. She thought of Rafael's cold remark. *'I am not the only one with blood on my hands.'*

'What do you mean, it didn't work out?'

'It doesn't matter,' Jennifer dismissed. 'It's in the past. But be careful,' she added in an unusual display of motherly concern. 'Your father didn't trust his, and I… I wouldn't trust him either.'

She didn't trust him. Didn't want to trust him. And

yet... 'I trust Rafael to care for his child,' Allegra said, because that, at least, was true.

Out in the living area Rafael looked up from his laptop when she emerged from the bedroom.

'You called your mother?'

'Yes.' Allegra paused, wondering how much she wanted to probe the past. 'She mentioned that your father did business with mine, and that it didn't work out.'

A lightning flash of emotion sliced across Rafael's face, too quickly for her to discern what it was, and then he carefully closed his laptop. 'Yes, that is true. They worked together on a mobile phone technology that would now be considered laughably obsolete, and they fell out over it.'

'Fell out?' Allegra regarded him uneasily, sensing something dark flowing beneath his calm surface, and nervous to dip a toe into it. 'Is that why you decided to take over my father's company? Some kind of revenge for what happened before?'

'Justice,' Rafael corrected swiftly. His face remained bland, but Allegra saw that his eyes were watchful and hard.

'What do you mean, justice? What are you not telling me? And why... why did you make that comment about blood on your hands?'

Rafael's jaw tightened, his eyes like chips of amber. 'Now is not the time to delve into the past.'

'But it's obviously important—'

'What is important is your health and well-being.' He rose from the desk. 'I have booked some spa treatments for you this afternoon to help you relax. They are aimed specifically at pregnant women.'

'Oh...' Allegra blinked, startled all over again. 'Thank you.' She felt as if her head was spinning. One moment

Rafael seemed as hard and unyielding as granite, and the next he was all softness and solicitude. Which was the real man? Who did she dare trust…if either?

Rafael paced the living room of the hotel suite, waiting for Allegra to return from her afternoon of spa treatments. He felt anxious, and he didn't even know why. At least, not *exactly* why. Since Allegra had catapulted back into his life he'd been struggling with a tidal wave of fury that she'd attempted to hide her pregnancy from him, and a stronger surge of both protectiveness and fear to keep both her and their child safe.

The memory of when he'd failed his family, his fists beating on his father's study door, his useless words. And then the aftermath. His mother's wan face, his sister's desperate defiance…their whole family falling to pieces, disintegrating before his eyes. It tormented him, when he allowed himself to think of it. The thought of failing Allegra and their child in a similar way or even at all was appalling. Unacceptable. And he wouldn't let it happen. He would do everything in his power to keep Allegra and their baby safe and well. *Everything*…for her well-being as well as his own.

He knew Allegra had questions about his father. His past. The deception and death that still haunted his nightmares and could ruin things between them. She still loved her father—that much was obvious—even though the man had abandoned her. He couldn't tell her the truth about him, not without jeopardising their own situation and Allegra's barely-there trust in him. The past, he determined, would have to stay buried.

The door to the suite opened and Allegra stepped inside, and the clear purity of her smile, the ivory blush of her skin made something twist hard inside Rafael's gut. He suddenly felt breathless, which was entirely a new feeling and made him feel poleaxed, reeling from the strength of his own reaction. He forced a smile.

'How was it?'

'Wonderful. I feel more relaxed than I have...well, ever.' She let out a little laugh, her grey eyes sparkling like silver. 'I've never even had a massage before. And look at my nails!' She held out her hands to him, her nails painted pale pink, and as a matter of course Rafael caught them up in his, drew her to him.

Allegra came easily, caught up in the moment, and he wasn't even thinking as he bent his head to kiss her, already anticipating the sweet, soft taste of her. Her lips parted soundlessly, her eyes fluttering closed, her golden-red lashes fanning onto her porcelain cheeks.

His lips brushed hers and Allegra let out a little sigh. Rafael pulled her closer and then he felt her stiffen in his arms. Her eyes flew open, filled with confusion. She shook her head and then drew away.

'No, I'm sorry...we can't...'

Of course they couldn't. The last thing they needed was this kind of complication...except he wanted it so badly. Rafael raked a hand through his hair, desire surging through his body. He was shocked by his instantaneous and overwhelming response, his heart thudding.

Allegra was still looking at him in dazed confusion, her pupils dilated with desire even as her mouth twisted with uncertainty.

The time would come, Rafael decided. Maybe not yet, not when everything was so uncertain, when their child's future hung in the balance. But the time would come. It had to.

CHAPTER SIX

'I HAVE A surprise for you.'

Allegra looked up from the book she was reading with a cautious smile. Rafael stood in the living-room doorway, the slight curve of his mouth softening his harsh features.

It had been a strange and unsettling ten days, living in the hotel with Rafael, finding a new and tentative normalcy. It had taken a little while, but eventually she'd been able to relax into a routine. Rafael had spent most of his time working in the hotel's business centre so Allegra hadn't seen him nearly as much as she'd expected to, which was, to her irritation, both a disappointment and a relief. He was often out in the evenings, although they'd shared a few rather tense meals together, neither of them completely comfortable co-existing in this weird limbo.

Rafael seemed as closed off as ever, his inscrutable manner giving nothing away, although towards her he was all solicitous concern, arranging for private museum tours, taxis and, recalling her shelf of cookbooks in her apartment, baking.

Rafael had insisted she order whatever ingredient or implement she wanted, and with a fully stocked, gourmet kitchen at her disposal Allegra was soon enjoying experimenting with new recipes. Her morning sickness was easing and she was actually starting to enjoy food again.

And then, of course, there was the almost-kiss they'd shared. She'd come back from the spa both buzzing and relaxed, and for a moment, with Rafael's warm gaze on her, it had felt so natural, so easy to fall into his arms. To tilt her head and wait for his kiss, that connection.

The shock she'd felt when his lips had barely brushed hers, the deep desire that had blazed a streak of lightning need straight through her, had thankfully made her take a step back. Getting involved with Rafael that way was far too dangerous. She was already well out of her comfort zone, simply being here with him, seeing him in passing in the hotel suite. She couldn't stand an even deeper intimacy, as much as her body craved it.

'A surprise,' she repeated now, her eyebrows raised. 'What kind of surprise?'

Rafael drew two tickets from the inside pocket of his suit jacket. 'Box seats to the New York Philharmonic playing Bach's cello suites at the Lincoln Center.'

'Oh!' She stared at him in unabashed delight—those were the kind of tickets that were usually well out of her price range, and she was touched that Rafael had thought to buy them. 'That's wonderful. When?'

'Tomorrow night.'

Allegra's smile faded as she admitted, 'But I don't have anything to wear...' Her maternity clothes consisted of a couple of pairs of loose cotton tops and shorts, and soon her burgeoning belly was going to require more.

'Problem solved. I've arranged for one of the top maternity designers to come here with a selection of evening gowns. You can take your pick.'

'Oh. Wow.' Not for the first time, Allegra was both touched and unsettled by Rafael's thoughtfulness and generosity. At times he seemed a million miles from the cold, hard stranger who had booted her out of his bed. But then at other times…

'Thank you,' she said now. 'For all of it. You're very kind.'

Rafael shrugged. 'I thought it might be nice to have a distraction. And when I saw it was a concert for the cello…'

'You're very thoughtful. And a distraction would be wonderful,' she said, smiling shyly. Rafael nodded and gave her the tiniest of smiles back.

The next morning a glamorous woman dressed all in black arrived with a couple of assistants carrying several plastic-swathed hangers each. While Allegra relaxed with herbal tea and croissants, the assistants laid out all the different evenings gowns—silks and satins, above-the-knee and full-length, in every colour of the rainbow. Allegra had never felt so spoilt for choice, or simply spoiled. She felt positively indulged as she stroked the dresses' soft fabrics and fingered exquisite lace.

'I don't know which to pick,' she admitted, and Amanda, the fashion designer, swooped in.

'With your colouring I'd advise the ice-blue. It will make your eyes pop and do wonderful things for your complexion.'

'Will it?' Allegra asked, bemused that a simple dress could do so much. Of course, the gown in question was far from simple, with its diamanté-encrusted halter-neck top and daring backless design. 'I don't know.' She nibbled her lip. 'It looks a bit…sexy.'

'Why can't a pregnant woman be sexy?' Amanda countered with a little smile. 'You're blooming and gorgeous. Let people know it.'

Allegra laughed. 'I haven't felt either all pregnancy. I've felt as worn and wrung-out as an old dishrag.'

'You don't look it now,' Amanda said firmly. 'And you won't look it in that dress.'

Persuaded, Allegra tried on the ice-blue gown and was amazed at how different she looked. The dress clung to her fuller breasts and slight swell of her bump before flaring out from her thighs to swirl about her feet. The backless design left the entire creamy expanse of her back bare, right to the swell of her bottom. She blushed to imagine Rafael seeing her in something like this. What if he thought she was trying to impress him? *Was* she? Suddenly her feelings were in a ferment.

'I don't know...' Already she was reaching for the diamanté ties, doubtful as to whether she could carry off something like this. Amanda stayed her hand.

'Trust me, no man could resist you in this dress, and certainly not the father of your child.' Her small, knowing smile made Allegra blush.

Did she want to be irresistible to Rafael? Sex was out of the question, and even kisses would complicate their already ambiguous relationship. The last thing she wanted was to be hurt...again. And yet...she'd felt worn out and ugly for months. The thought of looking good, *really* good, and having Rafael's eyes widen with surprise and then flare with desire...

She was tempted. She was seriously tempted.

That evening, as Allegra got ready for their night out, she started to doubt the wisdom of picking such a blatantly sexy dress. What if Rafael was put off by it? What if he thought she was throwing herself at him? What if she *was*?

And, really, the whole ensemble, from the diamond chandelier earrings Amanda had insisted she wear to match her father's sapphire necklace to the four-inch silver stiletto heels encasing her feet, felt a little much. Some people wore jeans to the Philharmonic. She didn't need to be quite so OTT.

And yet it was nice to feel beautiful. The silky material slithered over her skin and the diamonds winked at her ears. The heart-shaped sapphire nestled in the hollow of her throat, winking and glinting. Amanda had arranged for a make-up artist and hairstylist to finish her look, her hair held up by diamond-tipped pins, with a few curls cascading down to rest on her shoulders. She'd never, Allegra knew, looked so good.

Even so, she was still battling doubt as she left the safety of the bedroom. Outside the Manhattan skyline glittered, the entire city spread out before them. Rafael turned, his eyes narrowing as he took in the sight of her.

Allegra tried to smile but she felt so nervous and exposed that she wasn't sure she managed it. Rafael looked almost unbearably sexy in a midnight-black tuxedo, the snowy white shirt offsetting his olive skin, his hair brushed back from his forehead, his eyes glittering like polished bronze, everything about him radiating that restless energy that had drawn her to him nearly five months ago.

'Is it too much?' she asked with an uncertain laugh. 'The dress, I mean?' Her hands fluttered at her sides and she lifted her chin, trying for pride. She'd chosen this dress. She'd wear it no matter what Rafael thought... and yet she wished he'd smile or say something. He was practically *scowling*.

'You look...' Rafael stopped, his voice hoarse. Allegra waited, her heart fluttering like a trapped bird in her chest. 'Magnificent.'

A smile unfurled like a flower across her face, and

then she was beaming. She couldn't help it. A distant voice in her head was telling her not to be so obvious, not to let Rafael affect her. Why should she care what he thought? Why should she want to please or impress him? She shouldn't. She most certainly shouldn't.

And yet as Rafael grinned back that voice was silenced. Tonight she was a beautiful woman, and he was a handsome man, and they were going to hear the most wonderful music together. Allegra wanted to let herself enjoy it without trying to stay safe or sensible. She wanted to forget that she didn't trust him, wasn't even sure she liked him, and that the future was entirely uncertain. Tonight she wanted to leave all that behind and enter into the magic. And so she would.

Rafael had never seen Allegra look so beautiful. She was more than merely beautiful—she was incandescent, breathtaking. The ice-blue of her gown flowed like cool water over her perfect curves, the faint bump of her belly making a deep, protective urge rise within Rafael like a primal howl of possession. She was *his*. No matter what the results of the amniocentesis were, no matter what the future held. His to protect, to provide for, to possess. *His*.

Then he saw the sapphire pendant at her throat and it slammed into him yet again who her father was, who his was, and all the hard history that lay between them… dark, difficult history Allegra didn't know about, but which marked every moment of Rafael's life. History that reminded him that letting someone into your life, even just a little, was a terrifying responsibility as well as a formidable risk.

A faint frown marred Allegra's brow and Rafael banished the memory, the realisation, the fear. Those were not for tonight, when all he wanted to do was enjoy the evening…and Allegra. He stretched out his hand and she took it, slender fingers sliding between his. She squeezed his hand, and it felt like a promise, an agreement. Tonight was for them, for magic.

Wordlessly he led her downstairs to the waiting limo.

The evening felt expectant, although for what Rafael couldn't say. Despite their near-kiss over a week ago, he didn't actually expect anything physical to happen between them. He didn't want it, not if he forced himself to think rationally. If he let his libido lead the way, he'd peel that slippery dress from her creamy skin and have her in the back of this limo.

Yet far more unsettling than his desire for her was his desire to please her. He'd found himself arranging small treats and pleasures for her all week, simply to see her reaction. He told himself it was part of his duty, his responsibility to take care of her. The feeling inside him, as if his heart was a balloon floating higher and higher, was just a fringe benefit.

In any case, he wasn't going to start *feeling* things for Allegra Wells. After losing everyone he cared about, he was hardly going to let someone else get under his skin. Into his heart. No matter what happened with their child.

The Lincoln Center was glowing with lights as the limo pulled in front of the concert hall where the Philharmonic was playing. Rafael saw more than one man steal a speculative or even lascivious look at Allegra as she moved through the crowd, a stunning goddess with her red-gold curls tumbling artfully onto her bare, creamy shoulders.

She turned to glance back at him, grey eyes sparkling like silver stars. 'This is amazing, Rafael. Thank you.'

Every time she said his name he felt an arrow of satisfaction pierce him sweetly. He told himself it didn't matter.

They took their seats, Allegra excitedly perusing her programme like a child on her first trip to the circus.

Her enthusiasm made Rafael smile as he leaned forward to ask her, 'Haven't you been to concerts before?'

She wrinkled her nose. 'Oh, dear. Is my newbie status showing?'

'It's charming,' Rafael replied, 'but I would have thought, as a seasoned New Yorker, as well as a music-lover, this would be old hat to you.'

She shook her head, curls bouncing. 'No, not really. Not at all. I've been to concerts, but they've been free ones in churches and things like that. I've never heard the Philharmonic play live.'

'Never?' He was surprised.

She gave him a laughing look. 'Not everyone's a millionaire.'

Billionaire, actually, but he wasn't going to debate the point. He sat back in his seat, legs stretched out in front of him. 'Your father had plenty of money.' Not that he remotely wanted to talk about her father.

'My father did,' Allegra agreed quietly, some of the sparkle gone from her eyes, 'but we didn't. My mother didn't get anything from the divorce.'

Rafael frowned. 'She must have had some financial settlement.'

'Nope, not a penny.' Allegra shrugged. 'I don't know why.'

'She didn't sue for alimony?' It didn't make any sense.

'I was only twelve, I didn't ask. And I haven't asked since then because, to be honest, it just gets her going. She's always been bitter about it. All I know is my father managed to arrange things so we were left with nothing.'

Rafael supposed he shouldn't be shocked; he knew how heartless Mancini had been. But he was surprised, on Allegra's behalf. Why did she still care about him when he'd treated her so badly? 'So how did you survive?'

'My mother sold some jewellery to start, and she also had various boyfriends who helped.' Allegra made a face. 'That sounds awful, doesn't it? But my mother was used to living in a certain style, and it still makes her furious that she can't.'

'And what about you? Does it make you furious?'

Allegra shrugged, her gaze sliding away as her fingers touched the sapphire nestled at her throat as if it was a talisman. 'I don't care so much about things. And I've supported myself since I was eighteen.'

'Eighteen.' Another surprise. 'Did you go to university?' He realised that, despite having spent the last week and a half in her company, he didn't know that much about her or her life. Not that he'd actually spent much time with her. He'd intentionally stayed away, not wanting to complicate matters. Not wanting to get close. Now, however, he realised he wanted to know more about her... even if it unwise.

'No, I didn't.' Allegra pursed her lips, her gaze shadowed. 'I decided it wasn't for me.'

Rafael felt sure there was something she wasn't saying, but he had no idea what it was. 'What about you?' she asked. 'Did you go to university?'

'No, I went to work when I was sixteen.' He felt his chest go tight, his jaw hard, just because of the memories. His fist bunched on his thigh and he forced himself to relax. 'We needed the money.'

'Then we have something in common.' Allegra gazed at him in sorrowful compassion, and Rafael knew she was keeping herself from asking about their fathers on purpose. Neither of them wanted to prise open that Pandora's box right now.

'Yes, I suppose we do,' he said, and smiled. She smiled back and he felt the tension in him ease.

Then the lights dimmed, and they both settled back in their seats as the music began. Rafael wasn't that much of a connoisseur of music, but he loved seeing the look of rapt attention on Allegra's face. She was utterly arrested, a pearly sheen in her eyes, her hands clasped to her chest. He'd never seen someone look so thoroughly enthralled, and it touched a place deep inside him, a place he hadn't accessed in a long time. It made him yearn and mourn, just as he had when they'd listened to Shostakovich. Watching Allegra, he wanted to feel as much as she did. He wanted to let himself.

The concert came to an end, the last notes of music fading away into an aching stillness, and Allegra rose from her seat, dashing the tears from her face with an embarrassed laugh. 'Sorry, music always affects me like that.'

In the space of a second he was catapulted back to that night in Rome when she'd said the same thing. When he'd felt as powerfully as he did now, wanting this woman with an intensity that both thrilled and terrified him.

He'd wiped away her tears then, and she'd let him, and then they'd made love. It had been the most incredible sexual experience of his life, and he could remember every exquisite detail of that evening, of Allegra's response, of the way she'd felt under his hands and mouth.

He watched a rosy blush sweep across Allegra's skin and knew she remembered it all too. They stared at each other for a prolonged moment, eyes wide, hearts beating hard, the moment spinning on and growing in strength.

The desire was still there, and more powerful than ever. More dangerous too. Would they act on it as they had before?

Neither of them spoke in the limo on the way back to the hotel. Rafael couldn't keep from imagining himself reaching out one hand to tangle in Allegra's hair, drawing the diamond-tipped pins out one by one and then anchoring his lips to hers. He pictured sliding his hands under her gown, hauling her onto his lap so she was straddling him. With a suppressed groan he shifted on his seat, trying to ease the now persistent ache in his groin. He was torturing himself with these kinds of thoughts.

Allegra was quiet, her face pale, her expression thoughtful as she gazed out at the traffic streaming by in a bright blur of light. He thought she was feeling what he was, but even now he couldn't be sure. She'd drawn away from him once already. Even if she desired him, he knew that she didn't want to.

It was a pertinent reminder that, no matter what, sex would be complicated between them. Fraught and maybe emotional. And he didn't need or want to feel more for this woman than he already did. Then his leg brushed hers and an electric current zinged through his body. He couldn't help but feel.

They rode up the lift in silence, and then he was swiping the key card and they were in their suite, the rooms dim and hushed, as if everything was waiting for this moment.

It would be so easy to take her into his arms. To plunder her mouth. To peel the dress away from her body. All the things he'd been imagining, wanting…

Everything, anything, felt possible. He heard Allegra draw a shuddering breath and knew she felt it, just as he did. Just as much.

'Allegra…' His voice was an ache in the darkness, and he reached out one hand, fingertips brushing her shoulder. Her skin was as soft and silky as he remembered. She shuddered again, a ripple of longing that went through her whole body, and he knew, he *knew* she would yield. And he wanted her to, desperately. So desperately.

Then Allegra's phone pinged with an incoming message and in a split second the mood shattered. She slipped away from him, taking her phone out of her clutch and then frowning as she looked down at the screen. A new, different kind of expectation tightened Rafael's gut.

'What is it?'

She swallowed audibly. 'It's a voicemail from the doctor.'

'He called in the evening? While we were out?' His voice was sharp and tense.

'No, this afternoon. I missed the phone call and the voicemail just came in now.' She slid him a quick, worried glance. 'My phone's old. The messages don't always come in right away. I should have checked…' He heard the recrimination in her voice, along with the fear.

'What does he say?'

Allegra swiped a few buttons and then listened to the call. Rafael watched her face, noticing the way her lips pursed and her eyes clouded, pale red-gold brows drawing together.

'Allegra…?' he prompted when she ended the call. Everything in him felt coiled tight, ready to snap.

'No real news.' She let out a shuddering breath. 'Just that the results from the amnio are in and he wants to discuss them with us tomorrow morning at ten o'clock.'

'All right.' They stared at each other, the weight of the information pressing down making it hard to breathe. The insistent desire Rafael had been feeling had vanished, leaving only cold trepidation in its wake. 'At least then we'll know.' And then what? What would happen to their child, to *them*?

'Yes.' Allegra tossed her phone and clutch on a chair and wrapped her arms around herself. With her tumbled, fiery curls and her ice-blue gown she looked like a slender, burning flame, and Rafael wanted to wrap her in his arms, not out of desire now but to offer her comfort. The compulsion was so strong it felt like a pain, breaking open a scar deep inside him, a barely healed wound from when he hadn't been able to help. To save anyone.

'I should go to bed,' Allegra said softly. 'It's late.'

'Allegra…' He wanted to say something of what he felt, desperately needed to offer her some comfort—and yet what comfort could he give? Tomorrow would bring whatever news it did, and there was absolutely nothing he could do about it.

A shudder racked her body and it felt like a wound to his heart. He hated seeing her suffer, knowing she was afraid, just as he was. Then she lifted her head, regarding Rafael with tear-damp, pain-filled eyes. 'Goodnight, Rafael,' she whispered, and walked out of the room.

CHAPTER SEVEN

ALLEGRA COULDN'T GET to sleep. She lay on her bed, staring gritty-eyed at the ceiling, everything leaden inside her. It had been such a magical evening, going to the concert with Rafael. All night excitement had been fizzing like champagne through her blood, bubbles popping inside her head. The music. The mood. The moment when Rafael had looked so sexy and intent…and then the realisation, cold and hard, that this was all ephemeral and tomorrow reality would return with a dreadful thud.

She pressed one hand against the soft swell of her bump. *Oh, baby. Stay strong. Be safe.* Yet she knew it wasn't in her baby's power to be healthy. It wasn't in hers either.

Around two in the morning she finally rose from bed, knowing sleep wasn't going to come. She was planning to make herself a cup of herbal tea and then sit out on the terrace, watching the city settle down to sleep, but she stopped on the threshold of her bedroom door, for Rafael was sitting in the living room, dressed only in a pair of loose, drawstring pyjama bottoms, a tumbler of whisky cradled in his hands.

He looked up at her quick intake of breath, giving her a smile that was both sad and wry. 'You couldn't sleep either?'

'No.' She shook her head. 'I was going to make some tea. I'd ask if you wanted some, but I see you've got something stronger.'

'I need it.' Rafael's voice was hoarse, and pain flashed like lightning across his face.

It surprised her, because although Rafael was doing what he saw as his duty by her, Allegra had assumed, rightly or wrongly, that he didn't really want this child. He'd said as much back in Rome, and he'd refused to talk about the *what if?* scenarios until they knew more. She realised she'd assumed he hadn't really cared, not the way she did, and yet now, looking at the set of his jaw, the slump of his shoulders, she wondered if he shared her fear, her agony. If he longed for their child to live and be strong and healthy as much as she did.

In the kitchen she brewed a cup of chamomile tea and then brought it to the living room, curling up on the opposite side of the sofa from Rafael. He looked unbelievably sexy, stubble shadowing his strong jaw and the perfect, sculpted muscles of his chest on glorious display, a sprinkling of dark hair forming a V down to the low waistband of his pyjamas.

But Allegra wasn't thinking about how handsome he looked. She was realising how sad he seemed, and it made her ache.

'I've felt the baby kick,' she said quietly. Rafael turned to look at her, his mouth dropping open in surprise.

'You have?'

'Just in the last few days. I didn't know what it was at first. It feels like bubbles popping inside me. Little flutters.' She took a deep breath. 'But they've become a bit stronger in the last day or two, almost…almost as if the baby knows. As if he or she is telling me…' She broke off, her chest tight with the force of her feeling, the strength of her emotion.

Rafael leaned closer, his expression intent. 'Telling you what?'

'Telling me that he—or she—wants to live.' She scanned his face, looking for clues to how he felt, what this could mean—for both of them. 'That this baby wants to live, no matter what.'

His expression was both intense and unreadable as he stared at her. 'What exactly do you mean?' he asked in a low voice.

Allegra let out a shuddering breath. 'I mean that no matter what the results are tomorrow, even if we know this baby's life is going to be short and hard, I want to keep him. I want to know this baby, I want to hold him, I want to love him. Or her.' She let out a trembling laugh and brushed at her eyes. 'I seem to be rather emotional lately. It must be the pregnancy hormones.'

'I feel emotional,' Rafael said, his voice hoarse. 'This is hard, Allegra, and it might only get harder, for both of us…if you mean what you say.'

'I do, and I know.' But did she, really? The words were easy to say—sort of—but the actions that might test them in later months would be far harder. *Was* she strong enough? There was only one way to find out. 'What about you?' she asked quietly. 'Do you…do you feel differently? Because I won't hold you to anything, Rafael. You didn't ask for this. You didn't even want a baby…'

'I didn't want you to be pregnant,' Rafael corrected. 'And I imagine you didn't either. We were strangers, Allegra.'

'We still are,' she said softly.

'But this child is real and growing and I want it as much as you do.' He took a deep breath, meeting her gaze directly. 'Do you honestly think I would leave you to cope with this alone?' She was silent for a second, and he drew back, deep hurt scoring his face. 'Is that the kind of man you think I am?'

'I don't know what kind of man you are,' Allegra confessed. She knew she was hurting him with her words but she had to be honest for both of their sakes. 'You left me once before, Rafael. You pushed me away, dismissed me out of hand. I'm scared…' *That you'll do it again.* She couldn't say the words, admit so much.

Rafael's mouth twisted. 'We had a one-night stand, Allegra. I admit my exit lines could have used some work, but you can't judge me by a single conversation.'

'Or lack of conversation.'

'If you are going to carry this baby to term,' Rafael stated, 'then I am staying with you. No matter what.' His tone was flat and determined, unyielding as stone. Allegra didn't know whether she should be heartened or alarmed by the strength of his conviction. Was this simply a matter of responsibility and duty, or the heart?

And what was this going to mean for both of them? For their future? She'd intended on going this alone, because that's how she did everything. She didn't want to invite someone into her life, someone who had the power to hurt her, who had already hurt her once before. And yet she couldn't kick Rafael out either. He was this baby's father. He had a say, a right, just as much as she did.

Allegra stared down into the fragrant depths of her tea, her emotions a tangled web of confusion, of opposite desires to stay strong, safe and alone—and to run straight into Rafael's arms. To seek a comfort there that she didn't even know if he could give.

Inside her their baby kicked, and with a tremulous

laugh of surprise she pressed one hand against her belly. Rafael drew a quick breath. 'Did you feel…?'

'Yes.' She looked up, a new shyness coming over her. 'Do you want to…?'

'Yes.' His tone was heartfelt, emboldening her to reach over and take his hand, pressing it over her bump, their fingers interlaced. His palm was warm and strong and she liked the feel of it there. 'Wait,' she whispered, and they both remained still, holding their breaths, *hoping…*

And then it happened. A light kick, right into his palm. Rafael laughed, a sound of total joy. Allegra smiled, feeling tearful again. Everything about this was so *much…* Rafael, their baby, *them*.

Rafael kept his palm on her belly and their baby kicked again, stronger this time. He looked up at her, his smile now one of fierce pride. 'He's a fighter.'

'It might be a girl.'

'Then she is. I don't care either way, boy or girl. I just want the baby to be…' He trailed off, a confused torment creasing his features, and Allegra squeezed his hand.

'Healthy,' she finished softly. 'I know.' Wasn't that what all parents said? *I just want the baby to be healthy.* The words sounded trite when you felt assured of the outcome. In this moment of terrible uncertainty they were painfully earnest, and yet it was the not knowing that drew them together, that made Allegra feel as connected to this man, or even more so than she had during that terrible, wonderful night in Rome.

They remained on the sofa, hands interlaced on Allegra's bump, as minutes ticked past. Their baby kicked a few more times and then settled down, and after a while Allegra fell into a doze, only to wake when she felt Rafael scoop her into his arms.

'Sorry,' she mumbled. 'I didn't realise I'd fallen asleep…'

'You're tired.' His voice was gruff, a thrum in his chest as Allegra pressed her cheek against the steady and comforting thud of his heart. She felt so treasured and small in his arms, in a way she hadn't felt in years, if ever.

Rafael carried her into her bedroom, depositing her gently down on the bed. Allegra looked up at him, still half-asleep, missing the feel of his strength and warmth all around her, barely aware of what she was doing and yet knowing she needed him now more than ever. And maybe, just maybe, he needed her as well.

'Rafael,' she whispered. 'Stay with me. Please.'

A look of surprise flashed across his face and then Rafael slid into bed next to her. He pulled her into his arms, drawing her back against the solid wall of his chest so their bodies were like spoons in a drawer, fitting perfectly. With a sigh of contentment Allegra settled against him and drifted back to sleep. She didn't know what tomorrow would bring, but tonight she felt safe and happy and hopeful.

Rafael sat in the doctor's office, Allegra looking pale and tired next to him, both of them incredibly tense. Now was the moment of reckoning.

Last night had been one of the most intimate and intense experiences of his life—first feeling their baby kick and then holding Allegra in his arms all night long. The ache of desire at feeling her body so tantalisingly close to his had been overwhelmed by the fierce need to comfort and protect her. She needed him, and he wanted to be needed. Wanted to provide for her what only he could.

But this moment, he acknowledged with painful certainty, was outside his control.

The doctor came into the room, her bland expression giving nothing away. 'Miss Wells, Mr Vitali.' She smiled at them both before sitting down at her desk. 'I have the results of the amniocentesis, and there is good news and bad news.'

Allegra's hand snaked out, searching for his. Her skin was icy cold as Rafael clasped her fingers between his own, trying to imbue her with his warmth, his strength. 'Yes?' he asked, wanting to hear the worst and get it over with. Once they knew they could figure out how to move forward. What to do, even how to feel.

'Your baby does have a heart defect,' the doctor explained gently, her smile seeming kind. 'But it is not as serious as it first looked. We'll need to do some tests, but I believe the condition is operable and there is every chance your child will live a full and healthy life.'

Rafael stared at her in shock, barely taking in the words. He'd been bracing himself for the absolute worst news and now he felt blindsided by this wonderful surprise. Next to him Allegra let out a small, soft sob and brushed at her eyes, clearly overcome.

'What kind of heart defect?' Rafael asked. 'What kind of operation?'

Rafael and Allegra both listened as the doctor explained the situation. Allegra would need to have some tests done in the next week, but if all went well then her pregnancy could continue normally to term. She would be scheduled for a C-section to avoid the traumatic effects of labour and delivery on their baby, and then a few days after birth an operation would be performed to fix their baby's heart. The recovery would take several months but then their baby would, God willing, be healthy and whole.

'Besides the heart defect,' the doctor continued, smiling, 'your baby is perfectly healthy, and everything looks normal. Do you want to know the sex?'

Rafael glanced at Allegra, saw a shy hope lighting her features, making her look radiant. She nodded.

'It's a boy,' the doctor said. 'A healthy baby boy.'

A boy. Rafael's mind was reeling with the news.

Instead of the baby most likely doomed to die that they'd both been expecting, the awful outcome that Rafael had been bracing himself for, they could hope to have a healthy child. A baby boy whose condition could be healed, who was going to live and grow and know him. A *son.* He was filled with an incredible, overwhelming joy, almost too great to contain, and then realisation slammed through him, leaving him breathless.

This changed everything.

Allegra walked from the doctor's office in a daze of hope and incredulous relief.

'I can hardly believe it,' she said as they climbed into Rafael's waiting limo. 'Our baby is going to be *healthy...*' Again she was both laughing and blinking back tears, overcome by it all as she had been in the doctor's office.

It had been such an intense twenty-four hours, with the concert last night and then learning they would discover the amnio results today. And then those wonderful moments when Rafael had put his hand on her belly and felt their baby kick. Everything in Allegra had ached at the look on his face, and when he'd held her for the rest of the night she'd felt so safe and secure. She'd never wanted that feeling to end.

Since then she hadn't let herself think about any of it or what it meant, because the doctor's appointment had taken precedence. Now she glanced at Rafael and saw the frown that settled between his brows, noted the hard line of his mouth, and unease rippled through her.

She'd opened a part of herself to Rafael last night, had let him in, let him affect her, let him *matter*. All the things she'd promised herself she wouldn't do. It had felt so right, but now she feared she was going to pay the price for her trust and need. And so she scrambled to erect some barrier, find that much-needed distance. And yet how could she, when their baby was healthy? When every emotion she had was scraped raw?

'Rafael?' she asked cautiously. 'You…you are pleased, aren't you? About the baby?'

'Yes, of course. Pleased and relieved.' He paused, swinging his hard, amber gaze towards her and pinning her with it. 'But you realise, Allegra, how this changes things.'

It was more statement than question, and it made her blood freeze. The look on his face was hard and unrelenting. He looked as he had when he'd ordered her out of his hotel room, and she felt the way she had then, uncertain, vulnerable, confused. 'What…what do you mean?'

Rafael's gaze remained unyielding as he answered. 'Before this news the situation appeared temporary. It had an ending point, sadly.' His gaze flicked away from her to the window where traffic streamed by in a blur of colour and sound. His jaw hardened, his profile reminding her of a Roman statue, perfect and cold. 'Now the situation is ongoing and permanent, and that changes things between us, naturally.'

Allegra swallowed hard. Yes, she understood that. Now they would have a healthy child together, a child who would, God willing, live to adulthood. A child they would somehow have to raise together, because it was obvious Rafael wanted to be involved. And Allegra wanted him to be involved. She knew the searing loss of a father. She wouldn't subject her child, her son, to it, if she didn't have to.

And yet…how was this going to work? What was Rafael saying?

And what if he walked away from her and her son, just as he had before?

'Of course,' she said stiffly, 'we'll have to come to some arrangement.' Surely they could, although right now she could not imagine what kind of custody arrangement would actually work. She was in New York and Rafael lived in Sicily. They could hardly pass a baby between continents like some parcel, and she wouldn't want that anyway. Anything else, however, was unthinkable.

'Arrangement?' Rafael swung back to subject her to a cold stare. 'I am not interested in *arrangements*.'

His eyes resembled shards of glittering amber as he kept his gaze on hers. 'I… I don't understand,' Allegra said, although she was afraid she was beginning to. Here was the ruthless man who got what he wanted, who took over a failing company, who kicked a woman to the door. Here was the father of her child.

'I'm not going to be fobbed off with some custody agreement,' Rafael stated. 'I would not wish such a thing on any child, and certainly not mine. I'm not going to be satisfied with weekends or holidays, an evening here or there.'

'I think you're being extreme,' Allegra protested. 'Plenty of children have divorced parents and they grow up well adjusted and happy. We can find a way forward that suits us both…'

Rafael arched an eyebrow. 'Was that your experience?'

She bit her lip, caught by the admission. 'That was different.'

'How?'

'Because we wouldn't be getting divorced. Our child wouldn't know one thing and then have to learn another. There wouldn't be a sense of loss, because it would be how it always was, our son's normal.'

His lip curled. 'My lack of involvement would be normal?'

Allegra looked away. 'Why does it have to be your lack of involvement? Surely we can work something out.'

'How? You live in New York and I live in Sicily. A baby's place is with his mother, I recognise that. So what happens? I get our son when he's two or three? Four? Five?'

'No.' The word was torn from her, trembling and indignant.

Rafael gave a nod of cold satisfaction.

'You wouldn't want that either. You don't want to share our child, and neither do I.'

Realisation crept coldly through her, a seeping mist obscuring rational thought. She understood what he was saying, and yet… 'Then what are you suggesting?' she forced herself to ask.

'I want to be involved in our son's life, Allegra,' Rafael stated. 'Completely involved. You cannot deny me that. You will not.'

Allegra stiffened, hearing an implied threat in the words. 'And if I do?' she dared to ask.

'Do not even think of it.' Rafael's voice was a low thrum of grim intent. 'You do not want to experience the full force of my anger and power.'

'Wow.' She let out a shaky laugh, amazed and horrified at how they'd got to this place. Last night he'd held her so tenderly, she'd been halfway to caring about him. Trusting him. Today he was the merciless stranger who had kicked her out of his bed. There was a lesson to be learned here. She'd thought she'd learned it already, but it seemed she hadn't taken it in, not fully. 'You're bringing out the big guns, aren't you? And I thought I'd felt your *anger and power* once before.'

'Not even close,' Rafael answered coolly. 'Trust me.'

Never. The limo had pulled up to the hotel. Allegra gazed at the elegant building overlooking Central Park, and felt as if she were about to enter a prison, one to which Rafael held the keys. She couldn't go inside, not willingly.

'We can discuss the necessary arrangements,' she told Rafael in as dignified a tone as she could manage. 'Of course I want to accommodate you as best as I can. I want our baby to have an involved father as much as you do. A completely involved father. We can work something out, Rafael. I know we can.' A bellboy came forward to open her door. 'But I also want to return to my life,' Allegra said as firmly as she could. 'My apartment, my job. Now that we know things are okay there's no need for me to stay here.' And she could use some distance from Rafael and his autocratic commands, his unsettling presence. She moved to get out of the car and Rafael stayed her with one powerful hand encircling her wrist, the proprietary touch shocking her.

'You don't understand, Allegra,' he informed her in a lethal tone. 'You're not going back to your apartment or your job or even your life. As soon as possible you're coming to Sicily to live with me...as my wife.'

CHAPTER EIGHT

ALLEGRA STOOD IN the centre of their hotel suite, her whole body trembling. *As his wife?* The words he'd spoken moments ago in the limo reverberated through her. With no choice but to get out of the car and deal with this head on, she'd stalked up to their suite and then turned to face him, every atom of her being radiating outrage. Shock. *Fear.* Rafael, on the other hand, looked cool, calm and completely in control.

It was impossible. *He* was impossible. How could he issue such an outrageous command without batting an eyelid? Even now Rafael was shrugging off his jacket and heading for his laptop, as if it were a normal business day. As if their whole world hadn't shifted on its axis.

'Rafael.' Her voice trembled along with her body. 'You can't… *I* can't…'

He didn't even look at her as he answered, 'You can and you will.'

'Just like that?' Her voice rang out. 'You want me to leave everything and marry you? That was your *proposal*?'

Irritation flickered across his face as he turned to her. 'Don't be melodramatic.'

'Don't be *insane*,' she snapped, well and truly angry now. Anger felt better and stronger than the fear that surged right beneath it. Because even now she was afraid Rafael would win. He was richer, stronger, more powerful. And so far he'd achieved everything he'd wanted. Nothing stood in his way, and yet Allegra clung to her ground. She had to, because the alternative... 'I'm not marrying you.'

Rafael regarded her levelly for a long, tense moment. Then he shrugged and went to sit down on one of the plush sofas. 'Fine, let's talk about it. What are your alternatives, do you suppose?'

On shaky legs Allegra moved over to the sofa opposite him and sat down. 'To stay in New York and live my life.'

He arched an eyebrow. 'Working in a café for most likely little over minimum wage, and living in a studio flat in an insalubrious neighbourhood?'

'It is not insalubrious,' Allegra snapped. 'For heaven's sake, talk about being melodramatic.'

'I am not having my child raised in a near-slum.'

All right, maybe her street wasn't the fanciest in Manhattan, but it was hardly a slum. 'You're being ridiculous.' In all sorts of ways.

'And I think you're being ridiculous,' Rafael countered coolly. 'What about your job, Allegra? How do you propose to continue working with a newborn baby, one that will have particular and crucial needs at the start, and maybe after that as well?'

'I'll take time off, naturally.' She lifted her chin, determined to remain strong. Defiant. She'd meet every challenge he threw at her.

'And do you get maternity benefits with your job? Proper healthcare coverage?' He sat back against the sofa cushions, the twist of his mouth belying the dangerous emotion she saw sparking in his eyes. Despite his level tone, his reasonable demeanour, she had the feeling that he was angry. Very angry.

He was also right. Her job provided healthcare, but it wasn't the best coverage and she wouldn't get much time off after their son was born, plus she couldn't afford the kind of childcare she knew she'd need. All things she hadn't yet had time to think about, much less sort out. She looked away, silently fuming, saying nothing.

'You clearly haven't thought this through, Allegra. Unless you intended to rely on your mother's scant generosity?'

'No.' The word was squeezed out of her throat. She hadn't thought through all these details, at least not enough, mainly because she'd just been trying to struggle through her pregnancy.

And now, thanks to Rafael, she had to think about them immediately. Allegra took a deep breath, trying to steady her jangling nerves. 'I'll admit there are some difficulties,' she said as calmly as she could. 'But that doesn't mean the only other option is living in Sicily as... as your wife.' A blush swept over her entire body at that thought. *Marriage.* In all the possible scenarios she'd envisioned, that one had never even crossed her mind. Yet Rafael now seemed to think it was a foregone conclusion.

'Then name one option that would be acceptable to us both,' Rafael stated.

'I can't,' Allegra retorted, 'because you're being so unreasonable.'

'*I'm* being unreasonable?' Rafael leaned forward, his tawny eyes glittering. 'What if you are the one who is being unreasonable, Allegra? You seem to think it is your right not to have to make any changes or adjustments to your life circumstances for the sake of your child. Is that reasonable?'

'I didn't say—'

'You want to stay in your tiny apartment, walking up and down six flights every day?'

'Plenty of women—'

'Where would you even keep a stroller? Or a cot? That place is minuscule. There isn't room for a baby, and you know it.'

Her lips trembled and she pressed them together. 'I could get a bigger apartment, then.'

'Can you afford it? Or are you expecting me to pay for it—to fund your freewheeling lifestyle while I take whatever scraps I can? What do you think is going to happen?' Rafael demanded, his voice like the lash of a whip. 'I fly over to New York for occasional visits? I don't get to know my son until he's school age? Impossible. I refuse.' He glared at her, his whole body radiating both determination and rage. 'That is not how I intend to be a father.'

Allegra glared back at him, caught between misery and fury. All right, yes, she saw there were problems with her unthought-out plan. Of course she did. But she hated being railroaded into a huge decision, with Rafael expecting her to acquiesce instantly. *Marriage*…she'd never considered it. Never wanted to be that close to a person, that vulnerable—and why would Rafael?

But of course that wasn't the kind of marriage he was talking about. Even so Allegra couldn't countenance it. Couldn't let Rafael have that much power over her. Because, she knew, it would be power. Already he affected her too much. Made her want too much.

'You're not being fair,' she said quietly. 'I'm only four and a half months pregnant, and I've barely been able to keep a mouthful of food down until this last week. I'm sorry if I haven't worked out every last detail of my plan yet. And anyway,' she added, her voice rising, 'I didn't even know you were going to be involved at all until a few weeks ago.'

'Which begs the question why didn't you tell me,' Rafael returned, clearly unmoved by her words. 'I asked you specifically to tell me if you were pregnant. I told you I wanted to be involved in my child's life. And you chose to ignore me.'

'You also booted me out of your bed,' Allegra returned. 'Is that the kind of man I want in my child's life?'

'Now you have no choice.' Angry colour appeared in slashes on Rafael's high cheekbones. 'And no matter how I treated you on that night, Allegra, you had no right to deny me my child. There is a world of difference between ending a one-night stand rather abruptly and refusing me access to my son.' His jaw was bunched, his mouth a hard line. 'Even you should acknowledge that.'

Allegra stared at him, chilled to the very bone by the dangerous glitter in his eyes, the harsh, implacable certainty in the set of his features. The man who had treated her so tenderly, who had cradled her last night was gone. Vanished, as if he'd never been, and perhaps he hadn't. Perhaps that Rafael had been no more than an expedient mirage. She knew what it was like for people to change. To show their true colours.

'And yet you want me to marry you,' she stated shakily. She felt sick and dizzy, her skin clammy and cold. All the relief at their son's good health had drained away, leaving a dark-edged terror in its wake. The future loomed, menacing and more and more certain. Rafael would not be dissuaded.

'Marrying me is the sensible option,' Rafael answered. 'The only option. I want to be involved in my son's life, Allegra. Completely involved. He's my heir—'

'Your *heir*? It's not as if you're some king,' she interjected. Rafael's gaze narrowed.

'I am CEO of a multi-billion-euro empire. I intend to pass that on to my son, raise him to follow me into what would become a family business. He is my heir, and he is going to be raised in Sicily by both his parents.'

Staring at him, seeing how utterly implacable he looked, Allegra realised how trapped she really was. Rafael had all the power, all the money. If he wanted to— and at this point she wouldn't put it past him—he could use the force of his influence to take complete custody of their child. She could resist all she wanted or dared, but she'd still lose in the end. Maybe even lose her own child.

She pressed her hands to her temples, a crashing headache beginning its aching pulse. 'I need to think,' she muttered. 'And I need to lie down. I'm tired, and not everything is certain, Rafael. The doctor said I'd have to undergo some tests later this week.'

She rose from the sofa, stumbling slightly, and in one quick, fluid movement, Rafael rose to grasp her arm and steady her.

'Rest is a good idea,' he murmured. 'I'll make you some herbal tea to help settle you. Chamomile is what you like, isn't it?'

She glanced up at him in confused disbelief. Who was this man? 'Don't do this,' she whispered. 'Don't be horrible one moment and kind the next. I don't understand it. I can't take it.' *Not again.* With what felt like superhuman effort she shook off his arm and walked alone to her bedroom, closing the door behind her.

Rafael stared at the closed door and swore under his breath. That had not gone as he'd hoped or wanted. Yet what else could he have done? He wasn't going to negotiate, not about something as important as this. He certainly wasn't going to settle for some custody arrangement. And trying to woo Allegra with false words and oozing sentiment had felt like a waste of time and, well, *wrong*.

When he'd learned their child would be healthy all his protective instincts had risen to a clamour inside him. He needed Allegra and their son with him. He needed to be in control. He needed to make sure nothing went wrong. Things would be different this time. He would be different. But first he had to get her to agree.

Impatient and yet resolute, Rafael stalked to the kitchen and switched on the electric kettle. He'd make her the promised cup of tea, at least, to show he wasn't a complete boor.

But when he tapped on Allegra's door and the quietly opened it, he found she was already fast asleep, her Titian hair spread across the pillow, one hand tucked under her cheek, golden-red lashes feathering her pale cheeks. She looks so vulnerable and lovely it made something in him twist and tighten, and he promised right then that he'd make it up to her, to *them*. They could make this work. They would.

Several hours later Allegra opened the door to her bedroom and appeared, yawning and sleepy. Rafael turned from where he'd been trying to do work on his laptop and mostly failing.

Now he tried for a neutral expression as he watched her stretch, the thin T-shirt pulling across her breasts. 'Did you sleep well?'

'Yes, surprisingly. I didn't realise quite how tired I was.' She went to the kitchen and returned with a glass of water, her hair tumbling about her face in corkscrew curls, her face now set in serious lines. 'You asked me what my life would look like if I stayed in New York,' she said as she curled up on the sofa opposite him and took a sip of water. 'So now I want to ask you the same thing. What would my—our—life look like if I come with you to Sicily?'

Relief and hope expanded in his chest, made his head light. *She was going to agree.* He kept his expression steady, his voice mild as he answered. 'We would live on my estate in the mountains above Palermo. It is spacious and comfortable, with every luxury to hand. A large garden, a pool, every amusement for a growing little boy.'

Allegra nodded slowly, looking less impressed than Rafael had expected or wanted her to be. 'And what about schooling?' she asked. 'When the time comes? And friends?'

'Of course those as well,' he answered. 'There are plenty of good schools in the area and if we could not find one that was to our satisfaction, I would be willing to consider other options.'

She arched a delicate eyebrow. 'Such as?'

Rafael shrugged, his mind racing. He felt that Allegra was looking for something from him and he didn't know what it was. 'We could relocate, within reason. To Rome or Milan, perhaps. I have offices in both cities.'

'Or New York?'

He hesitated, sensing a test. 'The majority of my business is in Europe,' he said finally. 'A relocation to New York is not out of the question for some time in the future, but not now.'

She nodded, her lips pursed, and Rafael waited. 'What about me?' she finally asked. 'What would my life look like in Sicily, Rafael?'

He hesitated, wanting to say the right thing—but what

was it? 'You will need for nothing,' he said with a shrug. 'Clothes, jewels, whatever you like. They're yours.' Her mouth twisted and he realised he'd said the wrong thing. Allegra had not been particularly impressed or even interested in clothes or jewels, as far as he could see. *So what did she want?*

The women he'd dallied with in the past had been only interested in material possessions, a diamond bangle, a funded shopping spree in a designer boutique, but he knew Allegra was different. 'And of course you can make the house your own. Decorate it as you wish. Garden...' What else might she want to do? 'Music,' Rafael said at last. 'You can have your own music room. Play as much as you want. Host concerts, even.' He was practically babbling, and was irritated with himself for being so pathetically *eager.* She regarded him quietly, saying nothing, offering no encouragement.

'Why don't you tell me what you want?' Rafael bit out. 'Instead of looking disappointed because I can't read your mind?'

She flinched at his tone and he silently cursed himself. What did she want from him? He could give her everything. Everything but love. Rafael stiffened, appalled at the thought. Was that what Allegra was holding out for? Some ridiculous, romantic fairy-tale? Surely not.

'I don't know what I want, Rafael,' Allegra said quietly. 'This is all so unexpected. I haven't had time to process any of it properly. I'm still reeling from the news about the amnio results.' She let out a weary sigh. 'I know you don't want to, but please give me a little time to catch up.'

'Fine.' He bit the word out, still tense. 'But I do need to return to Palermo as soon as possible.'

'Then maybe you should return and I'll come later,'

Allegra countered. 'Why must we rush things? We could at least get to know one another first…'

'With me in Palermo and you here? No.' Rafael shook his head, resolute. She would just find an excuse to stay in New York. The thought, stupidly, hurt. 'I want you where I can see you, Allegra. Where I can protect you and take care of you and our son.' His voice thickened, much to his shame. 'That is important to me.'

Her expression softened as her silvery gaze swept over him. 'You have far more of a protective streak than I ever realised.'

'I do. I don't want to let you or our child down.'

'And you're afraid you will?'

'No.' He rose from his desk, determined to end this conversation. It had all got stupidly emotional, and he hated that. He didn't do emotion. It was for the weak. He'd learned that to his eternal cost with his father, when he'd goaded him with his childish complaints. When he hadn't been able to stop what had happened next. *Enough.* There was nothing to be gained by thinking of that now. 'I will never let that happen, Allegra. At least in that, you can trust me.'

Allegra sat down across from her mother, her expression resigned and set.

'You're *what*?' Jennifer Wells screeched.

'I'm going to Sicily,' Allegra answered. 'With the father of my child.'

'But you don't even know him.'

'I know he'll take care of me and our son.' That was at least one aspect of Rafael's character that she was sure of. It had been three days since Rafael had issued his ultimatum, and Allegra had spent those days thinking long and hard about her future. *Their* future. When the further tests with a neonatal cardiologist had revealed the extent of their son's heart defect, which wasn't as simple as they'd hoped but still within the realm of good news, her choice felt even more limited.

She couldn't do this alone. She'd lived most of her life in determined independence, chosen isolation, *loneliness*, but she couldn't do this by herself, and she didn't even want to. But even more importantly she didn't want Rafael or her son to miss out. She'd been denied her father's presence in her life from the time she was twelve. Could she wilfully deny her son the chance to know his father, and Rafael the chance to know his son?

It would be the height of selfish cruelty to choose self-preservation over her family. Because it *was* a matter of self-preservation. Rafael held a power over her, one she didn't fully understand. She was attracted to him physically, of course, but she'd felt stirrings of something even deeper. When he held her…when he'd felt the baby kick… if she let herself, she could start to care for him, and that would be a disaster. Because there was every chance Rafael would walk away from her as her father had. But he wouldn't, she prayed, walk away from their son.

And so she'd told Rafael she would go to Sicily, but she wouldn't marry him—not yet, anyway. They needed to get to know one another before she made actual vows, agreed to that level of commitment. To her surprise, Rafael had acquiesced. Tersely, but still. She'd been half expecting him to frog-march her down the aisle.

Then yesterday she'd gone to her apartment and packed up what she'd wanted to take, which had been surprisingly little. Looking around the tiny space, she wondered at how she had ever thought she could have managed there with a baby. And yet how she was going to manage in this strange new life in Sicily? So much was unknown.

'I can't believe you're doing this, Allegra.' Jennifer's voice rang out in censure. 'This stranger…running away with him? Have you thought this through at all?'

'Yes, and it makes sense,' Allegra answered. 'Considering the alternatives.' She felt weary right down to her toes, and tomorrow evening they were leaving for Palermo. She'd already handed in her notice for her job, said goodbye to Anton, who had been her friend and boss for nearly ten years. He'd kissed her on both cheeks with tears in his eyes.

'Is Vitali being…difficult?' Jennifer asked after a moment. She looked on edge.

'Pragmatic,' Allegra said, even as she wondered why she was being loyal to Rafael. Perhaps because, in his own hard way, he was being loyal to her. And whether she liked it or not, they were a family now. 'As am I.'

'You remember what I told you about his father?' Jennifer said, and now she sounded diffident.

'He did business with my father and it didn't work out, you said.' But it was more than that. Blood on his hands. What had happened? How much did it matter? She couldn't ask Rafael now; things between them were tense enough.

'Yes, and your father didn't trust him.' Jennifer expelled a breath. 'I don't know the details, of course, but there has to be a reason for that. I got the sense that there might have been something…' She paused, pursing her lips. 'Criminal involved.'

'Criminal?' Allegra stared at her, appalled by this new revelation. 'What do you mean exactly?'

Jennifer shrugged, her gaze siding away. 'I don't really know, but soon after they did business Vitali went broke. He lost everything, and narrowly avoided prison. That's…that's all I know. Perhaps it's better buried in the past.'

It was more than Allegra had ever known, and underscored how little she knew Rafael or his history. How little he'd told her. She'd have to ask sometime, and while she didn't look forward to that conversation, she needed to know what she was getting into. What their child was getting into. She needed to trust Rafael…yet how could she, when she didn't know him? When she didn't like to trust anyone?

'That might be so,' Allegra told her mother, 'but Rafael has his own business and I really don't think it involves any criminal activities.' At least she hoped not.

'But you can't be sure.'

'No.' She couldn't, Allegra knew with a pang of true fear, be sure about anything.

CHAPTER NINE

ALLEGRA GAZED OUT the window of the passenger jet at the hard blue sky, not a cloud in sight, and tried to bolster her courage as well as calm her seething nerves. They were due to land in Palermo in less than an hour, and after a sleepless night in the first-class cabin she felt exhausted and overwhelmed.

'Do you need anything?' Rafael asked as he looked up from his tablet where he'd been scanning the morning news. 'Herbal tea? A hot compress?'

'I'm fine.' He'd been all solicitousness for the flight, but it was a formal, distant concern that set Allegra's nerves on edge. She felt like his patient, or perhaps his possession. Maybe both. And she was conscious, more than ever, of how much she'd left behind. Her job. Her life. Freedom and independence.

'How far is your villa from the airport?' she asked, and Rafael put his tablet aside.

'About an hour. A limo will pick us up.'

She nodded, gripping the armrests, wishing she felt more at ease. More confident that she was doing the right thing. She'd be living in the lap of luxury after all. Rafael had promised her just about anything she wanted. And yet…he could be such a hard man. Even when he was being kind there was a distance to him, a remoteness that made her uneasy. And she knew no one in Sicily other than him. Their baby wasn't due for over four months. What would she do all day? Could she be happy?

'Please don't worry,' Rafael murmured, resting one long, lean hand on top of hers. 'It will all be fine.'

Allegra nodded again. Rafael squeezed her hand, and the simple touch had the power to affect her, reminded her that despite all their differences they did have chemistry. Chemistry Rafael no doubt expected them to act on...but when? She couldn't even begin to think about *that*. Sex seemed like an impossibility, although the doctor had, with a smile and a wink, given them the all-clear.

'There's no reason,' he'd said, looking at them both, 'why you can't have a normal pregnancy from now until your delivery...and a normal sex life.'

Allegra had blushed and stared down at her lap. Rafael had said nothing. She had no idea what to expect from him, from anything, and it made her feel uncertain. Vulnerable. Which was a feeling she hated.

'Please prepare for landing.'

Allegra put her seat up as the steward went through the cabin and the plane began its descent. Below she could see Sicily spread out in a living map: dusty, rocky hills and towns with red-roofed buildings that looked as if they were clinging to the mountainside. It was unfamiliar and yet it struck a chord, reminded her suddenly and sweetly of her childhood in Italy. A soft sigh escaped her and Rafael gave her a sharp look.

'Are you all right?'

'Yes, I was just thinking about when I lived here. That is, in Italy.' She gave him a small smile. 'It feels like a lifetime ago.'

'You lived in Rome?'

'I lived in Rome during the school year,' she answered,

'and spent summers at our estate in Abruzzi. I loved it there.' The land had been harsh and rugged and unrelentingly beautiful, snow-capped mountains piercing a brilliantly blue sky. She'd loved the quiet, the sense of solitude and stillness and peace. It had spoken to her shy, solitary spirit.

'You missed it?' Rafael asked after a moment.

'Yes, especially because my first year in New York was so awful.' She shook her head at the memory, her mouth twisting.

'What was so awful about it?'

'Everything. My English was terrible, and the school was big and rough—I felt lost. I was teased too, but it helped when I kept myself to myself. Then I was just invisible.'

Rafael frowned. 'That doesn't sound like much fun.'

'No, but I've always liked my own company.' She paused. 'It's easier, isn't it, not to depend on anyone? Not to care.'

Rafael didn't respond, merely frowned and looked out the window. Allegra wondered what he was thinking and decided not to ask. Better not to share any more feelings than she already had.

The plane touched down with a bump, and for the next hour they were kept busy clearing Immigration and collecting their luggage.

By the time Allegra slid into the limo she felt exhausted, and although she'd meant to take in the scenery on the drive to Rafael's estate, she ended up falling asleep as the limo climbed narrow, twisting roads, making the steep ascent into the mountains.

When Rafael nudged her gently awake she discovered she was lying on the seat, her head in his lap, her cheek resting on his powerful thigh. Rafael's hand rested lightly on her hair. It felt wonderful and alarming at the same time, and she scrambled up to a sitting position as quickly as she could. 'Sorry,' she mumbled as she pushed tangled hair away from her eyes. She felt thick-headed, her body clock completely out of synch, and she had a feeling she looked like a disaster. 'I didn't even realise I'd fallen asleep.'

'You were tired. We're here now, and after the doctor checks you out you can have a proper rest.'

Allegra looked at him in confusion. 'The doctor?'

'I've put a doctor on retainer for the duration of your pregnancy. He's living in one of the estate's cottages. It seemed sensible, considering the remoteness of our location. Of course, Palermo's emergency medical facilities are less than an hour away, and I have a helicopter on the estate.'

She stared at him in surprise. 'But the doctor in New York said my pregnancy was normal, Rafael. This seems a bit excessive.' Which was massive understatement. She didn't need a doctor on call, surely. And yet Rafael looked obdurate.

Rafael flicked a glance at her. 'There is no harm in taking precautions. You want what's best for our son, don't you?'

Once again he was playing that trump card. Allegra decided not to argue. She was too tired, and she supposed there was no reason to mind having a doctor around.

Rafael opened the door to the limo and ushered her out, one hand resting on her elbow as he guided her towards the villa. Allegra paused on the portico, breathing in the warm, fir-scented air as she took in the curving drive that snaked through dense trees, the rolling, rocky hills visible beyond.

She turned to the house, a sprawling and imposing

villa of weathered stone, its double doors of ancient, scarred wood now flung open. A smiling, red-cheeked woman, her greying hair piled on top of her head in a round bun, gave them both a wide smile while next to her a tall, lanky man nodded and bowed.

'This is Maria and Salvatore, my housekeeper and groundsman,' Rafael explained to Allegra. He spoke in Italian, which he hadn't done with her all the time they'd been in New York, and even though it was her native language, after so many years in America it took Allegra a moment to make the adjustment.

Maria came forward, exclaiming about her bump, and then kissed her soundly on both cheeks. Salvatore bowed again. The exchange heartened Allegra, and made her feel a little less alone.

'Now is not the time for a tour,' Rafael said. 'Since you are tired. I'll show you your room and then summon the doctor.'

'I'm fine…' Allegra protested, because now that she was here she wanted to explore. From the soaring foyer she could see a comfortable-looking lounge with huge sofas in cream linen and French doors overlooking a terrace. On the other side she saw the cheerful yellow walls of a large kitchen, and another set of French doors leading to what looked like a large vegetable garden. All of it made her want to see and know more. She felt the stirrings of excitement, which was a welcome change from all the apprehension.

'You need to rest,' Rafael said, clearly brooking no argument, and with his hand on her elbow he guided her up the curving stairs to a large bedroom. While he went to fetch the doctor, Allegra explored the room—it was every bit as luxurious as the one she'd enjoyed in the hotel back in New York.

There was a huge king-sized bed on its own dais, a massive fireplace that would make the room cosy in winter, and wide windows whose shutters were open to the tumbling gardens below. She rested her elbows on the stone sill as she took in the infinity pool sparkling under the sunlight, and the tangle of bougainvillea and hibiscus that covered the steep hillsides. The air was warm and dusty, scented with rosemary and pine. She felt as if she'd stumbled into paradise.

'The doctor will examine you now.'

Allegra turned to see a stern-looking, white-haired man with an old-fashioned black bag standing in the doorway, and her heart sank. Determined to be as accommodating as possible, she submitted to a battery of routine checks while Rafael watched.

'I really am fine,' she said as the doctor tucked his stethoscope away. 'Everything's fine.'

'Well?' Rafael turned to the doctor for his verdict, and Allegra gritted her teeth. Since when had she become incapable of speaking for herself?

'She's a little dehydrated,' the man said. 'And she needs some rest.'

Rafael nodded. 'Thank you.' He turned to Allegra once the man had thankfully left. 'I'll have Maria bring up some water. You should drink at least two glasses.'

Allegra folded her arms. 'I'm capable of making my own decisions, Rafael.'

His mouth thinned as he arched one dark eyebrow. 'You are fighting me on this small matter?'

'Yes, because you're treating me like an idiot. I don't need to be fussed over by a doctor every moment.'

'I simply wanted you to be checked out after our travel. What is the problem?'

She stared at him, frustrated, because he made it

sound so reasonable. It was his attitude she didn't like, the high-handed way he dealt with everything. With her.

'The problem is you're being aggravatingly bossy.'

'I am caring for our child.'

'Which is very important to you, I know. I get that, trust me. But you can't…you can't be in control of everything.'

Rafael bit back a response and then looked away. 'This is important to me, Allegra,' he said after a moment. 'I don't want to fail in my duty as a father. Please…indulge me.'

A bleak look had come into his eyes, and it made her wonder what hidden hurts Rafael was keeping from her. Or was she just being fanciful, and he was simply an arrogant, autocratic, domineering man? From the obdurate look on his face Allegra knew she'd get nowhere pressing the point now.

'Fine, I'll indulge you,' she said wearily. 'At least in this.'

Several hours later she woke from a deep sleep and stretched languorously. Long, golden rays of late afternoon sunshine slid across the floor. She'd been asleep for hours, so clearly she'd needed the rest.

Allegra got out of bed and went to explore the huge en suite bathroom, enjoying the enormous marble walk-in shower. Dressed in a strappy sundress, her hair damp and curling about her shoulders, she headed downstairs in search of Rafael.

She didn't find him, but she did see Maria in the kitchen, and the housekeeper bustled around to have Allegra sit at the round kitchen table and then plied her with iced tea and fig cookies.

'Something smells delicious,' Allegra said.

'Ah, it is a welcome feast for Signor Vitali and his lovely lady,' Maria said with a smile. 'It has been a long time since I have been able to cook so much!'

'Is it?' Allegra nibbled a cookie, wondering how much she could press the housekeeper for information. 'Has Rafael not had...guests here before?'

Maria gave her a shrewdly knowing look. 'Signor Vitali has never had anyone here before. He has always been a very solitary man. Salvatore and I have served him for more than ten years.' She smiled fondly. 'He worked so hard, he had little time for anything else.' She nodded meaningfully towards Allegra's bump. 'Perhaps now that will change.'

'Perhaps.' Although Rafael had certainly immersed himself in work since he'd come back into her life. Despite his insistence that he wanted to be an involved father, Allegra wondered if he simply wanted to be in control.

Replete with cookies and tea, she wandered out of the kitchen to explore the villa—and find Rafael. She discovered the lounge she'd seen earlier and a media room with a huge flat-screen TV and a state-of-the-art sound system. A dining room with a table that easily seated twelve was empty, as was a smaller room with a cosy table for four. She slipped through the French windows onto the terrace that overlooked the infinity pool, breathing in the scents of bougainvillea and rosemary. The sun was setting, painting the sky with livid violet streaks, and she heard birds chirping in the tall, stately firs that surrounded the villa on most sides, the mountains towering above them.

But where was Rafael—and why did she want to find him so badly? Perhaps he intended for them to live separate lives here in Sicily, a prospect that filled her with a treacherous disappointment. She wanted to know what their future was going to look like…and, she realised, she wanted to know Rafael. It had been all right to maintain a holding pattern while they'd waited for the amnio results, but now they were meant to have some kind of life together. Rafael was insisting they marry, and while that prospect still filled her with fear, it also made her want to get to know the man she might be spending the rest of her life with, at least a little. So where was he?

Maria had started to serve dinner in the smaller dining room, several fragrant dishes that made Allegra's mouth water. Then she noticed the place setting for one.

'Is Rafael not eating?' she asked, hating how small her voice sounded.

Maria made a face. 'Signor Vitali said he needed to work tonight.'

So the feast was for her alone. Allegra sat at the table and nibbled course after delicious course, feeling sorry both for herself and for Maria, who had gone to so much effort for her employer. Why had Rafael refused to come down for dinner? Surely his work couldn't be that important. Was he avoiding her on purpose, setting the pattern for their married lives?

Loneliness swamped her at the thought. Already she was losing that sense of independence she'd maintained for so long. She wanted Rafael with her, needed his presence in a way that made her feel unsettled. She wasn't used to needing people. Depending on them. Perhaps it was better this way…except it didn't *feel* better.

At the end of the meal she took her decaf coffee out onto the terrace, curling up on a lounger as she watched the stars appear in the sky, like diamond pinpricks in a bolt of black velvet. He was avoiding her, she acknowledged with leaden certainty. He had to be. To absent himself all afternoon and then through the evening… He was telling her how he intended things to be, and Allegra didn't like it. If he was going to leave her alone, she might as well have stayed in New York.

She liked it even less when she woke up the next morning to an empty-feeling house. Maria was in town at the market and Salvatore was outside, working in the garden. Rafael was nowhere to be found.

She decided to go for a walk—only to be told, regretfully, by Salvatore that Signor Vitali had forbidden her from leaving the formal gardens, as the mountainside was steep and dangerous. Allegra looked at the high stone walls, the whole world shimmering out of reach, and realised she was truly trapped.

She stalked inside the villa, fury rising in her like a tidal wave. So she'd been brought to this beautiful estate to be kept as a prisoner. She didn't know what hurt most—Rafael's controlling attitude or his deliberate absence. She stewed for most of the morning while Rafael kept his distance, and then finally she'd had enough. She'd find him, and, by heaven, she'd tell him what was on her mind.

'Where is Signor Vitali?' she asked Salvatore, who looked shocked by her strident tone.

'He is working…'

'Where?'

'In his study, but he does not wish to be disturbed.'

'Perhaps he needs to be disturbed,' Allegra answered. 'Could you please tell me where his study is?'

'I don't think—'

'Tell her, Salvatore,' Maria said quietly, coming into the room behind Allegra. 'She is carrying his child. She deserves to talk to him. And Signor Vitali…he needs company too.'

With a shrug of his thin shoulders Salvatore pointed upstairs. 'The top floor. A room on its own.'

Allegra stalked upstairs, her anger giving her a boldness she hadn't known she'd possessed. A narrow, twisting staircase at the end of the corridor led to a single room on the villa's top floor, its heavy, oak door shut fast. She knocked on the door hard enough to bruise her knuckles.

After a pause she heard Rafael's gruff voice. 'Salvatore?'

'No. Allegra.' She turned the handle, gratified when it opened, and walked into the room.

Rafael's study was spacious, with wide windows on three sides offering stunning views of the mountains. A huge mahogany desk took up the centre of the room, and Rafael sat at it, his eyes narrowed, his mouth compressed.

Allegra planted her hands on her hips as she faced him. 'If I'd known you were going to imprison me here, I wouldn't have agreed to come.'

'Imprison?' Rafael arched one eyebrow. 'I'd hardly call this a prison.'

'I'm serious, Rafael. Since we've arrived you haven't shown your face once—'

'I have much work to catch up on.'

Allegra hesitated for a second, wondering if she was overreacting. Wondering why she wanted his company so much, why she felt so *hurt*. Then she took a deep breath and ploughed on. 'So why can't I even take a walk?'

Rafael's nostrils flared. 'These are simply measures to ensure your safety.'

'I'm not made of glass,' Allegra burst out. 'I'm not going to *break*.'

For a second Rafael's face contorted, and then he looked away. 'You don't know that,' he said quietly.

'Anything could happen, Allegra.' His voice went hoarse. 'Anything.'

Allegra stared at him in confusion, her heart twisting at the look of bleak despair on his face. 'Rafael...' she asked softly. 'What is it that you're so afraid of?'

'I'm not...' he let out a shuddering breath, wiping his hand over his face '...losing you. Losing our child.' He turned away, dropping his hand, the set of his shoulders resolute once more, that brief glimpse of raw vulnerability gone. 'We came close to losing this baby, Allegra, or at least thinking we were going to lose it. Him. I don't ever want to feel that again.'

She stared at him, wishing she understood more. Wishing she knew how to reach him. 'You can't control everything, you know,' she said quietly. 'You can't prevent accidents from happening, or just life. I need to live, Rafael—'

'You are living,' he cut her off dismissively. 'Enjoy the villa and all it has to offer. Lounge by the pool.'

'I don't want to spend every day *lounging*.'

His expression closed up. 'I really do not know what you are complaining about.' And with that he angled his body away from her, pulling a sheaf of papers towards him. So she was being dismissed, like some unruly servant. He wouldn't even look at her any more. This was how Rafael dealt with people. He wasn't overprotective, he was compulsively controlling. And it hurt to realise she was just a cog to him, something to move and manipulate accordingly. Stupidly it hurt, because she hadn't wanted to let herself care. Yet here she was, caring. Hurting.

She stood there for a moment, watching him work, seeing the way he'd completely blanked her out. It was as if she no longer existed. His gaze didn't flick to her once.

She felt the fury rise again, but with it something far worse. Despair. She couldn't fight this. Arguing with Rafael, just trying to have a reasonable discussion with him, was like battering her head—her heart—against a brick wall. Because now that she was here, now that she'd come into his life and brought him into hers, she wanted more than this. And she had no idea how to get it.

Without a word she turned on a heel and left his study, slamming the door behind her. The loud thwack as it crashed against the doorframe was satisfying even though she knew the gesture was pointless and childish.

She walked downstairs, fury still pounding through her, along with the despair. She wrenched open the French doors to the terraced gardens, causing Maria to bustle in from the kitchen, her expression alarmed.

'*Signorina*—'

'I'm just going for a walk.'

Maria frowned. 'Signor Vitali—'

'I don't care about Signor Vitali.' Allegra cut him off, wishing it were true, and she walked out of the house.

CHAPTER TEN

FROM THE WINDOW of his study Rafael watched Allegra stride through the gardens, her entire body rigid with affront. He fought the urge to run after her, insist she return to the villa. Keep her safe. He couldn't control everything, but he'd damned well try. The alternative was unthinkable.

His gaze narrowed as he saw Allegra make her way through the garden to the latticed gate in the high stone wall. He'd forbidden her from leaving the formal gardens, didn't want her to navigate the steep and rugged mountain terrain surrounding the estate. Cursing under his breath, he saw Allegra wrench open the gate and then stride through the forest, swallowed up by the trees and the dark.

He waited an hour before he went out looking for her, just to show how reasonable he could be. A tense, endless hour when his mind raced with worst-case scenarios and he did his best to stave off the panic he felt skirting the edges of his mind, blurring rational thought. Memories danced like shadows in his mind, of his mother, his sister, his father. Their faces, their words, closed doors, shattered hope.

With a muttered curse Rafael flung open the door to his study. He yanked on a pair of hiking boots and headed outside, the air hot and dusty and dry, the sun beating hard on his head. She shouldn't have been out in this heat. He didn't even know if she'd put on sunscreen. And what about a sunhat and proper walking shoes? What if she'd tripped or fallen? His stomach clenched hard and he tasted the metallic tang of fear as he followed her path through the gate, picking up her trail through the broken ferns and grasses along the mountainside. With each step his anxiety grew and his fists clenched at his sides. He felt deep in his gut that something was wrong, that something had happened on his watch. *Again.*

For a second he could see his mother's empty eyes, his sister's wasting body. His *father…*

Dammit, he couldn't keep opening the door to all that remembered pain. What was it about Allegra that brought it to the surface? He needed to lock that door tightly, so tightly, before the memories surged around him and he drowned.

He'd been walking for about fifteen minutes, calling Allegra's name, his voice starting to grow hoarse with panic, when he saw her. She was crumpled up at the bottom of a large boulder, one leg awkwardly angled beneath her, her head lolling back. Her eyes were closed but they fluttered open as Rafael ran towards her, cradling her head in his lap as he said her name over and over again, tears of grief and self-recrimination springing to his eyes.

Her eyes fluttered open and fastened on his. 'Next you're going to handcuff me to my bed,' she murmured. Her face was pale and waxy with a pearly sheen of perspiration but her tiny smile made Rafael's heart turn over. 'Just spare me the I-told-you-so, please.'

'Are you hurt?' Rafael demanded, his hands shaking as he ran them lightly over his body, looking for bruises or broken bones.

'My ankle,' Allegra answered on a shuddery sigh. 'It's not broken. At least, I don't think it is. But I tripped on that stupid rock and went sprawling.' She pressed one hand to her bump, her voice trembling and her face crumpling as she added, 'I think the baby's all right.'

Rafael's insides felt icy as he bundled her in his arms. She felt light and precious, a treasure he wanted to cling to for ever. *The mother of his child.* 'Let's get you home,' he said, and, scooping her up, he started back towards the villa.

The trip back to the villa was a blur; Allegra curled into Rafael, resting her cheek against the hard wall of his chest, taking comfort from the steady thud of his heart. The last hour she'd spent trapped in the woods, the trees dark and menacing all around her, her ankle throbbing, had been truly awful. She'd been afraid for their baby, afraid for herself, and she'd cringed to think of what Rafael's reaction would be. Yet it wasn't her freedom or lack of it she was worried about, she realised—it was Rafael. Something was driving him to act in so domineering a manner, something dark and desperate, and she feared in her impetuous folly she'd made it much worse.

To his credit, Rafael didn't lambast her then. He treated her tenderly, carrying her through the woods, and then calling to Maria to bring cool cloths and compresses and tea as soon as they arrived back at the villa.

The doctor came and looked her over, pronouncing the baby well, the steady thud of his heart on the Doppler wonderfully reassuring. Her ankle was sprained and the doctor bound it up and then gave her strict instructions not to put any weight on it for at least a week, which would undoubtedly please Rafael.

After the doctor had gone Allegra fell asleep, grateful

to retreat into oblivion for a little while. When she woke up Rafael was sitting by her bed, his head in his hands, his long fingers driven through his dark, unruly hair. The sight of him looking so exhausted, so unguarded made her heart squeeze in a way she wasn't used to. A shaft of yearning pierced her sweetly, although what she wanted she couldn't say. To comfort him, perhaps—but would Rafael even accept her comfort? What was between them now? What *could* be between them?

'Hey.' Her voice sounded scratchy and she licked her dry lips. She must have become a bit dehydrated out in the hot sun.

Rafael looked up, his bloodshot eyes widening at the sight of her. 'You're awake. Here.' He reached for a pitcher of iced water and poured her a glass, holding it to her lips.

'Thank you,' Allegra murmured, and drank. She scooted up in bed, pushing her tangled hair out of her face as she noted the haggard lines of his face, the bleak set of his mouth. 'I'm okay, Rafael,' she said quietly, and to her shock his face crumpled almost as if he might weep. 'Rafael…' she whispered, reaching out one hand, and even more to her shock he took it, his fingers interlacing with hers.

'But you could have so easily not been.' His voice was a ragged whisper as he clung to her hand.

'I behaved foolishly,' she said. 'I'm so sorry.'

Rafael shook his head, the emotion reined in now but still visible in the lines of strain on his face. 'I am the foolish one. You wouldn't have gone off like that if I hadn't driven you to it. If I had been more reasonable.'

'You shouldn't blame yourself…'

'But who else am I to blame?' Rafael returned starkly. 'I am responsible for you, Allegra, and for our child, whether you like it or not. I cannot shirk or ignore that responsibility. I did once before and I will never do so again.'

'When...?' The word was a breath of sound. She realised she wanted, needed to know what drove Rafael. What made him the man he was. She wanted to know so she could understand him, but also so she could comfort him. So she could help. The strength of her own feeling surprised her, but she didn't back away from it. This was too important. *They* were too important. At least she hoped they were.

'My mother,' he said after a moment. 'My sister, in a different way.' He pressed his lips together. 'I lost them both, when it was my sacred responsibility to care for them. I failed them, failed my entire family.' He looked away, blinking fast. 'If I seem too controlling, it's because I can't contemplate the alternative.'

Allegra felt tears sting her eyes at the pain she saw in Rafael's face, heard in his voice. She didn't understand everything but she knew he was hurting. 'I'm sorry,' she whispered, reaching up to brush her hand against his cheek. 'For all you've suffered.'

Rafael closed his eyes, leaning into her brief caress, and then he pulled away. Opened his eyes and didn't look at her. 'In any case,' he said, a stiffness entering his voice, 'I will relax some of the measures I put in place.'

'That still makes me sound like a prisoner.'

'You're not a prisoner.' Now his tone was touched with impatience. Their moment of bonding was well and truly over. 'You're living in the very lap of luxury. I hardly see any reason to complain.'

Allegra tried to tamp down on the frustration she felt rising again. 'Don't *do* that,' she pleaded.

Rafael looked startled. 'Do what?'

'*Change.* One minute you're all solicitude and tenderness and the next you're acting as if you can't spare two minutes to talk to me. It makes my head spin. And it reminds me—' She broke off, biting her lip, and Rafael's eyes narrowed.

'Reminds you of what?'

'My father,' she said after a moment. She leaned her head back against the pillow and closed her eyes. If he'd shared something of his past heartache, then so could she. 'My father because…because after he divorced my mother I never saw him again, as you know.' Her throat thickened and she swallowed hard. 'And before the divorce…he loved me. He acted like he loved me, anyway. He called me his little flower. He tickled me, he tossed me in his arms, he gave me presents and tucked me in at night…' She gave a trembling laugh and brushed at her eyes. 'To have his love, to feel so important, and then to be cut off completely…it was awful, Rafael. The worst thing that ever happened to me.'

'The loss of a father is a very hard thing,' Rafael said after a moment.

'How did you lose yours?'

'He… An accident.' He looked away. 'A terrible accident.'

Allegra wanted to ask more, ask about the history between their fathers, but in that moment she didn't dare.

'Your father left you that necklace in his will,' Rafael said after a moment. 'He must have cared, at least a little.'

'Yes, but I don't even know why he gave it to me.' Allegra smiled sadly. 'There was a note…he asked for my forgiveness, saying he'd cared more for his reputation than for me. But I don't understand that at all.'

'Who can say?' Rafael answered. His voice was

guarded, his jaw bunched. Allegra wondered what he knew and wasn't telling. Or was she being paranoid?

'I keep telling myself he really did love me. He must have loved me, but something happened…something that made him act the way he did, cutting us off. But I can't imagine what it was.'

'And I remind you of him.' Rafael sounded cautious and diffident, and realisation scorched through Allegra.

'Only because you keep changing,' she said quickly. 'It's not as if— You don't need to worry, Rafael, I'm not going to fall in love with you or something like that.' She felt herself blush hotly as Rafael jerked back, almost as if she'd slapped him. Clearly the prospect of her falling in love with him was horrifying. Allegra rushed to fill the ensuing taut silence. 'I'm not looking for love,' she hastened to explain. 'I'm not interested… I mean, any… relationship between us wouldn't have to have that. I wouldn't want it to have that. I want us to get along, of course, but… I'm not looking for love, not from you, not from anyone.'

She finally, thankfully, managed to make herself stop speaking. Rafael had sat back in his seat, his expression terrifyingly inscrutable.

'Why not?'

'Because love hurts,' Allegra said simply. 'Doesn't it? To let someone matter that much to you. To let them hold your heart…because hearts can break.' She let out a shaky laugh. 'I sound fanciful, I know, but the truth is I don't believe that old adage about it being better to have loved and lost than never to have loved at all.'

'So you've never been in love? Romantic love?'

'No.' She drew a quick breath. 'Surely you realised that, considering…considering I was a virgin.'

'There's a difference between sex and love.'

'Yes.' Although for her she wasn't sure there was. Her one experience with sex had been far too intense and emotional.

Rafael fastened his resolute gaze on her. 'In any case, we will have a proper marriage.'

A flush swept over her at the thought of what a proper marriage would look like. Feel like. Could she keep herself from loving Rafael, loving the tender, caring man he could be when he wanted to, if she gave her body to him again and again? 'I haven't actually agreed to marry you,' Allegra reminded him.

'Yes, but it's only a matter of time. For our son's sake, Allegra.'

He was so aggravatingly arrogant. Allegra closed her eyes, overwhelmed by it all. 'I asked you to give me time to get to know you,' she said. 'And for you to get to know me. But we can hardly do that when you hide away in your study all the time.'

'I'm not *hiding*,' Rafael snapped.

Allegra opened her eyes. 'Rafael, as soon as you'd brought me here you disappeared. I don't care how busy you are, that's just rude. And cowardly.' His eyes flashed fire and Allegra wondered if she'd gone too far. 'Let's just spend some time together.' Surely there was no real danger in that.

Rafael was starting to look seriously uncomfortable. 'What exactly are you suggesting?'

'An hour or two every day,' Allegra returned. That felt safe. 'Meals spent together. Evenings…some conversation. We had a little bit of that in New York, didn't we?' A very little. 'But you need to stop avoiding me.'

'I'm not avoiding you. I am a busy man.'

'Well?' Allegra pressed, not to be dissuaded. As nervous as she was, she knew she wanted this. 'That's all I want, I promise.'

He leaned forward, his eyes glittering. 'That's all? Are you sure?'

Allegra's breath caught because she recognised the look of ferocious intent in his eyes. Of course she did. She also recognised the hot swirl of longing she felt unfurl inside herself, a languorous warmth that was lazy and urgent at the same time, wrapping her up and making her want. *Him.*

She licked her lips, her throat and mouth turning dry. 'I'm... I'm not ready for that yet, Rafael.'

'The doctor said it was safe.' His gaze roved over her, assessing, probing, demanding.

'That's not what I meant.'

'I know.' He leaned back in his seat, the heat in his eyes turning to a slow simmer. 'But think about it, Allegra. It could be very enjoyable for us both. It *will* be.'

'I... I know.' She had no doubts on that score. How could she, when the memory of their one night together still had the power to scorch her? And yet...the memory of the awful afterwards had the power to scorch as well, in an entirely different and unwelcome way. Things had changed between them since then, but Allegra still didn't trust Rafael—not in that kind of situation anyway. And, she acknowledged, she didn't trust herself.

Rafael's mouth curled in a lazy smile as his gaze raked over her once more. 'Let me know when you are ready. It will be soon, I think.'

She looked away, unable to stand the heat of his gaze. 'I will,' she answered shakily, and then wondered just what she had promised.

CHAPTER ELEVEN

RAFAEL STARED UNSEEINGLY at the screen of his laptop as Allegra's words ricocheted around his head, as they had been for the last three days, since she'd said them. *You don't need to worry, Rafael, I'm not going to fall in love with you.*

Words that should have filled him with sweet relief—and they did. Of course they did. But they'd surprised him too, because he hadn't expected such cold, clear pragmatism from her. Allegra was sensitive, emotional, romantic—whether she realised it or not. And yet she'd stated very clearly, with great certainty, that she would never love him. That she *couldn't.* What the hell did that mean anyway? Was that because of her—or him? Because he wasn't worth loving?

It was a question he hated asking, much less answering. It was a foolish, romantic question not worthy of his time. He should be thankful that his wife-to-be was so sensible. So like-minded. Moodily Rafael shut his laptop and gazed out the window of his study instead.

It was a day of lemon sunshine and blue skies, and he was tired of spending it inside. Tired of mulling over everything Allegra had said.

In the three days since their conversation he'd made an effort to spend more time with her. It wasn't always easy, and their conversations were sometimes stilted and jarring, but he had to admit to himself he actually liked being with her. Enjoyed hearing her clear, crystalline laugh, seeing her infectious smile. She'd had much sorrow in her life, but she was made for joy. Joy he wanted to give her, whether it was a gift or a touch…or more. But did she want to receive it? Receive him?

Why was he thinking like this?

The sound of crunching gravel had Rafael rising from his seat. A delivery van was approaching the front of the villa, and he knew what it held. A smile touching his lips, he headed downstairs.

'What is all this?' Allegra asked as the delivery man began bringing in boxes.

'Your things,' Rafael said simply. 'I had everything shipped from your apartment.'

'You did?' She looked flummoxed.

'Did you think we would leave it behind?'

'I don't know. I suppose I did. I knew you were terminating the lease on my apartment.'

'But I thought you'd want your things around you.'

'I do. Of course I do.' She shook her head slowly, smiling at him with a pure radiance that felt like a spotlight on his soul. 'You can be so thoughtful sometimes, Rafael. Thank you.'

'Only sometimes?' he teased. Their banter felt new and fragile, but kind of wonderful too. Allegra's smile deepened.

'Definitely only sometimes,' she teased back. 'But your rate is improving.'

He laughed, and with all of the boxes brought in Allegra began to open them, exclaiming over everything like a child at Christmas. 'My books…my cheese plant!' She looked up at him with laughing eyes, making something in Rafael's chest expand. 'I've had this thing for years, you know.'

'It looks like it needs a little water,' Rafael said, and took it from her. 'It's been in a box for days.'

'Everything came so quickly.'

'Expedited shipping.'

'That must have cost a fortune!' she exclaimed, and he shrugged.

'I can afford it.'

He took the cheese plant to the kitchen and when he went back to the lounge, Allegra was sitting on the sofa, her cello case in front of her, a thoughtful look on her face. She almost seemed sad.

Rafael propped his shoulder against the doorframe, watching the way her face softened as she opened the case and stroked the buttery-soft wood of the instrument.

'How long have you had that cello?' he asked quietly, and she looked up, blushing at being caught out.

'Since I was nine. My father bought it for me.'

'Did he?' Rafael said quietly.

'Yes…he loved to hear me play.' She let out a soft sigh. 'Even when I wasn't very good, sawing away at it. He'd always clap and say "Bravo."'

'Perhaps you'll play for me sometime,' Rafael said, and saw her eyes flare in surprise. Then she shook her head with sorrowful but firm decision.

'No, I can't.'

Rafael tried to hide the expression of affront and even hurt he feared was on his face. 'I see,' he said, unable to keep his tone from turning cool.

'I haven't played in almost ten years,' Allegra explained. She rested her hand on the cello. 'Not since I was eighteen.'

Intrigued, Rafael straightened. 'Why not?'

She shook her head, her eyes downcast, and he didn't think she was going to answer. 'Because when I was eighteen I auditioned for Juilliard,' she finally admitted on a little sigh. 'Or I should say I tried to audition.' She kept looking downwards as she continued, 'I'd sent an audition tape, and I was invited in for a live audition, which felt huge. It was my dream, to play music. I've taken lessons since I was a small child.' She bit her lip, and Rafael held his breath, waiting.

'It was a big step for me, to send the tape in. I know it might not seem like much, but I was so shy, especially after…well, after my parents' divorce. Music was a personal, even sacred thing to me. It still is.'

'So what happened?' Rafael asked. He felt anxious on her behalf, wanting to hear a happy ending to the story, even though he knew there wasn't one.

'I froze.' She let out a shaky laugh. 'I got there and I couldn't play. It was as if I was paralysed. I literally couldn't do it. The examiners were kind at first, but then they were impatient, and then I was dismissed. And that was that.'

'But why haven't you played since then?'

'I just couldn't. It's as if… I don't know. I just lost it. The desire as well as the ability. If I played now you'd probably cover your ears.'

'I wouldn't,' Rafael said, meaning it utterly.

Allegra stroked the cello again and then closed the case. 'Anyway, silly as it seems, I still like having my cello, so thank you.'

'You're welcome.' Rafael was silent, trying to sift through his emotions—the sorrow he felt for the shy, vulnerable young woman Allegra had been. Empathy, because her father had turned on her just as he'd turned on Rafael's father, his father, and just as with his father, his family, that rejection had had consequences. Protectiveness, too—because he never wanted her to feel that kind of anxiety again. And lastly, stronger than either of those two, desire, different and deeper than any he'd known before. He wanted her to play again. He wanted her to play for him.

But what on earth made him think he deserved such a privilege?

The next week passed in a lovely haze. Allegra felt herself relaxing into everything, especially the time she spent with Rafael. While he still spent a fair amount of time in his study, or going to Palermo on business, he made an effort to make time for her.

One afternoon when Allegra's ankle was feeling better they walked into the nearby hill town to shop at the market. Allegra enjoyed the simple pleasure of inspecting fat, red tomatoes and juicy melons while Rafael followed behind her, a wicker basket looped over one arm.

The ancient, cobbled streets were charming, and the view of the twisted olive trees and dusty valleys below truly magnificent.

Rafael suggested they have a picnic, and so they bought salami and bread, cheese and olives and grapes, and took it all to a stretch of grass overlooking the valley.

'This is wonderful,' Allegra said as she stretched out on the grass and Rafael fed her bread and cheese.

'As long as you don't get sunburned.'

'Don't fuss,' she chided gently, because she knew Rafael was trying, and it tugged at his heart. At moments like this, with everything relaxed between them and the sun shining benevolently above, she felt a marriage between them could work. Maybe it could even be wonderful.

Was she falling in love with him?

The question reverberated through her. When Rafael was kind and gentle and tender, she felt it would be easy to fall in love with him. Easy and amazing. But what if he changed? He had before, and she didn't know whether she could trust him yet. More and more she realised there were reasons Rafael acted the way he did—reasons he hadn't shared with her yet. Although they'd talked about many innocuous things, he hadn't spoken again of his family, and she hadn't asked.

Now, lying on the grass, feeling sleepy and secure, she decided to broach the topic. 'Rafael…what happened between your father and mine?'

Rafael tensed, his gaze turning guarded. 'Why are you asking that now?'

'Because it seems important. And because the more time we spend with each other, the more I want to have no secrets, no hidden things.'

Rafael was silent for a long moment. 'And if you don't like the answer?' he finally said, his voice toneless, his gaze shuttered.

Allegra felt the first stirrings of unease. 'Why wouldn't I?'

'Because your father treated mine unfairly. Very unfairly.'

Already she was prickling. 'How do you know—?'

'I know.' His gaze was opaque as he turned to look at her. 'But even that much is hard for you to hear.'

'Yes…but that doesn't mean I don't want to hear it.' Allegra took a deep breath. 'I know he wasn't perfect. Of course I know that. Look how he treated me.'

'Yet you're still protective of him.'

'I never wanted to hate him.' She looked away. 'Maybe because I always hoped he'd come back. But he won't now, and I want you to tell me. Please, Rafael.' She held her breath, waiting, and finally Rafael spoke.

'Twenty years ago our fathers were in business together.'

'The mobile technology you mentioned.'

'Yes. Your father provided the science, my father provided the parts. They were partners, friends.' He paused, his expression still shuttered, although Allegra heard the emotion in his voice. Felt the tension in his body next to hers.

'And what happened?'

'Someone embezzled a great deal of money from the company account. Your father blamed mine.'

She searched his face, looking for clues. 'But you don't think it was him?'

'I know it wasn't,' Rafael returned swiftly. 'I know. But your father insisted he had it on good authority, and he let it be known my father was a cheat, even though he couldn't prove it. No one would do business with him any longer. Within months he was ruined, and we were destitute.'

Shock sliced through her, and for a moment she struggled with what to say. How to respond. 'That's why you bought out the company.'

Rafael's mouth firmed. 'Justice was served.'

She sat up, hugging her knees, her mind still spinning. 'Why didn't you tell me this sooner?'

'I didn't know if you would believe me. And,' Rafael admitted, 'I didn't want to hurt you. I knew you loved your father, even if that love was misplaced. Things didn't feel strong enough between us…' He paused, searching her face. 'Do you believe me?'

'Yes,' Allegra said after a moment. 'I do.' And she ached for all Rafael and his family had endured. 'But I also believe that my father must have genuinely thought your father was in the wrong. I don't think he would have acted in such a manner without good cause.'

Rafael made a sound of disgust. 'And do you still think he abandoned you with good cause, Allegra? Why can't you see the man for what he is? *Was?*'

She recoiled, shocked by the vitriol in his voice. 'What does it matter to you if I choose to believe he was a good man?' she demanded stiffly. She felt hurt, and she wasn't even sure why. 'Why can't you let me love him still?'

'Because in my mind he is a demon,' Rafael returned flatly. 'And I will never forgive him.'

They didn't talk all the way back to the villa. The last few days had been so lovely, so promising, and now it all felt flat and strained. Over the last few days she'd actually been starting to care about Rafael. She *still* cared, which was why their argument hurt so much. And, Allegra acknowledged that evening as she lay in bed unable to sleep, it hurt because she knew there was truth in Rafael's words. Why did she have to believe her father loved her, when everything pointed to the opposite? Why did she cling to that frail, pointless hope?

Sighing now, Allegra shifted restlessly in bed. The baby kicked, and she placed one hand on her bump, taking comfort from those fluttery movements. Tomorrow they were going to Palermo for a scan, and she was looking forward to the reassurance of an ultrasound, that lovely whoosh of their son's heartbeat filling the air.

But tonight she wasn't thinking about their baby. She was thinking about *them*.

The sudden, soft strains of music floating from downstairs made Allegra still in her restless movements. It almost sounded like...

Holding her breath, she rose from her bed and slipped

on the silky wrap that passed for a dressing gown in this hot weather. Even at two in the morning the air inside the villa held a remnant of the day's heat, although the tiles were cool under Allegra's bare feet as she made her way downstairs, following the haunting strains of the cello she heard.

Downstairs all was dark save for a single lamp burning in the lounge. Allegra hesitated on the threshold of the room; she saw Rafael sprawled in a chair, his long legs stretched out in front of him, his button-down shirt several more buttons open than usual. His hair was rumpled and a tumbler of whisky dangled from his fingertips.

'It's Shostakovich,' Allegra said softly, and he glanced up, his eyes bloodshot and bleary. He was, she realised, a little drunk.

'The third movement of the cello sonata,' he agreed. 'It reminds me of you.'

It was the piece they'd listened to before they'd made love. Allegra was jolted to the core by the fact that he was listening to it now—that he'd remembered, that he cared. 'Why do you need reminding?' she asked softly. 'I'm right here.'

'Are you?' The question hung in the air between them, hovered like a ghost. Rafael gave her a long look before he glanced away, taking a large swallow of his drink.

'Is this about this afternoon?' Allegra asked after a moment. 'Our argument?'

'What do you mean, this?'

'You're sitting downstairs, listening to sad music and drinking whisky.'

Rafael looked away. 'I couldn't sleep.'

'I couldn't either.' She paused, then decided to up the ante, even if part of her shied away from being so vulnerable. Admitting so much. 'The truth is, I think you're right, at least partly. I want to believe my father still loved me because the alternative…' She stopped, catching her breath, her heart starting to thud. Confessions like this were *hard*. 'The alternative is he didn't love me, and that means… I'm unlovable.'

Rafael lifted his head to skewer her with a burning stare. 'You are not unlovable, Allegra.'

'My own father?' She tried to keep her voice light but it trembled. 'Come on. Parents love their children. That's a given.'

'Maybe your father was incapable of love.'

'You really think he was a monster,' Allegra said slowly. Rafael didn't answer. She stared at him, trying to divine something from the resolute, almost resigned set of his features. 'I don't want this to come between us, Rafael. Whatever happened…it's in the past. Let's leave it there.'

'You were the one who wanted to know.'

'And now I do.' She drew a quick breath. 'Is there anything more? To know?'

A pause, infinite, endless. 'No,' Rafael said finally. 'Nothing important.'

Allegra supposed she should feel relieved but she didn't. She felt anxious and also sad because, whatever Rafael had just said, she sensed that there was still something he was holding back. She could see it in his face, the set of his shoulders. He was carrying a world of sorrow, and she didn't understand it. She didn't know how to comfort him. But she wanted to.

'Our son is kicking,' she said softly. She pressed both her hands against her bump, laughing a little as their baby kicked against her palm. 'He's a fighter for sure. He's kicking me right now.' She looked up at him, a tremulous smile curving her lips. 'Do you want to feel him?'

He hadn't felt their baby kick since that night after the opera. They'd barely touched at all since then. It felt like a lifetime ago.

'Yes.' The single word was certain and utterly heart-felt. Rafael tossed his empty glass onto the table before rising from his chair and coming across the room to kneel in front of her. The warm wash of light caught the bronze strands in his dark hair, the glint of stubble on his jaw. Allegra held her breath, conscious of his closeness, his heat, the yearning inside her to reach him, comfort him. She touched his hair, threading her fingers through its softness, drawing him closer to her.

Slowly Rafael slid his hands along her bump, the warmth of his palms seeping through the thin silk of her nightgown and dressing gown. 'You're bigger,' he said softly. 'Even in just a few weeks.'

'He is growing,' Allegra answered with a little laugh. 'And I'm eating better.'

'You're beautiful,' Rafael answered, his tone almost fierce. 'I've never seen anything so beautiful as you—as this.' His palms curved around her belly, cradling their unborn child. Allegra's heart bumped unsteadily as desire and something deeper flooded through her.

And then their baby kicked, a sharp flutter, almost making her wince. Rafael laughed aloud. 'That was him.'

'Yes.'

'It feels so strong. Stronger than before.'

'Yes, he's quite a kicker.'

'He needs to be strong. He needs to be a fighter, with what's ahead of him.' Allegra thought of the planned surgery, the frightening uncertainty amidst the longed-for news—and the knowledge, sweet and sure, that Rafael would be by her side for all of it. Dependence—trust—could be a wonderful thing.

'Yes. We all have to be strong,' she whispered.

'It will be all right, Allegra.' Rafael's hands continued to cup her belly as he looked up at her, his gaze burning and intent. 'I'll make sure it will be all right.'

Tenderness flooded through her at his fierce expression. She knew he meant every word, and while the future held no promises or guarantees, she believed him. She believed *in* him, in his sincerity, and that faith compelled her to touch her hand to his cheek, her fingers smoothing across the gentle abrasion of his stubbled jaw. 'I know you will, Rafael.'

A brighter light blazed in his eyes and he turned his face so his lips brushed her palm. A shudder went through Allegra; her body shook with the force of it, and her breath came out in a ragged gasp. To be touched again, and so sweetly, so tenderly…

'Rafael…' His name slipped from her lips, and then he opened his mouth and sucked on the tip of her thumb, and her whole body twanged like a bow that had been beautifully plucked. Around them the music swelled, a crescendo of sound to complement the one of sensation Allegra could feel inside her, building, *building*…

Rafael let go of her thumb to turn back to her, and Allegra didn't know who moved first. With his hands on her belly and their baby between them their bodies bumped together, mouths clashing, hands tangling. The kiss went on and on, desperate, urgent and hungry, a symphony whose notes played their sweet music through her body.

Rafael's hands went from bump to her hair and then to her shoulders and breasts, touching her everywhere, and yet it wasn't enough. She needed him, needed now more than ever to feel the closeness, the connection she'd felt once before. And she thought he needed it too.

Then he pulled away, just a little, but it was enough to make her cry out with the loss of it, of him.

In the shadowy light from the lamp she saw his face, his expression resolute, ready, eyes like fire, a silent question waiting for her yes.

She placed one trembling hand against his chest, felt the steady, comforting thud of his heart. Pressed. Rafael glanced down at her hand, fingers spread out, seeking. He covered it with his own. They remained like that for a suspended second, everything about to tumble into free fall.

And then he bent his head, his lips a whisper away from hers, still waiting for her response. Her yes. And she gave it, leaning forward to kiss him deeply, her hands tangling in his hair, the action a promise, a vow.

He tensed under her hands and mouth, his body like a bow while she was the strings. And then the music began, a glorious symphony, as his hands came up to grip her shoulders hard and his mouth opened under hers, turning her whisper of a kiss into a shout, a plea, a demand—she answered all of them with her mouth, her body, her heart. An offering of everything she had.

His mouth moved on hers as he propelled her across the room and then up the stairs; she stumbled on a step and with a muffled groan against her mouth Rafael scooped her up into his arms, drawing her against his chest. Allegra nestled there, feeling both precious and small, as Rafael carried her easily up the stairs and then down the hall to the master bedroom.

He put her down gently, steadying her as she swayed against him. The room was dark, moonlight spilling through the latticed shutters over the window, and they stood there for a moment, silent, breathing, his hands on her arms.

Allegra couldn't see the expression on his face but she

felt the emotion thrum through him as he tightened his grip on her shoulders.

'Are you sure?'

Everything so far had been a resounding and overwhelming yes, and yet still he asked. Allegra placed one hand on his cheek, her thumb smoothing the line of his jaw, learning him, letting him know how sure she was. 'Yes,' she said simply. *'Yes.'*

He didn't ask again. He simply pulled her towards him, his smile gleaming whitely in the dark, and then her clothes fell away; she kicked off her pyjama shorts as Rafael slid her T-shirt over her head.

His breath hissed between his teeth as he looked at her, and Allegra didn't feel self-conscious or big with her belly on display. She didn't feel vulnerable or exposed. Under the heat of his gaze she felt only beautiful.

His hands followed his hot gaze, smoothing over her dips and curves, learning the feel of her with slow, thorough deliberation. She shivered under his touch, his fingers sending sparks along her skin, and then she grew bold enough to touch him, hands flat upon his chest, fingers spreading and seeking the sculpted ridges of his muscles.

'I like that,' Rafael whispered. He remained still under her questing fingers, and with shaking hands she slipped the first shirt button from its hole, and then another and another, until his chest was bare and she was pushing his shirt off his bronzed shoulders, revelling in his body, satiny skin over hard muscle. She hadn't touched him very much that first night. She'd been too overwhelmed by it all, both the pleasure and the grief. Now she revelled in the hot, silky feel of him, running her hand across his chest, down to his abdomen, fingertips brushing the waistband of his trousers.

Rafael let out a groan and Allegra laughed softly,

amazed at how she was able to affect him. Now she felt powerful as well as beautiful.

'You were beautiful before,' he murmured as he reached for her, hands cupping her breasts, thumbs sliding across their aching peaks. 'And you are even more beautiful now, carrying my child.'

'You make me feel beautiful,' Allegra whispered, and then he was bending his head and Allegra slid her fingers through his hair as his lips sought and found her, causing a lightning bolt of pleasure to blaze deep down inside.

He scooped her up again—she felt boneless, weightless—and carried her to the bed. Deposited her on top of the duvet, the silk cover slithering and sliding underneath her. He shucked off his trousers and boxers, leaving her breathless. She'd seen him naked before but the sight still overwhelmed and undid her. He lay next to her and drew her into his arms, their bodies bumping and touching in all sorts of places, making her shudder. It felt so much. She'd known it would; it was why she'd resisted this before, because the intensity felt exquisite and painful at the same time, and she had to brace herself for the tidal wave, to keep herself from falling, drowning.

She'd been telling herself he wouldn't feel the same way, that sex wasn't as important or sacred for him, but in that moment as his fingers touched her face and his body arced into hers she believed it was. He couldn't touch her like this, give of himself like this, without it meaning something. She felt it in his kiss, in his gentle hands, in the love he lavished on her body, finding and plundering all of her secret places.

And then—yes, finally—he was inside her, so big and right she gasped out loud and he lifted his head, his gaze blazing down into hers. 'Are you all right? I didn't hurt you?'

She clasped her legs around him, pulling him deeper

into herself, accepting him fully, feeling complete. 'I'm all right,' she said. 'I'm…' But she had no words, because the feelings were coming faster and stronger now, wave after wave as Rafael began to move and Allegra matched his rhythm, reaching, *reaching*…

And finding. Finally, gloriously finding, her body shuddering with the force of her climax, Rafael's face buried in her neck as he murmured words of endearment and promise, their bodies intertwined in every way possible. How could you be this close to another human being, Allegra wondered, and *not* fall in love?

She tensed, though, as their heart rates slowed and Rafael, who had been bracing himself above her so as not to press against her bump, rolled onto his back. The sudden whoosh of cool air on her heated skin felt like an unwelcome wake-up call.

What now?

She waited, barely daring to breathe, afraid of this moment and what had it had meant before. Would he dismiss her from his bed? Leave her here alone? Then Rafael reached out one arm and hooked it around her shoulders, drawing her against him so her bump was pressed against his side, her knees snugging into the backs of his thighs. Allegra expelled a silent sigh of relief. It was going to be okay. More than okay.

Gently Rafael caressed her bump, his palm curving around the taut roundness of her belly. He laughed softly as their baby kicked.

'I guess something woke him up.' A smile in his voice, in her heart.

'I guess something did,' she answered, and wrapped her arm around his chest.

CHAPTER TWELVE

HE COULD SMELL THE BLOOD. Sharp, metallic. He didn't recognise it, though, didn't understand as he pushed the now broken splintered door open with his fingertips and took a step inside the room.

'Papa?'

His voice was soft, scared, the voice of a child even though he was sixteen years old.

'Papa...'

He saw his father's hands first, slack, hanging down, fingers dangling. Then the drops of blood on the desk, a delicate spray, making him think ink had spilled. As if anyone used ink any more, let alone a bottle of bright red. And then his gaze moved upwards and he saw his father's shattered face. Heard a scream rip from his throat— except it wasn't his scream, it was his mother's; she stood behind him, hands raised to her blood-drained face, and the awful unholy sound went on and on.

'Rafael... Rafael!'

The hand shaking his shoulder woke him up; he came out of the dream like a bullet from a gun, the screaming still echoing in his ears. Next to him Allegra's face was as pale as his mother's had been, pale and frightened.

'Rafael...' she whispered, and he shook off her hand, roughly, and saw her flinch. Hated himself, but he couldn't keep from doing it, from turning away. He swung his legs out of his bed and strode to the bathroom, slamming the door behind him.

In the mirror his face was pale, his forehead beaded with icy sweat. Bile churned in his stomach and he thought he might be sick. Thankfully he swallowed it down, bracing his hands on the pedestal sink as he lowered his head and took several steadying breaths.

He hadn't had that dream in years. A decade, even. He hadn't let himself, had closed that part of his mind right off. *Don't think of it*, because if you did you'd be lost, lost for ever, no coming back. He knew that. Knew if he remembered how he'd begged, begged his father… You couldn't go back from that. You couldn't recover, and so he refused to think of it.

Except, he acknowledged as he looked at his pale reflection in the mirror, he thought of it all the time. Not consciously, but it remained, a canker inside him, destroying everything good. Allegra had asked how her father could leave her, if he'd loved her. Rafael knew the answer to that in his own case times a thousand.

Because he didn't love me. Because I couldn't keep him from destroying himself. Because it's all my fault.

He'd seen how his mother had gone, and his sister too. They'd been swallowed up by their nightmares, their memories, until there had been nothing left but a pale husk of a self, and then nothing at all. He couldn't let it happen to him. But why the dream, why now?

Slowly he lifted his head and stared at his reflection. The answer was right there in his dazed face, the acidic churn in his belly. *Allegra.* Their lovemaking had been both sweet and powerful, and it had woken up long-dead parts of him, parts of him that remembered and felt and feared. Parts of him that he'd iced over with thoughts of justice, kept frozen with cold, cold fury. Now everything was waking up, a spring of the soul, and this was the result. Dreams he couldn't bear to have. Memories he didn't dare think about. *Weakness.*

He turned the taps on full blast and washed his face, scrubbed hard as if it would make a difference, and then turned them off again. He stared in the mirror, his eyes opaque, hard, and then he nodded once and left the bathroom.

Allegra was curled up on her side, her back to him, one hand cupping her bump. Thankfully she'd fallen asleep, but even in sleep her face looked sad, her mouth puckered, a frown feathering her brow. Rafael reached out to smooth a red-gold curl away from her cheek and then stopped. No need for that.

Tonight had been intense, and now he needed to get things back the way they had been, comfortable, enjoyable, but not threatening. No danger of scars being reopened, him bleeding again, bleeding right out. Take a step back, make it safe. That was what he needed to do... and preferably without hurting Allegra too much. But hurting Allegra couldn't be his main concern any more. Keeping those memories locked tight away was.

Allegra woke slowly the next morning, blinking in the sunlight streaming from the windows, her body aching in delicious places. For a wonderful moment all she remembered was the pleasure, intense and overpowering, of being with Rafael. The way he'd held her, moved inside her...

Then another memory slammed into the first, leaving her breathless. The nightmare he'd had, the way he'd shut her out. She turned and saw that his side of the bed was empty, the duvet pulled tight across, as if he'd never been there. Had he even come back to bed?

Slowly she got out of bed, sorting through possibilities. What should she do now? How should she act? Despite what they'd shared together last night, she didn't yet know how to handle this moment. Whether to press or pull away. She pulled on the thick terrycloth robe hanging from a hook in the bathroom and then gathered her clothes up, tiptoeing back to her room. Downstairs she could Maria humming in the kitchen, Salvatore's tuneless whistle. Nothing from Rafael.

Back in her bedroom she showered and dressed; her mind sifting through memories, options. What to do? How to feel? Taking a deep breath, she went in search of the father of her child.

She found him in his study, forehead furrowed as he gazed at his laptop, his headphone set dangling from his neck. Allegra stood in the doorway for a moment, an ache in her heart, in her soul. She wanted to walk easily into the room and plop herself into his lap; she wanted to smooth away the furrows on his forehead and kiss that lovely, hard, mobile mouth. She wanted it to feel natural, right, and yet she simply stood there, wondering and waiting.

'Did you have a conference call?' she finally asked, her voice high and nervous as she nodded towards the headset.

Rafael's gaze flicked towards her and then away, revealing nothing. Giving nothing. 'Yes.'

'Are you able to manage most of your business from here?' He'd only gone into Palermo a few times over the last weeks.

'I'll need to start going into Palermo more often.' He

turned back to his laptop in a way that felt like a dismissal. 'As well as Rome and Milan.'

'I could come.' She kept her voice light. 'I'd like to come.' Rafael didn't answer, and Allegra took a deep breath. 'Rafael…about last night…'

His mouth tightened, his gaze still on the screen. 'Let's not do a post-mortem.'

'Post-mortem?' Hurt flashed through her. 'Really, that's what you'd call it?'

'You know what I mean.'

'I'm not sure I do.'

Finally Rafael lifted his gaze from his laptop, but then Allegra wished he hadn't. His eyes were opaque, fathomless, hard. 'Last night was pleasurable, Allegra, for both of us. That's all that matters. Let's leave it at that.'

'Rafael…' She took a deep breath, dared. 'What about everything we talked about? What about the dream you had?' As soon as she said the words she wished she hadn't. An emotion flashed across his face like quicksilver, gone before she could decipher it, but she knew it hadn't been good.

'Forget about that,' Rafael said flatly, and as he turned back to his screen Allegra knew she'd truly been dismissed. Still she wouldn't give up that easily.

'I have a doctor's appointment this afternoon in Palermo,' she said. 'An ultrasound. Will you come with me?'

He hesitated, and for that heart-stopping second she thought he wouldn't. That he was turning away from her and their child completely, for a reason she could not understand. 'Yes,' Rafael said at last. 'Of course I will.'

Rafael sat tensely by Allegra as the technician squirted cold, clear gel onto her stomach. They'd barely spoken on the drive into Palermo, which should have suited Rafael perfectly but instead made him feel restless and irritable.

He didn't know what he wanted. The remnants of his old dream still clung to him, ghost fragments he couldn't shake. They made him want to keep a little distance between him and Allegra, but another part of him howled in protest. Hated hurting her…and hurting himself.

'Everything looks good,' the doctor said as he prodded the ultrasound wand on Allegra's burgeoning bump. 'Baby is the right size…a growing boy.'

The fuzzy black and white shape on the ultrasound screen looked like a proper baby. Head, body, hands, feet, even fingers and toes. He was sucking his thumb and kicking his legs and the sight of him made a pressure build inside Rafael, a pressure he couldn't even begin to understand. His hands curled into fists at his sides and he had to fight to keep his breathing even.

What was happening to him?

He felt too much. Happy. Thankful. Afraid. All of it combined inside him, making it hard even to speak. He focused on practicalities instead, helping Allegra up from the table, listening and nodding as the doctor asked them to book another appointment in four weeks' time.

'What shall we do now?' Allegra asked as they left the doctor's office for one of the city's sweeping boulevards.

'Do?' Rafael looked at her cautiously. 'What do you mean?'

'I'm sick of being stuck at the villa,' Allegra said. 'It's lovely, of course, but I've never been to Palermo and I'd like to see it properly. Can we look around a bit?'

Rafael looked at the tremulous hope on Allegra's lovely face and knew he'd have to be a monster to refuse. 'Yes,' he said, the single word drawn from him with reluctance. 'I suppose.'

For the next few hours they strolled down boulevards to squares with sparkling fountains, explored narrow alleys with charming shops and market stalls, and ended up at a café facing the lovely Piazza Pretoria, with its iconic fountain.

Allegra had kept up a steady stream of innocuous conversation the whole time, and Rafael hadn't done much more than offer monosyllabic replies. He was trying to maintain that little bit of distance but it was hard…and becoming harder with every moment.

As they left the café Allegra bent over to reach her bag under the table and the sound of fabric splitting rent the air.

'Oh, no.' She straightened, her face fiery, one hand clapped to her back. 'I've split my skirt,' she whispered, looking mortified, and Rafael looked down at her clothes, realised she'd been wearing the same few loose tops and summer skirts since he'd seen her back in New York.

'I think you need some new maternity clothes,' he said, wishing he'd thought of it sooner.

'I definitely need a new skirt,' Allegra answered, laughing a little. 'I'm not decent!'

'I'll ring a boutique right now.' He draped his jacket over her as he shepherded her from the café into the waiting limo. Moments later they were stepping into one of Palermo's best boutiques on the Via Liberta, several assistants already waiting to serve them.

Allegra was whisked away to a dressing room while Rafael sat on a white velvet settee, sipping champagne and scrolling through messages on his phone. This was more like it; he could take care of Allegra in the manner he wished to—and that she deserved—without actually having to engage her. She wasn't even in the room.

'What do you think?' Allegra's voice was soft and hesitant and Rafael looked up from his phone, his brain instantly going blank.

Allegra stared at the nonplussed look on Rafael's face and wondered if she'd made a mistake. All afternoon she'd been trying to reach him, keeping up a cheerful one-sided conversation, determined to stay positive.

They'd shared a connection last night. She had to believe that, had to believe it had been real…and that they could have it again.

In the boutique's dressing room she'd tried on several outfits, and then paused when the assistant had given her a sexy, slinky cocktail dress in soft black jersey. This one, she decided, she would show Rafael. See if she finally got some kind of reaction out of him. And now she was standing here, feeling faintly ridiculous, and Rafael was looking blank.

'Well?' She managed a laugh, and then she did a little twirl. 'What do you think?'

'I think…' Rafael cleared his throat. 'I think you look…' He stopped, shaking his head as if to clear it. Allegra smiled. As far as reactions went, she'd take it.

She went back into the dressing room to change while the assistant took her clothes to the shop's till. She was just pulling off the dress when the door opened.

'I think I might need help with the zip,' she said, and then to her shock Rafael answered.

'I think I can do that.'

'What are you doing…?' Allegra began, her breath coming out in a soft sigh as Rafael gently tugged on the zip and then pressed his lips to the nape of her neck.

A shudder went through her and she swayed on her

feet, flinging one hand out to brace herself as Rafael's mouth moved down her back.

'Someone will see…' she murmured as he slid the dress further down so it pooled about her hips. She could feel the hard, hot strength of his body behind hers and she leaned back, sagging against him as he kissed the curve of her shoulder.

'No one will see.'

'They'll know.'

'I don't care. I can't see you in that dress and not touch you.'

Touch her but not talk to her. She'd spent all afternoon trying to reach him but it seemed he didn't want conversation. He wanted this.

And so did she.

Rafael pressed against her and Allegra's eyes fluttered closed. *This* was rather wonderful.

'Signor Vitali? We just need your card…' The musical voice of the assistant floated towards them and they both tensed. With what felt like superhuman effort Allegra moved away. She stepped out of the dress and reached for her clothes as Rafael left in search of the assistant.

They didn't speak on the way home, twilight cloaking the mountains in soft violet. Rafael had withdrawn into himself again, his expression shuttered and distant as Allegra curled up in a corner of the limo and dozed.

Back at the villa he disappeared into his office and with a sigh she went to put away her new clothes, sifting through the day's events in her mind. Was she crazy to try to break through the wall Rafael seemed determined on putting up? Foolish to try for more when for her whole life she'd settled for so much less?

Allegra sank onto her bed, her unseeing gaze resting on the moonlit hills outside the window. She'd come to

Sicily because she'd believed it was best for her child. It had felt like a sacrifice, one she had been ready and willing to make.

But now? Now, when she'd felt so much pleasure and happiness and connection with Rafael? When she sensed his overprotective, controlling nature disguised a man who could be tender and loving?

Now she didn't want to come to some *arrangement* where they married and raised their child together, but lived as virtual strangers. Now she wanted a proper husband…and not just in bed.

But how to go about getting it? Was she strong enough to reach Rafael, to keep trying even when he pulled away? To face failure and rejection and keep holding on? She wanted to be. She wanted to make this work.

The click of the door opening had her turning, her surprised gaze arrowing in on Rafael.

'Is everything all right?' she asked uncertainly, because he looked intent and serious and a little sad.

'Now it is,' he said, and relief rushed through her, along with desire, as Rafael came towards her and took her in his arms.

CHAPTER THIRTEEN

ALLEGRA GAZED AROUND the nursery with a smile of satisfaction. She'd made decorating the room her project over the last week, and she was proud of what she'd accomplished. Pale blue walls with stencilled white elephants cavorting across them, and a cot bed in blond oak with fresh blue sheets ready and waiting, although she didn't actually know when their son would sleep in this room.

The doctors had said he'd be in the hospital for several weeks at least, and then she planned to keep him in a bassinet next to the bed for easy feeding in the night. Still, she was excited about the room, could picture herself in the oak rocker by the window, her son cradled against her chest, sunlight streaming through the window, the perfect picture of familial happiness. Almost.

A sigh escaping her, Allegra moved to the window and looked out at the dusty hills. It hadn't rained in weeks and the air felt stuffy. Now in her sixth month of pregnancy, she felt huge and awkward and more than a little grumpy. She rested one hand on her belly, trying yet again to banish the fears that skirted her mind, threatened to swamp her heart.

For the last few weeks she and Rafael had reached a holding pattern of spending their nights together—and what wonderful nights they were—and the days mostly apart. While she couldn't fault Rafael for his solicitude and kind concern, the remoteness she sensed in him, the careful emotional distance he always kept between them, made her want to scream.

She wanted more. She tried for more, but at every turn Rafael foiled her obvious conversational gambits, her clumsy attempts to increase their intimacy. Was this what love was? Because she thought—she feared—that she loved him. Or at least that she could let him, if he'd let her. If he opened up.

But since that first incredible night he'd stayed remote. He didn't even spend the whole night with her when they made love. He held her for a little while afterwards, but he never slept with her and every morning Allegra woke to an empty bed and an aching heart.

She wanted more than this. She needed more than this. After a lifetime of trying to avoid intimacy and love, here she was, desperate for it. The very situation she'd been wary of had happened, and it felt as if there was nothing she could do about it.

'I have to go to Naples.'

Allegra started in surprise at the sight of Rafael in the doorway of the nursery. She couldn't tell anything from his usual, closed-off expression, but even so she felt a ripple of alarm. 'Naples? Why? Is it business?' He'd gone to Palermo several times a week, and Milan and Rome once each.

There was a slight, taut pause. 'No.'

Allegra frowned. 'No? Then…what? I mean, why?'

Rafael didn't answer for a long moment. Allegra thought he wouldn't. 'My sister,' he said finally, shocking her.

'Your sister…but…' She trailed off, unsure what to say. She'd thought he'd lost his sister, that she'd died. He'd spoken about her as if she was gone, and so Allegra had assumed the worst.

'She's not well,' Rafael said abruptly. 'I need to…go to her.'

Allegra stared at him, sensing the dark undercurrent of anxiety under his terse tone, and she ached to help. Wanted to comfort him, but knew he wouldn't let her. And yet…if he kept her apart in this, what hope was there? How could she ever get closer to him?

'Let me come with you,' she said, part entreaty, part demand, and Rafael's face shuttered.

'No.'

'Why not?' Allegra challenged. 'Please don't keep shutting me out, Rafael, and pushing me away. If we're going to have a child together, if we're going to marry…'

'You are being melodramatic. I haven't pushed you away.'

'Not at night,' Allegra agreed, lifting her chin. 'Not in bed. But in every other way you have. You know you have. I keep trying to reach you, and you keep refusing me. Please, Rafael, don't refuse me in this. I want to support you…'

Rafael stared at her for a long moment, his expression both hard and bleak, and then he finally gave one quick, terse nod. 'Fine,' he said. 'But I need to leave within the hour.'

He shouldn't have let her come. A deep unease settled into Rafael's gut as he climbed into the helicopter after Allegra. He hadn't intended to let her come, of course he hadn't. The last thing he wanted was for Allegra to see Angelica, see his shame.

But, he thought with a resolve tinged with despair, perhaps it was better this way. Perhaps, instead of hav-

ing to maintain that careful distance, it would yawn between them, gape wide, because finally Allegra would
see just what he was and how he'd failed.

The call had come that morning, from a doctor in Naples who had found his sister's ID in her bag, as well as
his name and phone number. She'd been discovered in
an alley, unconscious, unresponsive. The last time the
doctor had warned that another overdose could kill her.
Angelica didn't seem to care, and Rafael feared that was
because she wanted to die. His father's death had been
quick, a single shot; his mother a slow, deliberate wasting away. Angelica was choosing self-destruction. And
it was all his fault.

'Is your sister ill?' Allegra asked, shouting over the
sound of the helicopter that would take them to Palermo
for the short flight to Naples.

'In a manner of speaking.' Rafael turned to look out
the window to avoid answering any more of Allegra's
questions. She would see soon enough what Angelica
was like. What he was like.

And then? The unease he'd been feeling deepened into
dark regret. Then things would be changed between them
for ever.

They didn't talk much on the flight to Naples; Allegra
seemed to sense his mood and kept quiet, while Rafael
kept his head down, his eyes on his tablet, dealing with
work issues.

A car was waiting for them when they emerged from
the airport, blinking in the afternoon sunlight, the muted
roar of the city's traffic, the raucous honking of horns and
exclamations of passers-by hitting Rafael like a smack in
the face. He didn't like the busy, dirty streets of Naples.
He'd offered a dozen times or more to pay for Angelica

to move somewhere more congenial, but she'd always refused.

He gave the address of the hospital to the driver and then leaned back in the seat. Allegra looked at him in concern.

'Won't you tell me what's going on?' she asked quietly.

'What is there to tell?' Rafael shrugged, dismissing the question with a lift of his eyebrows. 'My sister is in hospital.' He paused, pressing his lips together. 'A drug overdose.'

He could tell he'd shocked her with that one. And that was just the beginning.

'What…?' Allegra's face crumpled with sympathy. 'Oh, Rafael…'

'Don't.' He shrugged away her compassion. 'It happens often enough. And there's nothing I've been able to do about it.'

Allegra lapsed into silence and Rafael looked away. He really shouldn't have brought her, but perhaps it would, painfully, be for the best.

Allegra's mouth was dry, her heart pinging in her chest, as she followed Rafael into the hospital lift. He pressed a button and then folded his arms over his chest, biceps bulging, face like an iron mask.

She'd been surprised and gratified when he'd agreed to let her come, but since he'd made that decision he'd seemed only to regret it, and he'd been colder and more remote that ever. She wondered if asking to come had been a mistake, and if Rafael would simply use this as a way to push her even further away.

The doors of the lift opened and Rafael strode out, while Allegra hurried to keep up. Then he was tapping perfunctorily on the door of a room before opening it and slipping inside. Allegra followed him.

The woman in the bed was asleep, dark lashes sweeping gaunt cheeks. Allegra stifled a gasp at the heart-wrenching sight of her—scars on each wrist and bruises and needle puncture marks scoring her arms in dozens of places. Her hair was dirty and tangled, her limbs scrawny, tendons sticking out like ropes. Rafael let out a shuddering breath. The woman's eyes fluttered opened and then focused on Rafael.

'You shouldn't have come,' she rasped out, her eyes burning like coals as she glared at him.

'Of course I came.' Rafael gazed at her for a moment, his expression closed and yet his eyes full of pain. 'Why, Angelica?'

Angelica shook her head, her eyes closed again. 'I don't want to talk to you.'

'Let me help you,' Rafael said, his voice taking on a strident edge. 'Please. There is a room waiting at the best clinic in Europe, in Switzerland. It's luxurious, Angelica, and discreet. You'd want for nothing.'

Angelica shook her head again, without opening her eyes. Allegra's heart started to splinter. She hated seeing Rafael like this, knowing how helpless, how hopeless, he must feel.

Rafael pressed his lips together, staring at his sister in a heart-breaking mix of grief and fury. 'I've only wanted to help you, Angelica. That's all I've ever wanted.'

Angelica opened her eyes, and Allegra stifled a gasp at the hatred and anger she saw in their depths. 'Help me? When have you ever *helped* me?' she demanded in a raw and ragged voice. Rafael flinched but didn't reply. Didn't defend himself. 'Do you know what he did?' Angelica demanded, turning to Allegra. She stared, speechless, unsure how to respond, how to feel. 'Do you?' Angelica's voice rung out. Allegra licked her lips.

'I… I don't…'

'He killed our father,' Angelica spat. 'He *killed* him. My brother only ever thought of himself. He didn't… he couldn't…' She turned away, sobs tearing her chest.

Allegra had no idea what to say. She didn't believe Angelica, the words of a vindictive and desperate drug addict, and yet…

Why wasn't Rafael saying anything?

'You can't deny it, can you?' Angelica said, her voice still coming in ragged gasps.

'No,' Rafael said after a moment. 'I can't.'

Shock rippled through Allegra. Rafael shot her a cold, hard glance. 'Now you know,' he said, but Allegra didn't feel she knew anything.

'Leave me,' Angelica demanded in a low voice. She seemed drained, lifeless. 'Leave me, I beg of you.'

Rafael gazed at his sister for a full minute while Allegra watched, her heart thudding in her chest. Then he turned and walked out of the room.

Allegra followed, her heart aching now, everything aching. 'Rafael…' she began when they'd entered a small waiting room, but he shook his head.

'Don't. I shouldn't have brought you here.'

'I asked to be brought here,' Allegra answered. 'I want to share your sorrows along with your joys. Please, Rafael…'

Rafael just shook his head again, pacing the small waiting room like a panther in a cage.

'How long has she been like this?' Allegra asked quietly.

Rafael didn't still his stride. 'Since she was fifteen. A year after my father died.'

'How…how did he die?'

He lifted his tormented gaze to hers, his mouth twisting. 'You heard her.'

'I don't believe her.'

'Don't you?'

'No,' Allegra said, but her voice wavered. She didn't believe Angelica, not really, but she knew something had happened, something that tormented Rafael, that made him the way he was, dark and distant, and she was afraid to find out what it was.

'Well, you should,' Rafael said, and turned away.

'Why don't you tell me your version?' Allegra asked quietly. 'What really happened?'

'What really happened?' He stopped, raking his hands through his hair and then dropping them in one abrupt movement. 'My father killed himself. I was the last to see him.'

Uncertainty mingled with sorrowful relief rushed through her. 'Then you didn't kill him…'

'I drove him to his suicide. And then I wasn't able to stop him from pulling the trigger.'

'Oh, Rafael…'

'And my mother and my sister blamed me. They blamed me, and they should have blamed me, because… because I couldn't…'

'But it wasn't—'

'You know what I was saying to him before he killed himself?' Rafael didn't wait for her to reply, not that she had any idea what to say. 'I was complaining about having to leave my private school, because there was no more money. My father had lost everything, everything, and I was whinging about school.' He shook his head slowly.

'Rafael, you were a boy…'

'A stupid, selfish boy. And it broke my father. He left

the room and locked himself in his study…' He stopped, shaking his head again. 'But there's no need to talk of it. Angelica won't see me again. You might as well return to the villa. I never should have brought you in your condition.'

'I'm not an invalid.' Her heart was aching, aching for this man she loved. And yet Rafael's expression was stony, and when she reached out a hand he jerked away from her.

'I'll arrange your flight.'

'What…what about you?'

Rafael shook his head. 'I won't come with you. I have business to see to.'

Allegra stared at him helplessly, knowing that Rafael was taking another step away from her, and this one far worse than any before. Yet what could she do?

'Please don't do this, Rafael,' she whispered, but he was already getting out his phone.

It was better this way. Rafael continued to tell himself that as he arranged Allegra's flight and saw her onto it. She looked at him with a face full of hurt and desperation, but he steeled himself against it.

She might want to make explanations, excuses, but he couldn't. And he wasn't about to open either of them to more pain. What it meant for their future, he didn't know. But now he knew he needed distance. Space.

He stayed in Naples for another two days, trying to reason with Angelica, but she wouldn't even talk to him. He called Allegra, and was reassured she had returned safely to the villa.

'When are you coming back?' she asked, her voice soft and sad.

'I don't know,' Rafael answered tersely. 'I have business in Milan and Rome.'

'I miss you,' Allegra said quietly, and he didn't answer. But after the call he spent several long minutes staring out the window at the dark night.

'I miss you too,' he said into the empty silence of his hotel room.

CHAPTER FOURTEEN

THE NEXT WEEK WAS ENDLESS. Allegra drifted around the villa, wishing she could make things better and feeling utterly powerless. She went over her conversation with Rafael again and again, considering all that he had and hadn't said.

Did he really blame himself for his father's suicide? If anyone, she thought with a bitter pang, he should blame her father, for ruining his. No wonder Rafael had been so driven to see justice served. His family had been utterly destroyed.

But *they* didn't have to be destroyed. She couldn't let this ruin them, and yet Rafael seemed hell bent on letting the past destroy any chance of their future.

She thought she understood now why he'd been so distant these last few weeks. Not because he didn't care but because he cared too much…at least, that's what she hoped. She hoped that it was fear of getting hurt that was keeping him away rather than brutal indifference.

Because that's how she'd felt for so long. Loving someone was risky. Loving *hurt*, because people left you. People hurt you. And Rafael didn't want to be hurt.

She hadn't either. She'd lived her life for safety's sake, never letting anyone get close, missing out because it was easier. Safer. But she didn't want to do that now. Now she wanted to risk. Now she was willing to risk everything, because she knew she loved Rafael. And love risked. Love fought. Love, she hoped and prayed, won. But first Rafael had to come back.

Rafael unlocked the front door, every muscle aching with weariness. He'd spent the last week working as hard as he could, in a desperate and fruitless effort to forget. To erase the memory of Allegra, the sweetness of her, so he'd be strong enough to come back here and maintain his distance. Stay separate.

It was late and the villa was swathed in darkness, everyone hopefully in bed. Rafael intended to creep quietly to his bedroom and avoid Allegra altogether. He'd barely taken a step before he heard a creak on the stair and then he turned to see Allegra standing there.

Her hair was tumbled about her shoulders and she wore a silky white slip of a nightgown that left frustratingly little to the imagination. Already desire was surging through him, and he wondered if he could make this simple. If he could make it about sex.

Then she took a step forward, one pale, slender hand held out in appeal. 'Rafael,' she said softly, and he tensed because there was no supplication in her voice. No accusation. There was just warmth. Acceptance. He turned away.

'I thought you'd be asleep.'

'I've been waiting for you.'

'You didn't even know I was coming back tonight.'

'I know.' She let out a soft, sad laugh. 'I've been waiting since you left, Rafael. A whole week.'

His chest felt tight and he tried to shake the feeling off. 'You shouldn't have.'

'Why not? Why are you pushing me away?'

'Why aren't you pushing me away?' The words burst out of him, revealing, and yet he couldn't keep himself from it. He turned to her, his voice ragged, his gaze burning. 'Why are you still here?'

She looked hurt, shocked. 'Do you want me to leave?'

'No.' He scrubbed his eyes with the heels of his hands. Something felt broken deep inside him and he couldn't articulate what it was, even to himself. 'I'm getting a drink.'

He stalked into the lounge, and after a taut moment Allegra followed him. Rafael poured himself a large measure of whisky from the crystal decanter and drank it down in one healthy swallow. He could feel Allegra's presence behind him. He could feel her confusion and hurt. 'You should go back to bed.'

He heard a sound, something he couldn't quite identify. She was moving or opening something, and he didn't know what it was. He stayed with his back to her, willing her to leave him alone even as a deeper part of him ached for her to stay.

Then he heard the first sorrowful note hover in the room, steal into his soul, and shocked blazed through him. She was playing the cello.

He turned slowly, his glass dangling from his slack fingertips as he took in the sight of Allegra, her hair tumbling about her shoulders in a fiery halo, her expression serious and intent as she drew the bow across the strings of the cello and another sonorous note flowed through the room.

'But…' His voice was hoarse, breaking the stillness. 'You said you didn't play. Hadn't played for ten years.'

Her gaze lifted and something deep in him trembled at the expression in her eyes, silvery and huge, clear and full of sadness. Full of *love*.

'I haven't. But I want to play for you, Rafael. Music…'

She paused, her voice choking. 'Music has been the greatest comfort to me. And I don't know of any other way to comfort you.'

She bent her head again and began to play once more, the notes sure and true and piercingly beautiful.

Rafael's throat thickened with emotion and he sank into the sofa as the music washed over him, note after perfect note, the music haunting and powerful, *breaking* him. He was broken inside, nothing but jagged pieces, his heart a handful of splinters. He let out a sound, a choking cry that would have shamed him if he hadn't felt so overwhelmed.

Allegra kept playing, each note touching his soul, undoing him. He let out another choked sound, and then Allegra was kneeling there in front of him, her arms around him, her face pressed against his chest as she whispered words that felt like sweet, sweet arrows, piercing the armour he'd surrounded himself with for so long.

'I love you, Rafael. I *love* you. Nothing matters to me but that. But you. Please believe me. *Please.*'

He let out a groan, defenceless against the onslaught of her heartfelt words. 'How can you love me…?' The words spilled from him, heedless.

'How can I not?' She pressed her lips against her jaw. 'I fell in love with you the night of my father's funeral.'

'I was only trying to seduce you…'

'And I wanted to be seduced. I saw glimpses then of the man you really are, the man you want to be. Don't turn away from me now, simply because you're afraid.' She laid her hand against his jaw, her skin silky and cool. 'Because that is why you've been keeping your distance, isn't it, these last few weeks, and even more so since we went to Naples? Because you're afraid of being hurt.'

He closed his eyes, not wanting to admit it, knowing it was true. He'd tried to separate his body from his heart but it hadn't worked. Allegra affected him in every way, right down to his core. And yet still he found himself saying, 'I didn't think anyone would love me. That anyone could love me…after my father…' He shook his head, his eyes closed, and Allegra kissed him again, her lips soft against his jaw. 'How could he do that? How could he walk away from me and kill himself? I begged him, Allegra. Pleaded with him with everything I had, pounded on the door, and still he did it, knowing the cost of it on me, on my mother and sister. How could he do that?'

The question rang out, the cry of a hurt child. It had festered inside him for twenty years, until his heart was nothing but scar tissue, barely healed over the old, old wound. And Allegra, and her love, had broken it all—him—open.

'I asked you something similar,' she whispered, her lips moving against his cheek. 'Do you remember? And you told me it wasn't my fault. Now I say the same thing to you, only even more so. Your father was a desperate man, Rafael, driven to terrible things because—because of my father. It wasn't your fault, just as my father leaving wasn't mine. Let's leave the past behind us and make our own future, for the sake of our child and for the sake of us.'

'But it was my fault,' Rafael groaned, his voice breaking on the word. 'Not his death, perhaps, but my mother… my sister…the choices they made, the fact that they felt compelled to make them. That they didn't trust me to provide for them, to see us through the darkness and the mess. *That* was my fault. I was the man of the family, I was in charge, and I failed utterly. I can't forgive myself for that. How can anyone else?'

* * *

Allegra squeezed Rafael's hands, holding on tight, wanting to imbue him with her strength, her love, because she felt as if everything teetered on this moment. Whether he would pull away for good or if the walls would finally come down for ever.

She recognised the core of honour and compassion that he'd kept hidden for so long, realised now that his withdrawal from her had not been from indifference but because he'd cared too much.

She knew that he now suffered from both guilt and hurt—just as she did, with her father's abandonment. Because when you were hurting, you assumed it was something in you that drove a person away. Something bad or wrong. And she would give anything now to show Rafael that there wasn't.

Slowly she leaned forward, still holding his hands, her bump pressing against him as she brushed her lips across his in a kiss of acceptance and healing. A kiss where she offered her whole self, there for the taking.

His body was still, his lips slack under hers, and her heart trembled at the terrible thought of his rejection, but then he opened his mouth and made the kiss his own, one hand coming to rest on the back of her head, and he took what she offered and gave even more back.

Moments later they broke apart and with a shuddering breath Rafael leaned his forehead against hers. 'When my father died,' he murmured, his breath fanning her face, 'I felt like my world had shattered…not just because we lost everything but because I'd lost him. Because he'd been driven to such despair, and I couldn't stop it. Couldn't stop him.'

'I'm so sorry, Rafael…'

'I felt powerless and out of control. And I never wanted

to feel like that again. But then I cruelly inflicted that pain on another family. I killed your father too, Allegra.'

'What are you talking about?'

'If what Caterina said was true...then your father died of a heart attack when he heard the news about me taking over the company. I killed him—'

'No, you didn't,' Allegra said quietly. 'You can't know exactly what happened, and in any case you can't blame yourself for my father's death along with everyone in your family.'

His eyebrows rose in disbelief. 'You absolve me?'

'I'm not the one to do that, Rafael. You don't need my forgiveness.'

'Whose then?' The question was genuine, yearning.

'Your own,' Allegra said softly. 'Rid yourself of these ghosts and demons. Your father chose to kill himself—there was nothing you could have done. Despair leads people to feel there's no way out, no hope. That was not your fault.' He opened his mouth to protest but she continued, her voice rising in strength and conviction. 'And your mother—that was her choice too. Perhaps she didn't want to live without her husband. It's not a reflection on you—'

'It is—'

'*No.* Maybe she should have wanted to live for her children, but some people are not strong enough. Don't blame her, Rafael, but don't blame yourself either. For your mother's death or your sister's addiction.'

'And your father?' Rafael asked after an endless moment of silence. 'Don't you...aren't you angry for what I did?'

Was she? 'I understand why you wanted to take over his business,' she said slowly. 'And I wish I understood more fully what happened back then. Did my father blame yours on purpose, knowing he was innocent? Who else could have embezzled the money?'

Rafael stiffened. 'It wasn't my father.'

'I know,' Allegra soothed. 'And maybe we'll never know who was truly responsible. But let's put it behind us, Rafael. For ever.'

He stared at her, and Allegra held her breath, waiting, everything in her aching. She'd given him everything. Her love, her heart, her body, her soul, her music. Everything. And she still didn't know what he was going to do with it.

'I want to try,' Rafael said at last, and Allegra nodded as she blinked back tears.

'Yes,' she said. 'Let's try.'

CHAPTER FIFTEEN

THE REALISATION WAS like a thunderclap, startling her awake. Allegra stiffened in bed, her heartbeat coming in thuds. Next to her Rafael slept on. They'd gone to bed together, holding hands, silent and accepting. It felt like a new start, fresh and fragile. Allegra hoped it would endure. That they would.

And then, in the midst of sleep, she'd had that sudden thought slam into her, leaving her breathless and reeling. *Her mother.* Her mother had embezzled that money. It made such horrible sense. Someone close to her father had taken the money; that same person had pointed the finger at Rafael's father. And it made her parents' sudden divorce understandable too, along with the lack of alimony, her father's concern for his own reputation. But where had the money gone?

Although Jennifer had always claimed poverty, after the divorce they hadn't been exactly destitute. It wasn't as if they'd been out on the streets. Looking at the situation now, a grown woman, Allegra doubted that a few pieces of jewellery could have really kept them afloat. Even the embezzled money wouldn't have lasted long in Jennifer's hands—the woman was a spending machine— but it would have tided them over for a while…until she'd found another man to fund her lifestyle. It seemed, all of a sudden, entirely, horribly possible.

If it was true…what would it mean for her mother—but far more importantly, for her and Rafael?

Allegra slipped from the bed, throwing on a dressing gown before reaching for her laptop. She typed in the Internet search box and within seconds she had the dates of both Marco Vitali's suicide and her parents' divorce. Weeks apart. *Weeks.*

Allegra pushed the laptop away as she stared unseeingly into the distance, her mind racing. If her mother had taken the money…if her father had discovered it… if he'd divorced her so abruptly because of that, wanting to separate himself from his wife but unwilling for his reputation to suffer…

There was only one way to find out. One way to truly know. She needed to talk to her mother. Allegra toyed with the idea of a phone call but she knew she wouldn't be able to get the truth over a telephone line. She needed to see her mother face to face, and see the truth, or lack of it, in her eyes. She needed to know. Because perhaps then she and Rafael could finally put the past to rest and move on as a family. Perhaps then he could find the closure he so desperately needed.

She glanced back at him, his face relaxed in sleep, his dark lashes feathering his olive-toned cheeks. He looked beautiful, like something out of a Renaissance painting, and he made her heart ache with love. But would he countenance a trip to America? What would his reaction to the possibility of her mother's crime be?

As if he could sense her thoughts Rafael opened her eyes. He blinked away the dazed confusion of sleep, his amber gaze arrowing in on her. 'Allegra? Is something wrong?'

She licked dry lips, her heart starting to pound. What if he was angry? What if he blamed her somehow? Despite everything they'd said and shared, she still didn't know if Rafael actually loved her. He hadn't said the words. He'd fought against the feeling, even last night, everything in him resisting, but she'd pressed and pushed and tried so hard...

'Allegra?' Rafael said again, his tone sharpening.

'I think I know who embezzled the money. Back then.'

'What?' Rafael sat up in bed, his eyes narrowed as he raked a hand through his hair. 'How could you possibly know that?' He almost sounded suspicious. Of *her*.

Allegra took a deep breath. She felt nervous, even afraid. Why was she risking this—*them*—so soon? Before she even knew the truth or strength of Rafael's feelings? And yet, with this new truth lodged inside her like a stone, how could she not?

'It came to me last night.' She gulped, Rafael's stare still hard and unrelenting. 'I think... I think it was my mother.'

'Your *mother*?'

'It makes sense, in an awful way. She had some money, but she didn't get it from my father. And the divorce was so sudden, so abrupt...'

Rafael swung his legs out of bed, sitting so his back was to her, his hands raked through his hair.

'This doesn't have to change anything between us,' Allegra said quietly. 'Does it?'

'There's no proof, is there?' Rafael's voice was flat, toneless. 'We could never prove it.'

'I... I don't know. I thought, perhaps, we could go to New York. Confront her. Maybe...maybe then you'd feel...' She trailed off, uncertain and miserable. Why had she begun this wretched conversation? Yet she couldn't have kept such an awful suspicion, a huge secret, to herself. She didn't want there to be secrets or lies between them, ever.

'You can't go to New York in your state.'

'Rafael, I'm barely into the third trimester. And I want to be there. Let's do this together. Even if there's no proof, it would be good to know, wouldn't it? Maybe then... maybe then you could finally let the past go.'

'While your mother walks free?'

Allegra blinked at the savage note in his voice. 'I'm sorry,' she whispered, because she was, even if none of it was her fault. Still everything felt complicated and messy, painful.

'I'll book the tickets,' Rafael said, and then he rose from the bed and walked out of the room.

It felt like too much, on top of everything that had happened last night. Allegra's *mother*. She'd as good as signed the death warrant on his family. He didn't blame Allegra, knew she had nothing to do with it, and yet...

It felt bitter, almost too much to bear.

Rafael got ready in taut silence, booking the tickets, packing clothes, telling himself he'd feel better when he knew.

Salvatore drove them to Palermo; Allegra looked tired and miserable, huddled on one side of the limo, one hand resting on her bump. Guilt flashed through him, an acidic rush. She'd given him so much last night. She'd told him she loved him. And he'd fought her every step of the way, couldn't bear the thought of being that vulnerable. That exposed.

And yet he'd shown her the worst of him and she still hadn't walked away. Even now, when he was practically ignoring him, Allegra was there, for the duration, determined to stay by his side, to see this through.

And maybe she needed this as much as he did. If her mother was guilty, it had affected Allegra's life as much as his. They'd both been ensnared by the past—and perhaps the truth could now set them *both* free.

The thought was radical, shifting truths inside him, tilting the world so his perspective was sharper, clearer.

Rafael reached over and took Allegra's hand; surprise flickered across her face as he laced his fingers through hers. He didn't speak; he didn't think he had the words. But he hoped she knew what he was trying to say.

The city was resplendent with autumn colour as they took a cab from the airport to Allegra's mother's apartment in the less fashionable end of Park Avenue, skirting Harlem. Allegra had slept for much of the flight, taking comfort from Rafael's silent support. He hadn't said much, but the mood had shifted between them, the tension focused outward rather than inside. Allegra rested her hand on his shoulder as she dozed and prayed that this would be what she wanted it too—closure. Peace.

Jennifer's expression was almost comical in its shock as she took in the sight of both of them standing in the doorway of her apartment. Her hand fluttered towards her throat and her face paled. 'Allegra…and you must be Vitali.'

'Rafael Vitali,' Rafael answered in a low, gravelly voice. 'Marco's son.'

'I never met him.' Jennifer's expression had cleared, hardened. She was, Allegra realised with a sinking feeling, going to put up a front.

'Mother, may we come in?'

'Of course. Have you…have you come all the way from Sicily?'

'This very afternoon,' Rafael answered. They followed Jennifer into her sitting room where she perched on a white leather sofa, eyebrows elegantly arced.

'What a lovely surprise.'

'Is it?' Allegra asked quietly, and Jennifer's eyes narrowed.

'What is that supposed to mean?'

Allegra took a deep breath. 'Mother, Marco Vitali was accused of embezzlement and lost his business as a result.'

'I told you that,' Jennifer answered with a dismissive flick of fingers. She shot Rafael a quick, wary glance. 'I'm sorry for it, of course, but it has nothing to do with me.'

'He killed himself as a result.'

Jennifer's expression didn't change. 'Again, I'm sorry.'

'There was never any proof it was him, though,' Allegra continued, determined to see this through. She and Rafael both needed to have this reckoning. 'The only so-called proof was that someone close to Papa told him it was Marco.'

Jennifer shrugged her bony shoulders. 'So?'

'So, who was that person? And who really did take the money? Because it was someone close to my father, someone he trusted.'

'You flew all the way to New York to talk about this?' Jennifer demanded, her lips twisting in a sneer. 'I suppose he put you up to it?' she added with a glare at Rafael.

'I did not,' Rafael returned, his voice a low thrum in his chest. 'In fact, I did not want her to make the trip in her condition. But I realised I did want to know. Not for my sake,' he emphasised, his voice lowering to a growl of menacing intent, 'but for Allegra's.'

'What…?' Allegra turned to him, her lips parting in wordless shock.

'If your mother is guilty,' Rafael said, 'then she affected your life as much as mine.' He turned to Jennifer, skewering her with a gaze full of knowledge and accusation. 'Because that's why her father stayed away, isn't it? You made him.'

Jennifer's mouth dropped open and for a few seconds she struggled to speak. 'I don't know what you're talking about,' she finally blustered.

'No,' Rafael answered, so firm, so sure. 'You do know. Because you tried to use Allegra as a bargaining chip.'

'What?' Allegra's mind raced. 'How do you know…?' she demanded of Rafael, the words torn from her.

'I don't. I'm guessing.' He nailed Jennifer with a look. 'And I'm right.'

Jennifer glared at him for a full minute, and then she rose from the sofa, flouncing over to the bar where she poured herself a stiff drink. Allegra watched her, her heart seeming to beat its way up her throat.

'Mother, is that true? Did you threaten Papa? Is that why—?'

'You always thought your father was a saint,' Jennifer said as she tossed back her drink in one swallow and then flung the glass on the table. 'Even when he walked away from you for good.' She turned around, her arms folded tightly against her chest. 'You can't prove anything. There's no paper trail, nothing. Trust me on that.'

'So you did do it,' Allegra cried, tears streaking down her face. 'How *could* you…?'

Jennifer pressed her lips together. 'Your father kept me on very short purse strings.'

'But why did Papa leave…?'

She looked away. 'I told him if he made me leave he'd

never see you again. He didn't want to go through the courts, didn't want the stain on his precious reputation. To have a criminal for a wife! He couldn't bear it. And I thought… I thought he'd change his mind, if he couldn't have you. I didn't know he'd be so bloody stubborn.'

Allegra leaned back against the sofa cushions, her whole body weak and trembling with shock.

'I never meant Vitali to be blamed the way he was,' Jennifer said defensively. 'I just suggested it once. I didn't expect Vitali's business to be ruined by it.'

'You destroyed the life of an entire family,' Allegra said, her voice shaking. '*You* have blood on your hands.'

'Is it my fault that he chose to do that?' Jennifer cried. 'He didn't have to.'

'No, he didn't,' Rafael interjected quietly. To Allegra's surprise he didn't look as angry as she expected him to. He looked sad and resolute, and the surest rock upon which she could depend. He put his arm around her, drawing her close to him. 'You are not to blame for his death,' he said to Jennifer. 'But you are a criminal all the same, and you know it.'

Jennifer's eyes shot sparks as she lifted her chin and said nothing. 'Tell me,' Rafael said quietly. 'Did Mancini ever try to contact Allegra?'

Jennifer looked as if she wasn't going to answer. 'There were letters,' she said finally, and looked away.

Allegra let out a gasp. '*Letters*… Did you keep them? Why didn't you show them to me?'

'I could hardly do that,' Jennifer dismissed. 'You would have started asking questions. But I'm not completely heartless, you know.' She pressed her lips together, and then she turned on her heel and walked out of the room.

Allegra pressed her cheek against Rafael's chest and

he put his arms around her. 'How did you know…?' she whispered.

'I guessed.'

'I never thought…never imagined…'

'Maybe now you'll find some answers.'

Allegra look up at him, her eyes wet with tears. 'I already have, Rafael. With you. In you.'

A brief, trembling smile touched his lips and he rested his forehead against hers. Allegra closed her eyes.

'I'm so sorry to interrupt this touching scene,' Jennifer said. She tossed a packet of letters on the table in front of them and Allegra took them up, scanning the faded envelopes. There had to be at least a dozen.

'We'll go now,' Rafael said, rising from the sofa.

'Wait.' Allegra touched his sleeve. 'Don't you have anything to say to Rafael?' she demanded of her mother. 'Do you know how much he has suffered? His family has suffered?'

Jennifer flinched a little but then pressed her lips together and said nothing. She wouldn't admit any more guilt than she had to.

'It doesn't matter, Allegra,' Rafael said quietly. 'This isn't about me.'

'But it is—'

'No.' He cut her off with gentle firmness. 'This was about you. You needed to hear this.' He gestured to the letters. 'You needed to see this.' He tugged her up to standing, his gaze intent and full of—dared she believe it?—love. 'And now we can truly move on.'

Moments later they were standing in front of her mother's building, blinking in the bright sunlight. Allegra pressed her father's letters to her chest as she shook her head in wonder.

'I never expected this…'

'I'm glad it has happened.'

'But what about you, Rafael? Does it…does it matter, knowing my own mother…?'

'Someone I love taught me that the sins of our parents do not have to affect or define us. The past doesn't have to destroy our future.'

A tremulous smile bloomed across her face, planted its roots deep in his heart. 'Do you mean that?'

'I love you, Allegra. I've loved you for a while, but I fought it because I am a blind, hard-headed fool. And I was afraid, just as you guessed and said. Afraid of being hurt. Of seeming weak. But you saw all my weakness and failure and you loved me even then. Even more.'

'I love you,' she said. '*All* of you.'

'And I love all of you.' He put his arms around her and drew her to him. 'Especially since you can forgive me when I act so foolishly, pulling away when I should have pushed closer.'

'I understood it was scary, Rafael. It was scary for me too.'

'But you wised up a lot faster than I did,' he said with a smile. He brushed his lips across hers. 'Now let's go home.'

EPILOGUE

Eighteen months later

'HE'S THE SMARTEST baby that ever was,' Allegra declared.

'Of course he is,' Rafael answered easily, as he joined her on the lawn, stretching his long legs out on the blanket. The sunshine bathed them in a golden glow, and above them the leaves rustled pleasantly. Their son, named Marco after Rafael's father, babbled excitedly as he attempted to heft his chubby self to his feet.

'He's trying to walk,' Allegra exclaimed. 'And the doctors said he wouldn't walk until he was at least two.'

'Yes, but what do they ever know?' Rafael teased.

It had been a long, hard year and a half in many ways. Little Marco had spent four months in the neonatal unit, first getting strong enough to handle heart surgery and then recovering from that surgery. There had been a few scary moments along the way—a bout of pneumonia that had tested his lungs, and an infection after his surgery. But he'd grown stronger and stronger and finally, when their son had been nearly five months old, they'd brought him back to the villa to begin their life together as a proper family.

Three months ago they'd got married, a small, intimate ceremony in the nearby town, with only a handful of guests. Allegra hadn't wanted a big do, and neither had Rafael.

They were happy as they were, living quietly, with Rafael commuting to Palermo for work. Allegra had started offering cello lessons to local children, and enjoyed playing more than she ever had. The local priest had asked her to play a concert in the church in the nearby town, and Allegra had agreed.

Love, she realised, made her bloom. Made her believe more in herself, because Rafael believed in her. And she saw the same unfurling in Rafael, the lightness and sheer joy in his face, his eyes. Love made you bloom and love also healed.

In recent months Rafael had taken new steps with Angelica, talking more honestly to her than he ever had before. Last week Angelica had moved into the clinic in Switzerland and was undergoing several months of rehab and therapy. So many miracles.

'Allegra, look!' His voice filled with amazement, Rafael pointed to their son who, with a look of both determination and terror on his face, was taking his first step.

'He's amazing,' Rafael declared, and, laughing, Allegra reached out to clasp Marco's hands.

'Just like his father, then,' she said, and, smiling, Rafael leaned down to kiss her.

* * * * *

THE VIRGIN'S
SHOCK BABY

HEIDI RICE

To Bryony, who made sure I gave this story the depth it deserved.

And Daisy, who talked me off the ledge a few times while I was doing that!

Dario, Megan and I thank you both sincerely.

PROLOGUE

'DARIO DE ROSSI IS escorting you to the Westchester Ball tomorrow night and you need to seduce him while you're there.'

'What? Why?' Megan Whittaker was fairly sure she'd just been transported into an alternate universe. An alternate universe that was two hundred years past its sell-by date. Either that or her father had lost his mind. Whichever way you looked at it, the demand he had just levelled at her from across his walnut desk in the Manhattan offices of Whittaker Enterprises, without even the hint of a smile on his face, was not good news, because he did not appear to be joking.

'To save Whittaker's from possible annihilation,' her father snapped. 'Don't give me your whipped puppy look, Megan,' he added. 'Do you think I would ask this of you if there were another option?'

'Well, I…' She wanted to believe him, even though she knew his love for Whittaker's had always taken precedence over his love for his daughters.

But unlike her sister, Katie, Megan understood that. Having spent the last four years working her way up to head her own tiny department at Whittaker's, she didn't begrudge him his dedication to the company that had been in their family for five generations.

She also didn't really begrudge him a request so outside the norm for a father to a daughter, or indeed a boss to his employee. She knew that to be successful in business your personal life had to suffer, and personal loyalties could be tested. But this was… Well… It wasn't even rational. What possible reason could there be for her to seduce any man? Let alone a man like De Rossi, a corporate wolf who had risen through the ranks of New York business society in the last ten years to become one of its prime movers and shakers.

Quite apart from anything else, if her father was looking for a femme fatale, surely he must know Megan was not the best candidate for the job.

She simply did not have the necessary temperament, equipment or experience. She had always been more comfortable in business suits and flats than cocktail dresses and heels. She found going to the beauty salon tedious, the concentration on her appearance a waste of time and money. Her intellect and her work ethic were so much more important. And after the few fumbled encounters she'd had at college, she'd been beyond grateful to discover she comprehensively lacked her mother's voracious and indiscriminate libido. At twenty-four, she was still technically speaking a virgin, for goodness' sake! These days she would much rather spend her small amount of free time watching TV boxsets with a nice glass of Pouilly Fuissé, than finding a man—especially as the judicious use of a vibrator could take care of her needs without all the awkwardness and disappointment.

'Someone's buying up all our stock,' her father said, the vein pulsing at his temple starting to disturb Megan. 'I'm almost certain it's him. And if it is him, we're in serious trouble. We're exposed. We have to stay his hand. That means making sacrifices for the good of the company.'

'But I don't understand how…'

'You don't have to understand. What you have to do is get an invitation back to his penthouse so we can discover if it is him. If you can find out which of our shareholders he's targeting that would be even better. Then we might have some hope of keeping the bastard off our back until I can secure new capital investment.'

'You expect me to seduce him for the purposes of industrial espionage?' Megan tried to clarify where her father was going with this, as something became devastatingly obvious to her. He had to be exceptionally stressed to believe she could pull such a plan off with her limited skills, which meant the company must be in serious financial difficulties.

'You have your mother's face and figure, Megan. And you're not a lesbian… Are you?'

Her face coloured, the heat racing up her neck, the impatient enquiry mortifying her. 'What? Of course not, but…'

'Then what's the damn problem? Surely there must be enough of that oversexed bitch in you somewhere to know how to seduce this bastard. It's built into your DNA, all you have to do is locate it.' Her father was becoming increasingly frantic. The bitterness in his voice at the mention of her mother made Megan's stomach knot.

Her father never mentioned her mother. Not ever. Alexis Whittaker had abandoned all three of them—her father, herself and her little sister, Katie—not long after Katie's birth, and had died ten years ago when her Italian boyfriend's Ferrari had plummeted from a clifftop road on the island of Capri. Megan could still remember her father coming to tell her the news at her boarding school in Cornwall, his face white with an agonising combination of grief, pain and humiliation. And she could remember the same hollow sensation in her stomach.

Her mother had been a social butterfly, stunningly beautiful, flamboyant and reckless—with everyone's life including her own. Megan could barely remember her; she'd never come to visit her daughters, which was why their father had shipped them off to board at St Grey's as soon as they were old enough.

The hollow confusion had turned to panic though, when paparazzi photos of her and Katie at the funeral had appeared on the Internet. They had been forced to leave the only real home they had ever known, chased out by the photographers wanting to get a glimpse of the 'grief-stricken' Whittaker sisters, and the salacious whispers about their mother's infidelities, spread by some of the other girls at St Grey's. Her father had moved them to an apartment ten blocks from his own on Fifth Avenue in New York, employed a housekeeper and a security guard, enrolled them in an exclusive private school and made the effort to visit them at least once a month. And eventually the media storm surrounding Alexis Whittaker's wicked ways and her untimely death had died down.

But ever since Megan had been ripped away from St Grey's, she had promised herself two things: she would protect the sister she loved from the fallout of her mother's disgrace, and she would work herself to the bone to prove to her father that she was nothing like the woman who had given birth to them.

And up until this moment, she had thought she'd succeeded. With her second objective at least. Katie, unfortunately, appeared to be almost as wild as their mother, despite Megan's best efforts to tame her rebellious temperament.

Megan, though, had concentrated on making her father proud. She'd got a first at Cambridge two years ahead of her peers in computer science. And then an MBA at

Harvard Business School specialising in e-commerce. To prove herself worthy, not just to her father but to her colleagues at Whittaker's, she'd refused his offer of a vanity position and had instead started on the ground floor of the building in Midtown. After six months in the mailroom, she'd applied for an internship in the tech department. It had taken her three years to work her way up the ladder from there, rung by torturous rung. Her recent promotion had put her in charge of the company's small three-person e-commerce department, finally proving once and for all that her mother's shameful behaviour had no bearing on who she was. Until this moment.

How could her father even consider asking her to seduce De Rossi? Did he expect her to have sex with the man, too?

'I can't do it,' she said.

'Why the hell not?'

Because I'm about as far from being De Rossi's ideal woman as Daffy Duck is from Jessica Rabbit.

'Because it wouldn't be ethical,' she managed, recoiling from the hot flash of memory from the only time she'd ever met De Rossi in the flesh.

He'd certainly made an impression.

She'd heard of him, but the gossip hadn't prepared her for the staggeringly handsome man who had arrived at the Met Ball with supermodel Giselle Monroe hanging off his arm like the latest fashion accessory. The brute force of his powerful body had barely been contained by the expertly tailored designer suit, and his bold heated gaze had raked over her when they'd been introduced by her father. The knowledge in his ice-blue eyes had disturbed her on a purely visceral level. And set off a thousand tiny explosions of sensation over every inch of exposed skin.

She'd been careful to avoid De Rossi for the rest of the evening, because she'd known instinctively the man was not just tall, dark and handsome, but also extremely dangerous—to her peace of mind.

'Don't be naïve.' Her father flicked a chilling glare at her. 'There are no ethics in business. Not when it comes to the bottom line. De Rossi certainly doesn't have any, so we can't afford to have any either.'

'But how did you even persuade him to take me to the ball?' Megan said, becoming desperate herself.

'It's a charity ball. He's paying for a table. You're going to be Whittaker's representative there. I asked him to escort you as a courtesy to me; he's a member of my club.'

So she had officially become a pity date—which would have been mortifying, if her father's ulterior motive wasn't a thousand times worse.

'De Rossi's only weakness that I could find is for beautiful women,' her father continued in the same deceptively pragmatic tone. As if he were talking sense, instead of insanity. 'Not that it's exactly a weakness. He's never been foolish enough to marry one of them, unlike me. And he never keeps them longer than a few months. But he's between women at the moment, according to Annalise, who keeps up with this nonsense,' he said, mentioning his mistress. 'And he never has one out of his bed for long. Which gives you all the opportunity you need. He'll be on the hunt and I'm putting you in his path. All you need to do is get his attention.' The dispassionate statement had shame burning the back of Megan's neck. 'Get an invite to his penthouse on Central Park West,' her father continued. 'Once he takes you there, you can get access to his computer and his files. Computers are your forte, are they not?'

That he'd thought this scenario through in such detail wasn't helping the chill spreading through Megan's abdomen—or the flush of awareness flaming across her scalp.

'But anything he has on there will be password protected,' she said, trying to be practical.

'I have his passwords.'

'How?'

'It's not important. The important thing is to get access to his computer before he changes them. Which means acting quickly and concisely.'

And setting her up as some kind of Mata Hari? The idea would almost be funny if it weren't so appalling.

'You can't ask me to do this,' said Megan. She'd always strived so hard to please her father, to prove herself worthy of his trust. There weren't many things she wouldn't do for him, but this request scared her on so many levels. 'You wouldn't ask me to, if I were your son,' she added, trying to appeal to her father's sense of justice. He wasn't a bad man, he was fair and, in his own gruff, distant way, he loved her and Katie. Obviously he was so stressed he had completely lost his grip on reality. But he had to be under a huge amount of pressure, if De Rossi was sniffing about the company.

She knew enough about De Rossi's business practices from the financial press to know that once his conglomerate got their hooks into your stock you were as good as dead in the water. He was famous for asset stripping. If he really was planning a hostile takeover, he could reduce Whittaker's to rubble in weeks, a legacy company destroyed in a heartbeat simply to feed his insatiable appetite for wealth at any cost. But her father's solution was beyond desperate, not to mention illegal, and doomed to failure. She had to make him see that, and find another way.

'If I had a son and De Rossi was gay, that would be an option.' Instead of looking persuaded, the tic in her father's cheek went ballistic. 'As neither is the case, it's a moot point.'

The blush seared her skin, the knot in her stomach tightening into a hollow ball of anxiety. It was no good, she was going to be forced to state the obvious.

'De Rossi might as well be gay for all the interest he's likely to take in me. He dates supermodels.'

And I'm hardly supermodel material.

At five-foot-five, and with the lush curves she had inherited from her mother, Megan had felt like an over-endowed pixie next to the slim, stunning woman who had fawned over De Rossi at the Met Ball.

But Megan's lack of appeal to men had always felt like a boon. She didn't want to become any man's decorative accessory. Especially not a man like De Rossi, who even on their brief acquaintance she suspected was as ruthless with women as he was in his business dealings.

She could control those mini explosions. They were nothing more than a biological reaction.

'Don't sell yourself short.' Her father huffed, looking exasperated now as well as desperate. 'You have enough of your mother's charms to attract him if you put your mind to it.'

'But I—'

'If you don't do it, there's only one other person I can ask.'

Megan's panic downgraded. Thank goodness, he had someone else he could ask. She would not have to even attempt something that was bound to humiliate and degrade her, and was extremely unlikely to be successful. 'Who?'

'Your sister, Katie.'

The panic went from ten to ninety in a nanosecond.

'But Katie's only nineteen,' she cried, shocked. 'And she's in art school.'

After an endless string of school expulsions and acting out against their father's authority, Katie had finally found her passion as a talented and brilliant artist. And she didn't give a fig about Whittaker's.

'An art school I pay for,' her father remarked, the dispassionate expression chilling Megan to the bone. Katie and her father had been at loggerheads for years—ever since the sisters had moved to New York after their mother's death. It had taken Megan months to persuade their father to pay for the exclusive academy that had only offered Katie a partial scholarship—something she had never told her sister. She didn't know how Katie would react if she discovered their father was paying some of her tuition fees and was prepared to pull the plug on the dreams she'd worked so hard for to save Whittaker's. But Megan doubted it would be good.

'Your sister is also as reckless and wild as your mother,' her father added. 'Given the right incentive, I think we both know she'd pass this assignment with flying colours.'

No, she wouldn't, she'd be crushed, Megan thought.

Katie was as lively and spirited as Megan was cautious and grounded. But for all her recklessness, she also had an open and easily bruised heart—and absolutely no regard for business ethics or expediency. Katie would be appalled that their father could ask such a thing of either one of them. And Katie's own worst enemy was usually Katie. She was volatile and unpredictable, especially if she was hurt. So much so that Megan had no idea what she'd do if forced into this situation by their father. She could have a mad passionate affair with De Rossi or annoy him so much he'd destroy Whittaker's just for the hell of it. But one thing was for sure, putting a hothead like Katie into the path of someone as ruthless as De Rossi would be a car crash of epic proportions, and Katie would be the one who got destroyed.

'The only reason I haven't already asked her is because

she knows nothing about computers,' her father said. 'And De Rossi likes his lovers more mature, according to Annalise,' he added. 'You've got a better chance. But if you leave me with no choice I will have to explain to your sister that if she wants to stay at her fancy art school she will have to—'

'Okay, I'll do it,' Megan jumped in, before her father could state the unthinkable. 'I'll give it my best shot.'

Even if her best shot had very little chance of being a success, her pride and her ethics felt like a small price to pay to save her sister from heartbreak—and Whittaker's from guaranteed annihilation.

'Good girl, Megan,' her father said. 'Take the day off tomorrow. Annalise will accompany you to select an outfit suitable for the occasion and take you to her beautician to get you properly prepared.'

'Okay,' she said, feeling dazed at the enormity of what she had just agreed to—and how ill-prepared she was for the challenge. Annalise's alluring sense of style and supreme sexual confidence had always intimidated Megan.

'Don't disappoint me. Whittaker's is counting on you,' her father finished, dismissing her as he turned back to the papers on his desk.

'I know and I won't,' she murmured, trying to sound confident.

But as she returned to her small office on the building's tenth floor, the pressure of what she had to achieve sat in her belly like a brick. An annoyingly hot brick seeping an uncontrollable and completely unregulated warmth throughout her body.

She didn't feel confident; she felt like a sacrifice, about to be staked out in the wolf's lair, with nothing to protect her but a designer gown and heels and an overpriced beautician's appointment.

CHAPTER ONE

'No way, Katie. You need to stay in your room when he gets here.' Megan's hand trembled as she picked up one of the diamond drop earrings Annalise had loaned her to match the sleek, blue, satin, floor-length gown it had taken her father's mistress an eternity to select during their endless shopping expedition that afternoon. The sting as the thin silver spike penetrated the rarely used hole in her lobe did nothing to calm the rapid flutter of Megan's heartbeat. She breathed deeply and picked up the other earring. She needed to stop hyperventilating or she was liable to pass out before De Rossi even arrived.

'But I want to meet him, to make sure he doesn't take advantage of you,' Katie said, the fire in her eyes accompanied by a petulant pout. 'He's rich, arrogant and scarily gorgeous. You've got zero experience of guys like him. Did you see the cover shot of him on that boring business magazine you get? He even looks hot in one of those stuffy suits.'

Yes, she had seen the magazine, she'd even re-read the interview with De Rossi to give herself some useful topics of conversation. But all the article had really done—illustrated with all those photos of him looking broad and muscular and indomitable—was make her panic increase. And Katie's misguided attempts to protect her were not helping.

'What if he tries to ravish you?' Katie added, the battle she'd been waging for the last two hours—to stand between Megan and De Rossi's super-human seduction skills—starting to wear on Megan's already frazzled nerves.

De Rossi was due to arrive in less than five minutes and Katie's misguided reading of the situation was the last thing Megan needed. But she would never tell Katie the truth. That the only thing standing between them and financial ruin was Megan's mission to seduce De Rossi—not the other way around—because that would only make Katie worry more about Megan's date in the lion's den. And Megan was already panicking enough for both of them.

She'd spent most of her life shielding her sister, ever since the day she'd stood beside a nine-year-old Katie at their mother's graveside and held her as her little sister shed real tears for a woman who had abandoned them.

She was not about to stop now.

But sometimes shielding Katie from the realities of life could be very trying. Megan poked the second earring into her earlobe with an unsteady hand and absorbed the sting, attempting to tune out Katie's next offensive.

'I can't believe you won't even let me meet him. All I want to do is make sure he knows not to mess with you.' Katie stood defiantly behind her, every sinew in her slim, coltish body fraught with challenge and righteous determination. 'At least promise me you won't let him lure you back to his love nest on Central Park West.'

'His *what* nest?' Megan would have laughed at the term, if her heart hadn't just jumped into her throat.

'Don't look like that.' Katie rolled her eyes, frustrated. 'That's what they called it in Giselle Monroe's piece in the *Post*. Didn't you read it?'

'No, I did not, and you shouldn't have either. It's salacious gossip.' The last thing she needed to read was the model's kiss-and-tell account of De Rossi's sexual prowess when she was nervous enough already.

'According to Giselle,' Katie continued undeterred, 'the guy's insatiable in the sack. He can make a woman—'

'Katie, for goodness' sake, shut up!' She swung round on the stool. 'I didn't read it, because I didn't need to. This isn't a proper date.' Even if the memory of one look from the man was still giving her goosebumps a month after the fact. 'Dad asked him to escort me. He may not even turn up.' The hope that he might have forgotten the arrangement had guilt coalescing in her stomach to go with the panic.

She was Whittaker's only hope. She'd promised to do this thing, even if the computer codes buried in her purse were burning a hole in her conscience.

The sound of the front door buzzer made them both jump.

'So he's not gonna show, huh?' Katie said, looking triumphant.

Megan cursed under her breath, and stood to check out her reflection. The gown was sleek and simple in its elegance, the bias-cut satin snug enough to enhance her curves without offering them up on a platter. Or at least, that was what Annalise had insisted.

Diamonds sparkled in the thin straps that held up the bodice, which plunged low enough to entice but not low enough to give Megan an anxiety attack. Yet. A faux-fur wrap to hold off the night-time chill in late April, and four-inch heels—which were as high as she could go without risking a twisted ankle—an elaborate up-do that held her unruly hair in some kind of order, a five-hundred-dollar make-up session and the delicate diamond drop earrings completed the outfit. Annalise had told her the ensemble screamed sophistication and purpose, rather than panic and desperation.

Megan wasn't so sure.

She heard the front door of the apartment being opened by their housekeeper, Lydia Brady, and the low murmur of a deep masculine voice.

Awareness rippled up her spine and she grasped her sister's wrists. 'Stay here, Katie, I'm warning you. This is going to be humiliating enough without you there making me feel even more self-conscious.'

Katie pulled her hands free, the spark of defiance disappearing for the first time in hours. 'Why would it be humiliating?'

'Because I'm not his type and he's only taking me as a favour to Dad.'

And Dad expects me to seduce him. Somehow. And then commit a crime to save Whittaker's.

'What do you mean, you're not his type?' Katie's gaze travelled over Megan's outfit, the appreciation in her wide green eyes making Megan's heart pound even harder. 'You look absolutely stunning. Just like Mum. I wish I had at least a few of your curves.' She flung her arms around Megan's shoulders, holding her tight for a few precious seconds. 'You're going to knock his designer socks off, you silly moo,' Katie whispered in her ear, before she drew back. Warmth suffused Megan.

Even when she was being a pain in the backside, Katie was Megan's greatest cheerleader and her best friend.

'Which is precisely why you need me there to make sure he doesn't get any ideas,' Katie added, in case Megan hadn't figured that out already after the four-hour campaign. 'Are you absolutely sure you don't want me to threaten him with my kick-boxing skills?'

'You gave up kick-boxing after two sessions,' Megan pointed out.

'What if I threaten to macramé him to death instead, then?' Katie offered—probably only half joking. 'I did a killer macramé piece for my course.'

The chuckle that popped out of Megan's mouth was part gratitude and part hysteria. Whatever happened with De Rossi, her life was likely to be irrevocably changed once tonight was over. Because she'd either be in his bed, or in a prison cell. Her sister's silly joke helped to ground her, though, and confirm what she already knew: that protecting Katie and her dreams, and protecting Whittaker's, were worth sacrificing her self-respect and throwing herself at De Rossi tonight.

All Megan had to do was figure out how to do that without having a nervous breakdown.

Lydia Brady stepped into the room. 'Mr De Rossi has arrived, Megan.' The older woman smiled. 'You look beautiful, dear.'

'Thank you, Lydia.' Nerves screamed across her bare shoulders, and the hot brick in her stomach sank lower.

Letting go of her sister's hands, she walked towards the dressing-room door, affecting the expression she had practised in the mirror for hours last night. Polite, confident and, she hoped, at least a little alluring.

Her heels echoed on the marble flooring as she made her way down the corridor, but as she turned into the apartment's plush lobby area all the air seized in her lungs and her steps faltered.

Dario De Rossi looked up from adjusting his cuffs, his crystal-blue eyes locking on her face like a tractor beam, and sending a sizzle of electric energy through her body.

The man looked devastating in a tux. Tall and broad, his powerful body only made more intimidating by the classic black tailoring, which emphasised the magnificent width of his shoulders, the leanness of his waist and the length of his legs.

How tall was he? At least three inches above her father's six feet.

She took a careful breath and forced herself to carry on walking, grateful her wrap covered her cleavage when the assessing gaze roamed down, setting off a series of mini explosions and making her insides grow hot.

'*Buonasera*, Megan.'

His English was so perfect, with only the slightest hint of his Italian heritage, it felt strangely intimate to have him greet her in his native language. The way the deep husky rumble of his voice skated across already oversensitive flesh, though, was not as disturbing as the dark flash of hunger in his eyes as she drew level.

'*Buonasera*,' she said, answering him in Italian automatically.

He lifted her fingers to his mouth, startling her, and pressed his lips to the knuckles.

The gesture should have been polite, gallant even, but for the way his thumb slid across her palm as he lowered her hand, sending arrows of sensation darting up her arm, and into her torso.

She tugged her hand out of his grasp, shocked by her response, as his gaze roamed up to her hair.

'The colour is natural?' he asked.

'Yes,' she replied, disconcerted by the approval shining in his eyes.

His firm lips lifted in a smile that managed to be both amused and predatory, as if he were a panther, toying with his prey.

'I hope I did not offend you,' he said, the intimacy of his gaze contradicting his apology. The bright blue gaze then dipped to her toes and back, sending seismic ripples over her skin and igniting every pulse point like a firework.

'Relax, *cara mia*.' The rough chuckle scraped across her nerve-endings.

A fiery blush crept up her neck. Was he mocking her?

She looked down at her hands, and forced her fingers to release their death grip on the diamond-encrusted purse. Annalise had told her that looking like a lamb being led to slaughter would not entice any man.

Breathe. Remember to breathe. Breathing is good.

But when she raised her head, he was doing that laser-beam thing again, as if he could see right through her—to the soon-to-be felon beneath.

'I'm sorry, I'm tired,' she mumbled. 'I've had a very busy day.'

Could she actually sound any *more* inane? Where was all the scintillating conversation about his business acquisitions that she had been working on for hours?

'Doing what?' he asked.

'Shopping for this dress, mostly. And getting my hair and nails and stuff done,' she replied honestly. Until today she'd had no idea that trawling the designer boutiques of the Upper East Side and spending four hours getting waxed and plucked and pampered to within an inch of her life was more exhausting than hiking up Kilimanjaro.

'Have you, now?' he said, the wry tone making her realise the statement made her sound like a spoilt debutante fishing for a compliment.

Humiliation washed over her.

She knew from the articles she'd devoured about him in the last twenty-four hours that he had been born into one of Rome's most notorious slums. He had to know what true exhaustion was. Everything else about his origins was sketchy, something he refused to talk to the press about, but that simple nugget of information had only intimidated her more. She could well imagine how hard De Rossi must have fought to escape his origins—and how hard he would fight now to keep hold of what he had. And what he wanted to acquire.

Her skin burned, her nipples tightening as his gaze met hers. The cool blue was not as icy as she remembered it from their first brief meeting. His lips quirked.

'It was time and money well spent,' he said, the casual compliment making the flush flare across her collarbone.

Then, to her astonishment, he lifted a hand and tucked his forefinger under her chin. The soft brush of the knuckle was like a zap of electricity, firing down to her core as he lifted her face.

She stiffened, stunned by the enormity of her response to a simple touch. She struggled not to jerk her head away, to submit to the proprietorial caress, despite being brutally aware of the heat now blazing on her cheeks.

What was going on here? Because the amused quirk on his lips had disappeared. Why was he looking at her so intently?

He drew his thumb across her bottom lip.

'You are very beautiful in your own unique way,' he said, his gaze lifting to her chignon. 'Especially that hair.'

He sounded sincere. Why did that make tonight seem all the more terrifying?

She forced a smile, trying desperately to pretend she wasn't burning up inside. But she couldn't resist the involuntary flick of her tongue to moisten lips dried to parchment. He focused on her mouth, and a soft indrawn breath escaped her at the hunger in his eyes.

'The colour reminds me of a naked flame,' he said. 'I wonder if you're as fiery in bed?'

The heat swelling in her abdomen settled uncomfortably between her legs at the boldly sexual comment. She ought to say something provocative back.

But she didn't feel provocative, she felt stunned. And hopelessly aroused. And completely out of her depth. Already.

Dario De Rossi wanted her. And while that should have been very good news, because she was supposed to be seducing him, the power dynamic did not feel as if it was in her favour. Surely her thighs wouldn't be trembling under that hard, heated gaze if it were? She searched her mind for something to say that wouldn't clue him in to how inexperienced she was.

Annalise had told her in no uncertain terms that De Rossi would not find her gaucheness appealing.

Think, Megan, think. What would Mata Hari do?

'That's for me to know,' she finally managed, allowing the desire her body couldn't seem to control to show in her voice. 'And for you to find out, if you dare.'

'There's not much I wouldn't dare, *cara*,' he said, the cynical edge in his tone disturbingly compelling.

His hand dropped, and she couldn't prevent the tiny sob as her body softened in relief.

She was playing a very dangerous game. But she had no choice. She had to brazen this out, pretend she was much more knowing and experienced than she actually was.

Sweeping his hand out in front of him, he smiled, and she became a little fixated on those firm sensual lips.

'Let's get you to the ball, Cinderella.'

She pushed out a strained laugh and walked past him, only to tense as his hand settled on the base of her spine. Sensation flashed down to her bottom, but she carried on walking, acting as if the feel of his hand wasn't burning through her clothing.

The ride down in the lift was excruciating, the deceptively light touch driving her insane. He kept his palm there the whole time, guiding her where he wanted her to go, and not letting her stray more than an inch from his side with the subtlest of gestures. But even so, the heat grew.

As they walked out of the apartment building, past the doorman, her nerves were screaming, the controlling pressure so light it was torture not to stretch against his hold. Her body waged a battle between wanting to kick off her heels and race away from him down the street, while another, much more elemental urge had her longing to ease closer to him and let the heat of his body overwhelm her.

The night chill caught her hair, making the tendrils the stylist had spent an hour carefully teasing out of the chignon dance against her neck. She shivered, the skin there already oversensitised by the feel of his gaze boring into her from behind.

The sleek black limousine was parked at the kerb, a man in a dark suit and a cap waiting for them. The chauffeur opened the door and tipped his hat, giving her a polite smile.

She eased into the shadowed interior, the split in the long skirt of her dress pushing open to reveal her thigh almost up to the hip.

She heard a gruff intake of breath. And had to tamp down on the desire to escape out of the other side of the vehicle. The cool leather pushed against the backs of her knees through the dress.

'The guy's insatiable in the sack…'

'What if he tries to ravish you?'

Katie's foolish observations came back to haunt her as De Rossi folded his big body into the seat beside her. His wide shoulders filled up the opposite side of the car and made the spacious, luxury black leather interior feel unbearably cramped and claustrophobic.

He leant across her to grasp the seat belt. She pulled back, his face inches from hers, his scent surrounding her. Sandalwood and musk and man. But as his eyes met hers he only smiled again and pulled the seat belt down to click it into place, his knuckles brushing her hip.

'Why are you so skittish, Megan?' he asked.

'I'm just a little nervous, Mr De Rossi,' she blurted out, then glanced around the car searching for a plausible excuse. She was supposed to be flirting with him, making him think she was available for a quick fling, not quaking like someone standing on a fault line. 'About the ball. I don't want to let my father or the company down. It's my first time representing them at such a prestigious event.' Which was actually true; ordinarily that responsibility alone would be reason enough for her nerves.

The warm proprietorial palm settled over her leg, and gave her knee a quick squeeze, touching her again in a way that made her feel owned.

'My name is Dario.' His jaw clenched and she noticed the bunched muscle, twitching. Was it possible she was affecting him as much as he was affecting her?

The thought thrilled her on some visceral level, but disturbed her more.

The possibility of playing him at his own game was almost as terrifying as the endorphins careering through her for the first time in her life.

'We are on a date, remember,' he murmured.

'Thank you for agreeing to escort me,' she said, finally remembering her manners. 'It was nice of you.'

'Nice?' He seemed amused and surprised by the suggestion. 'Not many women have accused me of that.'

She could well imagine. 'My father really appreciated you doing us this favour.' More than De Rossi would ever know. Hopefully.

'There is nothing to appreciate,' he said, cryptically. 'I only do favours when I expect something in return.'

'What do you expect from me?' she said, then realised how suggestive it sounded a moment too late. 'I don't mean...' she stumbled. 'I just...'

'I expect nothing from you, Megan.' He cut into her rambling denials with the skill and precision of a surgeon wielding a scalpel. 'I did this favour for your father.'

Those staggeringly blue eyes studied her, the knowledge in them unnerving her even more. Sensation skittered down her spine, making her breath seize in her lungs, the car's interior now devoid of oxygen. Did he know the real reason her father had asked him to escort her tonight? Was this charade already doomed to failure?

'Don't look so terrified, *cara*,' he said, and she tried to school her features not to give away her fear.

'I promise not to bite. Unless you want me to,' he said, before touching the intercom button to inform the driver to proceed.

Pinpricks rioted over her skin as the car whisked away from the kerb and she imagined those straight white teeth nipping at all her most sensitive places.

She forced a smile, attempting to shake off the sensual fog he seemed to weave around her so effortlessly.

This was going to be the longest night of her life. Her physical reaction to him was too intense, too overwhelming. How was she supposed to survive an evening in his company without telling him every one of her secrets?

CHAPTER TWO

DARIO DE ROSSI WATCHED AS his date finally appeared from the bathroom on the far side of the ballroom. That was the third time in the last hour that she'd deserted him to go to the powder room. And freshen up, as she'd put it.

She didn't need freshening up. Her dewy skin was lightly flushed, the colour riding high on those apple cheeks, on the rare occasions when she'd been close enough for him actually to see her face. And when she wasn't in the powder room, she was engaged in the most vacuous of conversations with everyone but him, her light breathy laughter making every pulse in his body stand on high alert.

She was not what he had expected.

He had known, of course, the second that Lloyd Whittaker had approached him in the club yesterday morning and asked him to escort his daughter to the ball, that the request was part of the man's last-ditch attempt to save his company. The fool had finally realised who was buying up his stock and had probably thought throwing his daughter at Dario would soften the blow. It wouldn't be the first time a business rival had believed that he could manipulate Dario through his enjoyment of the opposite sex—or believed the garbage written about his love life in the tabloids. Giselle's recent hissy fit in *The Post* hadn't helped in that regard.

It also certainly wouldn't be the first time a powerful man had used and degraded a woman he was supposed to love and protect.

The brutal flash of memory had his gut twisting sharply. He took a sip from the bottle of Italian lager the hosts had imported especially for him and waited for the sensation to pass, while he watched Megan Whittaker make her way towards him.

She took the most circuitous route through the crowd, he noted, stopping to talk to a series of her father's acquaintances, every one of whom, Dario observed as his fist plunged into the pocket of his trousers, seemed to think it was okay to look down her cleavage.

The dress—plunging low enough at the neckline to leave not nearly enough to the imagination—had made his heart slam into his throat and dried up every molecule of saliva in his mouth when she'd walked down the hallway of her apartment. And quite literally taken his breath away when she'd eased onto the seat of the limousine and revealed a mile of toned, tanned thigh. Which had to be an optical illusion, because the woman, despite all those impressive curves, didn't even reach to his collarbone in her ice-pick heels.

He downed the last of the beer, and dumped the empty bottle on a passing waiter's tray, deciding that he'd let Megan off the leash long enough.

He'd only agreed to this date out of curiosity. Because he was bored. He'd wanted to see what foolishness Whittaker had planned—especially as he had remembered the daughter from a tedious event a month ago that he'd attended with Giselle. Strangely he had remembered her eyes, that deep intense green had captivated him, but only for a moment, before she'd ducked her head. She'd avoided him for the rest of the evening. So he'd found it amusing that Whittaker had decided to push her into his path to-night. To do what exactly? Seduce him into releasing his stranglehold on a company her old man had been running into the ground for years?

The idea was so preposterous he had been convinced it couldn't actually be true. That such an apparently inexperienced girl should be used for such a purpose seemed beyond even Whittaker's ability to mismanage the situation. But he'd decided to play the scenario out, mostly for his own entertainment. He'd had no date for the ball, Megan Whittaker had already intrigued him, and he would enjoy proving that he was not the barbarian her father obviously assumed him to be. He was perfectly capable of resisting the charms of any woman—even if he hadn't had one in his bed for over a month.

But then his date had surprised him. Stunned him even. And he didn't like to be surprised, much less stunned. She was nervous, yes, and had an artlessness about her, which might have been why he had considered her so inexperienced a month ago, but beneath that was an awareness, a physical response to him that was so intense and unguarded it had done a great deal more than simply captivate or intrigue him.

He didn't like it. He hadn't expected to want her. Or certainly not this much.

But now he had to decide what to do about it.

If Whittaker had sent her on some cock-eyed mission to seduce him, he wasn't about to take advantage of that. But on the other hand, if her response to him was genuine, why shouldn't they enjoy each other for an evening? She couldn't possibly be *that* inexperienced. She was twenty-four, well-travelled, and she'd dated at university in the UK, according to the background check he'd had done by his friend Jared Caine, the owner of Caine Securities.

And he'd felt the way she'd stretched against the palm he'd rested on the slope of her back as they'd left her apartment—like a cat desperate to be stroked.

She wasn't an accomplished flirt, but her instinctive response to a simple touch suggested a rare chemistry. What if she was as wild and vibrant as that russet-coloured hair if he got her into bed?

He hadn't had such a basic reaction to a woman in years, maybe never. He liked sex, he was good at it, but something about Megan had sunk claws into his gut, tearing at his self-control, which he was finding it increasingly difficult to ignore.

He'd sensed her nervousness in the car, so he'd backed off when they'd arrived at the ball, deciding to observe her, and give himself time to figure out what exactly he was supposed to do about the driving need inside him.

But that had obviously been a mistake, because all it was doing was frustrating him more. Truth was, he hadn't expected the avoidance tactics, but as he watched her pause to strike up a conversation with Garson Charters, the senile old judge who seemed to be as fixated on his date's cleavage as every other man in the place, Dario knew that was exactly what her frequent trips to the powder room were about. She was wary of him, not all that surprising if her father had told her to come on to him.

The conniving old bastard probably expected her to wheedle information out of him about their business dealings.

So now he had two choices: he could escort her home, or play with the fire between them regardless of her father's ulterior motives. Whatever happened, though, backing off wasn't an option, because it went against every one of his natural—and a few unnatural—instincts.

He heard the string orchestra in the adjoining ballroom

start up a waltz as he marched through the throng of guests sipping champagne and whispering loudly, and made a beeline for his date.

Her head popped up as he approached, almost as if she had a radar ready to alert her to his presence at a ten-metre radius. Her gaze locked on his for a millisecond and then flicked away, but not before he saw the jolt of awareness cross her features.

Her hunger was as real as his.

She said something to the elderly judge, who still had his beady eyes focused on her cleavage, then began to edge past the guy, heading back towards the bathroom.

No way, not this time.

He caught up with her in a few strides and hooked her wrist, drawing her to a halt. 'Not so fast, *cara*. Where are you going?'

The colour in her cheeks deepened, her eyes widening like those of a startled deer. The smoky perfection of her make-up and the hint of glitter on her eyelids did nothing to mask the unguarded sparkle of awareness in the emerald-green gaze.

'Hi, Dario,' she said breathlessly. 'I think I left something in the restroom.'

'What did you leave in the restroom?'

She scraped her teeth over her full bottom lip, for less than a second, but it sent a shot of heat straight to his crotch.

'Um…my…' She paused, obviously casting around for something.

Unlike her father, she wasn't an accomplished liar.

He stowed the thought. She might be Whittaker's daughter, but he'd seen little evidence this evening of any deviousness on Megan's part. She couldn't even seem to flirt with any degree of sophistication—her desire for him as blatant as her nerves whenever he got within a few feet of her. He could feel the slight tremors in her arm and the pounding beat of her pulse beneath the fingers he had on her wrist.

'Whatever it is, it will be fine in the restroom until after this dance,' he said, linking his fingers with hers as he made his way towards the dance floor in the adjacent ballroom.

She followed behind him as they weaved their way through the crowd, her reluctance palpable. Almost as palpable as the quiver of reaction in her fingers. He clasped her hand harder, not sure why he was seeking to reassure her.

'What dance?' she gasped. The confusion in her voice was almost as much of a turn-on as the tremor in her fingers.

He drew her into the ballroom and swung her into the crowd, deftly joining the other dancers as he lifted her arm high and then placed his other hand at the dip of her waist. 'This dance.'

She matched her steps to his instinctively. He gave her waist a light squeeze, leading her effortlessly into the turn, and dragged her closer. 'Put your hand on my shoulder, Megan,' he ordered, pulling her easily into his body, until the length of her pressed against him from shoulder to hip. Those impressive breasts plumped up against his chest.

She did as she was told.

He swallowed around the renewed jolt of lust, willing his crotch to behave itself. At least until they were off the dance floor and he could get her somewhere private. His decision had been made.

Playing with fire it is, then.

CHAPTER THREE

MEGAN WAS IN TROUBLE. In big, broad, six-foot-three trouble. And she didn't have any viable strategies left to get her out of trouble.

Because her first and only strategy, of hiding in the bathroom until she came up with a better strategy, had just gone down in flames, even though De Rossi had been surprisingly co-operative at first.

But now that strategy had crashed and burned. And she was far too aware of him to come up with another. The deliberate beats of the waltz reverberated in her ears, the sprinkle of light from the chandeliers dazzling her as he swung her around with practised ease.

With his body plastered against hers, she felt overwhelmed by the heat coming off him, the bunch and flex of his shoulder muscles as she clung to the fabric of his tuxedo; and the flare of arousal in his darkened pupils— all proof she wasn't the only one caught in this maelstrom.

His big body surrounded her, his heady scent frying the few functioning brain cells she had left and sending her hormones into meltdown. She could hardly breathe, let alone think.

The hard planes of his chest pressed against her breast as he whisked her round again. And she stumbled. His muscular forearm braced across her back, lifting her off the floor for a beat.

'Steady,' he murmured against her hair as her heels clicked down on the polished parquet. 'Follow my lead.'

She surrendered as he propelled her round the dance floor, past the envious stares of the women around her. He looked magnificent, lean and graceful in the tuxedo but with that air of raw, rugged masculinity that made the other men stand back.

She felt light-headed, her caution and control obliterated under the tractor-beam gaze she'd felt on her all evening, even when she was busy scurrying off to the bathroom for the umpteenth time.

The music swirled around them, the twinkle of light above them as they weaved in and out of the other dancers disorientating her. It was as if she were in the heart of a kaleidoscope, the colour and light dazzling her and leaving her dazed. Every inch of her skin stretched tight over her bones, so that she could feel each millimetre that touched his: the controlling press of his large palm on her hip, the rise and fall of his breathing, slow and steady against her own ragged pants; the thud of her heart, audible above the glide of cello strings marking the beat.

At last the music ended and he came to a halt. She stepped back as he let her go. Grateful for the space, even if his scent still enveloped her.

'You dance very well.' She forced the words out. Wondering if inane chatter might be a viable strategy.

'Do you wish to leave?' he replied.

Obviously not.

'Yes.' The word popped out on a breathless sigh.

He took her hand to lead her off the dance floor. A few people tried to waylay them, but he marched past as if he hadn't noticed. Maybe he hadn't, but she had. She felt as if she had a sign on her forehead—'woman being claimed'.

Her father's suggestion came back to haunt her. He'd wanted her to seduce this man, and she'd agreed to try, but why did what was happening now feel as if it had nothing to do with her father, or Whittaker's, or even rescuing Katie's dreams?

She wanted De Rossi for herself. No one else.

Her pulse battered her collarbone, her fingers clasped tightly in his rough palm, the prickle of awareness shooting all over her body. He paused briefly to pick up their coats from the cloakroom attendant at the entrance to the elaborate Westchester town house where the ball was held.

The chauffeur-driven car was waiting at the kerb as they descended the steps. Megan's heels clicked on the paving stones like gunshots, shooting down the last of her caution and control.

Dario didn't wait for the driver but pulled the door open himself. The dark interior beckoned, but she held back, scared to take the next step.

If she entered the car, this man would be her first real lover. And while that hadn't felt like an event of any significance up to this second, it felt significant now. Obviously this was just lust, some pheromonal trick her body was playing on her. She wasn't a hothead like Katie, and she wasn't a romantic either. She didn't need the conceit of hearts and flowers to justify a purely physical urge. But she'd never had this urge with any other man. And because of that, she couldn't do this thing while there was still so much deception between them.

'Get in the car, Megan,' he murmured, his voice deep with purpose. 'Or I'm liable to do something that is going to get us both arrested.'

She turned to find herself surrounded by him again, his arm braced against the roof of the car, her back flush against the door frame; she could feel the thick ridge touching her belly through their clothing.

'I can't... I have to tell you something first.'

'If it's about your father, and the reason he set up this date, don't bother. I already know.'

'You do?' She pressed a palm to his chest, shock overlaid with bone-deep relief.

The clatter of his heartbeat through the starched linen felt like a validation, silencing the cacophony of objections in her mind. He was as blown away by their chemistry as she was. That was all that mattered, surely? If he knew about her father's plan, this wasn't seedy, or underhand, or unethical. It was nothing more than two healthy adults fulfilling a need.

He nodded, his dark hair shining black in the streetlamp. 'Tell me, are you here for him, for his company, or for me?'

'I...'

For me. I'm here for me.

But even as the truth rang in her head, she couldn't voice it. Paralysed by words whispering across her consciousness from another April night, spiced with the juniper scent of gin and selfishness, the words her mother had whispered to her before she left. The last words her mother had ever spoken to her.

'I have to leave with him, baby. He makes Mummy so happy. Daddy will understand eventually.'

'I... I can't,' she finally blurted out.

She didn't want to be like her mother, she couldn't be. Maybe she had the same biological urges, urges she'd tried to deny for so long, but she couldn't sleep with her father's enemy and do nothing to try to save him.

'Why can't you?' De Rossi asked.

'Because it would kill my father if you destroyed Whittaker's.'

The dark scowl on Dario's face would have been frightening, if she still had some control of her faculties. Instead it only seemed to spike the fire in her blood. Would a man as ruthless in business as Dario consider changing his mind? Would he stop his pursuit of her father's company for her? Did he want her that much?

'I promise you, I have no intention of destroying your father's company.' He ground the words out.

She tried to control the foolish spurt of emotion at the concession. But she couldn't help it. As smart and sensible and grounded as she had always been about life and business, and as aware as she was of De Rossi's ruthlessness, and his cynicism, she was still moved that he would give her this, because she'd asked it of him.

'*Grazie,*' she said.

His brow quirked, then his lips tipped up in a feral smile that should have been terrifying but was instead terrifyingly exciting.

'Don't thank me yet.' He gave her a firm pat on the backside. 'Now get in the car.'

She laughed, she actually laughed, as she scrambled inside. All the stresses and strains of the last twenty-four hours floated off into the Manhattan night as the car sped through the evening traffic towards his home—his love nest—on Central Park West.

Whittaker's would be saved. Her father could stop freaking out about losing the company that had been in their family for generations and she could have this night of erotic exploration with a man who made her blood bubble and fizz beneath her skin, without a single regret.

It took ten minutes to drive through the moonlit park, a few hardy and fearless joggers still peppering the well-lit streets as they passed Belvedere Castle's fairy-tale turrets. Megan felt almost as fearless as those intrepid joggers when the car drew to a stop and Dario got out. He hadn't spoken during the journey, and neither had she. But the fever of anticipation stirring her blood made her fingers shake as he helped her out of the car.

'So this is your love nest?' she said.

'My what?' he asked as she tilted her head to take in the two towers of the art deco building, the ornate and opulent architecture a luxury statement from a bygone era.

But the laugh at his puzzled expression got trapped in her throat as he escorted her into the building, past the doorman and a receptionist, until he reached the antique lift. The intricate iron filigree gates opened as the uniformed operator beckoned them inside.

'Good evening, Mr De Rossi.' The man in his late-fifties tipped his hat at Megan. 'Miss.'

'*Buonasera*, Rick.' Dario's tone was clipped, his hand gripping hers so tightly she could feel her pulse punching. 'This is Megan Whittaker.'

'Nice to meet you, Rick,' she said, her voice distressingly husky. Heat scorched her neck. How many other late-night lovers had Rick been introduced to on their way up to Dario's love nest?

The term felt quaint instead of romantic—which was for the best, she decided. She wasn't here to make love, but to have sex for the first time.

Suddenly the enormity of what they were about to do occurred to her. They hadn't even kissed yet. What would that firm sensual mouth feel like on hers? How would his body look naked? She assessed the width of his shoulders in the perfectly tailored designer coat. He was a well-built guy; what if all of him was as generously proportioned? Would it hurt?

Should she tell him she'd never actually gone all the way before?

Her pulse rabbited against her collarbone as she watched the gold arrow above their heads swing in an arc signalling the floors.

Despite the antique design, the lift whisked them up to the twenty-sixth floor without a single creak. Too soon, and yet not soon enough. Dario bid the operator goodnight and led her into a palatial lobby area. Fresh flowers stood on a side table, the only touch of softness against the sleek modern lines.

Shrugging off his coat, he dumped it on an armchair, then lifted her wrap off her shoulders. Despite the warmth pumping out of a central air system, she shivered.

Callused hands settled on her bare shoulders and he turned her to face him.

His handsome face, rigid with desire, should have frightened her, at least a little bit. But somehow it felt compelling, for him to want her so much. His thumbs glided over her collarbone. His fingers curled around her nape with exquisite tenderness. And trapped her in place. Then his lips. Firm, sensual, and unapologetic, slanted across hers, triggering a tsunami of sensation.

Her breath got trapped somewhere around her solar plexus. The hard, unyielding line of his body imprinted itself on her curves, making her want to yield. Instead of demanding or devouring, his lips were coaxing, gentle, until her mouth opened on a huff and his tongue plundered.

He explored, exploited, taking control of the kiss. Shivers of awareness reverberated in her core, then his fingers fisted in her hair to angle her face so he could go deeper, take more. Her heart beat violently against her ribcage, like the wings of a trapped bird trying to escape. She plastered herself against him, absorbing the heat of his body, and kissed him back, her tongue darting out to duel with his. The sudden feeling of weightlessness was as terrifying as the desperate flare of longing, the shocking well of desire surging up her torso to obliterate everything but the sight, the sound, the taste of him. Earthy and raw and so staggeringly real.

The kiss could only have lasted for a few moments, but still she staggered, unsteady on her feet, when he lifted his head abruptly. His brows lifted, his eyes flaring hot, and she wondered for a second if he were as stunned as she was by the intensity of feeling that had passed between them.

Taking her hand, he led her down the corridor and into a huge, double-height room. A majestic sweep of stairs led to a mezzanine level, the deep leather sofas along the back wall the only furnishings. Huge floor-to-ceiling leaded windows looked out over the dark expanse of Central Park, the lake and the twinkle of lights from the East Side skyline beyond.

She could see her own reflection in the mullioned glass, her breath heaving in and out, her satin curves shimmering in the light from the hallway as he stood behind her. He glided his thumbs under the gown's diamanté straps.

'Yes?' The low question shattered the silence.

'Yes,' she managed around the thickening in her throat.

He eased the straps over her shoulder blades. The rasp of the gown's zip seemed deafening. Satin caught at her waist, and then slid down to pool around her feet, revealing the lacy royal-blue lingerie Annalise had insisted on buying to go with the gown.

Her breath hitched painfully as she heard the click of her bra releasing. He dragged the lace straps off her shoulders to slide down her arms. Her heavy breasts were released from their confinement. His lips caressed her neck, suckling on the pulse point as his hands covered the swollen mounds, his fingers circling her nipples.

Sensation tugged at her sex as he rolled the rigid peaks between thumb and forefinger, plucking then squeezing. Her knees went liquid, and a strong arm banded around her waist to hold her up. Her pale flesh shone white against his darkness.

His lips caressed the side of her neck as he growled. 'I can't wait any longer to have you.'

She pulled away and turned to face him. Her pulse was going berserk. She dragged a precious lungful of air into her lungs and tasted him, the subtle aroma of sandalwood and clean laundry detergent.

His thumb skimmed her cheek. The gentle touch had all her nerve-endings springing to high alert.

No man had ever looked at her with such hunger in his eyes. She absorbed the heat and intensity and it felt like a benediction, a celebration of everything she was that she had always been terrified to admit to.

The heat between her legs melted into a puddle of need, making her skin sensitive and her senses alert to the scent and taste of him, the rough sound of his breathing.

She squeezed her thighs together. 'Neither can I,' she said.

Dario stared at the girl in front of him—an artless seductress whose acute awareness of his touch had been torturing him all evening.

He had become spellbound by his own lust. He'd never wanted a woman this much, so much he wasn't sure he could be gentle—and that frightened him. He could actually read every one of her emotions as they flitted across her face, her attempts to wrestle them under control almost as bewitching as the hard peaks of her breasts, which begged for his mouth.

Need coiled hard in his gut, the pounding in his crotch unbearable.

He cupped her breast. She jolted but didn't draw away.

'Are you sure, *cara*?' He wanted no lies or obligations between them. He'd promised not to destroy her father's company. But it had never been his intention to destroy it, only to take it from the man…tonight, when the final deal with the last of Whittaker's shareholders went through at midnight.

'Yes,' she murmured.

He threaded his fingers in her hair, loosening the up-do. As the soft, silky strands teased his fingertips, her scent curled around him, fresh and vivid, and heat powered through his body. Her eyes widened, her breathing coming in harsh pants now. And he knew she felt it too, that tug of yearning, the driving need to finish what they'd started.

Her teeth sank into her bottom lip, mesmerising him, and calling to every one of his baser instincts, instincts he'd spent a lifetime trying to control.

Need overwhelmed him as he lifted her into his arms. Placing her on the couch, he lowered his head, unable to resist the pull of that lush mouth a moment longer.

He heard the soft gasp, tasted her excitement and her trepidation. It could only be a trick of the night, this veneer of innocence. No woman could be innocent and drive him this insane, but even so he enjoyed the challenge as he coaxed and cajoled, tempting her with his tongue.

Her lips opened at last on a shuddering sigh. His tongue swept into her mouth, exploring. Then she began to explore back. Tentative at first, then bold. Matching his hunger with her own. Driving them both mad. She tasted glorious, sweet and eager and new.

Her fingers glided beneath his jacket to cling to his waist. Heat slammed into him. He lifted himself up, yanking off his jacket and flinging it on the floor, pressing her back into the cool leather. Lifting her hands above her head, he bracketed her wrists in one hand to palm the pouting tip of her breast.

The nipple poked against his palm, standing proud as she arched her back, her breathing coming in desperate gasps as she pressed into the caress. He circled the tight bud, all thoughts of caution obliterated by her seductive response.

He trapped the peak between his teeth, tonguing it and then sucking it into his mouth. She sobbed something incoherent in the darkness, the desire in her voice rasping across his skin and sending the need spiralling out of control.

He wanted her, more than he'd wanted any woman, her artless response tapping into some primal desire to claim her, brand her, devour her.

'Please, I can't...' She jolted against him.

'Shh...' he crooned, desperate to relieve the throbbing ache in his crotch. She wanted him just as much. He could feel it in her body, which was tight as a bowstring, and in the staggered rise and fall of her breathing; he could see it in the flush of arousal spreading across the delicate skin of her collarbone.

'That feels so good—' Her voice choked off as he sucked the nipple against the roof of his mouth, tugging hard. She jerked against his hold, and pulled her hands free to plunge them into his hair.

The thin thread on his control snapped, primal desire charging through his system. Damn thought and sense and reason and anything that would stop him from making her come apart in his arms.

The madness to have her consumed him. He inhaled the delicate floral fragrance, like a narcotic drug. Pressing the heel of his palm between her thighs, to test her readiness, he felt her warm and wet through the lace. She quaked with need, daring him to take her, claim her, control her. Here. Now. And satisfy the need driving them both insane.

He plunged beneath the damp fabric of her panties, circling the tight bud. She cried out, bucking against the intimate touch. But the slick folds told a different story. She needed this. Needed him.

Ripping her panties, he grasped her thighs, spreading them wide to press the aching ridge against her centre.

'Let me have you,' he growled, the ferocity of the demand foreign to his own ears.

She looked dazed, her eyes unfocused, but she dropped her head in the tiniest hint of a nod.

The madness took over. He grappled with his zip and released his erection, then, positioning himself against the swollen folds, he thrust hard.

But as he surged deep, he heard the cry of pain against his neck, felt the tiny barrier, before she tightened on him like a fist.

He stopped dead.

He was buried to the hilt, the orgasm already licking at the base of his spine. But the hot clasp of her body was so tight. Too tight.

'What the...?' He swore viciously, shocked and sickened by the evidence of her innocence. 'You are a virgin?' he said, the shock only countered by the fierce unstoppable desire to move, to finish.

Megan buried her face in his neck, her whole body reeling from the shocking invasion. It had been so good, so bright, so beautiful, but now she felt impaled. He was too big, filling up every space inside her, all those empty places that had ached for so long.

She stiffened as he shifted, the thick heat branding her insides, stroking a place so deep inside, it spun her mind away from coherent thought again and back towards that glorious heat that had consumed her just moments ago.

'Cara...' He cradled her cheek. 'Answer me. Why you did not tell me I am...your first?' His perfect English seemed to have deserted him, the words clumsy, those deep blue eyes alive with stunned disbelief and raw aching need.

'I'm sorry,' she said, not sure why she was apologising, but he looked so horrified, she didn't know what else to say.

He held her hips, easing back, withdrawing that glorious heat. She gripped his buttocks, felt the muscles jump.

'Don't stop. It doesn't matter, really it doesn't. And it feels good.' It didn't exactly; it felt sore, and overwhelming.

'I don't want to hurt you.' He bit out the words, torn between temper and what sounded like torment.

Why did this matter to him so much? She wanted to ask.

But what she wanted more was for the bright, beautiful feeling to return. So that she felt empowered and special, not crushed and broken.

'I'm not fragile. I won't break,' she said, determined to make him believe it.

He swore softly in Italian, his fingers holding her thighs, poised at her entrance. 'Are you sure?' he asked.

She nodded, unbearably moved by the torment in his voice. 'Yes, I'm sure.'

He sank back into her to the hilt.

Her breath clogged in her throat. She could feel him everywhere, the stretching feeling unbearable again, but with it came the swift surge of pleasure as he nudged a place deep inside. He rocked his hips, and nudged it again.

'*Si sente bene?*' he asked, his English apparently having deserted him entirely.

'Yes, it feels good,' she said as the pleasure began to build in fierce undulating waves, sweeping away the pain, the confusion, until all that was left was the glorious swell of ecstasy, pure and perfect. The sensitive tips of her breasts rubbed against the hard contours of his chest through his linen shirt, sending arrows of sensation surging into her sex.

The slick sounds of their bodies slapping together, the scent of pheromones and sweat heavy on the air, the soft bump of her spine against the leather, faded into the background until all she could hear were the pants of her breathing and the grunts of his. He established a punishing rhythm, forceful, relentless, unstoppable. Then reached between them to press his thumb to the heart of her.

The huge wave crested, her whole being now focused on the burning core of her body, clambering for release.

She held on to him, terrified, frantic and overjoyed, all at the same time. He grew to impossible proportions inside her, his thrusts jerky and uncoordinated in their desperation.

She rode on that high wide plane between intense pleasure and unbearable pain for what seemed like an eternity, but could only have lasted a heartbeat. And her body soared.

Her thin cry cut the still air as the wave crashed over her, overwhelming in its intensity, and his shout of release echoed in her ear, the hot seed searing her insides.

What the hell just happened?

Sensation came back in small increments as Dario waited for his heart to stop battering his ribs like a wild stallion trying to kick its way to freedom.

The sultry scent of orange blossoms and sweat, the weight of her hands on his waist, the clinging cotton of the shirt he hadn't bothered to take off. The tight clasp of her surrounding him as the iron-hard erection finally began to soften and the ache in his groin subsided.

He buried his face against her neck, the soft skin damp and fragrant, and felt the hummingbird flutter of her pulse, as wild and erratic as his own.

He couldn't move, didn't want to move, grateful for the shadowy light as they lay cocooned together on the couch.

He'd had good sex before. Hell, he'd had spectacular sex before. He'd never had sex like that before, or an orgasm so intense it had felt as if it were ripping out a part of his soul.

Who is this woman? And what has she done to me?

He eased up on his elbows and felt her flinch beneath him. The sob of discomfort whispered against his face, making shame twist in his gut.

She had been innocent, and he'd ravished her like a man possessed. Not only that, but he had taken her without protection. Spilled his seed inside her. He should have stopped, withdrawn, but she had transfixed him somehow. And he had been unable to focus on anything but her. And the need to possess her.

Why hadn't she told him? She should have told him she was a virgin. He would never have—

Stop lying to yourself.

No force on earth would have stopped him, once she had given him her consent and unleashed the wild hunger inside him.

He climbed off her, careful not to jostle her. He couldn't make out her expression in the shadowy light, but he could see the tremors raking her body.

Lush and lovely, her pale skin looked somehow ethereal

in the soft glow of light from the lobby. He felt the renewed stirring of desire, and shame mixed with anger in his gut.

You are not an animal.

The admonition seemed like another lie though as he zipped his trousers and walked to pick up the jacket he had discarded. He returned to the couch to find her seated, her arms wrapped around her waist. He laid the jacket over her shoulders, and drew her close under his arm.

'Why are you shivering? Are you cold?' he asked, his voice hoarse.

She had to be sore, but was she also scared of him?

He tucked a riotous curl behind her ear, relief assailing him when she turned to him and smiled. The urge to kiss her gripped him again at the guileless tilt of her lips.

He resisted it. Not a good idea, given that kissing her would lead to other, more dangerous pursuits.

'No, I'm not cold. I just… I think it's a reaction…' She hesitated, biting down on that full bottom lip that had driven him wild, was still driving him wild. He forced himself to look away from her mouth.

'A reaction to what?' he prompted, determined to distract them both with conversation. He didn't usually like to talk much after sex, but this was different. He'd never been a woman's first before. It wasn't a responsibility he wanted or would have chosen, but he felt it nonetheless.

'A reaction to…' She hesitated again, but she didn't look embarrassed or unsure, just as if she were searching for the right words. 'Well, the orgasm, I guess. It was pretty intense. You're much better than my vibrator.'

The chuckle rumbled up from his chest, part amusement, part desire, but mostly relief. Her blunt honesty was ridiculously charming, especially when she blushed.

'*Grazie*, that is quite a compliment,' he murmured.

She gave a shy smile, looking embarrassed now but also amused. 'Sorry, I'm not very good at this.'

He looped the wayward curl behind her ear again, let his thumb linger on the smooth skin of her jaw, the laughter dying on his lips. 'On the contrary, you are very good at it, especially for someone with so little practice.'

The blush climbed up to her hairline, but she seemed pleased with the compliment. He felt a strange sensation in his chest and dropped his hand. What was he doing? Behaving like a besotted fool, when he needed to make sure that there would be no fallout from his irresponsible behaviour.

'Megan, we must talk about practicalities.'

'What practicalities?' she said, the guileless expression making him feel uneasy. Could anyone really be this innocent? Was this whole scenario some kind of set-up? Had Whittaker been devious enough to offer up his virgin daughter as a means of trapping him?

'I did not use a condom,' he said bluntly. 'Are you on the pill?'

The flush fired across her cheeks and her eyes widened. Either she was an actress worthy of an award, or the shocked reaction was not faked.

'No, I'm not, I'm sorry, I didn't—'

'There is no need for apologies.' He cut off her stumbling words, feeling oddly ashamed at the cynical direction of his thoughts.

Megan Whittaker was that rare thing, a person as genuine as they appeared to be—just as he had originally suspected.

'We are both responsible for the error,' he added. 'I am clean, I have a regular check-up and testing for my company insurance—and I never usually have sex without protection,' he continued, suspecting the threat of disease was probably the reason for her horrified reaction. His conquests after all had been well documented in the press, and made to seem much more indiscriminate than they actually were. Because, until Megan, he had always chosen his sexual partners with exquisite care. Which was precisely why he had never found himself in this position before. 'If you need proof,' he said, when she didn't respond, 'I can get my doctor to contact you.'

'No, that's not necessary. I trust you,' she said, marking out her innocence even more. He wanted to tell her not to trust him, not to trust any man, but before he could find the words she added, 'I don't either, by the way... Have sex without protection, I mean. Just in case you were wondering, and were worried too.'

The gauche statement was so earnest, his lips tipped up in a wry smile. 'With your vibrator, you mean?'

'Um, well...' The blush intensified on her cheeks, before she buried her hands in her face and groaned. 'Oh, God, I feel like such a clueless muppet.'

'Not at all, *piccola*.' He laughed, he couldn't help it; her found her reaction charming. 'We do still have one problem though,' he said, sobering. 'When did you have your last period?'

'Oh, I...' She raised her face, the blush still burning brightly. 'About a week ago. I think.'

'Then we are not quite in the middle of your cycle,' he said. 'But you should take emergency contraception. Yes? As a precaution.' He watched her intently for her reaction to the request, his anger at himself increasing. What would he do if she refused?

'Yes, yes, of course. I'll go to a pharmacy.' She jumped up from the couch, her panicked reaction easing the tension in her gut. 'I better go now. I'll need to find an all-night pharmacy. I don't even know if you can buy it across the counter.'

'Megan, there is no need to panic.' He rose from the couch too and tucked a knuckle under her chin. Raising her face to his, he touched his thumb to her mouth, the heat powering through him surprising him. 'And stop biting your lip. Or I will not be responsible for the consequences.'

She released her lip instinctively. 'But I should go, Dario. I need to get the contraception. I don't want…'

'You have up to a week to take it.'

'I do?'

'I believe so. Don't look at me like that, *piccola*.' He smiled again, captivated once more by how easily she was to read. 'I promise you, I don't make a habit of making love without contraception.' The truth was he had never made this mistake before, even as an untried boy, but she didn't need to know that. 'But I am a cautious man.' Or he had been until now. 'As I have no desire to father a child.'

'Yes, of course.' She nodded, her cheeks still as bright as beacons. 'I'm sorry, I'm making a hash of this, aren't I?'

'Not at all. This is new to you, I understand.'

She shuddered slightly, his tux jacket dwarfing her as she tucked her arms into the sleeves and held it close. 'I should probably leave now anyway though. I'll make sure I go to a pharmacy first thing in the morning.'

She was correct, of course, this had just been a chance for them to slake the lust that had sparked between them as soon as they had met.

But as she stood before him, beautiful and beguiling in the half light, he knew the spark hadn't yet been extinguished. And tonight would be their only opportunity, because he would not be contacting her again.

In a few hours, his agents would complete the hostile

takeover of her father's company, giving their encounter a one-night embargo.

It was of course dishonest of him not to clarify his earlier statement about Whittaker's, so there could be no confusion about what he'd meant. But he didn't mix business with pleasure. And for that reason, he did not feel guilty for giving her the cryptic answer he had. What happened in the boardroom had no bearing on relations in the bedroom—or rather the couch. What had passed between them, however wild and uncontrolled, could never be more than a physical attachment after all.

Once she discovered the truth, she would be upset. She might even feel he had got her here under false pretences. After all, his reply to her request had been deliberately ambiguous. But as his gaze drifted down her bare legs and he remembered the sweet shudder of her release, the feel of her thighs clasping his hips as she came, he knew he didn't want their one night to end so soon.

In fact, he almost felt regretful that she would no doubt hate him in the morning.

She picked her gown up from the floor and clasped it to her chest. 'Is there somewhere I could wash up,' she said, looking shy again and unsure.

He walked over to her, his mind made up. They would have this night.

He would show her the finesse, the reverence he had failed to show her so far. She deserved better than a frantic romp on a couch. He wasn't a romantic or a sentimental man, but he was a good lover.

The last of the shame drained away. He could keep the wildness in check; he would not ravish her again.

'There is no need to leave,' he said, tugging the cool satin out of her hands.

'But I...'

He placed a finger on her lips. 'No buts. We have all night. Why not let me show you all the other things your vibrator cannot do for you?'

The blush intensified, and he found the lightness, the laughter threatening to roll up his torso again. Not a response he was used to when in the process of seducing a beautiful woman.

No wonder this woman was so damn captivating. She was simply the opposite of his usual type. Her uniqueness would wear thin quickly enough, but he was enjoying himself for now. And he planned to enjoy himself a lot more tonight. While making sure Megan enjoyed herself too, of course. She might hate him in the morning, but eventually she would thank him for showing her that sex was much more enjoyable when not compromised by emotional entanglements.

'I'm not sure that's a good idea,' she said.

'Why not?' He cradled her cheek, enjoying the way she leant into his palm instinctively. And her pupils darkened dramatically. Did she know he could see exactly how much she wanted him?

'Because, to be perfectly honest, I'm a little sore.'

The delightfully gauche statement, delivered with complete sincerity, had him throwing back his head and laughing out loud for the first time in longer than he could remember.

'What's so funny?' she asked, grumpily.

He scooped her up into his arms.

She grabbed hold of his neck, her frown of protest only making him laugh harder as he headed to the stairs and the deluxe king-size bed and lake-size bath with power shower he planned to make good use of in the next few hours.

He placed a kiss on her forehead, enjoying the feel of

her bottom against his forearm. Why not keep her naked and wanting the rest of the night?

Why had he never considered before how arousing it would be to help a woman discover the frontiers of her own pleasure?

'Do not look so worried, *cara mia*,' he said as he took the stairs two at a time. 'There are many ways to make love, not all of them require penetration. Clearly your vibrator does not help with this either.'

'I wish I'd never told you about my vibrator,' she said. 'Now you're never going to stop making fun of me.'

'I am not making fun,' he said, although of course he was. 'But I do intend to remedy the situation. With your permission?'

She huffed out a breath, but the excitement and arousal dancing in her eyes told a different story, especially when she tightened her grip on his neck and said, with mock severity, 'Oh, all right, then—if you insist.'

CHAPTER FOUR

DIDN'T THE MAN EVER EAT?

Megan stared at the dazzlingly clean and startlingly empty shelves in the huge double wide fridge. Apart from a couple of bottles of pricey mineral water, a bottle of expensive champagne, some imported Italian lager, some milk and an untouched box of expensive chocolates, there was nothing to eat. She searched the cupboards a second time. Nope, still nothing there except some strong Italian coffee.

She turned in a circle. The oversized Italian football shirt she'd fished out of a drawer in Dario's walk-in closet skimmed her bare thighs as she took in the acres of granite and polished steel. The tingle of sensation as the material brushed her nipples had a memory flushing through her. Of Dario ravishing her breasts in the shower.

Moving swiftly on.

She concentrated on the sun, which had begun to climb over Central Park, shining off the lake and adding to that magnificent view. She'd woken up with Dario's big body wrapped around hers in sleep. He'd tucked her against his chest after he'd brought her to a stunning orgasm for the fourth time in one night… She lifted the glass of mineral water she'd poured herself from the meagre supplies in the fridge and took several gulps to ease the dryness in her throat.

Dario De Rossi a snuggler. Who'd have thought it?

She smiled to herself, feeling a little giddy. It was a Saturday, so she didn't need to go to work today. She knew her father would want her to call him to confirm if she had discovered anything, but there would be no need for that now. Dario had told her he wasn't going to go after Whittaker's. Maybe he had never intended to.

But unlike last night, she didn't feel the need to run off and hide. He'd been so solicitous after they'd made love that first time. And so devoted for the rest of the night. He'd soaked with her in the bathtub, then done things to her body that had proved that, yes, vibrators could not replace a flesh-and-blood man.

The sex had been hot, intense and unbelievably intimate. But she had adored every minute of it. Was this what her mother had been so addicted to? Now she understood. Something fluttered in her chest. Something sweet and seductive and more than a little bit silly.

She set about figuring out the state-of-the-art coffee maker and ignored the feeling. Their liaison was unlikely to last past this morning—so there was no point in getting carried away. She needed to be pragmatic. Really, she ought to be heading home. She had to find a pharmacy en route and take care of the practicalities—as Dario had put it. Her cheeks heated as she recalled their excruciating conversation from the night before. Her hand strayed to her belly. And she wondered, just for a split second, what it would be like to have the child of a man like Dario De Rossi.

Not going there.

She shook off the foolish, fanciful thoughts and let her hand drop.

She didn't want Dario's baby. She didn't want anyone's baby. She was fairly sure she wasn't cut out for motherhood, any more than her own mother had been. And if by chance Dario's seed had found fertile ground last night, she would remedy the problem as soon as she got back home. But first she needed coffee.

She concentrated on filling the machine's in-built grinder with coffee beans. It didn't take long to have the strong, chicory scent filling up the kitchen. If only she had more clothing, she could pop out and get something for breakfast. She liked to cook. And she felt she owed Dario. He'd made last night magnificent. And she hadn't exactly held up her end, so to speak. She frowned as she poured a steaming cup of coffee into one of the demi-cups in the cupboard. He'd been so controlled, so focused, it had been flattering and exhausting and beyond amazing. But somehow the times after that first time hadn't felt quite as, well, quite as equal. She'd felt oddly like a pupil, being played by a master. Her attempts to touch him, to caress him, to drive him crazy back, rebuffed.

'I'm impressed.'

She jerked round, sloshing hot coffee over the counter, to find Dario standing behind her, his broad, muscular chest making her pulse race. He wore a pair of sweat pants low on his hips—revealing the most mouthwatering V she had ever seen in her life—and nothing else. His olive skin was deeply tanned, even down to the line of his low-riding pants. His dark hair stood up in clumps on one side of his head, but unlike her hair—which probably resembled Frizz City this morning—the rumpled, just-out-of-bed look only made him sexier. Add that to the jaw sporting a five o'clock shadow that had given her whisker burn in some interesting places last night, and the man wouldn't have looked out of place in a million-dollar cologne ad.

'Still skittish, Megan?' His sensual lips tipped up on one side in a boyish smile as he leant past her to pour himself a mug of coffee and the giddy feeling in her chest fluttered again.

She breathed in his scent, the sandalwood aroma a brutal reminder of everything they'd got up to together in the shower.

'You have a habit of creeping up on me,' she said in her defence, but she smiled. Had she actually spent all night in this man's arms? This god among men? No fair.

He laughed, that deep rusty chuckle that had enthralled her last night, when she'd had the oddest sensation that he didn't laugh nearly often enough. It had made her feel special. When she knew she wasn't. But still.

'Why do I impress you?' she asked, shamelessly fishing for a compliment.

The tanned skin around his eyes crinkled, as if he knew exactly what she was up to. 'You figured out the espresso machine without an hour-long tutorial.'

She laughed and glanced back at the complex contraption. 'It's not that hard for a computer geek.'

He sipped his coffee, hummed low in his throat, the sound sending the familiar pinpricks darting down to her sex. Heavens, she was a hopeless case.

'Sexy and smart *and* a great coffee maker.' He leant down to kiss her, the teasing licks sending her senses reeling, his rich coffee taste making the hunger in her gut intensify. But as she opened her mouth to take him in, he pulled back.

'Damn, what do you do to me, *piccola*?'
Little one.
He'd used the same endearment last night. It was probably something he called all the women who slept with him. It didn't make her special or different—she needed to remember that. But even so, the deep blue of his irises seemed to sparkle just for her when he said it. This play-

ful, provocative side of him made her feel as if she was getting a glimpse of something he never showed to anyone else.

'Nothing you don't do to me,' she replied, because it was true.

'Hmm, I doubt that,' he said enigmatically, before he walked round and perched on one of the bar stools by the kitchen counter.

'I thought I could cook us breakfast, before I go,' she said, trying not to sound too eager. 'But you don't have any food.'

'I use a caterer when I entertain. Otherwise I eat out.'

'I see.' Although she didn't really. Surely for any house to be a home, you had to eat in occasionally? 'Well, I guess I should be going, then.'

'There is no need to leave yet. I can get groceries sent up. I like the idea of you cooking me breakfast.' He glanced at her shirt. 'Especially in my Roma shirt. Maybe I will ravish you afterwards on the countertop.'

The arrogantly male statement and the wicked intention in his eyes should have unsettled her, but instead it only excited her. But then every damn thing about the man turned her on.

'If you're going to be a caveman about it, I may have to rescind my offer,' she teased back.

'We will have to see if I can persuade you,' he said and she knew she was sunk. They both knew her resistance when it came to him was zero. 'How much time do you have?' he asked.

She glanced at the clock on the glass wall next to the eight-ring cooker…that he never used. And blinked, shocked to realise it was inching towards ten o'clock. She had to get back to her apartment before Katie woke up. Katie was not an early riser on a Saturday when she didn't have to go to college, thank goodness. But she didn't want her sister asking probing questions about where she'd been all night. And she definitely didn't want her finding out about the morning-after pill debacle—which meant making sure she bought it and took it before Katie got out of bed.

'I didn't realise it was so late,' she said, unable to keep the regret from her voice. 'I really need to go home and change and handle the other…um…practicalities we talked about last night.'

'This is a shame,' he said, and seemed to mean it—which didn't help with the giddy flutter in her chest.

But then her phone buzzed on the counter. She picked it up. A message from her father.

What the hell happened with De Rossi last night?

Guilt washed over her as she glanced up at Dario. Her father sounded as if he was freaking out again. This couldn't be right. Dario had told her he wasn't pursuing Whittaker's, that there would be no takeover.

'I should probably take this,' she said.

A strange chill settled in her stomach as she walked to the other side of the room and texted her father back.

Don't panic Dad, everything's okay. Dario assured me he's not attempting a takeover. I spoke to him.

She stared at the text, then quickly scrolled back to delete Dario and replace it with Mr De Rossi. Then she pressed send. She'd done a lot more than speak to Dario, but her father did not need to know that. Their liaison had nothing to do with the company. Not now.

The reply came back within seconds. And the sinking

feeling in her stomach became a black hole. The vicious words felt like a punch in the gut she couldn't defend herself against.

Stupid little slut! You slept with him, didn't you? After he stole my company. You're no better than your bitch of a mother.

'He shouldn't say such things to you.'

She swung round to find Dario watching her, his expression grim. She whipped the phone behind her back, humiliated and sick at the same time. Had he read that?

'He's upset. I think… He's under a lot of stress at the moment,' she said, instantly jumping to her father's defence. He didn't mean to be cruel. He wasn't a bad man, just an extremely stressed one. 'But I should go, and explain things to him. He's obviously got the wrong end of the stick. He thinks De Rossi Corp is involved in a hostile takeover. And obviously that's not the case, because you promised me yesterday you have no interest in Whittaker's.'

Dario took the phone from her and grasped her hand to lead her to one of the kitchen stools. 'Sit down, Megan. I need to explain something.'

She sat down. Confused now and wary. Why did Dario look so serious? Where had the sexy man of a moment ago gone to? The man who had worshipped her with his mouth, his hands, his body, last night? And why had her father texted her so viciously? None of it made any sense. The company wasn't under threat; it had all been a misunderstanding of some sort.

'Megan, you must understand, I never mix business with pleasure.'

'I know. I'm sorry, I shouldn't have brought it up, it's just he texted me and I—'

'You misunderstand me.'

'Sorry?'

'Last night was about us enjoying each other, not about your father, or his company.'

'I know that, but you promised me that—'

'What I promised you was that I would not destroy Whittaker's. That is what you asked me and I answered truthfully.'

'I know, and that's good.'

'I have no plans to destroy it. Because, as of last night, I now own it.'

She blinked rapidly, the black hole in her stomach opening into a huge pit. A huge gaping pit full of vipers. As he continued to speak in that calm, pragmatic voice, his words became barely audible above the hissing in her head.

'Whittaker's is still a viable company with the right management. It is a heritage brand with excellent prospects. The right management, though, is not your father. E-commerce is the way forward. He has refused to develop that side of the business to any great degree. I only asset-strip companies that have no future.'

He had taken the company away from her father.

He hadn't lied, but he had been economical with the truth. And she'd fallen for it. Because she'd wanted to. She'd heard what she'd wanted to hear in his qualified denial, because she'd wanted him. Her father had every right to call her a slut. Because that was exactly what she was. She'd put her own pleasure above the good of the company. The good of the family. Just like her mother.

Tears stung her eyes, making her sinuses throb. She wouldn't cry. She didn't deserve that indulgence. She had to get back to her apartment, get changed and then go to see her father and try to make this right. She and Katie had the money from their mother's trust fund, but her father administered it. He was bound to withdraw Katie's tuition now, to punish Megan for this folly. For this betrayal.

She sniffed, struggling to pull herself together, to ignore the hollow ache in her gut. The same sick feeling that had paralysed her the night her mother had left, when she was convinced her mother's departure was somehow her fault, because she hadn't been a good enough daughter.

She clambered off the stool, but as she tried to walk past Dario he held her arm, and pulled her round to face him. 'If you are angry with me, you should say so.'

'I'm not angry with you. I'm angry with myself. I've betrayed a man I love and now I have to tell him what I've done and hope he doesn't hate me.'

'Why would you love a man who speaks to you like that?' He sounded annoyed. She didn't understand.

'Please, I have to go.' She tugged out of his grip, and rushed over to pick up her gown. She would have to wear it home. The walk of shame really did not get any worse than this.

'He doesn't deserve your loyalty,' he said, the cynical edge in his voice cutting through the last of her defences. 'No man does who would use you in such a way.'

But you used me, too.

She pushed the self-pitying thought to one side. Dario hadn't used her, he had taken what she had offered freely. But even so, she couldn't bear to look at him as she took off his football shirt and slipped into the satin sheath. She should have been embarrassed that he was watching her. That having those eyes on her, cool and blue and full of heat, still aroused her. But she was way past embarrassment—everything she had ever known or believed about herself and her own integrity ripped to shreds.

She deserved her father's scorn.

'We slept together,' she said, pushing her feet into the torturous heels. 'I made a choice to sleep with you. It was the wrong choice. I see that now. I let what I wanted get in the way of what was right.'

Not only that, but she'd allowed herself to believe that a man as ruthless as Dario would put his desire for her above a business deal.

She wasn't just a clueless muppet. She was a hopelessly naïve and narcissistic clueless muppet.

'Don't be foolish,' he demanded. 'This isn't about right or wrong. Or you and me and what we did together last night. This is about your father and his inability to run a company competently. The two circumstances are not related.'

'They are to me.' She picked the wrap up from the floor of the living room and took one last glance at the wide green canopy of Central Park. There would be families down there, on this bright spring day. Families who loved and respected each other. But her father would never respect her again. She'd failed him. Failed herself. Thanks to her hunger for a man who was so far out of her league it was ridiculous.

He snagged her arm again. 'This is madness, Megan. We satisfied a perfectly natural urge last night. Nothing more. There is no need to punish yourself.'

She shook her arm free, blinking furiously to stop the tears from falling—because she would feel even more wretched if he ever found out the truth.

That somehow during their wild night together, she had come to believe she and Dario were doing more than just satisfying a perfectly natural urge.

'I have to go.'

She rushed down the long corridor towards the door,

pathetically grateful he didn't try to stop her. The sound of her heels clicking on the inlaid wood flooring mocked her. Along with the scattershot beats of her heart. And the nausea rolling in her belly.

As she took the lift down, she felt sick at her own stupidity.

But as the cab drove away from the art deco apartment building, she also felt a strange sense of pity. For Dario.

Because for all his wealth and power, for all his good looks and potent sex appeal, his indomitable confidence and charisma, it was clear he did not understand the importance of family.

CHAPTER FIVE

'MEG, WHERE HAVE YOU BEEN?' Katie pounced on her forty minutes later as she let herself into their apartment.

'Oh. My. God. You spent the night with him, didn't you?' Katie hissed as she took in the creased satin gown, the haphazard wrap, and the hastily knotted bundle of frizz on Megan's head. 'Sheesh, is that whisker burn on your cheek?'

Megan placed a hand over the raw skin, ashamed all over again. 'I can't talk about it now.' *Or ever.*

Her head hurt, the deep ache matched by the smarting pain in her tear ducts from the disastrous end to her wild night with Dario De Rossi—and all the tears she refused to shed.

That was nothing though compared to what the company would face now. She would lose her job, and she'd deserve it. A part of her—the small, sane part of her that could still think straight—had reasoned that it wasn't her fault De Rossi had targeted Whittaker's, or that her father's wild scheme to discover Dario's intentions through some sort of computer hack wouldn't have made a difference. But even so, she felt unbearably guilty. For sleeping with a man who had destroyed what her family had spent years building.

'Actually, you don't have to talk about it, I already

know…' Katie grabbed her hand, and tugged her into the alcove off the hallway. 'Dad's here, and he's behaving like a lunatic. He called you all sorts of horrid names and dismissed Lydia. Just sacked her on the spot.'

'Oh, no.' Was Lydia going to be made to pay for her mistakes too?

'Did he say anything about your tuition?' Megan asked, praying that she might be able to limit at least some of the damage.

'Yeah, he's pulling the plug on that. You could have told me he was paying for it,' her sister said, but she didn't look nearly as devastated as Megan had expected.

'Don't worry, Katie, I'll find a way to fund it.' Somehow.

'Forget it, I'll figure out a way to fund it myself,' Katie said dismissively. 'Believe me, that's the least of our worries. We have to deal with Dad first. I think he's lost his marbles. I'm not kidding. He's been ranting and raving about Mum, and you and De Rossi. He's behaving like King Lear on a bender. I think he's on something. He's dangerous.'

'What?' The vice around Megan's temples tightened.

'I tried to call you, to warn you.' Katie's head swivelled round to peek past the column that edged the hallway and gave her a direct view of the living-room door. 'But I kept getting the answer-machine.'

Because Megan had switched off the phone when she'd left Dario's—too much of a coward to bear her father's wrath before she had to. She'd delayed the inevitable still further by stopping at a pharmacy en route. But the chemist's judgmental look as she'd bought the emergency contraception in a crumpled satin ball gown had been more than enough of a guilt trip to remind her of all her transgressions.

'Don't worry,' Megan murmured wearily. She really didn't need Katie's ongoing battle with their father resurfacing and turning this crisis into a catastrophe. 'Dad's mad with me, that's all. I did something he may never forgive me for...' Just the thought of that had the guilt clawing at her insides like a rabid dog. 'He's lost Whittaker's.' Of course her father was distraught. He must have just found out about the takeover when he'd texted her this morning. 'But he's not going to hurt either one of us.'

'Don't be so sure,' Katie whispered, her eye darts and head swivels becoming increasingly frantic. 'Please, you have to go. Don't let him catch you here. He smashed up the living room already. You have to run away and hide until he calms down. I can stall him. He hardly knows I exist. He won't hurt me. But you...'

'Megan, get in here now!'

Katie shuddered as their father's voice boomed down the hallway.

Weariness and regret added to the guilt tying Megan's stomach into tight greasy knots. But as she went to step into the hallway to face her fate, and the dressing-down she no doubt deserved, Katie grabbed her arm. 'Don't go, Meg. For God's sake, what's wrong with you? He's nuts.'

'He's not nuts,' she said, although he did sound a bit deranged. But losing a company that had been your father's, and his father's before him, could probably do that to any man. 'And he's not going to hurt me.' Their father had always been distant, preoccupied with the company and his commitment to making Whittaker's a success, but he had never raised a hand to either one of them.

She dislodged Katie's fingers from her arm and walked down the hallway to the living room. The first shock came when she walked into the room. For once, Katie hadn't exaggerated. The room Lydia Brady always kept so spotless looked as if a hurricane had hit it. The photos of her and Katie growing up that she'd framed and hung on the walls had been smashed. A table had been up-ended, leaving fresh flowers crushed and water splattered over the broken glass, but it was the wanton destruction of one of Katie's artworks—the beautiful painting was lying in tattered pieces across the floor—that shocked Megan to the core.

Her father stood by the window, with his back to her. She had expected him to look bowed, to look devastated, had been willing to apologise profusely and then try her best to soothe and persuade and maybe even come up with some kind of solution, if he would let her. But when he turned, his fists clenched at his sides, his usually perfect appearance horribly dishevelled, he didn't look sad, or angry, he looked wild; the whites of his eyes were blood-shot.

'About time the little slut got home.' He strode across the room, the broken picture frames cracking beneath his shoes.

Megan stepped back, the pain in her temples scream-ing now. He leant past her and slammed the living-room door shut on Katie, who was hovering outside the room. Then propped a chair against the door knob.

'Daddy?' Megan said, the first darts of fear combining with the guilt sitting like a lump of lead in her stomach.

The blow came from nowhere, cracking in the air like a missile shot. She reeled backwards, the pain excruciat-ing as it exploded in her cheekbone.

'You stupid bitch! I'm not your daddy. I kept you two around because I had to—'

She scrambled onto her hands and knees, ignoring the pain in her jaw, the prickle of glass in her palms. He stood over her and hit her again, his fist knocking her shoulder and forcing her down. His foot glanced off her hip then caught the hem of her gown, the blue satin now spattered with blood. Was that her blood?

The metallic taste permeated her mouth.

She couldn't move, the gown twisted around her legs. She could hear her sister's cries, the pounding of her fists against the blocked door.

'Megan? Megan? Answer me, are you okay?'

She tried to shout back, but no sound would come out, the scream locked in her throat as she rolled and saw her father, standing over her, yanking the belt out of the loops on his trousers. He flexed it, snapped it against his palm, as if testing it.

'It was a condition of the damn trust fund your slut of a mother left you.' He was talking, his voice tight with bitterness, but so calm, almost conversational, unlike the wild light in his eyes.

Katie was right. He had gone mad.

'I'm calling the police.' Katie's muffled shouts came through the door. 'Hang on, Megan. I'll get help.'

She heard Katie's running footsteps retreat into silence. *Run, Katie, run. Don't come back.*

Her mind screamed as her father ripped away the wrap she had clutched in one hand, then wheeled his arm back. She rolled onto her front, so as not to take the blow on her face.

Pain sliced across her back, the leather biting into her shoulder. She raised her hands, trying to protect her head and the belt cut into the skin of her arm.

'Please, stop.' The plea burst free of the blockage in her throat.

'You deserve this, Lexy,' he screamed her mother's name. 'You did this to me.'

Megan curled into a ball, trying to escape the barrage

of blows. His grunts of exertion, the brutal slap of leather against skin, the scent of lemon polish and blood swirled around her, retreating into darkness, nothingness.

Dario's face appeared, the memory sultry and vivid.

What do you do to me?

The jagged pain in her heart was the last thing to fade as she fell down, down—away from the agony, and the shouts of her mother's name over and over again—into a safe place where no one could find her. Unless she wanted them to.

CHAPTER SIX

'COULD YOU INFORM Miss Megan Whittaker I'm here to see her?' Dario announced to the officious-looking building receptionist.

He didn't like the way Megan had run out on him. He needed to speak with her again. She hadn't done any of the things he had expected of her. He'd been prepared for temper, recriminations, even a guilt trip for deliberately misleading her. He had been ready for all those things and had had all the arguments on hand to explain to her, sensibly and dispassionately, why she was wrong to have read too much into their liaison.

But she hadn't done any of those things. And he couldn't get the picture of her, looking devastated and furious, not with him, but with herself, out of his head. It was foolish of him to feel guilty. He really had nothing to feel bad about. But still he couldn't shake the feeling that he owed her at least a visit.

The memory of her sobs of fulfilment, her sighs of pleasure, her body so sweet and trusting nestled in his arms all through the night, couldn't quite allow him to leave it the way it had ended.

He didn't have to explain himself. They were adults, consenting adults, and everything they'd done together during the night had been mutually pleasurable. But still he felt responsible.

'I'm sorry, sir, there's no answer from the apartment.' The receptionist frowned, the officiousness dropping away to reveal concern. 'Which is odd, because I saw Miss Whittaker go up there ten minutes ago and I know Mr Whittaker and Katie are there, too.'

'Try it again,' he said, the back of his neck prickling.

Something wasn't right. The lift pinged and out of it flew a girl dressed in skinny jeans and a scanty top that left her belly bare. 'De Rossi!' she yelled, racing down the steps leading to the lift and coming to a shuddering halt in front of him. 'You have to rescue her! He's going to kill her, and it's all your fault!'

She grabbed a fistful of his sweater, the fear in her eyes, deep green eyes so like Megan's, searing him to his soul.

'Who are you?' he demanded as he marched towards the lift. But he had already guessed. The prickles became a swarm.

'What's wrong, Katie?' the receptionist shouted out, jettisoning the formality as she confirmed that the frantic girl was Megan's younger sister.

Dario broke into a run, stabbing the lift button ahead of the girl, who shouted to the receptionist, 'Call the police, Marcie. And an ambulance.'

'Which floor?' Dario demanded as they entered the lift together. Cold hard dread gripped his insides—as the memory of another time, another place, assaulted his senses.

Megan's sister punched the button herself. And kept stabbing it as the doors closed, tears streaking down her face now.

'Hurry up, hurry up,' she said in a broken mantra.

'Stop it.' He gripped her shoulders as the lift travelled

up to the tenth floor, her fear forcing him to push the flood of memory and his own terror back.

She collapsed against him, her whole body shaking, and wrapped her arms around his waist. Burying her head against his chest. 'Thank God, you're here. I couldn't get the phone to work in the apartment.'

He rested his palms on her thin shoulders, drew her away, her blind faith in him almost as disturbing as his own irrational fear. 'When we get there, you need to show me where they are.'

'He's locked the door. I couldn't get in.'

The lift finally arrived at the floor. She charged out ahead of him, leading the way to an open apartment door. He heard the sounds first, the rhythmic thuds. He raced down the hallway, kicking open the door the girl indicated at the end with all his might.

The wood shattered and the door flew inward. The explosion of sound startled the man inside, his fist raised, a belt wrapped around it.

Whittaker.

But then Dario saw the woman curled in a foetal position at Lloyd Whittaker's feet. And his mind stalled, the horror gripping his torso so huge and all-consuming he couldn't breathe, couldn't hear anything but the terrified screams in his own head.

'Wake up, Mummy. Please wake up, Mummy.'

'Megan!' The scream from behind him shocked him out of his inertia. The fear was replaced by a feral rage that obliterated everything it its path. Until he couldn't see Lloyd Whittaker any more, or the young woman he'd held in his arms all through the night. All he could see was the man he had fought so many times in his nightmares.

His fist connected with Whittaker's jaw and pain ricocheted up his arm. Whittaker flew backwards and crumpled into a heap, the one punch sending him sprawling into an already broken table, which shattered beneath his weight.

Dario wanted to follow him down, to keep on pounding until the man's face was nothing more than a bloody pulp, but the small mewling cry, like a wild animal caught in a trap, stopped the rage in its tracks.

He watched Katie crouch beside her sister. Megan's beautiful gown, the one he'd eased off her body last night, was torn, the red welts of Whittaker's belt scoring the delicate skin of her shoulders and back.

'She's hurt.' Katie's cries pierced the fog in his brain, dulling the choking fear, the incandescent rage. 'He hurt her. I hate him.'

The fury finally dissolved into a mist—the surge of adrenaline retreating to leave Dario feeling hollow and shaky. He knelt on Megan's other side and gathered her into his arms, determined to concentrate on the task at hand.

They had to get Megan downstairs, to an ambulance. She needed medical care.

Her fragile body curled into his chest as trusting as a child, the bodice of her dress drooping to reveal the dark blue lace that had captivated him the night before.

Ave, o Maria...

He prayed to the virgin mother, the prayer that had been drilled into him as a child by his own mother as he carried Megan's unresisting body through the wreckage of the apartment.

This is not your fault. You are not responsible for the behaviour of a madman.

He kept repeating the words in his mind, his throat dry, his knuckles raw, his arms trembling as he used every ounce of his strength to keep the dark thoughts under control.

As he held her in the lift—Katie stroking her hair and begging her to be okay—Megan shifted in his arms.

He thanked God and all the saints.

'*Cara*, can you hear me?' he asked, gently.

Her eyelids fluttered open, the vicious mark reddening on her check making the rage and pain gallop back into his throat.

'*Stai bene, piccola?*' he said, and willed her to be all right.

Please let her be okay.

'*Grazie.*' Her bruised lips tipped into a shy smile—guileless and innocent. She winced, as her eyes closed again.

And the crippling guilt he had been holding so carefully at bay stabbed him right through the heart.

CHAPTER SEVEN

'WE'VE PUT HER into an induced coma, Mr De Rossi. The CT scan was inconclusive and we want to be certain there is no swelling on the brain from the head injury she sustained during the assault.'

Head injury?

The doctor's words whipped at Dario's conscience.

He hated hospitals—the chemical aroma of cleaning fluids and air freshener almost as disturbing as the feeling of powerlessness. He'd been waiting for nearly twenty minutes to see the doctor, his self-control on a knife-edge for a great deal longer—ever since the paramedics had whisked Megan away from him in the foyer three days ago.

After watching Whittaker being treated by paramedics and then taken away in handcuffs, he'd spent hours dealing with his team of lawyers and the police to ensure any assault charges against him would be dropped. He'd then spent further hours being questioned as a witness to Whittaker's assault on his daughter. And after that he had been forced to give a press conference, the media swarming around the hint of a juicy story like flies on a rotting carcass. There had already been a barrage of reports on the Internet, and photographs of him and Megan dancing at the Westchester and their subsequent departure. All of which had fuelled speculation about how Megan had ended up being rushed to hospital the next morning, and how her father had ended up in handcuffs.

As soon as the press conference was over, Dario's first instinct had been to rush to Megan's bedside at the exclusive private hospital in Murray Hill where he'd insisted she be transferred to avoid the press hordes. But he'd forced himself not to give in to that knee-jerk reaction.

Going to see Megan in the hospital would only increase the press speculation about them, he'd reasoned. He and Megan were not a couple, they were never meant to be anything more than a one-night stand—and, despite the horror of her father's attack and his own cursory involvement in it, he was not responsible for her.

But after he had been waiting three torturous days for news of Megan's recovery, Dario's ability to be patient and circumspect about the situation was at an end.

He wanted to know what the hell was going on, because the reports he'd been getting had been inconclusive, contradictory and wholly unsatisfactory. She should be awake and lucid by now, surely?

Unfortunately, the decision to go to the hospital and see for himself how she was had not helped calm his temper in the slightest—because he'd been thwarted by a brick wall of white coats and medical jargon as soon as he'd arrived and now the good Dr Hernandez, all five feet nothing of her, was the last straw.

'I wish to see her,' he reiterated.

The truth was, he *had* to see her, to be sure she was okay. The faraway look in her eyes, that bruised cheek and bloodied lip, the welts left by her father's belt on her shoulder blades had been tormenting him for days. He needed to touch her, feel her skin warm beneath his fingers, before he would be able to breathe again.

'Her sister is her only authorised visitor, Mr De Rossi.'

'Is Katie with her now?' he asked.

'No, I insisted she went home to rest.'

'Then Megan's alone?' He didn't want her to be alone. What if she woke and no one was there? Wouldn't she be scared after everything she'd been through?

'Miss Whittaker is still unconscious and will remain so, until we're ready to bring her out of the induced coma later today.' The doctor continued dispassionately, 'But when that happens I am only going to authorise close family to visit her.'

And of course she had no other family than Katie, and her bastard of a father. Every protective instinct Dario possessed, instincts he'd never even realised he had, rose up inside him. They had been as close as any two people could get four nights ago, but he could see that wasn't going to wash with Dr Hernandez.

'I am paying for her treatment. I insist on seeing her.'

Maybe it was irrational, the fear that had gripped him ever since he'd stormed into her apartment building to find her being brutalised by her father, but he couldn't wait to see her any longer.

Dr Hernandez drew herself up to her full height, which did not reach his chin, and levelled a sanguine look at him. She didn't look intimidated in the slightest.

'This isn't about what *you* want, Mr De Rossi. It's about what's best for my patient.'

'And leaving her alone is best for her?' he demanded, his frustration increasing. This woman hadn't seen her curled on the floor like a terrified child.

'That doesn't alter the fact that you're not related to her, Mr De Rossi, and I can't authorise a—'

'We're engaged,' he said, grasping at the only connection he could think of to give him the access he needed. 'And I'm not leaving until I see her. Does that alter things?'

The doctor's features softened and she gave a weary sigh. 'Okay, Mr De Rossi, you can see her when she wakes up. But that could be a while.'

'I'll wait.'

She tucked her hands into the pockets of her white coat, the sympathetic look annoying him more. 'Why don't you go home first and get some rest? You look exhausted.'

Of course he was exhausted; he hadn't slept for three damn days. 'I'm not leaving.'

'It could be several hours before your fiancée wakes up.'

The quaint, romantic term gave him a jolt, but he ignored it. Seeing Megan was the only way to make the anxiety that had been lodged in the pit of his stomach ever since the attack go away. 'And I intend to be here when that happens.' On that point, he refused to budge.

If he returned to his penthouse, the memories of that night would be waiting for him. Memories he couldn't seem to shake. The sweet sighs of her release, the hours spent touching and tempting her. And worse still, if he closed his eyes, the nightmares would chase him. He would see her bruised and battered body, feel her dead weight in his arms as he carried her into the lift, trying not to hurt her more.

'Then sit down before you fall down,' the doctor said, not unkindly, indicating one of the waiting area's leather armchairs. The pity in the woman's warm brown eyes added discomfort to his frustration—and the dazed feeling that had started to descend without warning.

'I'm not going to fall down,' he said, locking his knees, just to be sure.

'Good, because I have no intention of catching you,' the doctor returned. Gripping his elbow, she led him to the armchair she had indicated. 'What Miss Whittaker needs now most of all is rest,' she added, her voice floating somewhere over his head and not quite coming into complete focus any more. 'She's suffered a terrible trauma.'

'I understand that,' he said, his knees giving way as the adrenaline that had been charging through his veins for days finally deserted him. 'Which is why I intend to stay.'

'I suppose it can't do any harm to have her loved ones close by.'

Her loved ones?

The doctor's softly spoken words made no sense.

But as she left the room Dario sank his head into his hands. He raked his fingers through his hair and gripped his head to stop it dropping off his shoulders. He didn't have time to worry about the doctor's misconceptions. He'd said what he had to say to give him the access he needed.

He had to make sure Megan was okay. And that Whittaker paid for his crimes. Then he would be able to forget about the attack—and get a decent night's sleep again.

His smartphone buzzed and he fished it out of his pocket. He scrolled through the list of missed calls and texts. His gaze snagged on Jared Caine's text.

Saw the news. Nice work knocking that creep unconscious, buddy. Here if you need me.

The simple, succinct message made his chest tighten—which had to be the exhaustion.

He and Jared were friends. They went way back. Ten years back to be exact, to a dark rainy night in the West Village—when Dario had been a twenty-year-old Italian upstart with a fledging investment corporation making a name for itself on Wall Street and Jared had been a fifteen-year-old street punk who'd made the mistake of trying to pick another former street punk's pocket.

Dario had taken Jared under his wing after that night because the boy's cynicism and street smarts, his thirst for something better in life and his too-old eyes, had reminded Dario of himself.

But somewhere in the last decade, as Jared had forged his own path, shearing off all but a few of his rough edges, to become a smart, erudite and ambitious security advisor with a growing portfolio, Dario had come to rely on the younger man's friendship and loyalty.

And right now he could use Jared's professional help, because his buddy owned and operated one of the best, and certainly the hungriest, private security and investigative firms in the city.

Dario keyed in a quick text, requesting a meeting soon to discuss Whittaker's case. Not that Dario didn't trust New York's Finest, but the NYPD didn't have the resources of De Rossi Corp. Dario wanted Megan's father prosecuted to the full extent of the law.

He had seen the look in Whittaker's eyes when he'd punched him. He knew exactly what that wild glassy sheen indicated. And if the fifty-something CEO had a substance-abuse problem he had managed to keep secret, there would no doubt be other stuff they could use to crucify him.

Jared's reply came back.

I'll get working on it. Then we can arrange a meet at my place. More private.

The tightness in Dario's chest eased.

He laid his head back against the armchair, his galloping pulse slowing to a canter, but blinked to keep the foggy feeling at bay.

No sleep yet, not until he'd seen Megan. And assured himself once and for all she was okay.

Because only then would he be able to get the picture of her cowering at Whittaker's feet, beaten and brutalised, out of his head.

CHAPTER EIGHT

SHE COULD HEAR VOICES.

The first was her sister's.

'Meggy, please come back, you have to wake up now.' She could hear the panic and fear in Katie's voice. But she didn't want to come back just yet. Couldn't she stay here?

But then she heard another voice, much lower and more assured, which didn't plead, it insisted.

'Open your eyes for me, *cara*.'

She frowned. She wanted to be a little bit annoyed. Why did she have to come back? Staying where she was felt so much easier. But that voice, it was so compelling. It made her feel important. Significant. Special. It sounded so sure. And so safe. And so deliciously seductive.

The tingling sensation in her fingers became something more. A ripple of sensation. Warmth spread over her hand and her eyelids fluttered open.

Dario?

Heat flushed through her at the memory of that seductive mouth on hers. But why did he look so different from the last time she'd seen him, in his penthouse apartment, after they'd made love?

His hair had been dishevelled then too, but it looked a mess now. His jaw was covered in dark stubble and his eyes… He hadn't had those bruised smudges under his eyes, had he?

'*Ciao*, Megan. *Come va?*' The lyrical Italian washed over her. But then his sensual lips tipped up at the edges as he translated. 'How are you feeling?'

That smile, she remembered that smile. So sexy. Heat settled in her abdomen and she tried to speak. But all that came out was a husky croak.

He held her hand and pressed it to his lips. The prickle of stubble against her knuckles made her aware of a few other aches and pains. A lot of other aches and pains. Where had they come from? She remembered being sore after their lovemaking, but not this sore.

'Water?' he asked.

She nodded.

Cradling her head, he held a cup to her lips, directing the straw into her mouth. She took a sip, the cool water easing the rawness in her throat. Why was she so thirsty?

'Okay?' he said.

'Yes,' she said, despite all those unexplained aches and pains. 'Where are we? Is this your bedroom?' Had he taken her upstairs? She was sure he had. She could remember the slow glide of his fingers over sensitive flesh, the prickling spray of the water in his power shower, the scent of sandalwood soap that had clung to his skin and hers later, much later, as they lay together on Egyptian cotton sheets. But everything else felt so disjointed. And this didn't feel like his bedroom, the cloying scent of roses and the persistent sound of something beeping confusing her.

'You're in hospital,' he said, placing the cup back on a bedside table.

'I am? Why?' That didn't sound right. What was she doing in a hospital? 'Did I have an accident?'

'You don't remember?' he asked.

'No, I… I remember being with you and…' The heat suffused her skin. Should she tell him? But he looked concerned. She didn't want him to worry. She didn't want him to think for even a second that she hadn't enjoyed herself. It had been a little sore at first. Just as she had suspected, he wasn't a small man…anywhere. But it had been glorious after that. She wanted him to know that. She thought she'd told him this already, but maybe she'd only thought it.

'I remember it was wonderful. You were wonderful. But that's all I can remember.' Had she made a complete muppet of herself? Fallen over in his power shower? Tripped down the stairs leading up to the mezzanine? That would be just like her, to knock herself unconscious after the best sex of her life. The only proper sex of her life.

'What accident did I have?' she asked, when he simply stared at her, his gaze searching her face as if he was looking for something. Something important.

'Meg, you're awake.' Katie's excited voice pierced her aching head before her sister bounced into view beside Dario.

He started to move aside to make room for Katie, who looked overjoyed to see her. But as he went to let go of her hand, Megan's grip tightened.

'No, don't. Don't go.'

She didn't want to let go of him, not yet. She liked having him there. Something dark and scary seemed to be lurking just out of reach, and she didn't want to let it come any closer. With Dario there, holding her hand, she knew it wouldn't be able to. He was such a force of nature. He would never let it hurt her, whatever it was. And he cared about her. She knew he did. Because she could hear his voice in her memory telling her everything would be okay.

He squeezed her hand back. 'What is it, *cara*?'

'Could you stay with me?'

He hesitated for a moment, but then he sat back down, still holding her hand. 'If you want.'

She could see Katie swivelling her head between the two of them, her eyes widening. But she didn't have the energy to care. She had known she would have to tell Katie about Dario, and everything that had happened last night at the Westchester Ball, because it was impossible to keep anything secret from her sister. But she was more than happy to let Katie draw her own conclusions now, because she wasn't exactly sure herself what had happened any more. Except that it had been glorious. And just having Dario look at her like that, as if he would keep her safe no matter what, was enough to make the aches and pains from her mysterious accident fade away.

Along with the dark, scary thing lurking in the shadows.

A short, rotund, middle-aged Hispanic woman with a friendly face and gentle hands appeared and introduced herself as Dr Hernandez.

She checked Megan's pulse, shone a light into her eyes and then spoke to her in a soft, even voice.

She asked Megan all sorts of silly questions, like her age and her name, and Katie's name and their relationship. And where they lived. And what year it was. The doctor asked her about Dario and if she remembered him. Of course she did, she said, as the blush spread up her chest.

Thank goodness the lighting was muted in here. Or this interrogation could become really awkward, especially with Katie sitting there listening to every word.

But then the questions became more confusing.

'Do you remember your relationship to Mr De Rossi?'

She felt Dario's hand clench hers, his jaw stiffening.

'I...' She wasn't sure how to answer that. She didn't want to seem even more gauche, or clueless, than she did already, but at the same time he was here, holding her hand, so maybe he wouldn't mind her mentioning it. 'We're lovers,' she said, deciding that sounded a little less embarrassing than *We shared a night of the hottest sex I've ever had.*

'Do you remember that you're engaged to Mr De Rossi?'

Huh?

'What? Seriously?' Katie said, echoing Megan's confused thoughts. 'You're kidding?'

Her little sister crowded in on her and Dario and the doctor again.

Really? They were engaged? That was, well, surprising. Astonishing even. She couldn't remember the exact details, but hadn't they only met last night?

Dario's grip stayed firm, though, and he didn't jump in to deny it. The look on his face was guarded somehow but intense.

Even though she couldn't remember falling in love with Dario—which was probably a bad thing—being engaged to him, having him fall in love with her, felt like a good thing. Or at least not a bad thing. It made her feel protected, coveted, the way she hadn't felt since she was a little girl and her mother— She cut off that thought.

No, she wasn't going to think about her mother. Because it would take away the happy, floaty buzz, the giddy excitement in her chest that thinking about Dario gave her.

And being with him. Now. For ever. That felt pretty good too. Because as well as him being there to protect her, he could give her lots more of the hot, sexy times that she *could* remember from their night together—their apparently very eventful night together.

Really, it was all good. Except the not remembering part. But that would come back in time. Surely no woman would forget falling in love with Dario De Rossi for long?

'I...' She paused. She didn't want to lie to Dario, but she

didn't want to hurt his feelings either. And if they were engaged, she must have agreed to it. 'I think I remember it.'

'Do you remember anything about your father? About what happened?' the doctor said.

Thoughts butted into her head. Not happy, or floaty thoughts, this time, but sharp, discordant, jarring ones. Panic tore at her raw throat, and she began to shake.

The beeping in her ears got louder, more persistent.

'I don't…' She couldn't speak past the blockage in her throat, that dark, scary figure lurking nearby, encroaching on her peripheral vision. 'I don't want to think about that.'

She didn't know why, but she knew thinking about her father would be bad.

'Shh, Megan.' Dario leant over her, still holding her hand; he stroked her hair back from her forehead, the intense look pulling her away from the fear. 'It's okay. Look at me, *cara*.' He caught her chin in firm fingers, making her concentrate on him, that turbulent blue gaze forcing the fear back. 'You're okay. Do you understand?'

The words echoed in her heart, folding around her like a soft blanket, keeping her safe.

'Yes, but don't go.' She wanted to go back to sleep, but she couldn't stop shaking, the terror still too close.

'I won't,' he said, his voice so determined she knew he meant it. *'Te lo prometto.'*

I promise you.

'Relax, Megan,' the doctor said. 'I'm going to give you something to help with that.' A warm tingling feeling seeped into her vein, spreading up her arm and enveloping her in a beautiful fog. She floated on it, sinking into the cloud, soothed by the pressure of Dario's hand and his deep compelling voice telling her again that everything would be okay.

She held on to his hand, knowing it was true, as long as she didn't let him go.

* * *

'What just happened in there?' Dario could feel his frustration levels rising as he stalked after Dr Hernandez. He and Katie had been double teaming for ten hours, waiting for Megan to come out of her coma. And now this. 'How can she remember nothing of the attack?' he demanded as the doctor stopped at the nurses' station.

He shoved his fists into the pockets of his trousers, the fear on Megan's face still haunting him. How had this happened? He didn't feel less responsible now, he felt more so.

'Your fiancée has suffered a serious emotional and physical trauma, Mr De Rossi,' the doctor said with complete equanimity as she jotted something down on Megan's chart. 'It's quite possible she has blanked some of the events from that day.' The woman's clear brown gaze focused on his face. 'The good news is, she remembers you and your engagement. Your presence calmed her down considerably, which will be useful in the weeks and months ahead as she recovers.'

Months. He couldn't be responsible for her for months. He wasn't even her real fiancé. He knew he should point this out to Hernandez, but the memory of Megan clutching his hand and looking at him with such faith in her eyes made the words clog in his throat. He could not deny the connection now.

Until Megan was well again, and she had her memory back—*all* her memories back—she would be defenceless.

'I can't believe you proposed after one night!' Katie appeared at his elbow. 'That must have been some night.' The girl's scepticism was, of course, entirely justified, but the astonished look spiked his annoyance.

'Your sister is a remarkable woman,' he heard himself say.

'I know she is,' the girl said. 'But I'm surprised you do.'

He could hear the bite of cynicism in her tone. And it occurred to him that, although Katie was the younger sister, she had none of Megan's faith in the inherent goodness of people.

'He certainly never did,' she added.

'I am not your father,' he said, the comparison annoying him more. 'I appreciate your sister.'

'I get that, or I guess you wouldn't have asked her to marry you,' she said, not sounding convinced. 'But you still don't strike me as the sort of guy to fall hopelessly in love in the space of one night.'

She was certainly correct about that.

'Who said anything about love?' he asked, his temper kicking up another notch. He didn't need the fifth degree from a teenager. 'Megan and I are well matched. And she understands this engagement is one of convenience.' Or she would, as soon as she regained her memory and he could break it off.

But until then he would have to maintain this fiction. He could not leave Megan so vulnerable.

There was the police investigation to consider, the subsequent trial and, on top of all that, the press, who had been camped outside the hospital for days. How could he leave the young woman who had gripped his hand with such fear in her eyes to fend off all that alone?

Maybe he had not wanted the job, but who else was there? A nineteen-year-old art student was the only other candidate.

'I don't believe you.' Katie interrupted his thoughts. 'Underneath all her pragmatism and business savvy, Megan's a romantic. If she agreed to marry you, she must think she's in love with you.'

'She needs someone to protect her. I have the money and resources to do that until she is well. She understands that.'

Megan had struck him from the first as a pragmatic young woman, astute and intelligent. Maybe she had a blind spot where her father was concerned, but however fragile her mental state she must have made a choice to agree with Dario's deception in there. A subconscious choice maybe, but a choice nonetheless. However faulty her memory, she could hardly have remembered a proposal that did not occur.

He flexed his fingers, recalling the feel of her hand, so small, clasping his, as she begged him not to leave her. And another memory swirled in his consciousness, making his lungs squeeze in his chest.

Please save me, Dario.

He took a steadying breath, forcing himself to shake off the debilitating images from his past.

He had to concentrate on the present. The way forward was simple. He could not abandon Megan until she was well. But their situation had nothing to do with love. He and Megan understood that, even if Megan's sister did not.

'I'm sorry. I don't know why I'm having a go at you,' Katie said, as the fluorescent lighting caught the bluish smudges under her eyes. The girl was exhausted. She'd been keeping this vigil a great deal longer than he had, he realised. She dragged her hand through her hair. 'I'm the one who let her walk into that room.'

'It is pointless to blame yourself.' He gave the girl an awkward pat on the shoulder. Then shoved his hand back into his pocket.

Consoling distraught teenagers was as far out of his comfort zone as pretending to be someone's fiancé.

'You should go home, get some sleep,' he said. 'I will stay and ascertain what is to be done next and contact you in the morning.'

Katie looked at him, then back at the door to Megan's

room, clearly torn. He was struck by the closeness of the
bond between the two sisters, despite their personality differences. He would do well to remember that.

'There is little more either one of us can do now,' he
added. He might not want this responsibility, but he was
not about to shirk it—until he had come up with a coherent plan for Megan's recovery.

'Okay, I guess she trusts you,' she said. 'And you did
save her life.'

The words should have made him feel more burdened,
but, oddly, instead he felt strangely relieved as he watched
Megan's sister leave. As long as he had complete control
of the situation, he would be in a position to resolve it, to
everyone's satisfaction.

'Dr Hernandez…' He turned to the doctor, who had
been scribbling on Megan's chart while he and Katie
talked. 'Can you tell me when Megan's memory will
return?' The first order of business was to discover the
depths of the problem.

'I'm afraid not. Medicine is not an exact science, Mr De
Rossi. We'll run some more tests, have her speak to a psy-
chiatrist to ascertain as much as we can about the amnesia.
If there is no neurological cause, though, I would expect
Megan to remember the events in more detail once she is
emotionally strong enough to deal with them.'

'Get her whatever she needs. Money is no object,' he
said, prepared to pay whatever it took.

'Either way, she should be ready to leave the hospital in
a week or so,' the doctor continued. 'Her physical injuries
are healing well. And she'll be able to get the rest and recuperation she needs much better in a home environment.'

He swore under his breath. The doctor was right, of
course, but what home environment did she have? She
could not return to her old apartment, which had been

repossessed as soon as Whittaker had been arrested and the state of his finances revealed. And anyway, it was the site of the attack. Katie was now staying with the girls' old housekeeper in Brooklyn, having refused his offer of financial aid. But Megan couldn't stay there—it was too small and would not protect her from press attention. He and Katie had been running the gauntlet of photographers and reporters while taking it in turns to visit the hospital. Megan would need somewhere far away from the media spotlight.

'By the way, Mr De Rossi,' the doctor cut into his thoughts as she finished writing on Megan's chart and handed it back to the nurse. 'You mentioned the possibility of Megan being pregnant. We ran the test as requested and it came back negative.'

Thank goodness.

Dario's lungs released, the relief making him lightheaded. He'd requested the test a few hours before, his mind finally functioning well enough to realise that Megan might not have had time to take the necessary precautions before her father attacked her. Maybe she hadn't even needed the emergency contraception. Either way, this at least was good news.

But before he could suck in another calming breath the doctor added, 'Of course, there's always a slight chance of a false negative this soon after possible conception, but it's unlikely.'

A false negative? What on earth did that even mean?

CHAPTER NINE

'HEY, MAN, WASN'T expecting you tonight.' Jared yawned, then squinted at Dario out of sleep-deprived eyes.

Dario glanced at his watch. And winced. Two a.m. 'Sorry, I did not realise the time.'

'No problem. Come on in.' His friend wearing only a pair of sweat pants pushed open the heavy metal door to his loft apartment. 'Want a beer? You look like you could use one,' Jared added, padding into the apartment ahead of Dario.

He probably shouldn't have come over at this hour. But for the first time in his life, he needed help and complete confidentiality, and Jared was the only person he trusted that much.

The guy was the closest thing Dario had to family. Or what Dario figured a brother would be like. Someone who would help you out in a jam, no questions asked, but didn't pry into your private life. And that was what he needed right now. Because he'd been roaming Murray Hill like a zombie for a couple of hours, ever since he'd left Megan at the hospital, trying to figure out a work-able solution.

'You look terrible,' Jared said as he cracked open a beer and handed it to Dario.

'It's been a long four days.' Dario took the beer and

chugged a mouthful of the yeasty lager. Had it really been only four days since he'd had Megan in his arms? Soft and sweet and sobbing for release?

Stop right there, amico.

He took another long pull of lager, struggling to ignore the inevitable swell of heat.

He needed to stop torturing himself with thoughts of that night, because he wasn't going to have Megan in his arms again. The only way to square the subterfuge with his conscience was if he didn't sleep with her. She was fragile, emotionally as well as physically, so until she was fully recovered he couldn't even consider making love to her. He swallowed. Sleeping with her *again*, he corrected.

And not even then.

She was trusting and innocent and this situation had become far too complex already. He preferred women who knew the score, so that he could keep his sex life simple and his affairs shallow and short-lived. Megan had got under his skin to an extent that no other woman ever had, and circumstances had done the rest. All of which made him supremely uncomfortable.

'Yeah, I gathered that from the press reports on late-night TV.' Jared took a swig of his own beer and leaned against the counter top, the searching look only winding the knot in Dario's gut tighter. 'How's the new fiancée doing?'

The beer hit Dario's tonsils and he jerked forward in mid-sip.

Jared gave him a hearty thump on the back.

'The press got hold of that already?' Dario managed at last, his voice a hoarse whisper. Someone at the hospital must have leaked the information—which was all the more reason to get Megan out of there, out of the city, as soon as she was well enough to travel.

'So it's true?' Jared said dispassionately, but the relaxed pose was history. 'You guys are engaged?'

'Yes,' Dario said, his tired brain starting to knot along with his gut. He needed to get some sleep. He'd been running on adrenaline for hours; it was dulling his thought processes.

'You want to tell me how that happened?' Jared said.

'It's complicated,' Dario said.

'I gathered that.' Jared picked his beer back up off the counter, and used it to point at the long leather couches that made up the apartment's seating area. 'Let's take a load off.' He led the way across the large open-plan living space. Dario followed.

Jared settled on one of the luxury couches. The leather creaked as he propped his bare feet on the coffee table. And waited for Dario to speak. The younger man's pragmatic presence helped to settle the nerves dancing in Dario's stomach as he stared out at the night time NoHo cityscape visible through the wall of glass that had replaced the old loft's loading bay doors. But the compulsion to explain the situation to Jared still surprised him.

He never talked about his personal life to anyone. He'd been a self-contained unit since he was eight years old. Had forced himself to be. Leaning on other people, relying on them, just made you weak. But his personal life hadn't been this complicated ever. And he hadn't been blindsided like this, by events beyond his control, since he was that eight-year-old boy. And he didn't like it, because that was a feeling he'd promised himself he'd never have again.

'Megan doesn't remember what happened with her father,' he said, fixing his gaze on the blinking light of a plane above the dark shapes of the city's skyline. 'They ran some tests, got the opinion of the top psychologist in NYC and a head trauma specialist from Baltimore who's supposed to be the best in her field.' He'd had the woman flown in especially, to give a second opinion. 'They don't think the memory loss is to do with her head injury, which was minor.' The relief he felt at that piece of information was still palpable. 'More likely it's to do with the emotional trauma. A form of PTSD. A man Megan loved and trusted turned on her like an animal, so she's blocked it out.'

He drew his thumbnail through the label on the beer bottle, watched it tear into jagged pieces.

There was only one thing to do. It didn't matter if it would complicate his life for a while. Seeing Megan's anguish when Hernandez had mentioned her father, her vibrant hair rioting around that alabaster face and her deep emerald eyes wild with terror, had pulled at something deep inside him that he could not deny. She'd gripped his fingers as if he were the only solid object in the midst of a hurricane. She needed him and he couldn't simply desert her.

'I see what you mean by complicated,' Jared said.

Dario looked up from his contemplation of the beer bottle, remembering his friend was there.

'She needs rest and as little stress as possible, according to the doctors,' he said. 'The press furore is only going to get more insane when Whittaker is charged. I think it is best if I take her out of the country. If she is my fiancée I am in a position to make those arrangements, to keep her safe and protected until she recovers.'

Jared sent him a level stare. 'If? So this isn't a real engagement. Does she know that?'

'Maybe, maybe not. But she has accepted it without question, so it hardly matters,' Dario said. Maybe it was complicated and confused, but it all made perfect sense if you looked at it rationally.

Megan was in no position to make these decisions for

herself. And even if she hadn't been assaulted, Dario didn't trust her to make sensible decisions about her own safety. She was far too trusting at the best of times, and these were not the best of times.

'Okay.' Jared leant forward, resting his elbows on his knees—accepting Dario's reasoning.

But then, he hadn't expected Jared to question him.

His friend was even more cynical about relationships than he was. To the best of Dario's knowledge, Jared had never kept a lover for more than one night. Manhattan high society was strewn with the bruised hearts of women Jared had cast off before they could mean anything to him. He suspected that emotional isolation had something to do with Jared's childhood, or rather the lack of it, but he'd never asked; any more than he had asked about the cigarette burns on his friend's forearms, which were barely visible now, or the other scars that had faded in the years since he'd offered Jared a bed for the night in his apartment, before referring the homeless boy to the proper authorities. Because Jared's past was none of his business.

'I was going to work up a report for you on the case,' Jared said. 'You want the high points, before we discuss the particulars of how you're going to get your new fiancée out of the country?' Jared asked, the efficient, down-to-earth approach reassuring.

Dario nodded. 'Yeah.'

'Just as you suspected, Megan's father was high as a kite when he attacked her,' Jared began. 'According to my contact in the NYPD he's had a major cocaine habit for years. His girlfriend Annalise Maybury—now his ex-girlfriend—told the detectives as much under questioning. And there's something else, something I found out on my own after doing some digging,' Jared continued, the cynicism in his voice even sharper than usual. 'They're not his daughters.'

'What?'

'Megan and her sister, they're not his biological kids. He's known for years—got them paternity tested without their knowledge when they were children after the mom ran off with one of her lovers. Whittaker only kept them around, pretended he was still their old man, because he was busy mooching off the trust fund their mom left them. Which is all gone now, just in case you were wondering.'

'*Bastardo!*' Dario's anger curled around his heart, turning from red-hot rage to ice-cold fury.

He'd known Whittaker was a poor excuse for a CEO, and an even worse excuse for a father. But he'd never suspected the cocaine use, or the violence, so adding embezzlement and exploitation to that didn't seem like much of a stretch. But how much more vulnerable did this make Megan?

Megan and her sister had no money. And the press were bound to find out the truth about her parentage and splash it all over the papers and the Internet to feed the public's insatiable hunger for scandal. He'd seen the paparazzi shots of her as a teenager at her mother's funeral. She'd been scared and alone but also fiercely protective of her little sister.

When the press got hold of this story, it would be worse.

The memory of the welts on Megan's shoulder blades leapt out from the recesses of his tired mind, only to blur into a bloodier, more terrifying image. The sickening thuds of fists hitting flesh, the high-pitched sound of his mother's screams and the scent of stale cigarette smoke and cheap chianti assaulted him.

'Hey, man, are you okay?'

Jared's question drew him back to the present.

He blocked the image out, the way he had learned to over the years. But the return of the old nightmare left him shaken. His hand trembled as he took a last swig of his beer. Something he did not need Jared, or anyone else, to see.

'Yes.' He placed the bottle on the table between them. 'Can you give this information to the police?'

'Sure. I'll send them a copy of my report. Anything else you need on this?'

'I need your help to get Megan and her sister, Katie, out of the country without alerting the press as soon as Megan is well enough to travel. And me as well.' His mind was made up. There was no other solution. And with Katie there as a chaperone, he ought to find it easier to keep his mind out of the gutter.

Megan's memory would return soon, he had to believe that, because he intended to do everything in his power to ensure she felt safe and secure and well rested enough for that to happen—which included him being by her side. And when her memory did return, he wanted to be there. Just in case there were other complications.

The possibility of a pregnancy was small, according to Hernandez, after she had dropped her bombshell about a false negative on the test, and he wasn't going to worry about it overmuch. But he also wasn't taking any chances.

'I'd advise against taking the kid sister with you,' Jared said, interrupting Dario's thoughts.

'What? Why?'

'She might need to be available for Whittaker's arraignment,' he said.

'But surely our sworn statements are enough until the case comes to trial?' Dario asked. Witnesses weren't usually called for an arraignment.

'True enough, but I wouldn't risk it. Whittaker might

be low on funds, but he's no fool. He's managed to beg, borrow and steal enough for a top-flight legal team. He's saying you inflicted the wounds on your lover in a jealous rage. Neither the police nor the prosecutor's office are buying that. But if Megan's lost her memory, Katie is the only reliable witness to the actual assault. You can make a good case for taking Megan out of the country to recuperate until the trial, and if you're her fiancé it makes sense for you to go with her. But you spirit Katie out of the country too, just before the guy's arraigned, and I guarantee you Whittaker's defence team will try and use it. The kid sister stays, or you're taking a risk of this case not even getting to trial.'

Dario swore, his head starting to pound. 'Okay, Katie stays. I'll tell her tomorrow. She won't like it.' And neither did he. Being alone with her big sister wasn't going to make resisting Megan any easier. 'We cannot risk having Whittaker weasel out of paying for what he has done. Katie will understand that.' Because he suspected, unlike Megan, Katie had never had any delusions about their father. Or rather, the man who had pretended to be their father. 'Can I ask you another favour in that case?'

'Fire away,' Jared said.

'Can you protect Katie from the press once we're gone?' The girl was brave and bold, but she was also reckless and unpredictable and young.

Jared nodded. 'Consider it done.'

'I should warn you though,' Dario said, recalling his run-in with Katie earlier that day. 'She may not be co-operative. She is not as trusting or as amenable as Megan.'

'I think I can handle a hot-headed kid,' Jared said. 'I happen to be a professional.'

Dario's lips lifted in what felt like his first smile in days at the wry tone. 'Thanks.'

Downing the rest of the beer, Dario got up from the couch and shook Jared's hand. 'I'll speak to Katie tomorrow.' Not a conversation he was looking forward to. 'In the meantime, can you liaise with the police and the prosecutor's office to let them know what's going on? Then work up a plan to get us out of the country undetected.'

'Got it,' Jared said as he walked Dario to the door of the apartment. 'Where are you guys headed?'

'Isadora.'

He'd bought the island off the coast of Sicily five years ago, when the company had made its first billion in turnover. And had finished renovating the five-bedroom villa on it over a year ago. He'd already had a visit scheduled to the island once the Whittaker takeover was finalised, to check up on the many investments he was making in the island's infrastructure. And get some much-needed R and R.

'Nice,' Jared said, before bidding him goodbye.

Dario wasn't so sure. When he was not so tired, he might appreciate the irony that his visit to the island was now likely to be the opposite of relaxing.

CHAPTER TEN

THE HELICOPTER TOUCHED down on a helipad hewn out of volcanic rock. Megan breathed in the scent of sea salt and citrus, her eyes expanding with wonder at the heart-stopping view as the blades whirled to a stop.

A path meandered through terraces of lemon groves to a white sand beach. Dario's villa stood on the clifftop, its elegant stone walls adorned by grapevines and wisteria, the dark wood shutters open to let in the sunny spring morning, which was a good ten degrees hotter than Manhattan.

Dario leaned over her to undo her seat belt. 'You're awake? Are you feeling well?' he asked, solicitous and concerned.

'Yes, I woke up a while ago,' she said. She'd noticed him sitting beside her when she opened her eyes, busy keying in data on his smartphone, apparently uninterested in the staggering view as the helicopter swooped over the Mediterranean and then hugged the coastline of the stunningly picturesque island.

She hadn't wanted to disturb him, so she'd gazed out of the window and absorbed the breathtaking vistas while trying to get her careering pulse and erratic heartbeat under control.

It all seemed like a strange and wonderful dream. So strange and wonderful, she didn't know what to make of it.

Everything had happened so fast. Ever since Dario had told her they were engaged in the hospital three days ago. And yet at the same time, in a sort of delayed motion, each new and astonishing experience leaving her struggling to make sense of them. Frankly, it was all a bit too wonderful. As if she couldn't quite believe it was real.

She had led a privileged life, having attended private schools and lived in well-appointed homes in London and New York. She considered herself to be fairly cosmopolitan, with a smattering of Italian and French, having spent her childhood and adolescence living on two continents.

But nothing could have prepared her for the opulence and luxury of the world Dario lived in.

They'd been whisked from the hospital to JFK in a fleet of limousines in the middle of the night, then transported across the Atlantic on a private jet. The cordon bleu meal served on bone china crockery with sterling silver cutlery, followed by a night—alone—on a king-size bed in the sleek aircraft. The helicopter ride had been yet another new experience—as exhilarating as it was unsettling. But by far the most daunting thing had been having Dario by her side during every waking hour.

He'd been so careful with her, as if she were made of spun glass and might break at any minute. But while his care had made her feel cherished and safe in the hospital, now it was starting to feel stifling. He was such a commanding man, both physically and professionally. And she knew she wasn't yet one hundred per cent, because she still couldn't remember a thing about their engagement, or her accident. She didn't want to seem ungrateful, but she couldn't help wondering how Dario had managed to fall in love with her, when he obviously thought she was a bit pathetic.

She also couldn't quite fathom how she'd agreed to

marry him, when he made the air seize in her chest and her stomach do backflips every time he looked at her with those piercing blue eyes.

How were they going to have any kind of married life together, when his presence by her side made it hard for her to breathe?

Then again, at least she wasn't the only one who found him a bit intimidating.

He never raised his voice, but everyone they came into contact with on their journey—his PA, the drivers, the pilots, even the passport authorities—did his bidding without question. Everyone except his friend Jared, who'd talked to Dario like an equal when he had come to tell Megan he would be keeping an eye on Katie while they were away, on Dario's instructions.

She had wondered why Katie would need anyone keeping an eye on her, and debated warning him that Katie wasn't the easiest person to handle. But, in the end, she'd decided not to say anything. After all, Katie was more than capable of speaking for herself, and it had been so thoughtful of Dario to worry about her sister's welfare.

A car and driver arrived at the heliport as Dario helped her down from the cockpit. His firm fingers on her arm made her pulse jump and jive. She concentrated on the spurt of adrenaline as he left her side to go to talk to the pilot.

Gift horse—mouth? Hello? Stop looking! Why can't you just enjoy the thrill? You're tired and a little overwhelmed, that's all. A staggeringly gorgeous man is in love with you. This is not something to have a panic attack about.

A team of staff members arrived in a fleet of SUVs to unload a series of bags, boxes and trunks from the helicopter's hold. Luggage Megan had never seen before.

'*Cara*, are you ready?' Dario said, returning to lead her to the car.

'Yes, but… I just realised I didn't pack anything for the trip.' She didn't recognise the luggage, so it must be Dario's. 'Do you think I could order some clothes?' There had been some expensive clothes waiting for her on his private jet to change into when she'd arrived from the hospital, which had been wonderful and had made her feel a little teary—her fiancé appeared to think of everything. There had even been a ton of expensive creams, makeup and haircare products for all her toiletry needs, and a designer negligee in the plane's bedroom—although the seductive confection of silk and lace had seemed a little pointless when Dario had worked through the flight on his laptop instead of joining her.

But she couldn't expect the luggage fairy to keep providing her with everything she needed.

Dario had told her they would be staying for at least a fortnight as he had a series of meetings planned with his business contacts on the island. He was a busy man, and she knew she had a demanding job too. Although every time she tried to think about her job, the dark shadow lurking at the edge of her consciousness threatened, so she had decided not to worry about that. But if Dario had brought all this stuff with him, she would need more clothing, too. She didn't want to embarrass him with her paltry wardrobe.

'I've only got the hospital gown, and my negligee and this,' she said, sweeping her hands over the ensemble of slim-fit jeans, a camisole and linen shirt he'd already provided.

She sank her teeth into her bottom lip. Dario's lifestyle was extremely glamorous, way too glamorous for a woman with no luggage. No wonder she felt overwhelmed.

'Stop worrying, *cara*,' Dario said, his thumb glancing over her bottom lip.

She stopped biting it, the goosebumps going haywire at his tiny touch.

'There is nothing you need that isn't already purchased.'

'But I didn't bring…'

'The cases are mostly yours.' He swept his hand to encompass the luggage still being transported by several burly men to the fleet of cars. 'Della, my PA, assured me it was all you would need.'

Megan gaped, feeling like Alice, having just plopped down the rabbit hole.

All she would need? There was enough luggage here to dress the entire catwalk at Paris Fashion Week.

'But I… I'm not sure I can afford it,' she said, desperately trying to scramble out of the rabbit hole, and plant her feet on solid ground. Or solid*ish.*

'Shh… Do not concern yourself with money.' He captured her chin, forcing her gaze away from the never-ending parade of designer suitcases. The slow sexy smile that spread across his handsome face wasn't any less disturbing. 'I can provide what you need while we are here.'

She knew he was just being thoughtful again, but the insistence in his voice brought back the flutter of frustration. 'That's very generous of you, but I prefer to pay my own way.'

In the hospital, he'd told her she was his responsibility, and, while she'd found it comforting then, it was way past time she let him off the hook now. She still had some interesting bruises—her back was covered in them, which made her sure she must have fallen down his stairs. Obviously, he'd taken the whole responsibility thing too far because she'd had her accident in his home—which was touching, but it was getting a bit over the top.

'I certainly don't think you should pay for my clothes. I can do that.' Of course, she wasn't sure she could pay for those clothes, because from the logos on the bags they looked way out of her price range. 'You must let me pay you back.' *Once I've secured a loan.*

Dario's brows furrowed, the offer clearly confusing him. Obviously Giselle hadn't been much of a pay-your-own-way kind of gal. Maybe she didn't have Giselle's supermodel face and figure, but she did have financial integrity. And an unimpeachable work ethic.

Or at least she thought she did.

One of the luggage handlers arrived to tell them everything was ready.

Dario replied in Italian, instructing them to take the luggage to the house and have the housekeeper unpack it in the bedroom.

She got momentarily fixated on the word *bedroom*, his rich, resonant voice making it sound ludicrously seductive.

The thought of what they would be doing together in the bedroom in the coming days, and possibly for two whole weeks, cheered her up considerably.

She couldn't wait to get started. Her body's constant hunger for Dario, the desire to feel his touch again—the one thing about their engagement that was straightforward and uncomplicated. Maybe she wouldn't need to wear all the clothes. Then she could return a few and get a refund.

'Come, we will talk about this on the drive,' he said.

'Okay,' she said, although she couldn't see what else there was to discuss.

But then he put a palm on the small of her back, caressing the base of her spine, to direct her to the car—and she had to bite her lip to hold back the purr.

As the car sped down the track towards his magnificent home on the clifftop, an infinity pool came into view nestled amid trellises of flowering vines as the road climbed towards the house.

'The clothes are a gift, Megan,' he said, in the velvet-over-steel voice she recognised as the one he used when instructing his employees. 'I am a very rich man. I enjoy purchasing things for you. Payment is out of the question. Do you understand?'

'Um...okay?' she said, because she was distracted by that delicious voice, and the thought of all the things they were going to be doing in his *camera* tonight.

The villa was beautiful. But she didn't get much chance to examine the sweep of living and dining rooms on the ground floor, before Dario had directed her to the second floor and a suite of rooms with a terrace that offered an awe-inspiring view of the pool and the terraces of lemon groves that led down to the sea.

The men carrying her luggage trooped in behind them.

But all Megan's attention was on the enormous bed. The four-poster, draped with gauzy muslin curtains, was the room's focal point, both romantic and exciting and a tiny bit intimidating. Her heartbeat throbbed in her throat—and a few other key parts of her anatomy.

'Megan, this is Sofia,' Dario announced and she turned to find a tiny bird of a woman in her fifties with lush chestnut hair standing beside him. 'She is the villa housekeeper and in charge of all the staff; she will take care of your needs. I have instructed her to serve you your meal in your rooms tonight, so that you can rest.'

'*My* rooms?' she asked, confused now. Wasn't this suite of rooms for both of them? Where was Dario planning to sleep? 'But...?' Her cheeks coloured. How could she ask him such an intimate question in front of all these people? 'Won't you be joining me?' she managed at last.

'Not tonight, *piccola*,' he said.

He cupped her face and gave her a proprietorial kiss on the forehead, making her feel like an over-eager puppy. 'You must rest. And I must work.'

He dropped his hands and stepped back so quickly she might almost have imagined the perfunctory peck, but for the prickle of sensation on her cheeks left by the calluses on his palms. '*Buonanotte*, Megan. I will see you tomorrow, at suppertime.'

At suppertime?

He marched out of the room, his back ramrod straight.

What about the rest of the day?

She stood in the centre of the beautiful room, feeling dazed and desperately disappointed.

Sofia chatted away in a halting mix of English and Italian about how overjoyed they all were to have their boss's *fidanzata* in residence, while directing a couple of maids to fold away the dazzling array of designer clothing and making menu suggestions for Megan's evening meal. But as Megan watched Dario, tall and indomitable, disappear down the steps of the terrace, she'd never felt less like a *fidanzata* in her life.

CHAPTER ELEVEN

'*BUONGIORNO,* SOFIA. *DOVE* DARIO?' Megan asked the house-keeper, hoping she'd got her tenses right—and trying not to be embarrassed by the all too familiar enquiry. Because she'd been asking the housekeeper every morning for almost a week where Dario was that day.

'*Buongiorno, signorina.*' Sofia smiled, busy stretching and pulling the fresh pasta dough, as she did every morning. '*Il capo?* He is with the fishermen, today,' she said. 'Tonight we will have *Pesce spada.* How you say that in *Inglese?* Swordfish? Yes?'

Megan nodded as her heart sank to her toes.

The swordfish season had started that morning. She had spotted the traditional long boat with its twenty-five-foot mast from the veranda in her suite of rooms as the sun turned the deep blue sea a ruddy pink.

So Dario had got up at dawn and would no doubt be gone all day. Again. She had hoped today, with no business scheduled that she knew of, he might be able to stay at the villa.

'*Delizioso.*' She did a smacking action with her lips and Sofia laughed.

'Only if the fish smile on us,' the housekeeper said. 'If they do not we have sardine ravioli.'

Megan smiled back, but it felt forced and tight.

She adored Sofia. The woman was friendly and efficient and had been happy to spend the afternoon yesterday teaching Megan how to make fresh tagliatelle, which had gone a long way in keeping her anxiety at bay. But she didn't think pasta making was going to cut it today.

She'd been at the villa for nearly a whole week now. And each day had begun to blend into the next. At first she'd forced herself to appreciate the chance to rest and heal, and had tried not to let Dario's absences from the villa—and indeed her bed each night—upset her.

The villa was in a stunningly beautiful location with every possible luxury at her fingertips and Sofia, along with her two young maids, Donella and Isa, were more than happy to accommodate Megan's every whim. She'd made herself relax and enjoy the late mornings spent lazing in bed or sitting on the veranda with strong coffee and a tray of Sofia's fresh pastries; the light lunches spent lounging by the pool reading the books she'd downloaded from the Internet; the afternoons spent swimming and exploring the secluded coves, picking wildflowers, and trying to identify the local fauna. It had all helped to fill up the empty hours and stop her from obsessing about getting the chance to talk to Dario. About their engagement. And about all the things she could not remember about him.

To be fair, the complete lack of any stress had been welcome at first, as her body healed from her accident.

She also called Katie using Skype each afternoon, but that had become an exercise in avoiding all Katie's probing questions about how everything was going with Dario.

In the last few days, she had tried to be content seeing Dario each evening, when they would sit down to the lavish four-course meal Sofia and her helpers prepared each day.

Last night, as the citronella candles burned, illuminating his harsh, handsome face, Megan had watched her fiancé devour Sofia's delicious food and finally drummed up the courage to ask him about himself.

But he had directed the conversation away from anything personal, and in the end she was just so pleased to see him, she had decided not to push.

The hunger inside her, though, had been like a dragon, breathing fire into every single erogenous zone, as she'd watched Dario's firm sensual lips consume a mouthful of Sofia's light, tart lemon zabaglione. She thought she'd caught his dark hooded gaze on her cleavage, but it had flicked away again so quickly she wasn't sure if she had imagined it.

Her confusion and desperation had increased as he had escorted her once again to her suite of rooms and bid her goodnight at the door. So much so that she had been unable to hold back the suggestion that he spend the night with her.

She'd waited patiently for him to make the first move. But her patience was at an end now. Instead of taking her up on her offer, though, he'd said nothing at all, his jaw rigid.

So she'd ended up babbling on about how much better she felt now and if she relaxed any more she'd turn into a narcoleptic… A very fat narcoleptic, because Sofia's cooking was to die for.

For a split second she thought she'd seen the flare of desire, burning even hotter than her own, but then he'd politely refused her offer and walked away—leaving her breathless, anxious, and hopelessly frustrated.

And now this.

After waking up feeing tense, confused and even more frustrated this morning, she discovered he'd gone again.

It was too much.

Ordinarily, she did not have a confrontational bone in

her body—that had always been Katie's forte. But after over a week of rest and recuperation at Dario's command she didn't think she could survive another night alone without exploding.

Bidding Sofia good day, she returned to her rooms and rifled through the swimwear she had found among all the other clothing. She picked out a stunning scarlet bikini, which she had shied away from wearing because of the purpling bruises on her hip and back. But the bruises were as good as gone now.

She squeezed herself into the two swatches of red Lycra, dismayed to discover that whomever had bought the clothing had underestimated Megan's bust size a fraction. Either that, or Sofia's pasta blow-outs had added a cup size.

Didn't matter. Dario needed to see the evidence for himself—that she was fully recovered from her accident. It was way past time she demanded more of his time and attention.

She packed her e-reader, some sun lotion and a towel into her beach bag, and headed to the two-tiered pool situated on the terrace below the villa, prepared for a long wait. Dario would have to walk up through the lemon groves from the harbour and past the pool when he got back from his fishing expedition—by which time she would be more than ready to confront him. She hoped.

Dario trudged up the last few stairs through the lemon grove, calculating the hour as close to four o'clock. He would wash the fish smell off, then take the Jeep over to Matteo Caldone's farm, to check on the new irrigation system he'd financed for Matteo's groves of blood oranges. His shoulders ached from reeling in fish for ten straight hours. And he was ready to collapse. But after last night, he was not about to risk seeing Megan any sooner than was absolutely necessary.

After today's back-breaking work, surely tonight he'd be able to sleep without being visited by the erotic visions that had woken him hard and aching every night since they'd arrived.

Walking away from her last night had nearly killed him. Once he'd returned to his own room, he'd had to resort to the sort of self-servicing that he hadn't indulged in for some time.

Unfortunately, it hadn't done much good. He'd woken sweating and swearing, with images of Megan on their one torrid night together turning his hunger into a ravening beast.

The salt air, perfumed by the tart, citrus scent of the lemon grove, filled his lungs. He let it go, the heavy sigh almost as weary as his aching body. Tonight he would sleep and he would not dream of Megan. Those high, full breasts with their pale, pink peaks as she begged for...

He blinked and wiped the layer of sweat off his forehead.

Dio! Basta!

Then he rounded the drystone wall that led to the pool terrace and all the air left his lungs in a rush. Sitting on a sun lounger, her wet hair tied on top of her head in a loose knot, her full breasts barely covered by the world's tiniest bikini, was the star player in every one of those erotic fantasies.

A small voice in the very recesses of his brain was whispering that he should step away, disappear behind the wall and then trek across the fields to approach the villa from the other side, before Megan spotted him standing there like a besotted teenager getting his first glimpse at a nude centrefold.

But he couldn't move, the blood powering down to his groin silencing that small voice while making the rest of his body scream in agony.

Then her head rose and she saw him.

Too late.

'Dario, I've been waiting for you,' she said. Or that was what he thought she said, because it was hard to tell over the sound of the blood plummeting out of his brain to destinations south.

Standing up, she walked across the sun-warmed terracotta tiles towards him, her gorgeous curves threatening to spill right out of the minuscule patches of scarlet fabric with each seductive sway of her hips.

After getting up at dawn to spend an entire day hauling fish so he could get a stranglehold on his libido, everything south of his belt buckle had lost the plot in less than a second. The throbbing ache in his groin was now even more pronounced than the aching pain in his over-tired muscles.

Next time I see Della I am going to murder her. What was she thinking, ordering Megan that pitiful excuse for a bikini?

'I need to speak to you about…' She paused. 'About what happened last night… I don't want to spend another night alone, Dario. I understand that you are busy, that you have work commitments. But there are so many things I need to talk to you about and I've hardly seen you since we arrived.' Her voice drifted through his mind but he could make no sense of what she was saying.

Was that excuse for swimwear actually *wet*? He could see the clear outline of her nipples through the fabric.

Madonna! Please kill me now.

Her conversation drifted into one ear and then right out of the other as he became fixated on taking each of those ripe, responsive peaks between his lips and torturing them until she begged for release.

'Dario, are you even listening to me?'

'*Scusami?*' he mumbled, forcing his gaze back to her face. Her pale skin had acquired a healthy sun-burnished glow in the last week, her cheeks now a bright scarlet hue even more tempting than that damn bikini. He wanted to lick that fluttering pulse in her collarbone so much he could almost taste her sweet, spicy aroma on his tongue.

The way he had every night in his dreams.

Her eyes widened. Was that trepidation or shock he could see in them, the misty green bright with stunned knowledge? Then she rolled her lip under small white teeth and everything inside him shattered. All the smart, practical, moral reasons why he couldn't taste her seemed to explode in a cloud of nuclear fallout.

'Stop biting your lip,' he said, his voice a low husky croak he barely recognised as his own.

'Dario! Don't speak to me like that.'

He wrapped his hands around her upper arms and hauled her to him.

Her eyes popped even wider as his heat and hardness rubbed against her naked belly through confining denim.

Then all coherent thought fled as his lips landed on succulent skin and his hands captured the lush curves that had finally pushed him over the edge into madness.

Megan sucked in a shocked gasp, the pulse point in her neck battering her collarbone as Dario bent his head to press his mouth to her neck.

Everything burst inside her, all the hopes and needs and wants that had been escalating for days.

Pulling free of his controlling hands, she plunged her fingers into his thick hair, and dragged his face up.

He wanted her too. She hadn't imagined it. She hadn't.

The truth felt like a sunbeam, bursting inside her, as hunger darkened his hot blue eyes to black.

'Kiss me,' she demanded.

His tongue thrust into her mouth as he massaged her bottom, notching the apex of her thighs against the mammoth ridge in his jeans.

She almost wept for joy, kissing him back for all she was worth, her heart ready to explode right out of her chest.

He held her easily, forcing that thick ridge against the one place where she needed it the most. A guttural moan seemed to reverberate in her chest. Was that her or him? Did she even care?

The pleasure mounted, her whole body on fire now, her melting core seizing into greedy knots of desperation, coiling tighter and tighter.

She wanted him inside her, but before she could think or talk or even respond the wave crashed over her in one titanic surge of pure unadulterated bliss.

She tore her mouth from his, her broken cry shattering the harsh grunts of his breathing.

He swore suddenly and let her go, his eyes still turbulent with need. But instead of taking her back into his arms the way she wanted, the way she was desperate for him to do, he looked stunned.

'Don't stop,' she begged. 'Please don't stop.'

Her chin and cheek stung from the rough abrasion of his stubble. Her whole body shuddered from the force and fury of the spontaneous orgasm.

'I should not have touched you,' he said, his voice brittle.

'Why not?' What was he talking about? 'I wanted you to,' she added, in case he hadn't realised it. But surely he must have realised it. She'd had a climax from little more than a kiss, for goodness' sake.

She felt herself flush at the gaucheness of that. But she refused to care. Why should she be embarrassed by her wildfire response to this man? They were a couple, engaged to be married.

He raked his hands through his hair and took another step back. Why did he look so tortured? 'This cannot happen.'

'Why not?'

'I…' He hesitated, and for the first time ever he seemed unsure of what to say. 'I could have hurt you. I should not have put my hands on you.'

Oh, for— Not that again.

Temper, rich and fluid, and surprising in its intensity, rose up. 'I'm not made of glass, Dario. And I'm going to be your wife. I want your hands on me.'

He stared at her, as if he were lost for words. She could see the huge erection outlined by battered denim. Then he said, 'You have bruises still.'

'No, I don't. You can see, they're as good as gone.'

His gaze went all glassy again, before he suddenly jerked his head up.

'I smell,' he said, his voice a harsh croak now. 'I must wash off the scent of the fish.'

'You smell of the sea. And of you. Both scents that I love.' As much as she must love him in order to have agreed to marry him. Did he doubt her commitment to him? Was that it? Because she couldn't remember why and how she had fallen for him? But how could she know if he would share nothing of himself with her? Not even his body.

'Please don't do this,' she said, determined to find out why he was so reluctant to repair what seemed to be broken between them. 'Don't shut yourself off from me.'

She reached out a hand, wanting to stroke that rigid cheek, to reassure him. But he jerked back, out of reach.

'I must go and shower. I will be out this evening.'

'Why? Where are you going?' she asked, trying to stifle the bitter stab of rejection. And hurt.

'I have important business to discuss with Matteo Caldone, a local farmer... A new irrigation system. I will eat when I return, but don't wait for me.'

Before she could get in a word of objection, or shout at him that she did not want to wait any longer, he had marched past her and headed up to the house.

She stood by the pool, stunned by the encounter. But as she dug her teeth into her lip she remembered that flash of pure unadulterated need that had darkened his eyes to black before he'd swooped down on her, and she realised one incontrovertible truth.

The only way to bridge the huge chasm that had opened up between them was to get Dario back into her bed. Everything else would surely follow. Because wasn't that how they'd fallen in love in the first place? Through their shared passion for each other?

And if their mad kiss a minute ago had proved one thing above all others, it was that Dario De Rossi still wanted her as much as she wanted him.

All she had to do now was make him admit it.

There would be no more polite requests. No more sitting meekly every evening while he directed the conversation, staying obediently in the villa all day or standing silently while he gave her that one peck on the forehead and left her alone for another night.

The only way Dario would ever see her as an equal, the only way he would ever open up to her, was if she started behaving like an equal. And started demanding that he satisfy the hunger that was eating them both up inside.

No way was she going to let him run off to yet another crucially important meeting. A crucially important meeting she was fairly sure he had made up on the spot.

Rushing over to her bag, she stuffed everything inside. She dashed across the pool terrace and headed towards the villa.

Time's up, Dario. You're not running away from me again.

It took her ten minutes to find his suite of rooms in the opposite wing of the villa from hers. Rooms she had never been invited to. That was going to stop too. What was the point of her being here, if they spent no time together? She wanted to know everything about him—all the things she must have discovered that first night in order to have agreed to this engagement, but which she had forgotten about because of her accident.

She passed through a simply furnished but beautifully appointed office, equipped with all the things necessary to run a multinational business. That he'd had all this equipment installed in a holiday home gave her pause for a moment. Dario was a workaholic. But she had no idea why he was so driven.

Shouldn't she know about these parts of his life? She wanted to know why he couldn't settle, and what had turned him into a man so determined to succeed that he could never take a break.

She found the door to his bedroom closed. She knocked but there was no answer.

Gathering her courage, she pushed the door open.

A bed even bigger than her own stood in the centre of the room, but it had none of the romantic flourishes of hers. It suited him, she decided. The open shutters on high windows afforded him a glorious view of the cliff tops and the path leading towards the harbour. The room was enormous, but Dario was nowhere in sight.

Had he left already? Had she missed him?

But then she jumped at the sound of splashing water coming from a door in the far wall. She noticed a pile of clothes that had been discarded in a heap on the floor.

Her throat thickened, the eddying heat making the skimpy bikini feel tight and restrictive on her swollen breasts.

He was in the shower. Should she go and join him?

Vague memories of him naked and fully aroused, the muscle and sinew slicked with water from a different shower, blasted into her brain.

Don't overthink this. Just do it.

She knotted the summer wrap around her waist, and inched open the bathroom door.

Her breathing hitched, her heartbeat thudding against her ribs. The hot melting sensation detonated between her thighs and spread throughout her body like hot lava. Her knees shook, the sight before her bringing the dragon in her belly to scorching life.

Dario stood ten feet away in the walled shower, naked, with his back to her, the pounding of multiple jets of water meaning he hadn't heard her come in.

He had one hand braced against the mosaic tiles, his head bent, obviously concentrating on what his other hand was doing. Steaming water slicked down bunching muscles, making her throat close the rest of the way.

His masculine beauty was so breathtaking, each hard plane and muscular bulge so perfectly sculpted, it staggered her.

He was pleasuring himself. Heat flushed through her. Had their kiss done that to him?

What a waste.

'Dario?'

His head whipped round and the hot blue gaze locked on her face. His motions stopped. He turned as his hand fell away and her gaze dropped to the huge erection standing proud against his belly.

'You should leave,' he said, but the command in his voice was tempered by the rasp of longing.

She shook her head, unable to speak. Or move. Everything inside her gathered into that harsh, aching desperation to feel the thick length buried deep inside her again. Because the one thing she could remember with complete clarity was how glorious he could make her feel.

He turned fully now, allowing her to look her fill. He was magnificent. Moisture pooled in her sex, dampening her bikini bottoms.

'If you do not leave, I will have you,' he said, his voice so husky she could barely hear it against the beat of the water. 'Is that what you want?'

'Yes.' She found the strength from somewhere, even though her whole body was trembling now with desire and longing.

He nodded, his jaw hardening. His eyes took on a harsh glint that was both terrifying and exhilarating in its intensity. 'Then prove it to me.'

Wrapping long fingers around the hard shaft, he stroked himself—not fast this time, but with agonising slowness. The erotic display was almost more than she could bear.

'Take off your clothes for me,' he said, the tone harsh with demand.

Undoing the knot on the belt with clumsy fingers, she obeyed him without question. The wrap slid off her shoulders, the silk feeling like sandpaper as it whispered over her sensitive skin.

'All of it.' The commanding tone tightened the desire in her gut. 'I want you naked.'

She reached behind to undo the hook—unable to deny him now even if she had wanted to. The scarlet triangles dropped from her breasts, and the swollen, tender flesh burst free from its confinement. The breeze from the open window tightened her nipples into hard, aching peaks.

He dipped his head, still stroking that huge erection, to indicate she must lose the bikini bottoms too.

She plucked the tie on one side, and the fabric dropped away.

She couldn't breathe—anticipation warring with panic—as he finally released his erection and turned off the water. Wrapping a towel around his hips, he walked towards her.

Gripping her face, he forced her gaze to meet his and stroked his thumb across her cheek. 'Are you scared of me, *piccola*?' he said.

The nickname stirred a new memory of their first time. She had been a little scared then, of his size and what was to come, but she wasn't scared now.

'No,' she said.

'Then why are you shaking?'

'Because I want you so much,' she said, knowing if there was one thing she was sure about, this was it.

He swore, but then said, 'I want you too. Very much.'

Bending, he scooped her up and carried her quaking body out of the bathroom and into his bedroom. Another memory assailed her, of being in his arms before. Of being carried up the stairs in his penthouse… Bright, exciting, arousing. But something darker tickled at the edges of her mind. Not in his penthouse, but her apartment, the crunch of broken glass under his feet…

The shadow she had been avoiding lurched into view and she slammed the door shut on that memory.

Don't go there. Concentrate on the wonder of now.

Placing her on the bed, he dragged off the towel, releasing that magnificent erection. Reaching past her, he found a condom in the bedside cabinet and rolled it on.

She folded her arms over her breasts as he climbed onto the bed.

'Don't hide from me, Megan.' He moved her arms above her head, bracketing her wrists in one hand.

She cried out as he circled one swollen peak with his tongue, then nipped at the tip. The exquisite spike of sensation darted down to her already molten sex.

He played with her breasts, circling and sucking, releasing her wrists to stroke her slick folds.

Her moans turned to sobs of need, deep and guttural, almost animalistic as he circled and caressed, right at the heart of her.

He raised his head, releasing her tortured nipples, his erection prominent against her thigh. 'I must taste you. It has been too long,' he said.

'Yes,' she heard herself beg, not sure if he was asking her permission but desperate for him to know he had it.

Parting her thighs, he held her bottom, then knelt between her legs and lifted her. She arched, offering herself to him as his stubble brushed against her inner thigh. His hot tongue licked at the heart of her, delving and exploring.

Her sobs turned to ragged pants, the pleasure coiling tighter and tighter. His mouth found the pulsating nub at last and suckled hard.

She cried out his name as she shattered, the orgasm crashing over her in undulating waves.

He licked her through the last drops of her climax, as if gathering her taste. Then he let her go, to settle on top of her. Capturing her hips, he thrust deep in one shudder-ing glide. She stretched for him, the pleasure returning in a titanic rush as he rocked her back to orgasm with stag-gering speed.

His hands anchored her, forcing her to take the full measure of him. His penis butting that perfect spot he had found once before. The second orgasm swept through her, obliterating everything in its path—the trail of fire sear-ing through her from her head to the tips of her toes. She clung to his shoulders, her broken sobs matched by his shout of release as he followed her over at last.

It felt like a month but could only have been a few sec-onds before she returned to her senses, every part of her aching with the exhaustion of a body well used.

He shifted, still so huge inside her. And then lifted his head.

Why did he look so guarded? Surely he must know he'd just given her a multiple orgasm.

'You are okay?' he asked. As if he really didn't know.

'Are you kidding?' she said, even though she could see he was deadly serious. 'I'm spectacular.'

The deep chuckle—although slightly strained—was like music to her ears.

'Are you sure I did not hurt you?' he murmured.

'I told you, I'm not fragile,' she said. 'I love having sex with you. I really, really love it.'

His eyes narrowed, but the shadows retreated as he cra-dled her cheek and then kissed her nose.

'Ditto,' he said. Then he rolled off her.

She felt the loss of his warmth, his heat, immediately. Was this the moment when he told her he had to leave, to go to his irrigation ditch meeting? She was all ready to protest, to finally demand that he stay with her for the rest of the day. But instead of getting out of the bed, he hauled her close, wrapping his arms round her, and tucking her against his body, her back to his front.

She could feel the hard length of him nestled against her backside.

'You're not leaving to go to the lemon farm?' she asked tentatively, afraid to remind him of the engagement.

'It is an orange farm. But no, not tonight,' he said.

He leaned over her to grab his smartphone off the bedside table. Then keyed in a text.

Snuggling against her back, he nibbled kisses along her shoulder. Incredibly, after that shattering orgasm—make that two shattering orgasms—she felt the sleeping dragon wake again in her belly.

'Are you hungry?' he asked.

Talk about a loaded question.

'Yes,' she said.

'What are you hungry for?' he asked, and she could hear the smile in his voice.

'For food and for you, not necessarily in that order.'

The deep chuckle reverberated against her, sending a ripple down her spine as he cupped her breast and played with the nipple. The arrows of sensation shot straight back to her still tender sex.

'Sofia will leave us food in the kitchen for later. But first you must rest.'

The tenderness in his voice, and the feel of his thumb teasing her nipple, made her feel warm and languid, but far too turned on.

'Why must I?' she asked.

She didn't want to sleep. She'd had over ten days to sleep and now she finally had him where she wanted him, why would she waste time sleeping?

'Because you will need your strength for what I plan to do to you next.'

She shifted around, so she could look over her shoulder to gauge his expression. 'Really? You're going to make love to me again?' She could hear the eagerness in her voice and hoped she didn't sound like a nymphomaniac. But already the renewed stirrings of hunger in her belly were becoming unbearable.

Clearly satisfaction was a relative term, and, when it came to Dario De Rossi, she might never be satisfied.

He sighed against her hair. 'I have no choice. My will is not my own any more.'

It seemed a strange thing to say. Why would he choose not to make love to her, when he now had conclusive proof she was fully recovered from her accident?

Before she had the chance to debate the puzzling thought, or ask any of the many other questions that had tormented her about him, his hand slid off her hip, and sure seeking fingers found her sex, blasting into oblivion everything but the renewed surge of longing.

CHAPTER TWELVE

'CAN I ASK you a question?' Megan's eyes brightened, her voice eager, as she laid Sofia's antipasti onto an earthenware platter.

It was late, and Dario was ravenous. Unfortunately, it wasn't just for the array of cold food his housekeeper had left out for them.

How could he still want her? When he'd spent the last six hours with her in his arms—none of it catching up on the sleep he had lost in the last week.

He tore off chunks of the sesame seed bread Sofia made fresh each morning and added it to their midnight feast.

'You may ask,' he said, reserving the right to refuse her, the anticipation in her eyes making him instantly wary. He should never have touched her. He had promised himself he wouldn't. But ultimately he had been unable to stop himself from taking what she offered so eagerly. And now he would have to pay the consequences—by finding a way to deflect her curiosity again, without feeling like a bastard.

'There are so many things I want to ask you about that night.'

Dario carried the platter and their glasses to the moonlit terrace, the fresh scent of sea air and citrus fruit doing nothing to appease the clutching sensation in his gut.

Was her memory about to return at last? Perhaps the sex had finally jogged something loose?

'What do you wish to know?' he asked, cautiously.

Lloyd Whittaker had been charged and arraigned, thanks to Katie's testimony. He had been refused bail and would be standing trial in a few months. Megan hadn't mentioned him though, not since she had woken up in the hospital—convincing Dario her memory loss was centred exclusively on her father. If she asked about him now, it would surely mean her mind was finally healing as well as her body. But as she sat down opposite him at the table and began to serve them both from the platter, her vibrant hair the colour of rich red flames in the light from the citronella candles, he didn't feel as pleased at the prospect of her memory returning as he should.

Here was a chance to finally end this charade. To free them both from the obligations brought about by Whittaker's attack and Megan's subsequent amnesia.

But as he watched her tuck into Sofia's *verdure misti*—clearly considering what she wanted to ask very carefully—his mind spun back through the events of the past week. Against all the odds, and despite the knife-edge of sexual frustration that had been driving him insane for days, he had looked forward to seeing her each evening.

At last she looked up from her plate. The sheen of olive oil on her lips made them look even more kissable than usual. Dario licked his own lips.

This was just sexual desire, nothing more. His hunger for her was clouding his usually crystal-clear judgment. Anything she wanted to know he would be happy to tell her—because it would bring her memory back sooner and that was what he wanted.

'Would you tell me about yourself?' she said.

Anything except that.

His shoulders tightened. 'What do you wish to know?' he said, stalling.

She smiled shyly, the subtle shift of her lips as sexy as it was beguiling. 'Everything. All the things you told me that night about your hopes and dreams and where they came from.'

'But I told you nothing.' He never talked about his past, his childhood, because it had no part in who he was now. He'd made absolutely sure of that, erasing all but the most basic facts about his life from the media narrative of his success.

'Don't be silly.' She seemed amused at his attempt to correct her. 'You must have told me something for me to have fallen in love with you.'

The happy expression on her face made his heart kick against his chest in hard, heavy thuds.

They weren't in love. He had never loved anyone—not since… He shut down the thought.

'I expect I told you loads of stuff too,' she added in that effortlessly optimistic tone. As if love were something you would want, instead of something that would only hurt you. 'But I can't seem to remember that either. So you're going to have to help me remember.'

But there is nothing to remember.

'I don't know what you would want to know,' he said, still stalling.

'Then how about I ask you all the things I'm curious about now, because that's probably what I asked before?'

He didn't know how to reply to that, but she didn't really give him much of an opportunity before she had launched into her first question. 'The article in *Forbes* said you grew up in Rome.'

'I grew up outside Rome, in one of the government-funded housing projects constructed for the Roma community,' he said, reluctantly. The snap of bitterness in his voice that he couldn't control, though, surprised him.

He'd realised a long time ago that the experience of waking up to the scrabble of rats outside the trailer window and the sound of his own teeth chattering during winters in the slum, or the fetid smell of rotting trash and effluent from the urinals that marked the summer months, were the very experiences that had driven his need to succeed. He'd long ago come to terms with the terrible privations of his childhood. He wasn't embarrassed or ashamed of his origins, but still he had no desire to revisit that time in his life.

'You're of Roma descent? That's amazing,' she said, as if this were something to be proud of.

He frowned. Didn't she know that the Roma people had been treated like the scum of Europe—ghettoised and vilified, their way of life stigmatised for generations?

'My mother was.' The information slipped out, as he recalled the woman who had been so proud of her heritage, despite the hovel they'd lived in.

'She *was*?' Sympathy and compassion clouded Megan's eyes, making the antipasti in his stomach threaten to revolt. 'I'm so sorry, Dario. Is your mother dead?'

For a moment, the memories threatened to flood in on him. Memories he had spent a lifetime forgetting. 'Yes, but it was a long time ago.'

'Oh, no, were you a child?'

'No,' he said, because he had never been a child, not in the sense she meant. Grasping his fork in stiff fingers, he scooped up a mouthful of Sofia's grilled aubergine. It tasted like chalk as he swallowed.

'What about your father?' she asked.

'I never knew him,' he said, the lie coming much more easily this time.

He heard a groan, and looked up to see Megan digging a knuckle into her temple as if trying to erase something from her mind.

'Are you okay?'

'Yes, but… It's like there's a darkness lurking at the edge of my consciousness and I don't want to let it in.' Had the question about his father made her think of her own? And all the things she was trying so hard to forget?

He got out of his chair. 'Then don't.' Smoothing the unruly hair back from her brow, he took her other hand, and tugged her out of the chair. 'It has been a long day. You must get some rest now.'

'Really, it's nothing. I'm fine.' She dropped her hand. 'It's gone now.'

'I insist. You must rest.' Despite her protests, he scooped her into his arms, the desire to protect her from the demons that might be chasing her foolish in the circumstances, but there nonetheless. He needed her to remember, but if remembering still caused her pain…

She gripped his neck, looking a little perturbed. 'Put me down, Dario,' she said. 'You're overreacting. I can walk.'

He tightened his grip, taking her into the house. 'Let me carry you. It is my fault you are over-tired.'

She held on to his neck and stopped struggling, but the look she sent him was one of frustration. He didn't care. He was right. They had overdone things because where she was concerned he was incapable of keeping his libido in check.

'I don't see how it's your fault when I seduced you,' she said, indignant now.

'That is debatable,' he said, but he couldn't help smiling at the stubborn lift of her chin, or the combative light in her eyes. He was beginning to discover how brave and spirited she could be, for a woman who had been brutalised. Unfortunately, it only turned him on more.

He felt the familiar response in his groin and took a turn once he'd mounted the stairs towards her suite of rooms.

'Stop right there. I'm not going to my own rooms,' she shouted, and all but threw herself out of his arms—a bit too brave and spirited for his liking.

He swore as he scrambled to gather her back up. 'Come back here.'

'No.' She batted his hands away.

'You need to sleep. You must do as I tell you.'

'I'll do no such thing. You have to stop treating me like a child, Dario. I'm a grown woman. I can make decisions for myself.'

He could feel his own frustration kicking in. 'Not when you make the wrong ones.'

Like believing even for a second you could have fallen in love with a man like me.

'Will you listen to yourself?' Megan propped her hands on her hips.

How could she want to kiss him and strangle him at the same time? Seriously though, they were getting this straight once and for all. No more excuses and no more distractions.

'This is not the nineteenth century and you are not in charge of me.'

'You need rest. It is past midnight and you have reached orgasm six times today,' he shot back.

So he'd been counting. Why did that make her feel so much better?

He crossed his arms over his chest, looking like the poster boy for stubborn manhood, strong and indomitable. He who should be obeyed at all costs.

Well, not by me, buster.

His biceps bulged deliciously beneath the short sleeves of his T-shirt.

Her sex clenched.

Fine, maybe some distractions were going to be impossible to ignore. But that didn't mean she was going to let him get away with his high-handed attitude a moment longer. They'd come so far this evening.

The sex had been awesome, but the tantalising glimpse of intimacy had been even more so. Because the few things she had discovered about him tonight had intrigued and moved her in ways she couldn't explain.

Who would have believed that beneath the charming, charismatic sex god lurked a man who could look stricken when he was asked about his mother? He'd masked it quickly, but she'd seen enough to be touched—and compelled to wonder about so many things. Things she hoped to be able to discover about him in the days ahead. But she couldn't do that if she allowed him to push her away again—to compartmentalise their time together and keep her at arm's length.

'And I enjoyed every single one of those orgasms,' she said, something rich and empowering surging through her when his face flushed with aggravation. Sex was the key.

She knew sex, even great sex, didn't necessarily translate into emotional intimacy—especially with a man who was so adept at hiding his feelings. But it was a very good start. Not to mention rewarding in its own right.

'But we wouldn't have been at it for six hours straight if you hadn't denied us both the pleasure of sleeping together for a whole week,' she added.

'You were recovering from your accident,' he said.

'And now I'm not recovering any more. I'm recovered. I think we proved that comprehensively this evening.'

Something flickered across his face again, before he looked away. She touched his forearm, felt it tense beneath her fingers.

'How about a compromise?' she murmured. She didn't want to argue with him.

'What compromise?' he said grudgingly.

She smiled, amused by the muscle bunching in his jaw. For a moment he reminded her of a petulant child, so used to getting his own way he had forgotten how to bend. Only he wasn't a child, not in any sense of the word. Because…biceps.

'This is funny somehow?' The muscle in his jaw started to throb.

She bit down on her lip, trying not to let loose the smile that wanted to burst over her face.

Because instead of finding his taciturn show of temper intimidating, she found it exhilarating…and unbearably arousing.

His gaze glided down to her mouth, and she felt the spark of awareness leap between them.

'Here's what I suggest,' she said, deciding to ignore his rhetorical question. 'I'll consider taking your advice about my welfare, if I think it's warranted, but only if you agree to let us start behaving like a couple.'

No way was she letting him confine her to her own bedroom again.

'What does that mean? We are already together here.'

'I want to share a bed with you.'

His eyes narrowed and she could see he was about to refuse, so she jumped in before he could.

'I want us to sleep together…' She hesitated. Would this make her sound too needy? She frowned. How could it when they were engaged? Since when did engaged couples sleep in separate rooms? 'I like being in your arms. I want to go to sleep with you and to wake up with you. It's important to me.'

Dario knew he should refuse. She did not know what she was asking. They weren't a couple.

But before he could force the words out, she said, 'You make me feel safe, Dario. I don't want there to be so much distance between us. Or why are we even considering getting married?'

The plea in her voice made him feel like a bastard. He should tell her now that the engagement had been a ruse. A ruse that had got out of control. But somehow, he couldn't bring himself to do it. Something about the way she was looking at him, as if he could harness the moon and the stars for her if she asked him to, made him want to say yes.

She trusted him. When she learned the truth, it would crush that trust. But until then, he wanted her to feel safe and secure.

He cupped her cheek, his heart thundering in his chest when she leant into the caress and smiled.

'I can accept that compromise...' he said, touching his thumb to her bottom lip. 'But only if you promise to let me seduce you when we get to my bed?'

Maybe it had been a mistake to deny them both the physical pleasure that flared so easily between them? Perhaps this physical closeness was what she needed to find the strength to battle the darkness lurking at the edges of her consciousness. And really, what better way was there to distract her from her foolish desire to get to know him better? Which was all part and parcel of her foolish delusions that she loved him—or had ever loved him.

She smiled, the quick grin captivating and full of mischief. 'Absolutely—assuming of course I don't seduce you first,' she said, batting her eyelashes outrageously.

'*Dio!*' He reached for her hand and marched towards his own bedroom. Her seductive chuckles spurred the aching hunger in his groin.

Somehow or other he'd completely lost the upper hand in this negotiation, but the feel of her hand in his—and the thought of having her in his bed tonight, all night—was like a heady drug, making it hard for him to remember why exactly he had ever insisted on keeping her out of it.

CHAPTER THIRTEEN

MEGAN SQUINTED AT the sun shining through the shutters and stretched, disappointed to find Dario's side of the bed empty. Again. After over a week of waking up in Dario's bed she still hadn't managed to wake up before him. Her body protested, the desire to slip back into sleep almost overwhelming. She yawned, forcing the tiredness back. And grinned. Too much spectacular sex could be exhausting.

As she rolled over onto her belly, her grin widened at the sight of Dario's smartphone on the bedside table. He couldn't be far, probably in his study next door catching up on emails while she slept the day away.

Thank goodness he hadn't left without her. He'd mentioned a speedboat trip to the lagoon on the other side of the island today—one of the many trips and excursions they'd been on ever since she'd moved into his suite of rooms.

She'd used her newfound boldness to insist he start taking her with him each day on his different trips. And although he'd been reluctant at first, she was so glad she had insisted—because she'd discovered so many amazing things, not just about the island but about Dario, too.

Isadora had only a small fishing village on the other side of the peninsula on which the villa sat, many of whose inhabitants had to commute to the mainland to find work.

Dario had invested a lot in rejuvenating the island's once thriving community—building a new dock, constructing the villa itself and resurrecting the old olive, lemon and blood orange groves that had once thrived in the volcanic soil and had been a mainstay of the island's economy.

Each day, Megan would discover a new aspect to everything he was doing on the island, as he oversaw those projects with her in tow.

For a billionaire with a portfolio of international companies and investments, Dario had no qualms about getting his hands dirty. And the islanders hero-worshipped him, while also being comfortable treating him like one of their own.

Maybe she hadn't made much headway getting him to talk more about himself, or his past, but everything else she'd discovered had only made her fascination with him increase.

He was still bossy, but she had begun to realise that was all part of how focused and intense he was. He would never ask something of someone he wasn't prepared to do himself. And maybe he was still guarded about personal information. But his focus and intensity each night in bed—and on the occasions when they snatched a chance to make love in the daylight—showed a care and concern for her pleasure that made her sure what they were forging together was much more than just a physical connection.

She could make him laugh, lighten that dark, brooding quality that had once intimidated her, but now made her love him all the more.

And today she had a plan. To make a much bigger dent in that wall he seemed determined to keep erected around his emotions. And her plan was simple. Today was the first day they would be alone for one of their excursions. She would seduce him into a puddle and then pounce on him while he was floating on a cloud of afterglow—unable to resist her brilliantly subtle interrogation.

Of course, her plan was a risky one, because up until now she'd been the one who could barely remember her own name after they made love. But today she planned to get sneaky.

She'd asked Sofia to provide a picnic for their trip—to lull Dario into a false sense of security and satisfy his boundless appetite for food—and she was going to wear her scarlet bikini—to torture him with his boundless appetite for her.

She picked up the phone on the table to check the time.

Nearly noon? She frowned. How could she have slept so late when she had something so important to do today?

Throwing back the cover, she sat up.

Mission: Puddle of Lust, here I come.

The nausea came in a rush, the wave heaving up from her stomach so suddenly she was already gagging as she raced into the bathroom. She made it just in time before she lost last night's dinner in the toilet bowl.

Finally empty, her stomach settled into an uneasy truce as she sat on the cool tiles. Her whole body ached as she reached to push the flush button.

'*Cara*, what happened? Were you sick?'

Dario knelt down beside her and wrapped her robe around her shoulders to cover her nakedness.

'Yes, I think I must have picked up some kind of bug.' She placed a hand on her stomach. 'Although it feels a bit better now I've been sick.'

'Has this happened before?' The fierce expression made her heart bobble in her chest. Why did he look so disturbed? She hoped he wasn't going to use a little bit of nausea as an excuse to start treating her like an invalid again.

'No, not really.'

'No or not really?' he said.

Her stomach had been a bit queasy yesterday, and the day before when she'd woken up. But she hadn't been sick. And it had soon gone away. His brows drew down as he waited for an answer and she decided a white lie might be in order.

'No, it hasn't happened before.' Using the toilet bowl, she pushed herself to her feet, steadfastly ignoring the pitch and roll of her not-completely-calm belly.

She tied the robe around herself and brushed her teeth, before walking past Dario, who still looked concerned.

She escaped into the walk-in closet.

'I'll be fine,' she said, her voice deliberately light and cheery. 'All I need is a swim in the lagoon to make me feel better. I'm sorry I slept in so long.'

But when she came out of the closet, he'd disappeared into his office. She heard him talking in rapid Italian on his smartphone. She tuned it out. Thank goodness, he'd found some business thing to keep him occupied. She slipped on a summer dress and sat at the dressing table to slick on sun cream and a touch of lip gloss.

But when Dario returned to the bedroom, his face was still set in the same unforgiving lines. 'How is your stomach?'

'It's wonderful. Really, I'm great now. How long will it take to get to the cove?' she asked, still trying to inject as much brightness into her voice as she could, while subtly changing the subject.

'We're not going to the cove. The helicopter will be ready in ten minutes, to take us to the hospital in Palermo.'

The forbidding expression had her already dodgy tummy jitterbugging. 'Don't be ridiculous. I'm not going to hospital over a bit of nausea.' Why was he overreacting?

'Tell me, Megan,' he said, his jaw so tense she wondered he didn't break a tooth. 'Have you had a period since we arrived?'

'No,' she replied.

'Then we must go to the hospital for a pregnancy test.'

Shock came first, her stomach jumping right into her throat. 'But I can't be pregnant, we've used condoms the whole time. It's not possible.' It couldn't be possible. Except... The evidence started to reel off in her mind: her increased bust size, the tiredness and now her upset tummy. But more than that, something else niggled her memory.

Sofia tapped on the bedroom door. 'The helicopter is waiting, *signor*. Do you still want the picnic?'

The nausea charged back up Megan's throat at the mention of food.

'*No, grazie*, Sofia,' she heard Dario murmur as she shot back into the bathroom.

CHAPTER FOURTEEN

'YOU ARE INDEED pregnant, *signora*.' Dr Mascati smiled benignly at Megan. Dario tensed beside her, his expression as guarded as it had been throughout the never-ending helicopter ride from Isadora to the heliport on the roof of the exclusive private maternity centre.

'Are you sure?' Dario said, his voice curt. Not angry but not happy either.

Megan understood. This was shocking news. No wonder he'd hardly said a word to her since they'd boarded the helicopter. She hadn't known what to say either. However whirlwind their engagement, they hadn't even talked about their wedding yet, so introducing a pregnancy into that was bound to put huge pressure on them both.

But after the last week, the last two weeks, ever since waking up in the hospital, she'd come to terms with why she had agreed to marry him in only one night. Maybe it was mad. But the more she discovered about him, the more she got to know him, the more sure she was that she could love this man.

'The test is unequivocal,' the doctor said in his perfect English. 'There can be no doubt. We can do a scan in a couple of weeks so you can see your baby for yourself.'

'Okay,' she murmured, acknowledging the leap of joy despite her shock.

She placed a hand on her stomach, imagining the tiny life growing inside her. However unprepared for this they both were, this pregnancy felt so positive on some elemental level.

Perhaps it was her hormones talking. Or the endorphin high she'd been riding on for the last seven days. But whatever it was, she knew instinctively that despite the challenges and problems ahead they would be able to deal with them.

Maybe it had only been a few weeks, but Dario—so protective, so caring, so solid and sure of himself—would make an amazing father, and she… She would do everything within her power to be the mother this tiny life deserved.

Dario spoke to the doctor in rapid Italian, but the conversation floated somewhere over Megan's head as she caressed her invisible baby bump. And tried to contain the secret smile in her heart.

Dario was obviously unsure about this development; she could tell that already from his reaction to her sickness, which she realised now had been panic. Pure and simple. She just hadn't recognised it as such, because he always seemed so confident and commanding. But once they were alone together, they could talk about his misgivings. This pregnancy didn't have to be a bad thing.

'Megan, we must go now.' Dario's words jolted Megan out of her reverie.

'Oh, yes, thank you, Dr Mascati,' she said, trying not to sound too spacey. Even if she felt as if she were flying somewhere above the cosmos at the moment.

Dario rested an arm around her waist to guide her out of the doctor's office. They made their way back up to the roof, Dario gripping her hand as they crossed the heliport to the waiting chopper. He said nothing, his face now an implacable mask.

She stared out of the window on the flight back. The noise of the chopper's blades made it impossible to speak and she was grateful for that, because she wanted to get her thoughts together. He would need reassurance. Understanding.

But she was confident he would come around to the idea given time and encouragement. If he was sure enough of his feelings to ask her to marry him after only one night, no way would he be too scared to take on this responsibility once he knew how positive she was about it.

The sun dipped towards the horizon as they swooped over the villa and came into land on the cliff-top heliport.

Dario led her back to their suite of rooms in silence. Sofia arrived to lay out a meal for them on the terrace. The housekeeper sent her a gentle smile and Megan smiled back at her. Did she know already?

She stared out at the sea, the sky lit in a redolent array of red and gold and deep darkening blues. Isadora was such a beautiful place. What a wonderful place this would be to bring up a child.

No, that was silly, Dario had a life in New York, and so did she. But surely they could spend summers here—with their baby. She had to tell Katie. Her sister would be an auntie.

'Eat, Megan. You must be hungry.' She glanced back to find Dario watching her. She dialled down her excitement.

She was getting way ahead of herself. There was still so much to talk about. So much to discuss. She mustn't try and second-guess Dario's feelings. The doctor had said the pregnancy was still in the very early stages.

'Yes, of course,' she said, although the truth was she was far too nervous to eat. 'This looks delicious.' She picked up her fork and forced down a few bites of the aubergine and cherry tomato pasta she was sure Sofia had produced for her delicate stomach on Dario's orders.

'Do you want to talk about the baby?' she asked, as nonchalantly as she could, while she watched him closely, to gauge his reaction.

The impassive mask cracked, revealing something she didn't understand until he said, 'It is not a baby yet. It is a collection of cells.'

The flat words tore into the excitement that had buoyed her up through the helicopter ride.

Her fork clattered onto the plate. 'I know I'm only a few weeks pregnant, but…' She stalled, suddenly scared to say what she thought.

'But what?' he asked, not unkindly.

'It feels like a baby to me,' she managed around the feeling of dread suddenly pushing against her throat.

What would she do if he wanted her to have a termination? She hadn't even considered that option. Wasn't sure she could go through with it even if that was what he wanted. Had she been foolish, expecting him to be as happy about this unexpected event as she was? Probably, yes.

'Don't you want this baby?' she managed to say. Prepared for the worst, but desperately hoping for the best.

He looked away, across the terrace towards the sea, the breeze lifting the thick waves of his hair, lost in thought for a moment. But when he turned towards her, his gaze was shadowed and unreadable. 'That is not my decision. It is yours.'

The bright bubble of hope burst at the pragmatic tone.

Her hand strayed back to her tummy, and she looked down at the still invisible bump. Tears stung her eyes. She blinked furiously, desperate not to let them fall. It was just all so overwhelming. Not only the news about the baby, but how she felt about Dario. If she chose to have it, would it tear them apart? And if she chose not to, would it tear her apart?

Courage, Megan.

Dario was right: this was her choice to make and she'd already made it. She had to stand up for this child, and hope that, however early it was, this pregnancy wouldn't destroy what she was just starting to build with Dario.

Wiping away the errant tear that had slipped over her lid, she forced her gaze to his and smiled at him. 'I want to have your baby, Dario. Very much.'

He stiffened, and for once she could see his feelings written plainly on his face. He didn't look upset by her response—or particularly pleased either. He simply looked stunned.

He dipped his head, the nod almost imperceptible. 'I see,' he said.

She clasped her hands in her lap, but she couldn't stop her fingers from trembling, the emotion pressing on her chest too huge to deny as the bridge they had spent one glorious week building felt as if it were collapsing into a yawning chasm.

He didn't want this baby. She could see it in the rigid line of his jaw, the shadowed distance in his eyes.

'Dario, please tell me how you feel about it,' she begged, using every ounce of the courage she had left as another tear slid down her cheek.

He shook his head, then reached over to brush the tear away. The tender gesture made her heart ache even more.

Pushing back his chair, he stood up. 'You are tired, *piccola*. We can discuss this tomorrow.'

She should say something, anything—they needed to discuss this now, before he had a chance to retreat even further into that protective shell—but the last of her courage deserted her when he lifted her into his arms.

She clung to him as he carried her into their bedroom.

They would make love, she told herself desperately. That would make everything better. They were always so close when they made love.

He undressed her, but when she thought he would reach for her, he didn't. Instead he brought her one of his T-shirts, and helped her into it.

'Why do I need this?' she asked.

'Because your other nightwear tempts me too much,' he said. 'You need sleep, *cara*.' He tucked the thin sheet around her and stood up.

'Aren't you coming to bed, too?' she asked.

'Not yet, I have some work to do. I will be in later.' He kissed her forehead. 'Go to sleep. It has been an exhausting day.'

She wanted to argue with him, but her limbs were already melting into the bed. She curled up, taking in the comforting scent of sandalwood that clung to the sheets.

It was okay. She was still in his bed. And he would be back soon. Then they would make love. And all their differences would melt away.

'Don't be long,' she murmured as her eyes drifted closed.

But he had already left the room.

CHAPTER FIFTEEN

'SHE'S PREGNANT? FROM the look on your face, I'm guessing that's not good news,' Jared said, his voice as dispassionate as usual over the scratchy Internet connection.

Dario rubbed his forehead, trying to erase the picture lodged there of Megan crouched on the bathroom floor retching this morning. And the single tear drifting down her cheek this evening in the dusk as she told him she wanted to have his child.

He was shattered, the strain of trying to keep his emotions in check the whole day too much even for him. He had called his friend to get some advice. Even though he knew already, there was no advice that would fix this.

'No, it's not,' he said. 'It happened on our first night. We had agreed she would take the morning-after pill, but now she doesn't remember that conversation.' He raked his hand through his hair, and stared out into the starry night sky, the full moon reflecting off the bay.

The shock of this morning's discovery had left him reeling. He couldn't become a father. And Megan did not want to be a mother—something she would know when her memory returned. But as that hadn't happened, the way forward now was fraught with complications—and heartache.

And the last week had only complicated the situation more. It was all his fault.

He should never have given into his hunger for her and taken her back into his bed. And he should never have agreed to her requests to accompany him during the day. Because the time they'd spent together, instead of reinforcing all the reasons why they could never be a couple, had done exactly the opposite.

He'd become completely enchanted with her. Not just her enthusiasm and responsiveness in bed, but the way she behaved out of it.

He'd come to adore the bright, eager and surprisingly well-informed chatter about all the improvements he was making to the island. He'd been charmed by the way she had captivated the local fishermen with her faltering Italian or bonded with Matteo Caldone's wife over how to make gnocchi. And had come to rely on having her with him, having her by his side. She had made even the most tedious details of his working life an adventure. When he'd woken up this morning, he'd been stupidly excited about the prospect of taking her for a swim in a lagoon, knowing how much he would enjoy seeing her wide-eyed wonder at the cove's natural beauty. In the space of one short week, she'd managed to turn him into someone he didn't even recognise. Someone fun and playful and optimistic in a way he hadn't been in years. In short, a besotted fool.

But worse than that, in the past week, their fake relationship had started to feel real. Real enough that even the thought of her giving herself to another man had begun to torture him. And he had forgotten to be cautious and careful with her feelings as well as his own.

But this morning's bombshell had brought that illusion crashing down around his ears.

This relationship wasn't real.

He could never love Megan—however much he had enjoyed her companionship in the past week or the intense physical connection they shared. And Megan didn't really love him, because any feelings she had for him were based on a lie. But even knowing all this, when she had stared at him out of misty green eyes and told him she wanted to have his child, for one terrifying moment he had actually wanted it to be true.

It was all such a catastrophic mess, and he didn't know how the hell to get them both out of it.

'So she still doesn't remember that you were never engaged for real?' Jared said.

Dario shook his head.

'Maybe it's time to tell her the truth and see what happens, pal.'

Jared was right, of course. He should have said something tonight when he'd had the opportunity. Should have said something a week ago, before he'd taken her back into his bed. But still he kept second-guessing himself.

'What if I do that and it only confuses her more?' A tiny, foolish part of him almost wished she never regained her memory. It just went to show how far he had lost his grip on reality.

'Doesn't seem like you have much of a choice,' Jared said. 'It's either that or she has the kid and you pretend to love her for the rest of your life.'

'No, that is not an option, either.' His head felt as if it were about to explode, the fear that had haunted him since childhood making his heart kick his ribs in harsh erratic thuds.

'Sorry I can't be of more help, man,' Jared said, sounding as dejected as he felt. 'Good luck.'

Signing off, Dario turned off his laptop and walked back into the bedroom.

She lay curled on the bed, having kicked off the sheet. Her body looked small and defenceless as she moved restlessly in her sleep. He should sleep elsewhere, but as a small moan escaped he found himself taking off his clothing and slipping into the bed. He cradled her quaking body in his arms, and inhaled the flowery fragrance of her hair. Her breathing deepened as he stroked the soft strands to quieten her and the arousal that was always there became a dull ache in his groin.

'Shh, *piccola*,' he murmured as he struggled to find his own peace. And a way out of this mess—without hurting the smart, sweet, beautiful woman he had come to know.

'You stupid slut! You're worse than your mother.'

The darkness came to her in dreams, seeping into her consciousness where she couldn't defend herself against it. She saw her father's face contorted with rage, sweat dripping down his mottled skin as he screamed at her.

Pain rained down on her, striking her shoulders, her back, lancing through her heart, shattering everything she had ever known about herself and her place in the world.

'You're not mine! You and your sister were whelps from her lovers.'

Her broken sobs echoed in her head, as she begged her daddy not to hurt her any more. But her daddy wasn't her daddy now, and he hated her.

Just as the pain became unbearable, Dario's voice beckoned her out of the nightmare. 'Shh, Megan, it's okay, I'm here, you're safe.'

She awoke with a start in the darkened bedroom with Dario's arms around her.

Shapes formed in the moonlight. Familiar, comforting shapes. Dario's face harsh with concern. The giant bed where they had slept together in each other's arms. Luxury furnishings gilded by the light of the waning Mediterranean moon. The citrus and sea scented breeze brushed her naked skin through the open shutters. And for a moment she did feel safe. Secure. Loved… So happy.

But then the darkness unfolded as the dream returned. Not a dream this time though, but terrible reality: the kaleidoscopic colours of the ballroom as Dario spun her around in a circle on their pretend date; her sobs of fulfilment as he stroked her to orgasm; the wry tilt of his lips as they discussed emergency contraception; the shuddering humiliation as she received her father's text.

Nausea pitched and rolled in her belly. Clammy sweat covered her body. And horror hit her hard in the chest.

'*Cara*, are you okay?' he said, his voice gentle, coaxing.

But she knew the truth now. And his concern, his care, wasn't love. It was pity.

She could feel the phantom pain from her father's belt and see the dispassionate concern so clearly on Dario's face as he knelt next to her shattered body.

'Let me go.' Pushing against his hold, she wrestled with the cloying sheet, climbed off the bed.

'What's wrong?' he said, pulling back the sheet to follow her.

She scrambled away from him, her back hitting the wall of the bedroom, the cool plaster chilling her fevered flesh. 'You lied. Why did you lie to me? We were never engaged!'

For a moment he looked shocked, but then she saw the guilty flash of knowledge. Her thundering heart felt as if it were being crushed in her chest.

'Your memory has returned?' he said, his voice patient. And tightly controlled.

She gagged. Rushing into the bathroom, she heaved what little she'd eaten the night before into the toilet bowl. As she carried on heaving she heard him enter the bathroom behind her.

A dim light came on and warm hands settled on her shoulders.

She spun out of his grasp. 'Don't touch me.'

He stood in sweat pants, his magnificent body mocking her. How ridiculous she had been, to think for even a moment that a man like him would ever love her.

He had been nothing more than a glorious one-night stand—was never meant to be more than that—and because she had lost her memory, he had spun out a lie.

But why? Why would he do that?

He lifted a hand. Like a man trying to calm a frightened beast. 'You are over-emotional. Come back to bed so we can talk.'

She shook her head, trying to hold on to the tears making her sinuses ache. 'How could you pretend we were engaged? That we were in love? For all this time? Why would you?'

It had all been a lie. How could he justify it to himself? And how could *she*? She'd fallen in love with an illusion. None of this had been real. Her hand strayed to her stomach and the baby growing there. None of it except her child.

The child he didn't want, and now she knew why.

'You are overwrought. You need to calm down,' he said.

Anger flared. She clung onto it desperately, through the heartache and the weariness. 'Don't patronise me. Tell me the truth. Why did you tell me we were engaged? Why did you make me believe you loved me?'

He stiffened at the use of the word. And her already battered heart cracked silently in two.

'I never pretended to love you,' he said, and the last remnants of hope that she hadn't even realised she still clung to withered and died. 'I wanted you to get well,' he said. 'Which is why I brought you here. Away from the press, the trial, so you could recover. It was for your own good.'

'You slept with me, knowing I didn't know the true nature of our relationship. How could that be for my own good?'

His eyes darkened, his jaw tensed, and she felt the spark of electricity arc between them. She folded her arms across her chest, her swollen breasts tender and far too sensitive under that searing gaze. The T-shirt he had helped her into before bedtime suddenly felt see-through, every inch of skin prickling with the need to feel his touch as memories of that first night, of the past seven nights in his arms assaulted her.

'You offered yourself to me,' he said. 'And I should have resisted. But everything we did together we both enjoyed.'

It sounded reasonable, persuasive even. And of course, he was right. She had begged for him to make love to her. Except it had never been love. At least not for him. 'Did you ever care for me at all?'

'Of course I did,' he said, the frustration in his voice helping her to bury the agonising hurt deep.

'And what about the baby? Perhaps you should tell me how you really feel about that now.' But she already knew, the bitter truth turning her insides to jelly.

He heaved a deep sigh. Seeing the agony in his eyes made her want to weep. 'Megan, it is complicated. You must see that? Now you remember everything?'

He stepped forward, but she threw up a hand. 'Please don't, don't come any closer.' She couldn't stay strong, stay invulnerable, make any sense of this if he touched her. The chemistry between them had messed with her head all the way down the line. And made her fall in love with a phantom.

'My father attacked me because he hated me.' She pushed the words out past the thickness in her throat. The cruel, ugly words her father had said striking her all over again with more viciousness than the belt he'd used on her. 'He pretended to care about us for years because of the money in our trust funds. But this…' she swung her hand between them '…what you did, feels so much worse.'

Dario dragged a hand through his hair, cursed under his breath. 'I understand you are angry and upset,' he said. 'But let us talk about this in the morning. It's the middle of the night. You're tired. Come back to bed. I can make you feel better.'

'You think sex will make this better?' she said, stunned.

'I think it cannot hurt,' he said.

The wry twist of his lips made her heart shatter at her feet. That he had manipulated her with sex wasn't really the point, because she had revelled in her own destruction. That he thought it would make things better now, though, almost made her feel sorry for him.

How could anyone have such a jaundiced view of love and relationships that they thought sex was the only connection worth having?

He approached her.

But she held up her hand. 'No. I don't want to sleep with you, Dario.'

Of course, they both knew that wasn't strictly true. She only had to be in a room with him for her body to prepare itself for him. To yearn for him. It would be humiliating if it weren't so sad.

But she refused to give in to the yearning. She had to guard what little was left of her heart. In the hope that, one day, she would be able to heal. And move on from this.

'I need to think,' she said as her mind raced. She had to get away from him. Get away from Isadora. If for no other reason than to protect her child. 'I want to return to my own room.'

For a moment she thought he looked stricken at the suggestion, but it could only be an illusion like everything else. She had never been able to read him, or his feelings; her emotions had played tricks on her in the last few weeks, but that was the biggest trick of all.

She moved past him into the bedroom, pathetically grateful when he made no move to stop her. Her whole body began to shake, heat flushing through her, when she glanced at the bed, the rumpled sheets a testament to her foolishness and naiveté.

She had spent her whole life trying to please her father, a man who had never loved her. And if her memory hadn't returned, she might have done the same thing again with Dario.

'We will speak of this again in the morning,' Dario said from behind her. 'And find a solution.'

She turned around as she reached the bedroom door. The red fingers of dawn had begun to lighten the sky outside, shadowing his handsome face, and her heart squeezed tight in her chest. For just a moment, he looked like the loneliest man on earth.

'I never meant for you to be hurt,' he said.

The last tiny flicker of hope guttered out as she acknowledged something incontrovertible. Maybe he hadn't meant to hurt her, the way her father had. But the truth was he had.

She left the room as one of the tears she had promised herself she wouldn't shed slipped over her lid. She scrubbed it away with her fist.

After returning to her bedroom, she kept the exhaustion and the heartache at bay to dress.

She called Katie on her cell, and tiptoed out of the house, then rushed through the lemon groves down to the harbour, where the fishermen would be setting out for their morning catch.

As she stood on the deck of a small fishing boat, the aroma of fish and sea salt made her delicate stomach revolt. She retched over the side of the boat, but there was nothing left to throw up. As she raised her head she caught sight of the villa spotlighted on the hilltop in the early summer dawn.

She imagined Dario inside. And all the hopes and dreams that had never been real. Letting them go would be the hardest thing of all. But she had no choice.

While she had been falling hopelessly in love with a fantasy, he had managed to seal himself off from any emotion that would make him vulnerable.

So now she had to do the same.

Dario awoke, the pounding on his bedroom door disorientating him for a moment. He sat up, confused to find the other side of the bed cold. Then the details of the argument just before dawn came back to him.

He swore viciously, trying desperately to ignore the treacherous memory of Megan's face, white with shock and grief. And worse still, the deep sinking hole in his stomach when he had been forced to let her leave, and had lain in his empty bed alone.

But then he registered what his housekeeper was shouting through the door.

'*Signor! Signor! La signorina e andato, ha lasciato con I pescatori.*'

Megan has left with the fishermen? What the...?

He leapt out of bed, dragging a robe on as he raced to the door to find Sofia on the other side looking distraught as she explained in frantic Italian what she had heard from the young man delivering that morning's fish.

Dread spread through him. Megan had left? She had hitched a lift in a fishing boat in the middle of the night?

When she was still dealing with the emotional trauma of her memory returning? When she was pregnant? Was she mad?

He charged down the corridors until he reached her suite of rooms—to find the bed empty and unslept in, and a note addressed to him perched on the bedside table.

He picked it up, and flicked it open.

Goodbye, Dario.
I will take care of a termination.
Please don't contact me again.

No, no, *no.*

The note dropped from his numbed fingers and fluttered down onto the carpet.

He should have been relieved, he should have been grateful, that she had come to her senses, was going to do the sensible thing. But he felt none of those things as he clutched his head in his hands, and slumped onto the bed.

The cold, hard lump of devastation and grief in the pit of his stomach dragged him back to another time. He forced his mind to shut down as he lifted his head to stare out of the window at the new summer day, the dawn light spreading over the ocean.

And wondered if he would ever feel warm again.

CHAPTER SIXTEEN

Two months later

MEGAN SAT IN the chauffeur-driven car and watched the phalanx of photographers and reporters charging down the steps of the Manhattan courthouse towards them. Her sister, Katie, gripped her hand.

'Are you sure you're okay to do this, sis?' Katie's voice vibrated with the strength and maturity that she had gained ever since Megan had returned from Isadora.

Megan squeezed her sister's hand. 'We both need to do this to make sure Lloyd Whittaker stays behind bars as long as possible.'

The clamour outside the car became deafening as two burly security guards muscled their way through the crowd and one of them opened the driver's door.

He leaned into the interior. 'We have a detail to see you safely into the courthouse, Miss Whittaker. You both okay to go?'

The harsh flash of halogen lights blinded Megan as they stepped out of the car and were muscled into the courthouse, the noise becoming deafening as the reporters shouted questions.

'Are you here to testify against your father, Miss Whittaker?'

'Megan, tell us about your affair with Dario De Rossi? Are you two still an item?'

She clung to her resolve, tried to tune out the mention of Dario's name, to keep her nerves steady. But as they entered the main foyer she saw the tall, lean figure of Dario's friend Jared Caine standing beside the security checkpoint. And her heart careered into her throat.

'Well, if it isn't Mr Tall, Dark and Patronising,' Katie said, in a sing-song voice shot through with sarcasm as he walked towards them. Katie hadn't mentioned Jared before now, but she had never played nice with guys who told her what to do, so her animosity towards Dario's friend didn't really surprise Megan.

'Hello, Miss Whittaker, Katherine,' Jared said, in the confident, impersonal tone she remembered from the only other time she'd met him. If he'd heard her sister's jibe, he didn't let on.

'Why are you here?' Megan asked, anxiety gripping her insides.

'Dario's giving evidence at the moment,' he replied.

The news she had been dreading sliced through the defences she had been putting in place ever since running away from Isadora. But she maintained eye contact with Dario's friend, determined not to give away the turbulent emotions churning in her stomach.

She'd known this was likely. She'd just have to deal with it.

It didn't matter if she wasn't ready to see him again. He'd done what she'd asked, and hadn't contacted her since she'd left Isadora at dawn.

It didn't matter that she hadn't been able to stop thinking about him. Or stop going over every minute, every second she had spent with him since that first night. It was a weakness she would have to get over. Eventually. And it seemed today was the day when she was going to be forced to confront it. And him. For the first time.

She needed to move on from the time they had spent together on Isadora. To accept that it had all been fake. The way he obviously had. Coming to terms with the truth about their relationship as well as the truth about her father—or rather her ex-father—would eventually make her a stronger, more resilient person.

If only she weren't going to be forced to take that next step today, of all days.

One of the security guards who had helped them into the building appeared to Jared's right. 'What's next, boss?'

'Stick around. Miss Whittaker and her sister will need an escort when they leave the building,' Jared replied.

'Did Dario arrange the bodyguards?' Megan asked and Jared nodded.

The protective gesture was like a new knife through the heart—and her hard-fought-for composure. She didn't want any evidence that he still cared, when he had never cared enough.

'Please, tell Dario we don't need his help,' she said.

The tension in Jared's jaw drew tight. 'You should tell him yourself. He's not exactly rational where you're concerned.'

What did that mean?

But before she could ask, the prosecutor's intern appeared looking harassed. 'Miss Whittaker, you're up next. We need to get you into the courtroom.'

Her stomach continued to rebel as the intern ushered them through the security line, leaving Jared behind.

As she walked into the courtroom her gaze immediately connected with Dario on the witness stand. Her steps faltered, the blast of heat not nearly as disturbing as the pressure on her chest as his gaze swept over her.

From a distance, he looked as indomitable and intimidating as ever, the tailored designer suit, clean-shaven jaw and close-cropped hair a far cry from the intense and yet tender, even playful, man she had glimpsed on Isadora.

Her hand strayed to her stomach, but she forced herself to let it fall away as the intern directed her to the front of the courtroom and the seats behind the prosecutor's table.

But she couldn't take her eyes from the man on the witness stand. And as she drew closer, for a moment she thought she saw a flash of pain and longing in those pure blue eyes.

She broke eye contact, the pressure on her chest becoming unbearable.

You're wrong. Stop deluding yourself.

She needed to cut out that fragile, foolishly optimistic corner of her heart that still believed she loved him, or that he might have grown to love her.

She pressed her hand to her abdomen. She had her child to protect now. The child still growing in her womb.

The child she could never tell Dario about, because he had made it clear he had never wanted it, or her.

How can it still hurt so much to look at her?

Unable to detach his gaze from Megan's, Dario blanked out the defence attorney's questions.

But then Megan's gaze dropped away from his. And he felt the loss all over again, as he had so often since that fateful night on Isadora when her memory had returned and he'd seen the pain he'd caused in those expressive emerald eyes.

She looked pale and drawn in the tailored skirt and jacket. Had she lost weight? Her wild red hair was ruthlessly tied back. The style should have made her look severe and unapproachable—but only made her look more fragile and vulnerable to him.

His fingers clenched on the varnished wood of the witness box as he forced his attention back to the defence attorney. He had to concentrate on his evidence—as the man continued his campaign to convince the jury that Dario had been the one to attack Megan and not her father—and ignore the agonising parade of regrets that had plagued him since that night.

Stop trying to remake the past. She ran from you. And rejected your child. This was the outcome you wanted. Why can't you learn to live with it?

But then the defence attorney's mouth twisted in a grim approximation of a smile as he delivered a stream of questions that smashed into Dario's already faltering composure like physical blows.

'You maintain that you have never hit a woman, Mr De Rossi? That it is simply not in your make-up to do so? But is it not correct that you come from a family with a history of violence against women? That in fact your father was an extremely violent man, who hit you and your mother on numerous occasions? And that you indeed witnessed him beat your mother to death at a very impressionable age?'

Megan's head jerked up as the court broke into uproar— the barrage of questions, and Dario's shocked reaction to them, tearing away the stranglehold she had around her own heart.

Oh, please don't let it be true. Please don't let him have suffered like that.

Her chest imploded, the information delivered by the lawyer too traumatic to contemplate. But then her heartbeat rammed her throat in hard, heavy thuds as she registered the devastation on Dario's face—the mask of indifference ripped away to reveal the true horror of what he had once endured, clear for all to see.

And suddenly all the unanswered questions that had plagued her since that night, the questions that had made it so hard for her to move on, slammed into her all over again.

Why had he been so determined to protect her? How could he have made love to her with such passion, such purpose, and felt nothing?

Dario remained speechless, and utterly defenceless as the prosecutor's attempts to halt the line of questioning were dismissed by the judge.

'Mr De Rossi must answer the question. The prosecution can determine the relevance of this information in due course.'

The court fell silent, Megan's heart shattering.

'I did not consider him my father,' Dario said in a voice hoarse with raw emotion. 'The man was a monster.'

'Indeed,' the defence attorney said, the word laden with theatrical doubt. 'And yet it appears you resemble him in no small degree. Is it not the case that you seduced Lloyd Whittaker's daughter to secure a business deal? That you attacked her when she tried to return to her father? That you spirited her away while she had no memory to your private island in the Mediterranean? And then discarded her when she had outlived her usefulness to you.'

Dario's eyes met hers, the guilt and regret now so clear and unequivocal, the shudder of yearning and love that flowed through her was beyond her control.

'I did not leave Megan,' he said, the resignation in his voice destroying her. 'She left me.'

The poignant words pierced her heart. And the tug of war she'd been playing with her feelings for Dario was comprehensively lost.

Why had she run from him? Why hadn't she given him a chance? Given herself a chance?

What she had found with Dario on Isadora might have been built on a lie—but why hadn't she even considered staying and trying to make it real? Had what she thought was strength been nothing more than cowardice all along?

'Perhaps we should ask ourselves then why she would run from you, Mr De Rossi?' the defence attorney continued. 'And why she would choose not to inform you that she carries your child? Is it because she is terrified of what you might do to her?'

Megan leapt to her feet, her hand cupping her stomach, the puzzled shock on Dario's face at the news she still carried his child making the guilt lance through her.

What had she done to him? This man who had strived to protect her? The way he had no doubt once strived to protect his mother? All the lies he had told had been to protect her fragile mind from its own fears until she was ready to face them. But the lie she had told him had been to protect herself. Because she had been too weak, too scared, to admit she loved him. And now he was being crucified because of it.

'Stop, please stop,' Megan shouted. 'It's not true. Dario would never hurt me.'

Noise exploded around her, the judge's gavel echoing in her head.

'Meg, are you okay?' Katie's fingers gripped her arm as the surge of emotion threatened to choke her.

She swayed.

Her gaze remained locked on Dario's as he jerked to his feet in the witness box.

She heard the judge's call to order, the prosecutor's shouted demands for a recess next to her ear, but the blood buzzing in her head became a cacophony. Her knees dissolved as she dropped into the dark.

'I have you, *cara*, you are safe now.' Dario's voice beckoned her out of the darkness and into the light, as it had once before.

The clean, spicy aroma of soap and man enveloped her. The noise still surrounded her, but she was in his arms again as he shouldered his way through the crowd, protecting her from the shouted questions, the press of bodies, the bright flash of lights.

The sound of a door slamming cut out the noise until all she could hear was her heart hammering against her ribs.

They were alone in a cramped office, the large desk pushed into a corner surrounded by shelves loaded with leather-bound books.

The July sunlight shone through the window, lighting the dust motes in the air.

'Can you stand?' he asked.

'Yes, I think so.'

He put her down, holding on to her waist until he was satisfied she was strong enough to stand unaided.

'It is true?' he asked, his gaze focused on her belly, his fingers gliding over the barely visible bulge. 'About the baby? It still lives?'

She nodded. 'Yes, they... They think it's a girl.'

'Una bambina?' he said, the sound so full of stunned pleasure her guilt began to strangle her. *'Bellissima.'*

'I'm so sorry I lied to you in my note. It was cowardly and unforgivable and I—'

'Shh, *cara*.' He brushed the tears away with his thumbs. 'You are not the coward. I am.'

'Maybe we were both cowards,' she ventured.

His lips curved in a sad smile that melted her heart. 'I think, yes.'

She blinked, feeling the salty sting on her cheeks. 'Is it true, Dario? What he said happened to your mother?'

Dario stared at the woman in front of him, so brave, so bold, so beautiful. But the earnest question ate into the joy at the news their baby still lived.

He wished she hadn't heard about his mother, wished she would never have to know the truth of his past. But how could he tell her any more lies?

Guilt consumed him, not just for his part in his mother's death, but for his part in Megan's assault. A part he had never truly acknowledged to himself until now.

Maybe he hadn't been the one to wield the belt, but his actions had left her vulnerable. Left her at the mercy of a violent man—the way he had once left his own mother at the mercy of another violent man.

He stepped back, letting his hands fall from her waist. 'Yes, it is true. She died and it was my fault.'

'How could it be your fault?' Megan said, the sympathy and compassion in her eyes making him hate himself even more.

'I provoked him. My father.'

'I don't believe you,' she said, her dogged defence of him making him more determined than ever that she should know the truth. The whole bitter truth about who he was.

'And even if you did,' she added, 'it still wouldn't make what he did your fault.'

'You do not understand,' he said. 'He was a powerful man. A rich man with another family. He called me his gypsy bastard, and my mother his whore.' That the memory of his father's taunts still haunted and humiliated him only made him feel more ashamed. 'He enjoyed hurting her. When I woke that night, I saw him on top of her. And I could see how terrified she was.'

'Oh, Dario.' She touched his arm. 'No child should have to endure that.'

He shook his head, planted his fists into the pockets of his trousers, his insides churning with the long-forgotten memories—the hollow aching guilt that would never go away.

'I shouted at him to leave, to never touch my mother again. I was eight years old, nothing more than a proud, angry boy, and I thought I was man enough to protect her. He was furious. He lost all control, began to beat me with the belt he had used on me before. But this time, I don't think he would have stopped. My mother saved me. She fought him with the last breath in her body. She died protecting *me*.'

'Stop it.' Megan gripped his arms and shook him, her fierce expression forcing him back to the present, and away from the gut-wrenching guilt of memories. 'Don't you dare blame yourself. You were a child when your mother died. Do you understand me? And she died protecting you, because she loved you.'

He tried to absorb what she was saying. But he could not, because he knew his mother's death wasn't the only guilt he bore. History had repeated itself with Megan. Just as the defence attorney had implied.

He grasped her cheeks, looked into that brave face and forced himself to admit the final truth that he had been trying to deny for so long.

'Don't you see, Megan? I did the same thing to you. I lied to you to get you into my bed that night. I lied about my intentions towards your father's company. All I thought of was my own pleasure. And you paid the price. My actions provoked Whittaker, in the same way my actions once provoked my father.'

She reached around his waist and pressed her cheek into his sternum. 'Please stop it, Dario. It's not true. You mustn't blame yourself for what my father did to me.'

He placed his hands on her shoulders, wanting to believe her, yearning to hug her back, but terrified of all the emotions rushing to the surface. All the emotions he had spent two months struggling to comprehend.

She smiled up at him, the tender expression making his ribs ache, and his whole body feel as if it were perched on the edge of a precipice.

'I love you, Dario. So much.'

Gripping her cheeks in trembling palms, he pressed his forehead to hers, wanting to plunge over the edge, as the last of the walls shattered around him.

But how could he ever deserve her, or their child, after all that he had done?

'You cannot love me,' he said on a broken breath. 'I do not deserve it.'

Folding her arms around Dario's neck, Megan kissed him, tears streaking down her cheeks now. She had to make him believe her, had to make him see that he was worthy of her love.

At last, he opened for her and took her mouth in a deep, seeking kiss. She felt the emotion shuddering through him. And into her.

She loved him. And she suspected he loved her too. But he'd been too scared to acknowledge it to himself, let alone her, because of what had happened to his mother. She understood that now. She had to show him that he didn't have to be scared of love any more.

She drew back, taking in deep breaths as she saw the

torment still shadowing his eyes. 'Do you love me, too, Dario?' she asked. 'Do you want this baby?'

He sighed. 'Yes. And yes.' He rested a hand on her stomach as her heart filled with happiness. 'But I could not bear it if I hurt you again.'

She pressed her palm over his, hearing the raw emotion in his voice.

This was a struggle for him. A struggle that would take time and work to heal all the way, but knowing he loved her, and knowing where his anguish came from—knowing why it had been so hard for him to acknowledge his feelings—was surely the start of something magnificent. Something they could build a future on, with their baby.

'Dario, I know you're scared,' she said. 'And now I know why you're scared.' Because he had been traumatised by his mother's death as a child.

Her heart would always break for that little boy—who had learned to cope with the trauma by persuading himself he did not deserve to be loved.

She took a breath, her whole heart now lodged in her throat.

'I'm scared too,' she said, determined to get through to that little boy. 'Everyone is scared when they fall in love. Because love is a scary thing. But it's also a joyous, wonderful thing. And to have the joy, you have to overcome your fear. Can you do that, for me?'

'But what if I make a mistake?' he said, still unsure. Still scared. 'What if I cannot be a good father? A good husband? What if my love for you and our child is not enough?'

'There aren't any guarantees. Life isn't like that.' She gripped his hands, the love flowing through her so strong now she thought her heart might burst. 'And believe me—considering how new and untried this adventure is for both of us…' she smiled '…we're both going to make mistakes. The truth is we're probably going to make a ton of them. But it will be okay. As long as we make them together.'

He looked down at her belly. 'But I don't even know how to be a father. My own father was a monster.'

'And my mother was a woman who cared more about her next orgasm than she ever did about her daughters,' she replied, her smile widening. 'Look at it this way— however rubbish we are at this, we'll already be so much better than them.'

He nodded and let out a hoarse laugh, which had a wealth of bitter knowledge in it. 'This is true.'

'So what do you say, Dario De Rossi? Are you willing to go on this adventure with me?'

Her heart stopped beating, it simply stopped, as she waited for him to answer.

'You are sure you want to go on this adventure with me?' he said, the seriousness in his face making her heart jump and pound in her throat.

'Absolutely.'

He nodded again—the fierce passion that flashed into his eyes as he drew her into his arms choking off her air supply.

'Then I don't believe I have a choice,' he murmured against her hair. 'Even I cannot continue to be a coward in the face of your bravery.'

She wanted to laugh, the joy bursting in her heart almost more than she could bear.

He clasped her cheeks and lifted her head. 'I think now we must make this engagement real,' he said. 'Will you marry me, *piccola*?'

Her heart soared. 'Absolutely.'

His mouth swooped down to devour hers, the giddy

contentment making her head spin as warm hands cupped her bottom, and heat spread through her.

A loud thumping pulled them apart as Jared's voice came through the door. 'Sorry, folks, adjournment's over. And the judge is getting antsy.'

'Stall them a minute more,' Dario shouted back. Then he turned to her, his expression sober. 'Are you strong enough to take the witness stand after me?' he asked, searching her face for any signs of fatigue or fragility. 'If you are not, I will make them wait until tomorrow.'

'No. I can do it. I *want* to do it,' she said, knowing she was strong enough to do whatever it took to put the man who had pretended to be her father behind bars—because with Dario by her side, she was strong enough to do anything. 'For us.'

Cradling her head in his hands, he kissed her forehead, then her nose, then her mouth—the play of his lips full of sincerity and hunger.

'For us,' he vowed.

EPILOGUE

One year later

'SHH, *BAMBINA, PAPA* is here now.'

Megan stretched on the bed and plumped the pillows behind her as she watched her husband walk back into their bedroom, having retrieved their crying daughter from her crib in the room next door, which had once been his office.

She smiled as the baby quietened, happily settling into her favourite place in all the world, nestled on her father's shoulder as he rubbed her back with one large hand.

The little diva.

At six months old, Isabella Katherine De Rossi had her father—billionaire master of industry and feared corporate raider—wrapped firmly around her tiny little finger.

'She is not wet.' Dario frowned. 'Could she be hungry again?' he asked, rocking his daughter gently as he returned to their bed.

Megan yawned, and looked out of the bedroom window to gauge the time by the Mediterranean sun, which was barely creeping over the horizon. 'No,' she said. 'She had her morning feed less than half an hour ago.' Megan couldn't contain her grin at the confusion on Dario's face.

He was still sometimes unsure about his role as a husband and father, and so fiercely protective of them both it often led to him being a bit overzealous when caring for Issy. He was always the first to pick her up if she cried.

'Do you think she is unwell?' he said.

'I think she just likes having you hold her,' she said. 'And she knows that if she cries, you'll rush in there to pick her up.'

The frown eased from Dario's face and he chuckled as he lay down on the bed beside Megan. Lifting his daughter, he bounced her in his arms. The baby's delighted chuckle joined his deep laugh.

'You are a bad *bambina*,' he said, rubbing her nose against his own, the tone the opposite of chiding. 'You mustn't scare *papa* like that.'

He settled back, with the baby curled on his broad chest.

With her head tucked under her father's chin and her small fist stuck in her mouth, Issy dropped into sleep, secure in the knowledge that her father would hold her safe in his arms.

'Dario,' Megan said, smiling as Dario turned towards her. 'I need to talk to you about something.'

She'd held it off long enough. Had waited until they were on Isadora again, where the pace of life was slower, less pressured.

The last six months, heck the last year, had been idyllic. She'd never imagined when they'd made that commitment to each other, in the dusty clerk's office during her father's trial, that her love for Dario and their child would eventually become so overwhelming, so all-consuming. And because she'd been so content—and maybe also a little scared that this adventure was still so new and fragile, especially for Dario—she hadn't wanted to make any demands.

He'd changed so much though, from the cautious, guarded man she'd known. He'd been to therapy to help him deal with the lingering trauma of his mother's death. And they'd made a life for themselves in New York—in the huge brownstone he'd bought a block from Central Park. Their wedding had been a quiet affair on Isadora, with only the islanders and a few of his business associates as guests, plus Katie and Jared as witnesses.

Since their marriage, and even more so since Issy's birth, Dario had cut back on his business commitments, happy to spend long evenings and lazy weekends with her and Issy rather than building his business empire. Not that he wasn't still driven and focused, but he was now equally driven and focused about making his personal life as much of a success as his professional one.

And the bond he had established with his daughter was something that filled Megan with joy and wonder and gratitude every single day.

So the time was right to tell him about the interview she'd had last week in Brooklyn while their housekeeper Lydia Brady had looked after Issy. She'd held off and held off telling him about it, because she'd been concerned about his reaction.

Oh, just say it, Meg. For goodness' sake.

'Hmm…?' he murmured as he continued to stroke his daughter's back.

'I've been offered a job.'

His hand stopped moving as his head jerked round.

Well, that had certainly got his attention.

'A job where?'

'It's a charity in Brooklyn that administers a series of refuges for battered women and their children. They need someone to set up and then operate a new computer system to reduce the amount of time and money they spend on paperwork so they can spend more of it on setting up new refuges.'

He didn't say anything, but she could see the tension in his jaw. Instead of replying, he suddenly sat up and got off the bed.

'Dario? Where are you going?' she asked.

But he didn't turn to look at her, he simply walked out of the room mumbling, 'I should put Issy back into her crib.'

Okay, well, that didn't go according to plan.

Megan's heart sank as she flopped back onto the pillows, her excitement turning into a tangle of anxieties in the pit of her stomach. She didn't want to have a battle with him about this. But it looked as if she might have to.

Dario placed his daughter in her crib, and stroked the soft fluff of red hair on her head.

He wanted so much to say no.

He wanted to tell Megan she couldn't take the job. He didn't want her travelling to Brooklyn every day. Working for a charity that he could probably buy and sell several times over. He could fund the place himself. Throw money at them so they wouldn't need her computer expertise. If she needed a job, he could find her one at Whittaker's, preferably one that didn't require her to leave their house.

He wanted to insist that her daughter, their daughter, needed her mother at home. Where she would always be safe. And as their daughter grew, he would want to do the same thing to Issy. And all the other children he hoped they would have one day.

He wanted to wrap his perfect family in cotton wool and keep them locked away for ever from the outside world, so no one and nothing would ever have the power to hurt them. He wanted to protect them with his money, his resources and the last breath in his body. He wanted to cocoon them for ever in the love that still took his breath away every time he laid eyes on either one of them.

But that was the coward's way out.

Because he'd seen the look of excitement in Megan's eyes, seen how enthusiastic she was about this new opportunity. And he knew if he loved her, he could not kill that joy—however great his need to protect her from harm.

Damn it. But loving someone more than life itself— the way he loved Megan and Issy—was fraught with so many complications. Complications and difficult choices that he often found it extremely hard to even comprehend, let alone solve.

But then the words Megan had said to him a year ago, in the courthouse in Manhattan, echoed in his head. The words he had had to repeat to himself so many times since: when Megan had been curled over the toilet bowl and throwing up each morning through most of the months of her pregnancy; when he had endured the terror of watching her bring their child into the world through twelve gut-wrenching hours of labour; when he'd held the tiny, vulnerable and unbearably precious life they'd made together in his hands for the first time. The words he knew he would be repeating to himself for the rest of his life: when Issy took her first step; when he had to leave her on her first day of school; when he taught her how to ride a bike, drive a car, sail a boat, fly a helicopter; when she went off to Harvard or Yale—because, obviously, his daughter was going to be the smartest, bravest, most brilliant child the world had ever seen.

To have the joy you have to overcome your fear.

He kissed his fingertips and pressed them to the soft skin of his daughter's forehead; her tiny chest rose and fell in the regular rhythm of deep sleep. Relief eased some of the tightness in his chest. Thank goodness, he wouldn't have to face most of those fears with his daughter for a little while at least.

Walking back into the bedroom, he spotted Megan sitting up in their big bed, her arms wrapped around her drawn-up knees.

'Dario? I need to know what you think,' she said, her anxiety tempered with determination. 'About me taking the job?'

He climbed onto the bed, then gathered her into his arms. He held her tight, let the swell of arousal—that was always there when she was near him—help him to push out the words.

'You want to take this job?' he asked as he kissed her hair, even though he already knew the answer.

'Yes, I do.' She swung round in his arms, the eagerness on her face crucifying him a little more. 'I thought it all through about Issy's care while I'm at work. Lydia is fabulous with her, and she's happy to step in. And we've got more than enough other staff to take up the slack.'

He'd employed Lydia Brady as soon as he and Megan had moved into the new town house he'd bought on the Upper East Side—concerned that the penthouse apartment might not be suitable for a child. He'd also insisted on hiring three additional staff. Something he knew Megan still struggled with. He was forever coming home and finding the staff helping Megan with some charity project or other that had nothing to do with their domestic duties.

'And anyway, I'm only going to be working three hours a day to start,' his wife continued. 'I told them I want to take the time to wean Issy properly.'

'Shh, Megan.' He tucked her hair behind her ears, allowed his thumbs to skim down her cheeks. 'You don't have to say any more.'

Dio, *but I love this woman so much.*

'If you want to do this thing,' he added, 'I would never stand in your way.'

'Really?' She smiled. 'Because I thought… When you walked out with Issy like that, I thought you were upset about the idea. That you were going to object to it.'

He shook his head. He wasn't the only one with insecurities. Why did he find that so comforting all of a sudden?

'I could never refuse something so important to you,' he said, but then he smiled, enjoying the role of devil's advocate. 'But if I did, what would you do?'

The quick, seductive smile captivated him as she reached up to cradle his cheeks. 'Then I guess I would have to convince you,' she whispered against his lips.

She set her mouth on his. The heat surged at the seductive licks of her tongue.

He chuckled, the sound deep and so full of contentment. A contentment he'd never believed could be his. Her delighted answering smile made his heart thunder in his chest.

They would be okay. This job would be okay. He had to let her have her freedom despite his fears. And Megan need never know that he would hire one of Jared's security team to watch over her while she was in Brooklyn.

And if she did find out, they could always negotiate. Because if there was one thing his wife was an expert at, it was negotiation.

Scooping her up, he sat her in his lap, held her firmly when she wriggled, inflaming his desires still more.

'So you think you can convince me?' He cupped her breast, licking at the rigid tip through the sheer fabric of her nightgown. Arousal surged into his groin when she arched into his mouth, responding with enthusiasm to the erotic torture as always. 'Perhaps I will convince you first?' he teased.

She grasped his head and pulled his mouth up to hers. The kiss was long and deep before she drew back.

'You're on, big boy,' she said, clearly relishing the erotic challenge—even though she had to know she'd already won.

His loyalty, his trust and every single piece of his heart.

* * * * *

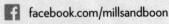

MILLS & BOON
MODERN
Power and Passion

Prepare to be swept off your feet by sophisticated, sexy and seductive heroes, in some of the world's most glamourous and romantic locations, where power and passion collide.